Niobia Bryant is the award-winning and nationally bestselling author of more than forty-five works of romance and commercial mainstream fiction. Twice she has won the RT Reviewers' Choice Best Book Award for African American/Multicultural Romance. Her books have appeared in *Ebony*, *Essence*, *New York Post*, *The Star-Ledger*, *Dallas Morning News* and many other national publications. One of her bestselling books was adapted to film.

Sheri WhiteFeather is an award-winning bestselling author. She lives in Southern California and enjoys shopping in vintage stores and visiting art galleries and museums. She is known for incorporating Native American elements into her books and has two grown children who are tribally enrolled members of the Muscogee Creek Nation. Visit her website at www.sheriwhitefeather.com

THE REBEL HEIR

NIOBIA BRYANT

HOLLYWOOD
EX FACTOR

SHERI WHITEFEATHER

MILLS & BOON

First Published in Great Britain 2021
by Mills & Boon, an imprint of HarperCollins*Publishers* Ltd
1 London Bridge Street, London, SE1 9GF

www.harpercollins.co.uk

HarperCollins*Publishers*
1st Floor, Watermarque Building,
Ringsend Road, Dublin 4, Ireland

The Rebel Heir © 2021 Niobia Bryant
Hollywood Ex Factor © 2021 Sheree Henry-WhiteFeather

ISBN: 978-0-263-28291-7

0421

MIX
Paper from
responsible sources
FSC C007454

This book is produced from independently certified FSC™ paper to ensure responsible forest management.

For more information visit: www.harpercollins.co.uk/green

Printed and bound in Spain
by CPI, Barcelona

THE REBEL HEIR

NIOBIA BRYANT

This one is dedicated to the wonderful thing called love.

One

Jillian Rossi pushed her tortoiseshell spectacles up on her nose as she looked over the rim of her cup of coffee at the spacious chef's kitchen of the townhouse in the prominent, historic Lenox Hill section of Manhattan's Upper East Side. She eyed the dark wood custom cabinets against the light walls, chrome appliances and bronzed fixtures. She loved the space. Knew it well from working as the private chef to its owners for the last year.

Not that she wasn't used to working for the wealthy and famous.

After many years of learning about cooking at the elbow of Ionie, her beloved grandmother, Jillian had gone on to culinary school with a dream of one day opening her own restaurant. Social media success garnered for posting home-cooked savory meals and delicious desserts led to her traveling the world as a personal chef for well-known athletes and celebrities—waylaying her restaurant dreams. Yacht parties. Elaborate dinners. Whirlwind events during award season. Private jets. Mansions. Penthouse apartments. Private islands. Celebrities.

"Lifestyle of the rich and famous," Jillian sighed.

Several years later she'd left being a part of the more glamorous side of life to finally open her restaurant, assuming her days serving as a private chef were over. Unfortunately, the venture had bombed, leaving her in massive debt just a year after its opening. The sting of disappointment and embarrassment from her failure was all too familiar, and the past year had not lessened it any—nor had the return to work as a private chef.

She loved cooking. And, considering the Cress family were world-renowned chefs, they seemed to enjoy the meals she prepared without question. Jillian took that as a feather in her cap. She just considered the position a step backward in her career path.

Been there. Done that. Now I'm doing it again.

Jillian crossed the kitchen to enter the large pantry to the right. Here there were custom cabinets filled with perfectly organized essentials. The counters were marble-topped and beneath one section there was an under-the-counter commercial-size freezer. There was also a large rinse sink to handle food prep if necessary.

As she moved to the office area set up for her, she checked the laser printer to ensure the cream heavy-bond paper with its gold, raised monogram was loaded. Using the touch screen computer, Jillian printed off copies of the breakfast menu. One for each family member's platinum-rimmed place setting.

She was used to the grand nature of it all.

Being in such luxurious surroundings by such an accomplished Cress family only furthered her desire to succeed. The former chefs now operated a multimillion-dollar culinary empire. They also owned this five-story, ten-thousand-square-foot townhouse, which was large enough to accommodate the entire brood. The parents, Phillip Senior and Nicolette. The five sons: Phillip Junior and his wife, Raquel, and their four-year-old daughter Collette, Sean, Gabriel, Lucas and—

"Morning, Jillian."

Cole.

At the deep sound of the voice of Coleman Cress, she paused for one telling second before reaching to remove the printed menus. The pace of her heart sped up as she looked over her shoulder to see him standing in the open doorway. Filling it with ease.

Like his four brothers, Cole was a handsome man with a tall, lean, toned warrior-like physique. He had almond-shaped eyes of a grayish-blue against his medium-brown complexion. His good looks were best described as *chiseled*—from his high cheekbones and broad nose to his square jawline. But there was a complementary softness to his full mouth and the long lashes framing those eyes. He kept his dark brown curly hair cut low, the shadow of a beard and mustache intensifying his magnetism. His clothing preference—normally dark T-shirts, denims and leather motorcycle jackets—gave him just the right amount of edge to draw long glances.

Often, Jillian found his looks similar to that of the actor Michael Ealy.

Just pure goodness.

Her pulse raced. "Good morning, Mr. Cress," she said as he stepped inside the pantry and closed the door behind him. She extended her arm to hand him a menu.

"Omelets for breakfast. Here's the list of the choices of ingredients."

Cole locked eyes with her and smiled, as smooth as syrup spreading across warm pancakes. A knowing smile. A charming one with just a hint of the wile of a wolf. "Mr. Cress?" he mocked as he strolled across the pantry to stand before her, ignoring the paper. "Why so formal? Last night it was Cole."

Cole, don't stop. Don't you dare stop.

She forced herself to break their gaze, shivering in her awareness of him, and flushed with heat at the memory. Over the last year they had shared many. Hotly. Secretly.

Cole eased his large hands beneath her monogrammed chef's coat and settled them on her hips. She felt the heat of his touch through the black leggings she wore. "Tell me you don't want to kiss me," he whispered against her mouth as he lowered his head.

She closed her eyes and waited to feel his mouth with sweet anticipation.

His kisses are the absolute best.

"We can't," she whispered, stepping back before that glorious mouth of his could land.

Cole paused before taking a step that would close the gap she'd put between them. "I hate that you're right," he admitted, letting his eyes linger with apparent regret on her mouth before turning and exiting the pantry, leaving the door ajar.

Jillian released a little breath and bit her bottom lip as she watched him walk away in his bow-legged swagger. She waited for her pulse to cease racing. Cole had that effect on her. With him near her or just in her line of vision, she lost control.

He had been hard to deny since the first time she'd laid eyes on him. Last January. When she'd been hired. For the next two months, they'd shared long looks that had hinted at their mutual interest. By March, they'd been in a deep, no-holds-barred, no-strings-attached fling. A year later, as a woman in touch with her sexuality and not looking for anything serious after two failed marriages in her youth, she was still enjoying her hot, passionate, secret affair with the rebel Cress son.

Still, anything serious with him was not a part of her plan.

Clearing her throat, Jillian collected the printed menus and carried the stack out of the pantry. She walked to the dining room at the rear of the house with its elaborate glass wall as Nicolette Lavoie-Cress stepped off the elevator in the corner to her right beside the staircase. "Good morning, Mrs. Cress," she said, giving a polite nod to the middle-aged, olive-skinned French beauty with silver-streaked blond hair and bluish eyes like Cole's. "I was just putting out the breakfast menus."

Nicolette nodded. "Very good," she said with her heavy French accent. "For dinner, I am expecting the entire family…except Gabe."

Jillian was well aware that Gabriel Cress had moved out of the family home after a massive fall out with Phillip Senior. He had not been back to the townhouse, not even for the fall and winter holidays. Cole had also revealed that Gabe was still with Monica, the Cress family's former housekeeper for the past five years.

But she made sure her face revealed none of that awareness or that the woman's regret was clear.

"The temperature is finally starting to warm up, so let's do some kind of pasta," Nicolette said.

Phillip Senior, a tall, solid, dark-skinned man with broad features and a bright smile, stepped into the kitchen. He was from England and had met Nicolette when they both attended culinary school in Paris. He shared an intimate look with his wife before he gave Jillian a formal nod of greeting and continued into the dining room. He claimed his seat at the head of the long table for ten, topped with charcoal leather and surrounded by steel-blue-suede armless chairs.

"How about seafood linguine with squid, mussels, clams, shrimp, scallops and lobster?" Jillian offered, wanting to reclaim the woman's attention.

Jillian found her to be sophisticated and composed unless communicating with her husband. Her love for Phillip Cress Senior was of no question, nor his for her. Neither tried to hide their affection for one another.

"*Merveilleux,*" Nicolette said, moving across the kitchen to the dining room, as well.

Jillian, pleased that she thought it *wonderful*, followed behind and quickly moved around the table to set a menu on each place setting. Cole, swiping through his phone, did not look up when she put one before him. She held no curiosity about what had his attention. She neither wanted nor claimed ownership to a wild, rebellious man like Coleman Cress.

That would be ludicrous.

Jillian no longer trusted her love goggles. In truth, she'd shattered them under her foot, determined not to have yet another failed relationship thanks to childhood fantasies of a romance like that of her parents, who'd been together since high school. For now, Cole Cress and his eight-pack abs were all about fun distraction and nothing more.

And what could be more fun than lovemaking made all the more daring with whipped cream, taking long motorcycle rides through Manhattan, or bathing together in hot, scented water filled with flower petals.

As the rest of the family entered the dining room, Jillian cleared her thoughts and headed to the kitchen.

"Good morning, Chef Jillian!"

She smiled down at the happy face of Collette with her dimpled cheeks, bright yellow spectacles and big toothy smile. Phillip Junior and Raquel's four-year-old daughter was completely adorable.

"No-no," Nicolette gently reprimanded her granddaughter from her seat at the end of the table opposite her husband.

"Oops," Collette said, giggling as she briefly pressed her hands to her mouth. "*Bonjour*, Chef Jillian."

Nicolette, Jillian knew, was teaching French to the little one.

"*Bonjour*, Collette," she returned warmly before continuing into the kitchen to retrieve a crystal carafe of her fresh-squeezed citrus juice and a warming carafe of Ghanaian coffee.

She eyed Felice, the live-in housekeeper who'd replaced Monica, in the den attached to the kitchen's east side in the spacious open floor plan. Like Jillian, the older woman focused on her daily duties. She wasn't as pleasant as Monica, but she got her work done, which was all that mattered.

"I see that you insist on dressing like a derelict, Coleman," Phillip Senior said in his British accent.

Jillian paused because the annoyance in the patriarch's voice was unmistakable. All of the other sons wore suits and held a more professional demeanor. Cole's insistence on not doing so was a constant thorn in his father's side.

Cole shifted his eyes up from his phone to glare down the table at his father. "If you mean comfortable and of my choosing as a grown man, then yes," he said, his tone cold.

It was like watching day transform into night in an instant. Cole was charming and friendly, a charismatic gentleman—except in his interactions with his father. He seemed to enjoy antagonizing him.

"Life is all about the choices we make," Cole continued.

Phillip Senior's eyes narrowed to slits and the movement of his cheeks evidenced his clenched teeth.

Nicolette looked over and saw Jillian standing there.

"Phillip, I'm sure this can wait," Nicolette said.

Translation: not in front of the staff.

At the woman's movement of her fingers to enter, Jillian walked into the room as Cole broke his hard stare with Phillip Senior to return his attention to his phone. The wealthy playboy was always quick with a joke or sardonic comment and seemed to relish being the rebel in his family. She doubted he took anything seriously.

And thus why, for her, their connection was all about really great, super-spontaneous, hot sex. Cole was beautiful with his muscled body and sexy as all get-out. And he knew how to please her—in fact, he seemed to thrive on it.

Damn.

Jillian fought the urge to shiver in desire. That was the Cole effect. Just the very thought of his lovemaking was enough to awaken her privates. "Okay…" she began with a lick of her lips. "We have a nice selection of ingredients for omelets along with Lyonnaise potatoes. Also, there are fresh seasonal fruit cups in a light honey and your choice of toast."

"Just egg white with spinach and a little mozzarella for me," Lucas said before reaching for the citrus juice to pour himself a small glass.

That wasn't surprising. The youngest Cress brother

had shed fifty pounds and seemed dedicated to keeping the weight off—and his string of pliable women on.

As she took everyone's choice, Jillian's eyes kept going to Cole. She could tell from the stiffness of his shoulders that he was annoyed. He'd always spoken highly of her pan-fried potatoes sautéed with caramelized onions and butter. She served them for breakfast or dinner, along with a steak.

He won't be ready to eat, though.

"Cole, what type of omelet would you like?" she asked.

He looked up at her. His shoulders softened and he smiled. A new switch from night to day. "I'll pass on breakfast. Just coffee is fine," he said with a seemingly polite smile.

Jillian's knowledge that she was right about his eating habit being affected by his mood surprised her. With a nod, she turned and walked back across the vast space to the eight-burner Viking stove to heat and oil eight omelet pans straight from the Cress, INC. line of cookware. Quickly she cracked two eggs into each of eight ceramic bowls, added salt and black pepper with heavy cream before whisking each swiftly then pouring them into the pans.

Leaving the eggs to set and cook on low-medium heat, she opened her leather case to reveal her engraved all-metal knife set…and a note card monogrammed with the Cress, INC. logo. She held the card to her nose and inhaled the subtle scent of Cole's cologne still clinging to it. Like her sheets after he spent a night at her apartment.

She opened the card and mouthed the words as she read them to herself. "Last night before I left you, I kept the panties you were wearing. I want to enjoy the smell of you."

The thrill she felt was addictive.

She looked over into the dining room and caught his eyes on her. He patted the pocket of the leather jacket he wore before raising his cup of coffee in a toast. She flushed with warmth. But, forcing herself to focus on flipping the omelets and adding the ingredients atop one side of each, she was unable to slow the pounding of her heart at the thought of Cole in possession of her sheer red panties.

Over the rim of his cup, Cole surreptitiously eyed Jillian as she left the dining room. She was a tall and slender bronzed beauty with her auburn curly hair pulled up into a topknot. The glasses she wore while cooking couldn't hide the long, thick lashes that framed her round brown eyes. Her cheekbones were high, and her chin narrow, giving her face a heart shape that lent emphasis to her full pouty, perfectly kissable mouth. The back and forth movement of her buttocks in her black leggings enticed him. He smiled into the cup. It was an even more glorious sight free of clothing and gripped in his hands.

Damn.

Jillian was beautiful and curvy. Funny and feisty. Sexy. Insatiable. And not searching for her happily-ever-after.

Perfect.

He thoroughly enjoyed flirting with her before they found hot moments to relieve the sexual tension that pulsed between them. But he was not looking for love.

Been there. Done that.

When he'd met Traci Mason during his senior year at culinary school, Cole had believed he'd found a stunning, intelligent, loyal beauty with whom he could plan a future. He'd even purchased a ring and planned a huge engagement surprise via hot-air balloon. Then his brother,

Gabriel let him know Traci was quite vocal with her friends that she had landed a big fish from the wealthy Cress family and planned to ride the wave to her own successful career.

Any doubts Cole had had about the veracity of the gossip were erased when Gabriel played him a video, taken without Traci's knowledge, of her saying just that. And more. Much more.

It was clear that she'd seen Cole as a pathway to success and not as a man to truly love.

That had been his last serious relationship and he'd preferred no strings attached ever since. His sexy, secretive dalliances with the family's beautiful chef for the past year had been his escape as his family had become unrecognizable. His father's announcement that he was stepping down as the chief executive officer of Cress, INC., and would name one of his five sons as his successor, had put the brothers at odds with one another. Gone was the notion of loyalty. Each was in search of Phillip Cress Senior's deeming him meritorious of the throne.

Cole couldn't deny that it was a worthy empire.

His parents had devoted more than fifty years to build a reputation as celebrated and well-respected chefs, won Michelin stars and James Beard awards, established many successful restaurants, and written more than two dozen bestselling cookbooks and culinary guides. In a calculated move that had paid off, they'd shifted their focus to establishing Cress, INC. And, within just a few years, had successfully diversified into production of their own nationally syndicated cooking shows, cookware, online magazines, an accredited cooking school and a nonprofit foundation.

Like their parents, the five Cress brothers had become chefs—all acclaimed, as well. Four years ago, upon their parents' earnest request, each son had left behind his career to claim a full-time role as a member of the business's executive team. The eldest brother, Phillip Junior, ran the nonprofit, the Cress Family Foundation. Gabriel had stepped down from overseeing the restaurant division to fulfill his dreams of owning and operating his own eatery. Sean supervised the syndicated cooking shows. The youngest, Lucas, was head of the cookware line.

And Cole served as president of Cress, INC.'s digital marketing and global branding, overseeing a small team that managed publicity and marketing as well as the company's websites and online presence. He'd taken the position at his mother's urging to participate in something along with his beloved brothers.

In time, he had come to enjoy the work and taken pride in the company's exponential growth in online traffic and analytics. In truth, he cared nothing about the CEO position and had only competed for it because he felt his father didn't believe he could do it. Unlike his brothers, his desire to create and cook was too strong to ignore. Thus, his food truck purchase and operation on the weekends—another bane to his father, who found the very idea of the food truck industry beneath chefs of Cress caliber.

An outdated and judgmental notion.

And he's the last man to hold everyone else to such damn high standards.

Cole set his cup down on the saucer as he spared his father a glance just as the man looked down the length of the table to give his wife a warm smile. The anger he felt with his father—the same ire that had spurred his rebellious nature since his teenage years—burned like fire in his gut.

Liar.

Phillip Senior was a formidable man who was very

aware that he was raising men. He loved his boys, but the only softness and warmth he showed in abundance was to their mother. There had been little tolerance for whining, misbehaving, mistruths or weakness from his sons.

Cole looked to one of the two empty chairs at the table. The normal seat of his older brother, Gabe, was empty. He was proud of him for standing up to the disparaging way his father had spoken of Monica upon discovering his son had dared to date the help.

Cole felt his stomach burn at the memory...

"Is she the reason for your insanity lately?" Phillip roared, the veins of his neck seemingly strained.

"She's the reason I'm happy," Gabe returned calmly.

"Happy or horny?"

"Both."

Cole chuckled, which incensed his father even more, yet his other brothers sat as if afraid to speak up. Their silence angered Cole. Gone was their alliance as brothers.

"There are women you wed and those you bed. Know the difference. And that goes for all of you," Phillip said.

Gabe angrily strode over to his father, standing toe-to-toe to confront him. "Don't disrespect her in that way." His voice was cold. "I tolerate a lot from you, but I will not put up with that."

Knowing Gabe was "The Good One," offering no trouble and never a cross word to his parents, it had been exhilarating to watch him challenge their father. In the same manner, Cole wished he had been brave enough to do the same in the past.

As his family members' conversation continued around the table, Cole, lost in his thoughts, took another deep sip of the brew. He barely noticed his grip on the rim of his cup had tightened. Once he did, he released it. The cup dropped down onto the saucer. He had to catch it before it tipped and spilled its hot contents.

Every eye was on him.

"Quelque chose ne va pas, Oncle Cole?"

At his niece's question, Cole looked down at her, looking up at him through her bright spectacles from her usual seat beside him at the table. He smiled at her with warmth. "Nothing's wrong, Collie," he assured her.

"You seemed moodier than usual," Nicolette observed, giving him an encouraging smile. "I know you love Jillian's potatoes. Not feeling well?"

"Don't spoil him, Nicolette."

Cole tensed at his father's terse reprimand. "Spoiled is believing you can have anything you want, when and where you want it," he snapped, sitting back against his chair.

Phillip Senior glared at him before shaking his head and returning his attention to the print newspapers he still favored.

Cole didn't miss his brothers Lucas and Sean share a look. Phillip Junior frowned and his wife pretended not to notice. Collette was lost to the tension.

The father-son contentious relationship was nothing new. In truth, the root of Cole's problem with his father was more than a rebellion. It was a bitter disappointment.

As a teenager, Cole had visited the family's restaurant and walked in on his father cheating on his mother with one of the waitresses. Visions of their half-clothed bodies rutting away flashed in his mind's eye and he winced at the memory and forced it out.

He'd never shared the secret of his father's affair. At times, he hated himself for that.

Cole looked at his mother. A devoted beauty whose

feelings for her husband were clear. Her love. And her loyalty.

He hadn't wanted to hurt her, but his anger at his father for betraying her had been stewing for years.

Cole had been determined to be a better man to Traci before he'd discovered she was using him. Although he knew his reputation in the press was now that of a playboy, Cole never juggled more than one woman at a time—he just kept his relationships strings-free.

"Can I get anything for anyone before I go shopping for dinner?"

Cole glanced up at Jillian, standing in the opening of the dining room, before he looked over his shoulder at the spring sun blazing down on the thirty-two-foot length of the garden. A long concrete table set beneath an arched framework covered with bamboo leaves offered privacy and shade. At night, he liked to sit outside, smoke a cigar and sip Uncle Nearest premium whiskey as he listened to the sounds of New York and watched the illuminated water fountain at the end of the garden.

There had been many a night that memories of stolen moments with the sexy chef had dominated his thoughts. More often than not, that led to a phone call or text before he was off on his motorcycle, zipping through the streets to reach her.

And stroke deeply inside her...

"That will be all, Jillian. Thank you," Nicolette said, breaking into his train of thought.

"We need someone to step in and take over the restaurant division in Gabe's absence," Phillip Senior said, wiping the corners of his mouth with his napkin before dropping it atop his half-eaten steak, mushroom and mozzarella omelet.

Cole glared at his father. "Good luck with that," he drawled. "I'm not filling a spot my brother left."

"Grow up, Cole!" Phillip Junior snapped.

Cole shot him a glare, as well. "Go to—"

"Oh no-oo," Raquel said, rising in a beautiful sheer red shirt and matching wide-legs pants to pick up their daughter's plate. "Come on, Collette. We'll finish breakfast upstairs."

"What's wrong?" the little girl asked.

"The adults need the room…and to remember *they* are adults." Raquel shot a meaningful glance at both Cole and her husband before leading the preschooler out of the room.

"This sullen brat routine is getting old, Cole," Phillip Junior said, looking even more like the former wrestler turned movie star Dwayne "The Rock" Johnson. He hated it when his brothers teased him about that.

"And so is figuring out just how you manage to breathe with your face buried so deep in Dad's behind," Cole shot back.

Of all the brothers, Phillip Junior was the most devoted to his father—and believed that being "The Eldest" guaranteed him a natural progression to the throne.

"Enough," Sean said sternly with a shake of his head.

Cole eyed "The Star." Everyone had a role. Sean relished his as the star of several of Cress, INC's most popular cooking shows. He believed his face as the brand was the winning ticket. "Enough what?" he asked.

"Enough making everything uncomfortable because it amuses you," Lucas answered.

I find humor to avoid rage. But Cole kept his thought to himself as he eyed the youngest Cress son, "The Favorite." All his life, Lucas had been doted on by their mother with love—and plenty of food. He'd packed the extra pounds on until recently.

Cole loved his brothers. His only anger with them was for their blind allegiance to their father, who was undeserving of it.

No one knows that but me.

"So, you all will just fill Gabe's shoes and make him feel we don't want or need him back?" Cole accused, eyeing each of his brothers.

"À la nourriture. À la vie. À l'amour," Nicolette said, filling the silence with her favorite French saying. To food. To life. To love.

The maxim was painted on the wall above all of her stoves—personal and professional—and on the base of every pan in the Cress line of cookware. It was the watermark of every letter from the various editors of their culinary magazines. It was also branded throughout their online presence. And it served as the closing statement for the cooking shows produced by Cress, INC.'s television division.

"Gabriel will return," she asserted. "His presence here and at Cress, INC. is missed. Until he decides that he wants his position back, someone must complete the work."

"I'll do it," Phillip Junior asserted. "A future CEO has to set the example and step in when left in a jam by someone else."

"Sycophant," Cole muttered, disgusted by the lack of loyalty among brothers.

Nicolette reached to cover Cole's hand with her own. "I miss him, too," she assured him.

"Then fix it," he demanded, locking his gray-blue eyes with her own.

Her gaze softened as she nodded. "I think you're right," she admitted.

"Nicolette!" Phillip Senior roared.

"Assez, c'est assez, mon amour," she said, looking down the length of the table at her husband.

Like their parents, the brothers spoke both French and Spanish fluently.

Enough is enough, my love.

And though her tone was soft, there was no denying the finality of her words.

Two

One month later

"Enjoying your meal?"

Jillian looked up at the striking figure of Lorenzo León Cortez, Gabriel's best friend. His voice was deep, and he was tall—well over six feet—with broad shoulders and bone-straight, waist-length hair that only accentuated handsome features of his Native American and Mexican heritage.

The man was truly magnificent.

"It was delicious," she admitted, smiling at her plate now empty of the short ribs.

Jillian had been surprised to receive an invitation to the opening night of Gabriel's restaurant. Of course, she knew Cole had been behind it and had seen the look on Nicolette's face when she'd arrived that his mother had been none too pleased. Nicolette Lavoie-Cress clearly didn't favor socializing with the help.

Tough.

She glanced over at the family's table in the center of the restaurant and caught Cole's warm gaze on her—or rather, them. She took a sip of her champagne with a smile before looking up at Lorenzo, who was standing beside her table.

"You look like you could use some company, Jillian," he said.

I must look as good as I feel in this dress.

Another shadow darkened her table. "Looks can be deceiving, Zo," Cole said.

Jillian frowned at the possessiveness of his tone.

Lorenzo nodded in understanding before turning to walk away.

The jazzy background music filled the silence.

"You crossed a line," she said, rising and picking up the sequined purse she'd picked to complement her red-satin wrap dress with its delicate spaghetti straps and a plunging neckline—a leftover from her time traveling the world. "Suddenly, this thing of ours has developed strings."

"Jillian—"

He reached for her arm, but she easily evaded his touch and walked away, clearly ready to leave the small, intimate restaurant with its clean, stylish décor of pale walls, dark furnishings and bronzed accents behind. She opened the copper-trimmed glass door and stepped out onto the street without looking back.

At the sight of Gabriel and Monica at the other end of the block sharing a kiss, she smiled before heading in the opposite direction toward her red Mazda Miata with its black-canvas convertible top.

"Let's go home, Cherry," she said before unlocking the door and giving it a hard jerk.

Once the restaurant failed, the flashy BMW she'd purchased during better days as a private chef was repossessed when the payments were more than she could handle. She had returned to driving the cute and sporty little Miata her parents purchased for her at eighteen. It was fifteen years old and a bit finicky at times. When the engine didn't start on the first try, she caressed the steering wheel and tried again. "Mama loves you," she whispered, easing onto the street.

The drive to her modest loft apartment in Brooklyn went well, and she was glad to pull into her parking spot in the garage. She quickly made her way to the elevator and up to the ninth floor. She loved the building's architecture: exposed brick, piping and ducts, beamed ceilings, wood columns and oversize windows. The blend of industrialized style with modern appliances and design gave it an aesthetic she had fallen in love with and had been pleased to be able to afford. She didn't have a lot of space, less than seven hundred square feet, but the ceilings were ten feet high, and the city's views were vibrant at night.

As soon as she unlocked her sliding metal barn door, Jillian began undressing, leaving a deliberate trail of sequined clutch, heels, flashy red-satin dress and then her panties. Nude, she walked across the hardwood floor to the kitchen to pour herself a glass of wine. She'd gotten all dolled up. Attended the event. Eaten delicious food. And now she was ready to relax.

Her front door slid open and Cole stepped inside, still handsome in his black suit and tie. Jillian took a deep sip of her wine. "What took you so long?" she asked with a glance over her shoulder.

He closed and locked the door, then came toward her with heated eyes as he undressed and dropped his clothing atop hers. "How were you so sure I was coming?" he asked, removing his boxers and kicking them away to slide across the polished hardwood.

Jillian gave him a look that said "puh-leeze" as she enjoyed the sight of his sculpted nude body. His inches, darker toned than the rest of him, grew in length before her eyes, with a slight lean to the right. And led him right over to her. She was already shivering in anticipation as he wrapped one strong arm around her waist and pulled her close to bury his face against her neck.

"Humph. You just wanted to make sure Lorenzo wasn't sniffing around," she teased.

He stiffened and raised his head to look down at her. "Really?" he asked in his deep voice.

She gave him a soft laugh before leaning back in his embrace and drizzling some of her wine across her breasts. "Thirsty?"

He bent his knees to tongue the moisture. "And hungry," he moaned against her soft flesh.

Jillian flushed with heat. "Cole," she gasped as she blindly set the glass atop the counter before pressing her hands to the hard contours of his back.

When he raised her body with ease to bury his face against her cleavage, she wrapped her legs around his waist. The first feel of his crafty tongue against her nipples rushed them to hardness. He suckled one of the tight buds into his mouth and she released a sigh of pleasure from deep within as she rolled her hips.

Her entire body felt alive with their sexual chemistry. The pulse they created was not to be ignored or denied. And it had been that way over the last year without hesitation or deceleration.

Jillian clung to Cole as he carried her over to the center of the loft and the brown-leather sofa that also served as her bed when there was time to open it. There wasn't. Passions unleashed, they needed quenching.

Cole sat on the sofa with her straddling his lap. She brushed the curls from her face as he leaned his head back and eyed her. Her face. Her breasts. Her belly. The close-shaved mound of her intimacy. He massaged her hips and upper thighs as she took his hard inches in her hand to stroke. He grunted at her touch and rocked his hips forward.

"It's so hard," she whispered, enjoying his wince of pleasure.

"It aches," he admitted.

Jillian took one of his hands and pressed it down between her thighs. He cupped her. The curve of his palm pressed against her warm, pulsing bud as the tips of his fingers stroked her lips. Heat and electricity infused her. She cried out in sweet release as she rolled against his touch. Her grip on his inches tightened, evoking a wild cry of pleasure from him that gave her such immense joy.

He straightened and pressed kisses from her jawline up to her ear. "Watching you in that little red dress all night, and not being able to touch you, was pure hell, Jillian," he rasped.

She trembled.

"All I could think of was getting it off you and me inside you," he continued before sucking her earlobe.

She panted sharply.

"Did you have on a bra?" he asked.

She shook her head.

"I could tell."

He leaned her upper body back and lowered his head to lick her nipple and then caress it with a cool, steady stream of air.

"Damn," she swore with a gasp.

He switched his wicked onslaught to her other breast.

"That. Is. Amazing," Jillian admitted as he tended to her with slow and deliberate care.

She pressed her hand to his head and leaned to the right to open the wood box atop the square glass end table to retrieve one of the dozen condoms inside. She was ready for him. Wet, throbbing and in heat.

Tearing the foil, she removed the ribbed ultrasensitive latex.

"You ready?" he asked, watching her work the protection along the length of his hard inches.

She nodded.

"I wanted to taste you the way you like," he said, his voice thick.

"*We* like," Jillian reminded him, rising on her knees.

"It's the best meal I've ever eaten," Cole said, his smile wicked.

"Really?" Jillian asked, easing onto him.

Slowly.

They stared into each other's eyes, mouths open at the feel of her tightness surrounding his hardness.

Cole swore as the thick base of his erection entered her.

She dropped her head back and looked up at the ceiling, feeling her eyes glaze over with passion. She took a moment to adjust to the feel of him pressing against her walls. He throbbed inside her. She liked it—a lot.

Cole pressed his hands to her back and pulled her forward to kiss her. First, a slow press of their lips, and then he deepened it with his tongue and a guttural moan as she rocked her hips back and forth. She ended each smooth glide with a Kegel that gripped and released him. He liked that—a lot.

With her hands pressed to the sides of his face and

his arms wrapped around her so tightly that her breasts flattened against his hard chest, they slowly ground against each other as they took turns sucking each other's tongues. Sweat coated their bodies. She felt his heart pounding hard, just like her own. He lowered one arm to grip a handful of one of her round buttocks. She whimpered into his mouth.

"So good," he moaned, his eyes searching hers.

She nodded with urgency before she licked at his mouth and suckled his bottom lip. "Damn good," she agreed, stopping to clutch and release his inches with her walls.

"Jillian," he moaned, leaning back against the sofa and drawing her forward with him.

She rose slightly on her knees and took the lead in riding home. Nice and slow. Wicked and deliberate. She always wanted to give as good as she got, and the truth was that Cole Cress was *the* best lover she had ever had. Attentive. Passionate. Lengthy. It was nothing after a long night of numerous climaxes for her to beg him to claim his own happy ending to bring the passionate torture to an end. It was commonplace for them to sex each other to sleep and then have him wake her not long after for more.

His stamina was beyond impressive.

And addictive.

She broke the kiss to look at him with soft eyes and a hint of a smile. "I really like having sex with you," she whispered.

"Same," he agreed.

"And the best part," Jillian said, quickening the back-and-forth motion of her hips.

"What?"

"Climaxing while you're inside me."

She felt his tool stiffen.

"Same," he said, lifting his head to capture her mouth with his own.

Together they moved in unison, fast and hard, as they drove each other headfirst into the electrifying white-hot spasms of their climaxes. Moans. Hoarse cries. Hurried and frantic movements. Mindless falls into the hot abyss together. Shaken. Stirred.

With one last high-pitched cry, Jillian collapsed against him and rested her forehead against the top of the sofa as he rubbed her back and pressed kisses to her shoulder.

The aftermath of their fiery connection had them both sweaty and spent.

Ding-dong.

Jillian frowned at the sound as she raised her head.

"Not Leon I hope," Cole quipped, a teasing light in his electric eyes.

She sat upright and lightly pinched one of his nipples. "You're sexier than you are funny, Cress," she said, rising to walk over to the door where she kept a tablet on a small metal table in the corner. On the screen was the video feed from her doorbell. And she was looking at the face of Nicolette Cress.

"It's your mother," Jillian whispered, her heart pounding at the shock as she galvanized into action, picking up their trail of clothing.

Cole stood and deeply frowned. "What?" he asked.

Jillian gave him a dramatic shove as she took quick steps to the sofa and slapped the clothing against his chest. "Bathroom," she ordered.

"What!" he exclaimed, now holding the pile in his arms. "I'm not hiding from my mother."

She turned to open the engraved armoire against the wall to remove a cotton robe. "Yes, you are. Because I need my job, and your mother is not firing me because she discovered The Rebel naked—"

"The Rebel?" Cole scoffed.

"Yes," Jillian stressed as she pulled on the robe and moved to push him across the apartment.

Ding-dong.

Cole's frown deepened as he back-stepped into the bathroom. One of her sexy heels dropped from the heap in his arms.

Jillian motioned with her hand for him to back up some more so that she could grab the doorknob. "Two rings? Your mother's a little pushy," she said before pulling the door closed.

Cole set their clothing in the sink before easing the door open a little. Through the crack, he watched Jillian sniff the air and survey the scene. She suddenly jumped, as if frightened, and rushed over to the sofa. Picking up the empty condom wrapper, she slid it into the pocket of her bright yellow robe. He looked down at the latex still clinging to him, filled with his release.

"Mrs. Cress?" Jillian said, feigning surprise. "It's a little late, and I was running a bath."

"You and I need to speak," his mother said.

About what?

"I'm curious what we have to discuss that couldn't wait until I got to work in the morning," Jillian returned coolly.

Feisty.

Cole covered his mouth to trap a yawn. A night of decadent food and champagne capped off with mind-blowing sex, he wanted nothing more than to sleep it off. He leaned against the sink and crossed his arms over his chest as he listened to their conversation.

"Your dealings with my son," Nicolette said.

Cole stiffened.

"Excuse me," Jillian said. "You're mistaken."

He stepped closer to peek through the slit of the open bathroom door. His mother and his lover were facing each other. Jillian's back was to him. He grimaced as he fought the urge to dress and leave his hiding place to admonish his mother for dipping into his business.

Her hiring of Jillian as part of her household staff was Nicolette's business.

"Tonight, at Gabriel's, was very revealing when Lorenzo and Cole seemed to bump heads about you," Nicolette said, looking around at Jillian's apartment before casting her blue gaze squarely on the chef. "That, plus Cole unable to take his eyes off you in that red dress, was telling."

Just deny it, Jillian, and send her on her way so we can go to bed.

Jillian shook her head. "Mrs. Cress—"

His mother held up her hand to stop her. "I don't have time for games or pretenses," she said in her heavy French accent. "I know my sons. Probably better than they like. He wants you or has had you. Either way, I want it to end."

Cole frowned as he straightened to his full height. Anger burned the pit of his stomach. He couldn't believe what he was hearing.

"And if you end whatever it is you two have going on, I will appoint you an executive chef at one of the Cress restaurants…in another state," Nicolette finished. "So, choose. Either way, you are done at the townhouse. I won't pay you to screw my son."

What the hell?

This was a side of his mother Cole had never seen before. Cold. Manipulating. Controlling.

"But you will offer me an executive chef position instead?" Jillian countered with a tinge of sarcasm.

"The only talents of yours I am interested in my family enjoying are in the kitchen," Nicolette said.

"Mrs. Cress, I refuse to be insulted in my home. It can fit inside your pantry, but it's mine," Jillian asserted.

No nonsense until the end.

Nicolette chuckled. It was mocking. "And my son might fit inside you, but *he's* mine, and I do not want this thing between you to get out of hand."

He turned and dug through the pile of clothing for his underwear and suit pants. He was ready to confront his mother. "This is bull—"

He paused in jerking on his boxers at the sound of the front door sliding closed. He felt like a fool, frozen like a deer in headlights in Jillian's cramped bathroom, waiting to hear what was going on. He pulled his boxer briefs up, dropped the black pants, and opened the door to step out.

Jillian, locking the front door, glanced back over her shoulder. "She's gone, Cole."

"I figured that out since I was in the only hiding place in here," he said, standing with his hands on his hips.

She smiled at him as she crossed her arms over her chest and made her way to one of the three expansive arched windows of her apartment.

"I'm sorry about that, Jillian," he said. "I had no idea my mother would ever pull such a stunt."

"It's not your fault, Cole," she said, leaning against the window, the city's nightscape as her background.

He walked to her and wrapped an arm around her waist to pull her back against his body. "She left before I could set her straight about this stunt," he said, eyeing

Jillian's reflection. "But I will as soon as I see her. I can't believe she insulted you like that."

He frowned at her continued silence.

"Cole—" Jillian raised her eyes to lock with his in the window "—I'm going to take the job."

His frown deepened as he stepped back, releasing her from his grasp. His jaw worked in rising irritation as he realized that Jillian was putting her ambition before him.

What was it she'd said at the restaurant? *Suddenly this thing of ours has developed strings.*

Right. They were never meant to last.

Although he and Traci had been in a relationship, Jillian's choice felt like a similar betrayal. Not as callously calculated as Traci's machinations...

Or was it?

She turned and leaned back against the window as she stared at him, asserting, "It's an opportunity that I can't pass up, Cole."

Still...

It stung.

He released a bitter chuckle and shook his head before turning to cross the room to enter the bathroom.

He dressed and made a conscious effort to not let his anger toss her clothing. That would be childish. He was sardonic at times and could find humor where most could not, but he wasn't silly. As he smoothed the lapels of his suit jacket, he eyed himself in the mirror above the sink. In the reflection, he saw the truth of his anger at Jillian.

And his hurt.

Cole cleared his throat and forced away the emotion lining his face.

It was not his first time looking betrayal in the face.

But it will be the last.

He left the bathroom. "Have a good life, Jillian," he said, taking long strides to the door.

She rushed across the space to stand in front of him. "Cole, talk to me," she urged, clenching his upper arms.

He brushed off her touch. "The way you did before you decided we were done without even talking to me?" His tone was so very cold.

"This was no strings, remember," she said. "We were just having fun. *Remember?*"

He looked down at her. "I'm clear about that," he assured her. "I just didn't know you would use me for your come-up. Excuse me if that's hard to swallow."

She looked pained by his words. "It's so easy to speak from your seat of privilege, Cole," she said.

He scowled. "Privilege?" he barked.

"Your family. Cress, INC. Your wealth." She ticked off each on her fingers.

"None of those things earned me my first James Beard at just twenty, and you damn well know that—or you should, *Chef*," he said, letting his ire drip off the word.

"Don't mock me, Cole," Jillian said, her voice soft.

"Don't shortchange yourself," he shot back.

"What do you mean?"

"Why not gain the position based on your skill and not a payoff where you collude with my mother to control my damn life?" His voice was hard, unrelenting.

"You made a scene tonight, Cole. Your mother discovered our personal business because of you. I lost my job tonight, Cole," Jillian said, her hands slashing the air as she pointed at him.

True.

"Why can't you see this from my point of view? Get out of your hurt feelings and see the position I'm in?"

"Hurt feelings!" he charged. "This is anger. Disgust. Disappointment. Not hurt. No strings, remember?"

They both fell silent. Somehow it was filled with turbulence.

He turned from her and paced as he slid his hands into the pockets of his slacks. He'd look over at her, feel the stab of her betrayal, and look away. Mixed with his anger was confusion.

Why does this bother me so much?

The old Cole would have laughed, popped champagne, and celebrated her new position with her before one last "sexcapade" to carry him through the dry spell until he met his next no-strings attachment.

Foolishly, there had been moments over the last year when he'd felt his time with Jillian was different, but he'd ignored them. Still, she was not his forever. He'd known that going in, and she'd made it clear as it came to a shattering end.

"Cole," Jillian called over to him.

He looked at her. Her robe puddled at her feet, she stood naked before him. Just as beautiful, alluring and tempting as ever. His body betrayed him and he began to harden. It would be easy to narrow the space between them, hitch her against the door, and fill her until he climaxed.

So very easy.

But things were different. His trust in her had been shattered. And if there was one thing he'd learned from life, it was that trust was everything to him.

"You made your choice, Jillian," he said, his voice low as he treated his eyes to one last intimate look at her body. A playground he had enjoyed with relish over the last year. He would miss it. "I wouldn't want you to go back on your word to my mother. Besides, your debt to my family and me is well paid."

Jillian gasped at the dig as she raced to him and slapped him soundly at the implied insult.

Whap!

It turned his head to the left. It stung. But not as deeply as the ache radiating across his chest. Or the betrayal he felt at himself for hating that he'd sunk low enough to insult her in such a manner. Still, he bit his bottom lip to keep from apologizing and instead breezed past her to leave the apartment and Jillian behind.

Three

Two months later

"Your new apartment is beautiful, Jillie."

Jillian turned her phone from her waterfront view in San Francisco to look at her family on the screen via FaceTime. Her father, Harry Rossi—whom she favored— her mother, Nora—from whom she got her humor— and her grandmother, Ionie. They were all huddled in front of the computer in Rochester, New York, in her parents' home.

"Thank you, Gram," she said, taking a seat on the L-shaped sofa as she eyed the petite senior with her short silver curls and her beloved fuchsia lipstick. She was vibrant, smart, and funny, but the grandmother she knew was beginning to fade a bit as a chronic heart condition weakened her.

Jillian fought the urge to ask her how she was doing, knowing it irritated her to be coddled.

"We miss you, Jillie, but we're proud of you," Harry said in a booming voice that matched his lofty broad frame.

Her mother lovingly called him Bear.

And their love, since the days they'd been in high school, was sickeningly adorable. Arguments were few and far between. Shows of affection were often. Lots and lots of laughter. Long hugs. And slow dances with whispered promises.

They loved and liked each other.

That was her childhood.

It was her search for her own "Mr. Right" or "The One" or her "happily-ever-after" that had led to Jillian's two failed marriages. The first at just eighteen to Warren Long, her high school sweetheart. A wedding at the county courthouse and a year of arguing over their lack of money as they both attended college made them realize they were too young—and had moved too fast—to be married. Thankfully once the hurt and bitterness had faded, they'd remained in touch over the years.

That had not been the case with her second husband, Chuckie Forge. They'd met when she'd been hired as a line cook in his small but popular restaurant in the Hell's Kitchen section of Manhattan. Their fiery, passionate three-month affair had led to a Vegas marriage that had crashed and burned when he'd disappeared for an entire weekend with his pastry chef. Unlike Warren, Jillian disdained Chuckie and was pleased to never lay eyes on him again.

"How are things going with the restaurant?" Her father's question interrupted her musings.

"Better," she said. "The shift between being a personal chef and an executive chef for a restaurant that is part of a brand is huge for me. There's less freedom."

"You understand that. Right?" her father asked.

"Absolutely," she assured him.

And she did. But still, she wished she could plan the menu without input from corporate or restaurant management. It felt formulaic, and she suspected it was why the position had been left open following the previous chef's exit. He now operated his own restaurant.

Her grandmother covered her mouth with a yawn. Jillian smiled. The three-hour time difference was taking some getting used to, as well. It was six in California, but on the East Coast it was nine at night. Definitely past her grandmother's bedtime.

But she wasn't ready to say good-night to them.

She was lonely.

Jillian looked past the phone to her spacious furnished apartment with its incredible waterfront views and just a walk from the restaurant, CRESSIII. Her new six-figure salary would pay off her debt within a year. And the press generated by Cress, INC.'s public relations team of her hire as executive chef might lead to even more opportunities.

None of it replaced the surprising hole left in her life without Cole.

She sighed.

"Everything okay, Jillie?" Ionie asked, leaning closer to the screen.

Jillian smiled when her grandmother tapped it. "I'm not frozen, Gram," she said.

"Oh. Okay," Ionie said. "I can't be right and hit it out of the park all the time to bat a thousand."

Ionie *loved* the New York Mets.

"Listen, Jillie, my bed is calling my name," she said, standing. "And I'm going to answer. Videophone me tomorrow."

"It's FaceTime, Mom," Harry said with a playful wink at the screen as his mother turned and walked away.

Ionie was filled with one-liners and it never took much to nudge one out of her.

"Tomato to*ma*to, Harry. Same difference, son," she called over her shoulder as she sauntered away with a sway of her hips.

They all chuckled.

The eighty-year-old retired schoolteacher was a spit-fire. They adored her.

"How is she doing?" Jillian asked.

"Better. The full-time nurse is great with both of us working," Harry said.

"We worry a lot less about her being home alone, so the *nurse* is a huge help," her mom told her. "And thank you for your help with the cost, Jillie. I'm proud of you for taking on that responsibility."

"No worries. We're family. It's what we do," she assured them.

"Why aren't you at work?" Nora asked as she licked the tip of her thumb and swiped at something on her husband's cheek.

"The restaurant is closed on Mondays," she explained, fighting the urge to rub her eyes since she was wearing her contacts.

Her brow furrowed when her father pressed a kiss to her mother's palm and they shared a look.

Jillian moaned, having seen that look a million times during her childhood and knowing a kiss was next. Just sickeningly sweet.

"Let me let y'all go," she said, zooming her finger in on the button to end the call.

"Bye," they said in unison just before the screen went black.

She released a heavy breath and dropped her phone onto the sofa. The silence of the apartment echoed. She leaned forward to pick up the remote from the leather ottoman serving as a coffee table to turn on the wall-mounted television.

Nothing held her attention.

And everything seemed to remind her of Cole.

A romantic movie where the couple shared a kiss.

Cole was an excellent kisser.

She switched the channel.

Click, click.

A commercial for soap.

Jillian smiled, remembering them squeezing into her small tub together to share a bubble bath.

She frowned and raised the remote.

Click, click.

A weather news story about a string of rainy days ahead.

I remember that weekend at my apartment when we stayed inside, cooked for each other, and had the most amazing rainy-day sex.

She shook her head to clear it of the steamy memories.

Click, click.

This time she turned the television off. She couldn't escape her thoughts of *him*. Cole. Cole. Cole. Cole.

She looked down at her phone.

Don't do it. Move on. You made your choice. Live with it. And stay off his Instagram.

Jillian pushed aside her thoughts and snatched up her phone. Her heart pounded, and she felt nervous butterflies as she scrolled through his feed. He hadn't posted in weeks.

She paused at a photo of him leaning against his high-end food truck. Serious face. Electric eyes in his brown complexion. All-black attire. Sexy as sexy could be.

I miss him.

The nights were the worst. They used to tease it was their "sexing hours." Jillian had lost count of those after-midnight hours where one would text the other. Within the hour, he would arrive and, not long after he was hard, she was wet, and their grunts of pleasure echoed in her loft apartment. On the door. The floor. The shower. The sofa—open and closed. Against the window.

She bit her bottom lip and closed her eyes with a deep moan at the visual of his hard buttocks clenching and un-clenching as he stroked inside her, her back and buttocks pressed against the windows. Her knees had clutched his sides and her fingers had dug into his shoulders as he'd delivered one deep thrust after another.

I could use Cole's special delivery.

But those days—and nights—were over, and her body was going through withdrawal.

Over the last couple of months, had she second-guessed ending her dalliance with Cole? Yes. But in those moments, she reminded herself forever had never been a part of their plans. Still, she had never intended for him to feel offended or put off.

Jillian had tried a few times in the weeks following her rushed moved to San Francisco to call him, but he'd never answered. She'd wanted to get it through to him that the hefty salary would allow her to assist her parents with the expensive medical care her grandmother required, to say nothing of help clear the hefty debt from her first restaurant closing. Her duty to her family and her success was interwoven—it had to be.

Wealth was not a part of her legacy.

Unlike Cole.

And now her life was moving on.

Without Cole.

Within the year, her feelings for the sexy rebel had deepened beyond just a fling. Hindsight was always twenty-twenty because that realization hadn't hit home until he'd been out of her life for good. She had thought she'd only wanted sex from him, but she ached with sadness for more than that, wanting to hear his deep voice, to make him laugh with her dry wit, or to have him surprise her with one of his notes.

Jillian rose from the sofa and made her way to her bedroom. On her bedside table was the carved wood box from her loft in New York. She opened it. Gone were the condoms. Instead it held every monogrammed note Cole had ever given her over the last year. It wasn't until she'd packed up her things that she'd found them all randomly placed around her apartment. In a cookbook. Mixed with mail. In the back pocket of jeans.

Anywhere and everywhere. She'd never thrown them away.

She sat on the edge of the bed and picked up the box, holding it up to her nose. The scent of his crisp cologne still clung to some of the notes. She smiled a little as she opened each folded card.

Some were funny.

"'What's black and white and hard all over?'" she read, chuckling at his play on his mixed-race heritage and his desire for her.

Most were steamy.

"'There is nothing better than the taste of you,'" she read, letting her finger stroke his slashing handwritten words.

She had taken the notes for granted.

As she sat with Cole's notes scattered on her lap, she fast realized she had taken the time they'd shared for granted, as well.

* * *

Bzzzzzz. Bzzzzzz. Bzzzzzz.

Cole ignored his cell phone vibrating in the inner pocket of his black tuxedo jacket as he placed his small stack of hundred-dollar chips on the roulette table of the luxurious, historic casino in Monte Carlo, Monaco. He kept his eyes on the ball after the dealer waved his hand across the table, signaling no more bets. He took a sip from his snifter of whiskey and, with a calm aloofness, watched the ball fall onto the winning number.

He smiled as the dealer pushed a sizable stack of chips next to his on the number four. "Luck be *my* lady tonight," he said, playing on the lyrics of the 1950's Frank Sinatra song.

"Then call me Luck."

Cole was waiting for the dealer to pay out all winners on the board. He looked to his right at the sultry feminine voice and found a beautiful, svelte woman offering him an alluring smile. Her skin was the color of dark chocolate. The crimson she wore on her lips and her body was electrifying. From her accent and the high cut of her cheekbones, he assumed she was of African descent—a regal beauty with the type of style that spoke of elegance and wealth.

He felt annoyance that he instantly compared her to Jillian. Two months later and thoughts of her still replayed on a loop in his mind.

"You've been here for a month, and you're always alone. It's time for you to make a new friend," the sultry beauty said, drawing his attention once again. She extended her hand. "Lesedi Osei."

He took her hand into his own. "Cole Cress," he said, easing out of their shake when her finger pressed against his inner wrist.

Before Jillian, he would have matched Lesedi's vibe, offered her an early morning breakfast as the clock struck four in the morning, and then taken her to his bed to make sure she never regretted her boldness in approaching him.

He retrieved all of his tokens before turning to her. "And if you know I've been here that long, then so have you," he said.

She tucked a metallic leather clutch under her arm. It matched the strapless minidress she wore. "My family is staying in Monte Carlo for the summer," she said, her accent giving her voice a lilting quality.

"Nigerian?" he asked of her heritage.

"Very good," she said with an incline of her head.

He watched her tuck her shoulder-length bob behind her ear and glance away. A flirty move that was subtle. He caught it. She was interested.

Am I?

He eyed her. But it was Jillian's shapely frame in the dress that he saw.

That angered him.

To be intimate with this beautiful chocolate woman before him would be nothing more than using her to relieve his sexual frustration and make him forget a woman whose past betrayal stung like it happened yesterday.

Damn.

Lesedi looked up at him with a regretful smile. "Whoever she is, she is truly the lucky one," she said.

"She doesn't deserve it," he mumbled, clenching his jaw.

Lesedi opened her clutch and removed a business card to extend to him between her index and middle finger. "*If* you ever fix it or forget it…" she said before walking past him with one soft pat to his chest.

As he slid the card into the front pocket with his phone, he turned and watched her walk away before she disappeared into the crowd. Deciding his night of gambling, drinks and fine food was done, Cole left the elaborately decorated casino to take the stairs up to the hotel lobby. Here, too, the architecture spoke to its long history and grandeur.

Last month he had been at the family's country estate in Paris when the house staff made his mother aware that he was staying there. Once her incessant calls bounced between his cell and the estate's landline, Cole had caught the first flight to Monte Carlo. Within hours, he'd been safely tucked away in the city of glamour, enjoying the serene quiet of the days and the endless opportunities of an active nightlife.

As he caught the elevator to his suite, he pulled his cell phone from his pocket. He wasn't surprised to see his mother's number. Nicolette Cress was on a mission to bring the wandering son back into the fold. She was huge on the family remaining close.

Thus, the townhouse large enough…for them all.

Same as the business…for them all.

Nicolette was so intent on family unity that she'd mediated Gabriel's part-time return to Cress, INC. as he'd put his primary focus on his restaurant and she'd capitulated on his relationship with Monica, the family's former maid.

Where Phillip Senior was stern in his demand for family loyalty, Nicolette used a different approach—knowing how to sway all the men in her life to bend at her will.

The night he saw his mother move with such calculating coldness for his feelings at Jillian's apartment, he had never returned to the Cress townhouse. He'd spent the night at a hotel in Midtown Manhattan and flown to Paris the next day. He kept in touch with his brothers to assure his mother that he was alive and well, but he had, thus far, avoided any direct communication with her and handled his business decisions via Zoom calls and emails.

No one knew that Jillian was at the root of his annoyance with his mother.

Cole entered his deluxe suite. With the linen curtains of the terrace door open, the moon cast the room's modern décor with light. The shades of white, powder blue and taupe matched the view of the sea. It was calming by day or night.

He kicked off his handmade leather shoes, undid the top buttons of his shirt and unlatched the band of his Piaget watch as he crossed the marbled entryway to make his way down the hall to the bedroom. His yawn was hard to deny because of the late hour, but he walked up the space between the all-white, king-size bed and the sitting area's suede chair to open the terrace door. The scent of the sea reached him. The sight of the moon's rays glistening upon the waters calmed him as he took in the views of the city's Belle Époque architecture among the surrounding green hills.

It was too magnificent to ignore.

And he could use the tranquility.

Thoughts of Jillian made him feel as if a storm was brewing inside him with no escape. He missed her. That truth caused him to clench his teeth and release a heavy breath filled with his frustration at her.

And himself.

He felt like a fool.

Cole walked back into the suite to pour himself two fingers of whiskey from the crystal decanter on the bar in the sitting area's corner. With a sip, he made his way back onto the terrace. In truth, he avoided slumber because she conquered his sleeping hours—through dreams and nightmares.

Had he known the first time he'd laid eyes on the beauty that it would end the way it had, he never would have made the first move that day…

Cole and his brothers were in the movie room on the second floor of the five-story townhouse. It was a rare night that they all were home, and when the youngest Cress family member requested that they watch her favorite animated movie, Moana, her wishes were the command of the family. She was everyone's soft spot as the inner struggle to be named heir to the Cress, INC. throne reigned.

Cole had been the last to come down from his bedroom suite on the fourth floor. Everyone was seated in one of the twenty leather recliners that faced the movie screen. Collette sat front and center, her cup-holders filled with snacks—a treat because her mother always plied her with healthy alternatives.

"Hurry, Uncle Cole," she urged, her cheeks stuffed with candy.

Cole moved to the fully stocked snack station along the far wall, next to the entry to the wrought-iron staircase. It was completely stocked with a variety of boxed candy, a popcorn maker, a soda fountain and an ice cream machine. He selected a box of Goobers from the stack on the glass shelves. "Where's Mom?" he asked before opening the box and tossing a few of the treats into his mouth.

"She's interviewing the new chef," Phillip Senior said, kicking the recliner back and elevating his feet.

"Oh yeah?" Cole said. "Franco will be hard to top."

Their chef of the last ten years had retired with plans to return to his native Brazil. His traditional dishes had impressed the family of chefs. Even Phillip Senior had begrudgingly admitted that Franco's feijoada—*a Brazilian beef, pork and bean stew—was better than his own.*

Who would top that? he wondered.

Curious, Cole moved to the tablet on the wood-paneled wall and accessed the house's security system. Every room of the townhouse was under surveillance. Except, of course, his parents' suite, which took up the entire third floor and the six personal bedroom suites on the fourth and fifth floors.

He found his mother in the living room, seated on the light gray velvet sofa across from a young woman on the other.

She sat with poise and confidence in a stylish black pantsuit, her ankles crossed as she looked his mother directly in the eye. Her curly hair had been pulled into a topknot and her spectacles were perched on her nose. With her plump lips covered in red lipstick, he couldn't help but think she had the air of a naughty librarian waiting to be untamed.

"Cole, close the curtains and kill the lights," Lucas called over to him.

Cole forced his eyes away from the woman's face to look over at the second half of the spacious floor that made up the library with its floor-to-ceiling shelves lined with books. Like the other four floors of the townhouse, the entire rear wall was glass. He used the button on the light switch by the stairwell to close the soft gray velvet curtains. He dimmed the lights as well, just as the movie started. Although night and its darkness reigned, his actions would ensure a better movie-watching experience.

Instead of claiming a seat, however, he used the darkness to descend the wrought-iron staircase. It opened directly into the first-floor living room, but he paused, crossed his arms and leaned against the railing to watch the stranger from across the room.

She was beautiful. Her voice husky. Her confidence clear.

"I'll be honest, Jillian, I am very impressed by your previous employers," Nicolette said.

Jillian.

"I am very interested in someone used to decorum and discretion," his mother continued.

"Of course," Jillian agreed with a nod just before she glanced past his mother's shoulder to look at him. Her eyes widened slightly in surprise.

He gave her his best smile—the one that had wooed many a woman over the years. Nice, easy, and charming, with the right amount of wile.

Jillian shifted her eyes back to his mother, but he saw the spark of interest before she did.

It made his pulse race, and he felt excited in a way that surprised him. He decided right then that he wanted Jillian, and he would charm the beauty right into his bed...

And he had.

And it had been glorious. Never had he had so much fun in a pantry.

Cole pushed away the hot memory. As he stood on the terrace of his suite in Monte Carlo, nursing her betrayal and his drink, he understood the chorus from the song *I Wish* by Carl Thomas because he wished he'd never met Jillian Rossi at all.

He felt used by her.

True, their relationship had been casual, but he'd still thought it had meant more to her than something to toss away without a second thought after more than a year of sharing time.

Bzzzzzz. Bzzzzzz. Bzzzzzz.

Cole eased his phone from his inner pocket again. It was Gabe. It was just after nine thirty on the East Coast.

His family had no way of knowing they were reaching out to him at odd hours where he was.

He answered the call. "Yeah?" he said.

"Hey, stranger."

He chuckled before he took another deep sip of his drink. "How can I help you, big brother?" he drawled to the man who was older than him by two years.

They'd grown up close and had remained so in their adult years.

"Asking just what spurned this journey you're on would be a waste of time, I guess?" Gabe asked.

Cole's grip on his glass tightened. Usually, he and Gabe were honest with each other. In fact, Gabe was the only family member who knew of his relationship with Jillian. He knew his brother would keep whatever secrets he'd shared with him, but he was hesitant to share just how much Jillian's and their mother's actions had angered and disturbed him.

"If you sneaked off to San Francisco, believe me, I understand," Gabe assured him.

Cole frowned as he sat on one of the lounge chairs. "San Francisco?" he asked.

"To be with Jillian."

Cole's gut clenched.

So that's where she is.

He had made it his business to avoid knowing Jillian's whereabouts. Out of New York was more than enough. "We're done," he said, his voice sounding cold even to his ears.

"You want to talk about it?"

She used ending things with me as a stepping stone for her career.

He could still feel her heel in his back.

"Nah," Cole said with a shake of his head even though his brother couldn't see him.

"You sure?"

"Yes," he admitted with a begrudging smile.

The line went quiet.

"Gabe?" Cole wondered if the call had ended.

"One sec," Gabe said, sounding distracted.

Cole knew his brother well, and Gabe was a thinker. That's what made him the best choice to take over as CEO of Cress, INC.—if he hadn't already turned down the position. "Leave it alone, Gabe," he warned, knowing he was putting the pieces to the puzzle together.

"You're not speaking to Mom, who pushed for Jillian's new executive chef position…"

Cole jumped to his feet. "Gabe," he snapped.

"Okay, okay." He acquiesced. "Listen, I called because I need you to attend the Chef Gala."

Every year Cress, INC. held a glitzy dinner party for all the chefs from across the country. Gabe served as the president of the restaurant division, and this event was essential to his brother. But it would put Cole directly in the room with the two women he was avoiding—Jillian and his mother.

"No," Cole said firmly.

"Listen, Monica and I are announcing our engagement. I *need* you there," Gabe stressed.

They had been brothers for thirty years. Never had they not had each other's back. Not once. And there had been plenty of times that Gabe had saved the behind of his rebellious teenage brother hell-bent on wreaking havoc.

Cole released a long breath before turning to make his way inside his suite to replenish his drink.

"I'll be there," he promised.

Four

He really hates me.

Jillian took a deep sip of champagne as she stared across the original CRESS restaurant at Cole. When she'd walked into the Midtown Manhattan restaurant filled with nerves but still feeling beautiful in her elegant attire, she never assumed his anger was still so visceral that he would barely glance at her when their paths crossed.

It was as if she hadn't existed.

"Hello, Cole," she'd said with a smile.

"Jillian," was his cold and clipped response as he'd barely broken his stride past her.

It hadn't helped that he'd looked dark and sexy in his tuxedo with a crisp haircut and groomed shadow of beard. Just a gorgeous man. With an equally devastatingly fit body. She remembered it well.

"Jillian! It's so good to see you!"

She shifted her gaze to find Monica walking toward

her in a white satin gown that fit her curvy frame like a
second glove. "Wow. Love and lots of money suit you.
You look gorgeous," she exclaimed as they shared a hug.

They'd both served at the pleasure of the Cress family as chef and maid. During that time, they had been
friendly but not close. Still, it was good to see her. And
in that moment of nursing hurt feelings because her former lover had treated her as a stranger; Jillian could use
a friendly hug.

"You're the one. I love this," Monica said.

She stepped back to eye Jillian from her upswept curls
to her sheer black, exposed-corset bustier draped with
black-sequined fabric across her breasts and around her
waist to trail down one leg of the satin palazzos she'd
paired with the daringly risqué top.

"Thank you," Jillian said, trying to forget she'd wondered what Cole's reaction would be to her ensemble
when she'd selected it last week from an exclusive wom-
en's boutique in San Francisco.

All for nothing.

"Congratulations on the new position," Monica said,
stopping one of the uniformed waiters who passed by
with a tray of flutes filled with vintage champagne.

Jillian remained silent to the praise. Her eyes had
locked on a beautiful redhead with reality-defying
breasts, uplifted by the bodice of her strapless emerald-
green dress, saunter up to Cole and press a kiss to his
cheek. She wound her arm around his. The move was
clingy and possessive.

"Ohhhhh," Monica said, drawing the word out.

Jillian glanced over at her. "What?" she asked, feeling her heart pound.

"So, it was Cole with the naughty note of the 'taste of

you lingering on his tongue'?" Monica asked with a sly look before taking another sip of her champagne.

Last year, Monica had been cleaning the kitchen and found one of Cole's sexy notes in Jillian's monogrammed cutlery bag. When she'd attended her first event with Gabe at the Cress townhouse as his girlfriend—surprising everyone including Jillian—she had asked which of the Cress men had written the note. Jillian had kept the truth a secret.

Until now.

"What gave it away?" Jillian asked.

"The look you just gave Cole and Kimber," Monica said. "So, I assume you kept your word of it ending once you left your job at the Cress townhouse."

Silly of me. "Something like that," Jillian said.

"Well, this should be good because the last thing Nicolette wants strutting around a Cress, INC. event is a woman with low IQ and high hem," Monica said.

"I'm sure he's just fine with both," Jillian drawled, chancing another look across the restaurant.

They weren't in the same spot.

CRESS, the first of the group of restaurants started by Cress, INC., was a beautiful, massive restaurant in hues of chrome and ivory with modern detailing and lots of lighting. A true showpiece.

Having been flown to New York, executive chefs from all eleven Cress restaurants had been put up in suites at a nearby five-star hotel. Phillip Senior and Nicolette were preparing a decadent seven-course meal for the gala dinner. It was a Monday and, with the restaurants closed, it was the perfect night to celebrate and motivate their chefs.

As she looked around the small crowd, Jillian was impressed by the attendees, including the stunningly handsome Lorenzo León Cortez. He looked so gorgeous in his light gray tux, matching silk tee and Native American neckpiece of black-braided leather and chunky turquoise. His long hair was pulled back from his handsome face.

"He is exquisite," Jillian said, remembering Cole being bothered by Lorenzo's attention to her the night of Gabe's restaurant opening.

"Zo?" Monica asked. "He's Gabe's best friend, so I plead the fifth."

"You could have just said he's not exquisite," Jillian reminded her.

"I'm not built to lie," Monica said, giving her a little wave before walking away with a wink.

Jillian cleared her throat and pressed her free hand to her belly before easing through the multitude of people toward Zo, who was standing at the L-shaped bar. He turned and did a double-take as she approached. She gave him a beguiling smile. He gave her a curious look.

Two can play Cole's game.

"Hello, Lorenzo," she said, looking up at his towering height.

He took a sip of his beer and eyed her with amusement. "Can I assume from the stares Cole is shooting at us that you're over here to make him jealous?" His deep voice seemed to rumble.

Jillian instantly felt childish and rightfully so. "Yes," she admitted, leaning her elbows against the edge of the bar.

Lorenzo chuckled as he bent a bit at the waist. "It worked," he said before walking away.

Moments later, she felt heightened awareness—like a shiver. She knew before Cole stood beside her that he was there.

"What games are you playing?" he asked.

The cool scent of his cologne teased her.

"So now you know me?" she asked before taking a sip of her champagne.

"I never knew you to play games, Jillian, but then I realized too late I never knew you at all," he said, his voice low enough for just her ears and cold enough to chill her to the bone.

Sadness waved over her, but she stiffened her spine and turned sideways to face his profile.

He's so damn handsome. And I miss him. I want him. I... I... I...

Jillian gasped at the realization of the depth of her feelings for Coleman Cress.

I love him.

Cole turned his head to look at her.

Their eyes met. She shivered and had to close her eyes to break the connection before her feelings for him tumbled from her mouth.

I love you, Cole.

"Jillian?"

The sound of her name on his lips was her undoing. She opened her eyes to turn and walk away from him as fast as she could on her heels without falling. Her heart beat faster. Her pulse sped up.

Missing him? Desiring him? Wanting to sex him?

Fine.

Falling in love?

That was not a part of the plan.

Jillian reached the door to the hall leading to the restrooms. She paused at the entry and looked over her shoulder, still trembling from her revelation. Cole's date was back at his side, but his eyes were on her across the restaurant.

With intensity.

I love him.

She turned quickly and raced down the hall, her hand on the wall, to reach the ladies' room. As soon as she entered, she pushed the door closed and leaned against it for a few moments before moving to the sink to grip the edge of the counter. She studied her reflection. She felt afraid and excited.

Her breathing labored. Her heart pounded. Her pulse raced.

Just like that, *everything* had changed. Absolutely everything.

Damn.

Cole took a deep sip of his coffee with Kahlúa as he sat back in his seat at the line of tables set up for a family-style dinner for twenty-six guests. His parents sat side by side at one end, with Phillip Junior and Raquel at the other end. He looked along the table's length, elaborately decorated with floral arrangements and candles, at Jillian enjoying a conversation with Xin Lao, the executive chef of CRESS VIII in the Napa Valley.

She glanced up and he shifted his gaze away from her.

Earlier, at the bar, something had happened.

He'd seen a shift in Jillian's eyes, and it had shaken his soul. As she'd rushed away, he'd had to fight the instinctive urge to follow her. Stop her. Question her.

Kiss her.

His gut clenched.

When she'd paused at the entrance to the hall and looked back, he hadn't been able to take his eyes off her—and had struggled to stand firmly in place. When she'd turned to disappear down the hall, he'd felt regret.

Jillian Rossi was still in his system.

The first sight of her entering the restaurant in that

strapless, almost revealing bustier with the wide-legged pants that emphasized her thick thighs, hips and rounded buttocks had him hungering for her. She was spectacular, and it had taken an Oscar-worthy performance for him to do nothing more than speak her name and move past her with a quickness when he'd first laid eyes on her.

All night, as his date had clung to him like Velcro, he'd watched Jillian without appearing to do so—something he'd learned during her days working in the family townhouse. He missed nothing. Every smile. Every laugh. Every introduction to a new person. Every handshake.

His desire and disdain for her battled deep within him.

"Cole? You okay?"

Kimber Locke drew his attention. He looked over at the Playboy model sitting beside him. Beautiful woman. Even pleasant to be around. Her role? To annoy his mother.

His parents had been busy preparing the elaborate meal for the night when he'd arrived. Once they'd stepped from the kitchen, free of their chef coats and in their designer evening wear, Cole had gently guided Kimber by her elbow through the crowd and into the direct line of vision of his parents. His mother's look had quickly shifted from surprise and pleasure at seeing him to fighting hard not to reveal her disgust at seeing Kimber at his side. Nicolette's private persona was different from the public one she'd carefully cultivated. For a brief moment, that façade cracked.

Nicolette Cress hated it when one of her sons paraded a nighttime liaison—especially at a business function.

"Yeah, I'm good. Thanks," he said.

Kimber gave him a conspiratorial wink. She was in on his hijinks. They'd briefly dated a few years ago, and she

was well aware that her very presence irked his mother—
making the ploy all the more enjoyable for her, as well.

The night was coming to an end. A decadent meal
of French cuisine relished. A dessert of individual fruit
tarts with different selections of exotic fruits devoured.
His parents' formal speech given, Gabe and Monica's engagement announcement celebrated. The annual bonus
checks much appreciated.

But beneath the jovial surface, hell was brewing—and
every Cress family member knew it.

Ding, ding, ding.

Cole turned his head to eye his parents rise from their
seats to his left. He covered his mouth to hide his humor
at his mother, fervently avoiding looking in his and Kimber's direction. Avoidance by Nicolette Cress was top-
tier hidden anger.

"We want to thank you all for joining us tonight and
allowing us to cook for you," Phillip Senior said with a
broad smile.

Cole stared down into his cup of coffee. His father
really could charm.

"Under the guidance of Gabriel and his team and the
entire staff at Cress, INC., we thank you for providing
the most important element—cooking delicious food,"
Phillip Senior continued. "Without your skill and love
of food, Cress, INC. would not have had its most successful year to date."

Applause filled the air.

Cole looked up as his mother cast a beautiful smile at
her husband. It was filled with love. He eyed his father
bend from his tall height to kiss her.

Scoundrel.

Cole was angry at his mother for her machinations in

his love life, but she was his mother and still deserving of his father's loyalty.

"Thank you all again. Have a good night. And safe travels in the morning back to your homes," Phillip said.

"If my family could just remain behind for a quick *bavardage*," Nicolette added, with an inadvertent glance at Cole before she forced a stiff smile.

Bavardage. The beautiful French word for chitchat, which she truly meant as "verbal lashing."

His parents and Gabe moved to the door to personally say goodbye as the chefs and their dates began to exit. Cole's eyes immediately went to Jillian as she tucked her clutch under her arm and made her way to the front. She didn't look at him.

He clenched his jaw, feeling dismissed and forgotten by her once again.

"Should I go?" Kimber asked.

"Definitely not," Cole said, watching as Jillian shook the hand of his mother and father before leaving.

Just outside the door, she paused and looked back over her bared shoulders. Their eyes met.

She gave him a hesitant smile, and his body betrayed him by desiring her in a rush.

His mother closed the door, breaking the connection. He eyed her, not doubting she had done it purposely.

Monte Carlo is calling my name.

Phillip Senior walked over to the bar and poured himself a Scotch.

His mother leaned against the door, released a heavy breath, and finally landed her cobalt eyes on him. Hard and intense.

They matched his own.

Her unspoken message to her son was clear. *Send her away or I will obliterate her.*

His mother's anger was nuclear and he knew Kimber's feelings would suffer collateral damage.

Cole leaned over. "Thanks for tonight. I owe you," he whispered near her ear.

Kimber smiled at him and pressed her hands to his cheeks as she tilted her head to kiss him. Deeply. And with a loud moan.

Cole fought not to laugh as she broke the kiss. She cleaned his mouth of her gloss with her thumb and then rose to walk away with sultry stride meant to annoy his mother.

Nicolette looked like she could spit bullets as she crossed her arms at her chest and moved away from the door with angry steps that sent her rose-gold evening gown fluttering behind her.

"I'll be waiting up for you, Cole," Kimber said with a wink and another blown kiss.

Nicolette released a cry and turned quickly to steer Kimber out the door before closing it.

He covered his mouth with his hand as he looked around the restaurant at his family members' expressions.

Phillip Junior looked pleased though his wife cast him an annoyed glare.

Sean had joined their father at the bar.

Gabe and Monica shared a look—she was clearly surprised by her first inclusion behind the Cress family veil.

Lucas was eyeing the fruit tart he'd ignored earlier.

Nobody wanted to be there.

"Bienvenue, Coleman. Je vois que tu as eu le temps de ramasser les poubelles," Nicolette said coldly in her native tongue.

Welcome back, Coleman. I see you had time to pick up the trash. He shook his head at her judgment.

"Kimber is not trash," he said, reaching for the anger

that sent him away from his family for months. "And neither was Jillian."

Nicolette stiffened. "What do you mean?"

Cole rose to his full height. "I was at Jillian's that night. In the bathroom. I heard everything. I know what you did," he said, enjoying the widening of her eyes with each word he spoke.

Silence reigned.

"What's going on?" Phillip Senior asked from behind him.

"Jillian?" Lucas asked. "Nice, Cole. *Real* nice."

Cole ignored his brother's praise as he came to stand in front of his mother and look down at her. "The last thing I needed was for you to interfere in my life," he said. "It was a side of you I had never seen before, and I *never* want to see again. You judged Monica. You judged Jillian. It's time you sit down before a mirror and take a long hard look at yourself."

Nicolette's eyes filled with tears. "Cole," she whispered.

He shook his head, his eyes ablaze and his jaw firm. "What you did was wrong and deplorable—"

"That's enough, Cole," his father said, moving to wrap his arm around his wife's shoulders.

He ignored him. "We are your sons. We're grown men. We can decide on our own without you pulling strings like Geppetto," he continued.

"I only want what's best for you." Nicolette extended her arm to reach for his hand.

He pulled back from her touch. "Who says you know what's best?" he asked. "You don't even know what's best for you."

Nicolette's forehead wrinkled in confusion.

Cole shook his head and shifted past her to open the

front door to the restaurant. "Kimber is waiting for me," he lied, leaving them all to ponder just what he'd meant.

Jillian looked at the two wedding photos she held. In both, she was so young.

And so naïve.

"Hey, you."

She looked up at her father standing in the doorway in T-shirt and pajama bottoms. They both looked over at Ionie, still asleep in her bed. "I wanted to be near her since I leave in the morning," Jillian admitted from where she sat on the rocking chair. She set the photos on her lap to reach over and lightly stroke her grandmother's soft silver curls.

Harry walked into the room and came to stand at the other side of the bed. "Yeah, I check on her every night before we go to bed," he admitted, talking low so as not to interrupt his mother's sleep.

Jillian gave him a soft smile. Her father was an only child raised by a single mother. His love for Ionie was boundless. She knew it was hard for him to see some of her spark fade.

"How was your party?" he asked, coming around the bed to pick up the photos from her lap.

Confusing.

"It was fun," she said instead.

"And the reason for the trip down memory lane?" he asked, sitting on the side of the bed.

"I was wondering the same thing," Ionie said, opening her eyes.

Their gazes went to her as she softly smiled. "All closed eyes ain't sleep," she said. "Besides, who could rest with all this company in my bedroom?"

"I didn't mean to keep you awake," Jillian said, reaching to hold her hand.

"I was just enjoying you being near me, like when you would spend the weekend with your granddaddy and me," Ionie said, her eyes twinkling with the moonlight streaming into the room. "We would wake up and find you sleep at the foot of the bed, on the bench, or on that cold floor. Like you couldn't stand not being near us. I loved it then and I love it now, Jillie."

That all was so true.

"Mama, you need anything?" Harry asked.

"For Jillie to tell us what's on her mind."

Jillian thought about admitting to her father that she'd had a no-strings-attached relationship and then ended it by accepting her executive chef position.

Hard pass.

"I was dating someone and we ended things," she said, skirting the full truth. "I saw him tonight—"

"At the gala?" her father asked as he scratched his full silver-flecked beard.

She nodded. "Seeing him again made me feel like I care for him more than I realized," she said.

"Do you love him?" Ionie asked, patting Jillian's hand with her own.

Jillian closed her eyes and bit down on her bottom lip as emotion swelled in her chest for Cole. "Yes," she admitted in a whisper.

"Does he love you?" Harry asked with the protectiveness of a father.

She shook her head, remembering Cole's anger with her that night. *And tonight.*

"What?" Harry snapped, rising.

"I broke things off," she said to ease his annoyance.

"Can you fix it?" Ionie asked.

Jillian looked out the window. "I don't want to. I'm not looking for love. Look where it got me before. *Twice,*" she said, her voice soft. "I've always wanted what you and Mom had, Dad. That love story you can tell your kids about thirty years later. But it's just not in the cards for me."

"Life is like a library," Harry said. "It contains so many books because there are many different stories to be told. Each one unique. And special. And needed. Your story may not look like ours, Jillian. Create your own."

She gave her father a teasing smile. "Oh, *Bear,*" she said, ribbing him with her mother's loving nickname.

Ionie chuckled. "Leave my son alone," she playfully admonished. "Because before he was Bear, he was my Sugar Toes."

Harry gave them both a withering look.

"Sugar Toes," Jillian teased. "Oh *my.*"

"I'm going where I'm appreciated," he said over his shoulder as he left the room.

"Might as well, because what she got for you, your Mama and daughter sure can't give you," Ionie called out.

Jillian chuckled as she leaned over to press a kiss to her grandmother's soft cheek. "I love you, Gram," she sighed, lowering her head to rest against her arm.

Ionie reached over with her free hand and rubbed Jillian's loose curls. She hummed them both to sleep with Jillian's heart and thoughts filled with Cole.

"Leave the bustier on."
At Cole's command, Jillian stood before him and un-buttoned her pants before letting the material fall to her feet in a satin puddle. She arched one of her brows and slowly slid her fingers under the rim of her lace panties with the skill of a burlesque dancer. She used tiny rolls

of her hips to ease the flimsy lace down around her hips and buttocks.

Cole sat on the bench, leaning back against the foot of the bed as he watched her by the light of the fireplace. She tempted and tantalized him with her slow, sensual movements as they locked eyes. His inches hardened, and stood erect as he ached for her.

Still in her heels, she twirled the flimsy lace on her finger before looping the panties around the tip of his hardness. She smiled and moved forward to stand between his open legs then playfully took a bow that lowered her head near his lap. With her teeth, she nipped her panties and removed them to drop to the floor, leaving the tip of his inches free to be covered with her lips.

Cole arched his hips off the bench at the feel of her tongue tasting him intimately. "Jillian," he gasped as he pressed his hands to her cheeks and raised her head, afraid he would burst. He wrapped an arm around her waist and drew her forward to sit on his lap. He kissed her deeply, his tongue slowly thrusting in her mouth the same way he wished he could stand his inches doing so.

"Give it to me, Cole," she pleaded against his mouth, taking his hardness into her hand to grasp and stroke.

"It's yours," he told her.

Jillian rose from his lap to lower her core onto him as she gripped the back of his head and licked at his mouth.

"All mine?" she asked, gripping him with her walls.

With one hard upward thrust, he planted all of himself inside her—

Cole awakened from his dream with a start. "Damn," he swore, sitting upright and looking down at his erection.

Bzzzzzz. Bzzzzzz. Bzzzzzz.

Another dream about Jillian.

Bzzzzzz. Bzzzzzz. Bzzzzzz.

He swore, ignoring his cell phone vibrating on the nightstand with calls from his family. It had awakened him. And now his waking thoughts were filled with Jillian.

That damn bustier of hers is torturing me.

With deep breaths and a wildly pounding heart, he looked around at his hotel suite. And then at his erection. With a grimace, he grabbed a pillow and pressed it against his hardness as he fell back on the bed, unsure if he was more frustrated at still wanting Jillian or at the interruption of his erotic dream of her.

Five

Two weeks later

Jillian used the handle of the pan to rotate it atop the fiery gas range. She grabbed the tall, slender glass of extra-virgin olive oil with her free hand to add it to the root vegetables she was sautéing. Quickly she set it down and grabbed a large pinch of pink salt to sprinkle across the baby carrots, sliced parsnips, leeks and matchstick-sliced rutabagas.

"Three-root-vegetable soup ready, chef," her sous chef called over to her.

She nodded as she turned and used tongs to divide the veggies atop three bowls of puréed soup carefully layered with the flavors of garlic, onion, chicken broth, butter and turmeric. "Run the dish," she ordered, wiping her hands with the dishtowel tucked into the pocket of her monogrammed chef's coat.

"Yes, chef!"

She turned back to the stove and wasn't sure who had obeyed her order as she'd turned it off. Their night at CRESS III was over. Now it was about cleanup and minor prep for the next evening. She allowed herself a smile and a deep exhale of breath, more than ready for a glass of red wine as she sat on her balcony and enjoyed the view.

And try not to think about Cole.

Better said than done.

Against the odds, she had fallen in love over her year of lascivious encounters with Cole. She hadn't planned it. Hadn't even fathomed it possible. She had been wrong. With each passing day now, she *knew* she loved him, but equally knew that she would keep her distance and allow the love to fade with time.

Between his anger at her and her reluctance for a serious relationship, loving him was futile.

And so very foolish.

"Chef, may I have a word with you?"

Jillian stiffened at the sound of Clark Newsom's voice behind her. She turned. His tone was filled with the same arrogance as the tilt of his chin and the slight lift of his left eyebrow.

"Sure," she said, aware of the furtive looks of her staff.

With a stiff smile, she followed the short and slender man in his three-piece suit to his office at the rear of the restaurant. She allowed herself a playful moment as she wrinkled her nose at him. "What's this about, Clark?" she asked the restaurant's manager once she entered the office and he'd closed the door to move past her to take a seat behind his desk.

The menu.

"The menu," he said, echoing her thought.

Jillian slid her hands into the pockets of her coat as she eyed him. "It was a special request, Clark," she said, already knowing that when a patron gave her carte blanche for the side dish with their chicken, she prepared her Lyonnaise potatoes—something not on the menu.

He looked grim and released a long drawn-out breath. "I am the executive chef, Clark—"

"Of your first restaurant that is part of an international brand," he said, cutting her off.

Jillian fought the urge to rotate her head to release the sudden tension. "When will the training wheels come off, Clark?" she asked, keeping annoyance from her tone.

He stroked his chin. "When you prove you will not let what happened to your first restaurant happen to this one," he said.

Jillian stared at him. Hard. Unrelenting. Cold. Even as the heat of embarrassment warmed her belly. "Until you step from under the protection of the Cress brand and attempt to build something on your own—to fly without a net and risk it all—then don't you dare sit there in your feigned glory and fool yourself into thinking you can look down your nose at me."

"And yet here we both are with that Cress safety net," he countered with a smug look.

Jillian gave him a withering glare before she turned to leave his office, slamming the door behind her. She paused on the other side, hating that he was right. She felt constrained by the reins Cress, INC. had on her culinary creativity. Being watched and scolded. Judged and found lacking to some degree.

But here I am.

She closed her eyes and pinched the bridge of her nose. *And I chose it over Cole.*

Her regret was visceral.

Jillian pressed a hand to her belly as she made her way back to the kitchen.

* * *

The next morning, Cole drove his all-black vintage Harley-Davidson motorcycle through the streets of Manhattan, enjoying the feel of the wind as he dipped in and out of traffic. Outside of cooking, he felt the freest on the back of his bike.

He slowed to a stop at a red light, sitting between a Land Rover to his left and a white convertible to his right. At the soft beep of a horn, he turned his head to the right to look through the tinted visor of his helmet at a beautiful caramel beauty with freckles and shocking red hair. She slanted him an admiring smile. He raised the visor to reveal his face.

Her smiled widened.

He gave her an appreciative look just as the light turned green, and she pulled off with a wink and wave. He chuckled before he lowered his visor and accelerated forward as well, guiding his bike between vehicles to leave her behind eventually.

By the time he reached the underground parking garage of the Midtown Manhattan building housing the Cress, INC. offices, he had forgotten the red-headed beauty. The moment of flirtation had been nice, but his focus was not on the sweet intimacies of a woman. Parking his Harley in his assigned spot, he locked it and made his way across the spacious, filled garage in his jeans, boots and a long-sleeved black button-down shirt of crisp cotton. Unlike his brothers, Cole shunned office attire—partly to annoy his father and partly because he found suits constraining and only wore them when necessary.

He rode the elevator up to the fortieth floor. Cress, INC.'s corporate offices occupied the entire floor of the towering building housing offices, a test kitchen, cafeteria, conference room and private dining room for the family. On days his mother wasn't at her renowned culinary school and worked from these offices; she prepared lunch for the family and staff. He stepped off the elevator and crossed the polished floor, pausing as the frosted automatic doors slid open.

Bzzzzzz. Bzzzzzz. Bzzzzzz.

He pulled his phone from the back pocket of his pants.

"Good morning, Mr. Cress," someone said.

"Morning," he said, raising his hand in greeting at the passerby as he looked down at his phone.

His mother was calling.

Their Cold War had to cease—he knew that. Especially with him returning to work.

"Hello," he said.

"Welcome back, son," Nicolette said.

Someone had alerted her to his presence. The concept of Big Brother had nothing on a curious mother—especially a powerhouse like Nicolette Lavoie-Cress.

"How can I help you, Mama?" he asked, aware that his tone was still cool and distant with her as he made his way down the wide hall to his office. He gave his brothers Luc and Sean a wave through the glass wall of their offices.

"The family is doing an interview and cover shoot for *Scrumptious*," she said of Cress, INC.'s flagship magazine.

He entered his office, pausing to take in the sight of the Manhattan skyline outside the floor-to-ceiling windows. The sun was bright and its rays almost blinded him.

Jillian had loved the feel of the sun on her naked body. He remembered mornings she would lie on a yoga mat beneath the loft windows to relish the beams as they warmed her body, giving it a golden glow. Never had he seen anything more beautiful.

"Cole?"

"I can't make it," he said, jarred from his memory. "You know I run my food truck on the weekends."

The chair behind his deck swiveled to the front, revealing his mother sitting in it.

"Rather dramatic. Don't you think?" Cole asked as he walked over to his ebony desk and set his phone facedown upon it along with his keys.

Nicolette stood, looking beautiful in a tailored black-silk pantsuit. "Not unlike you disappearing," she said before opening her arms wide and bending her fingers to beckon him. "I haven't hugged my son in months. Let's fix that ASAP, Cole."

He stepped into her embrace, towering over her height.

Nicolette rose on her toes in her heels. "I did things wrong, but I meant well," she said. "Forgive me?"

Cole stepped back and busied himself pushing his shirtsleeves up his arms before claiming his seat. "Forgive? Yes. Forget? Not yet," he said.

"Even if my actions revealed the flaw of blind ambition in Jillian?" she asked.

He stiffened as he stared at his mother hard. "You and I will never discuss Jillian Rossi," he said.

Nicolette held up her hands as if conceding. "We need you at the interview," she said, switching gears.

"I'm available at any time outside of the weekend," he said, logging on to his computer.

"Your food truck wasn't important to you during your…sabbatical," his mother pointed out as she walked around to claim one of the seats in front of his desk.

"So, you could imagine my urgency to get back to it as soon as possible," he countered.

Nicolette eased her hands into the pockets of her pants. "When you were a toddler, you clung to me more than any of your brothers—even Lucas once he was born," she said.

Cole steeled himself. She was going into full guilt mode and pulling at heartstrings. His mother was the best at it.

"You would love for me to pull you in my lap and read to you," she continued with twinkling blue eyes and a genuine smile. "It was the best. Just me and my little Cole Man. The sound of your little raspy voice asking me to read some more was better than a flawlessly cooked soufflé. Just perfection."

She sighed.

"What went wrong, Cole?" she asked. *"Pourquoi me deetestes-tu?"*

He chuckled and tapped his fingers atop his desk as he eyed her. "I don't hate you," he answered her question. "I was angry at you for interfering in my life, and I need to make it clear to you not to do it again. It feels disrespectful as a grown man."

She nodded in understanding. "It is not easy to accept that your boys—"

"Sons," he interjected.

"Fine, Cole," she snapped before releasing a long breath as she balled her hand into a fist and pressed the side of it to her mouth. "You're grown."

"Thirty," he stressed. "Your youngest is twenty-nine."

"Don't remind me," she muttered.

Cole chuckled again.

Nicolette eyed him and then offered the smile that made America love her. "Cole, this weekend is the only time available for *Scrumptious'* team to get in and get it all done to make the deadline for the mag to go to print."

He remained quiet.

She nodded, taking his silence for consent. "Thank

you," she said with emphasis as she stroked her hair, which was fast becoming more silver than blond.

He gave her a brief nod before turning his attention to his emails. His team's most recent analytics report showed a plateau or steady decline across all online social media platforms and the massive company website.

"I'll be meeting with my team today regarding a redesign and relaunch of the website," he said as he opened the site and frowned at its slowness to upload.

"I know you have no real interest in the CEO position—"

"At *all*," he insisted.

"My rebel," she said softly.

He glanced over at her. She was his mother and he adored her—flaws and all. So he offered her his smile.

"Knowing you don't want it, I'm proud of you for still taking the initiative, and I look forward to hearing more about your plans," Nicolette said.

In truth, he was looking for a diversion from his thoughts now that he was away from the intoxicating recreation of Europe. The project would help him focus on something else besides...

Missing Jillian.

Nicolette rose from her seat to walk across to the office's glass entryway. She paused beside his name etched in the glass. "Will you be home tonight, *mon fils*?" she asked of her son without turning around.

Cole frowned. He didn't enjoy hurting his mother. He had simply just respected the anger she'd caused in him and allowed himself time to forgive and move on. So he knew his next words would be a blow. "I have a real-estate agent looking for condos..." he began, opening and closing his hand into a fist that he was sure must feel like the grip on her heart. That comparison led him to press his palm flat against the desktop. "Until then, I'll be staying with Gabe and Monica."

She stiffened.

Her love for her children was not in question. Never.

"I need privacy. I'm a grown man, but maybe it's hard to respect that if I'm still living under the same roof as the entire family at thirty," Cole explained.

Saying no more, Nicolette left his office and walked away. The sound of her heels against the polished tiled floor soon faded.

Cole wiped his hand over his mouth, longing for the days when his life was much simpler. When annoying his father was the most demanding task of his day. Adoring his mother without question. Felt the loyal bond between him and his brothers. Enjoyed the time spent cooking in his beloved food truck. And finding the sweetest no-ties, uncomplicated passion with Jillian.

Now?

Everything seemed disjointed. He felt shattered into pieces and twisting in the wind.

He hated it.

One week later

"You look amazing, Jillian."

She gave her date a warm look as they danced to the jazz band in the club that had recreated the vintage feel of Harlem. "Thank you," she said, offering him a smile that belied the nervousness she felt.

Miles Fairmount was the handsome, well-built man who owned the market where they purchased live sea-food for CRESS III. After several offers for dinners, Jillian had finally accepted—desperately in search of a remedy for the "I love Cole Cress" blues. She needed all the help she could get.

Seeking a connection, Jillian raised her hand from his shoulder to his nape and leaned a bit closer to lightly rest her forehead against his chest. She inhaled his cologne and closed her eyes as they swayed to the music.

But all she could think of was that Miles wasn't as tall as Cole, who could easily rest his chin atop her head and whose height forced her to lean back to look up into his face. And his cologne was spicier than the cool notes Cole preferred. Because of Miles's bald head, there were no soft curls to tease on his neck. His hand on her back felt unfamiliar. They were not moving in sync.

He was not Cole.

Jillian released a heavy sigh.

Miles paused. "Everything okay?" he asked.

Her eyes studied his face. He was a handsome man. A nice man. Successful and charming.

But not Cole.

That blue-eyed playboy has me all messed up.

Miles chuckled and raised her arm above her head to slowly spin her before gently guiding her body back against his. "I don't have a chance. Do I?" he asked, sounding amused.

He's insightful.

Jillian offered him an apologetic look. "You would—"

"If…" he offered.

She nodded and bit the corner of her bottom lip.

"So where is he?" Miles asked as he danced them in a circle among the other dancers on the black floor with its red-hued lighting that harmonized the soulful ambience.

"Not with me," she admitted in his ear, feeling the loss of Cole as tangible as the pain of a deep cut.

"Is he on his way back?" Miles gently maneuvered

her into a dip and then lightly jerked her body back up against his.

Okay, this is fun, Jillian admitted to herself.

"No," she admitted to him.

"Then maybe you should go to him," Miles offered before he raised her arm for another twirl.

And say what?

Forgive me? Understand me? Have me?

I love you?

But did she want a relationship with Cole or anyone else? Did she want to put her heart out there just to be disappointed? Was Cole worth risking it all?

I'm already heartbroken.

And her biggest fear pulsed with a life all its own deep inside her, causing sleepless nights and nail-biting sessions.

Just because I love him doesn't mean he loves me.

As Miles twirled them around the crowded floor, her thoughts filled with Cole's anger. Their fling had lasted longer than expected. Why was he so angry at her? That she'd chosen her career over great sex? Or…

"Miles?" Jillian said. "Can I get a male point of view on something? Is that okay? It's about *him*."

"Sure."

Although she felt uncomfortable talking to her date about another man, she longed for a male perspective on something that had nagged at her of late. "What would cause a man to be so angry about a woman ending a no-strings attachment?" she asked.

He continued to sway as he considered her question. "Depends…" he began. "Could be I'm an egomaniac refusing to admit a woman would want to end things and feeling I should have been the one to do it."

That made her wince slightly.

"*Or...* I cared for her more than even I knew I did," he offered.

Hope sprung to life in her chest.

"*Or...* I felt betrayed," he finished.

Her gut clenched. At that moment, Miles had hit the nail on the head of her assessment and could be called MC Hammer.

"So, if she chose a great job in San Fran offered to her by one of his loved ones to ensure the end of their relationship?" she asked near his ear, her voice tentative.

Miles leaned back to look at her. "He may think you used him for a come-up," he suggested.

"Right. I didn't, but I can see how he may think that," Jillian admitted, feeling so weary that she allowed her head to rest against his shoulder.

Miles chuckled and patted her back consolingly.

Jillian you're on a date!

She jerked up her head. "I'm sorry," she said, regaining her composure.

"In the words of Usher, you got it bad," he said. "The only thing to do is a have conversation...*with him*."

It was her time to chuckle. "Am I the worst date ever?" she asked.

He spun her away and then pulled her back to him. "Sadly, not at all," he said dryly.

That drew a full laugh from her—head flung back and all.

"For tonight, let's enjoy some good fun and good music," Miles said. "And when I see you Tuesday at the market, we'll just share a friendly smile and remember we wished each other well in our love lives...apart."

"Deal," Jillian agreed.

Miles took several steps back as he swayed their hands between them. *Dance*, he mouthed.

She did, holding the flared skirt of her red dress as she gently rocked her hips. It felt good to focus on the music and not work, missing her family or Cole—for at least a little while.

Cole released a yawn and set his laptop beside him on the bed as he sat back against the tall leather headboard. He checked his watch. It was well after midnight. He had been going through mockups for the new web design and overseeing plans for a massive launch party. He'd been at it all day and long after arriving at Gabe and Monica's sprawling Tribeca condo.

Wearing navy pajamas that were totally for the sake of modesty while living with his brother and his fiancée, Cole left the bed and crossed the large room to use both hands to open the French doors. The heat of summer was fading quickly as early fall was approaching. He looked down at the street from the towering height, taking in the traffic, the bright lights and the still fast pace of New Yorkers even with the late hour.

There was a time when he would have been among them, searching for fast times and faster women to while away the late hours. Over the last year, Jillian's apartment had appealed to him more. Just being there with her— laughing, cooking, watching silly television shows, or lost in the heat of their desire for each other—had satisfied him. That year had led to him no longer seeking— or needing—the nightlife.

But, just as he'd feared, being back among the New York streets was a poignant reminder of Jillian. He ached for her and then felt anger at being so foolish to do so.

She made her choice.

He closed his eyes and grated his teeth. It *still* bothered him.

He hadn't been ready for their time to end, and it didn't sit well that she had. It felt so disloyal to him. So underhanded.

Even though they had always maintained a no-strings attachment.

Even though neither had talked about forever.

He hadn't even thought about it like that before.

That made him frown at his conflicted feelings. Was it that he'd wanted to be the one to end it? Was it all about his ego?

Cole thought about that. Searching within himself for his truth. In the end, he shook his head.

His lingering doubt: had getting an executive chef position at a Cress restaurant been Jillian's real motivation to work as their private chef or to get involved with him.

Did she use me?

His anger resurfaced.

Balling and releasing his hand at the tension in his body that fought for release, Cole reentered the guest bedroom. He crossed the hardwood floor with bare feet to leave the suite and walk down the darkened hallway to the kitchen in search of a late-night snack.

"Deeper, Gabe. Go deeper."

Cole froze at Monica's words echoing in the hall.

The door to the master suite was slightly ajar, and it was clear Gabe and Monica were having a late-night snack of their own. His stomach grumbled, but he didn't dare walk past their door. Turning, he returned to his suite and closed the door securely behind him, resigning himself to sleep off his hunger.

Long after settling beneath the covers in the cloak of darkness, he realized it was not just food for which he yearned. His brother had found love; they shared their lives. Loving each other. Taking care of one another. Making love to each other.

As he lay in his bed with nothing but his anger at Jillian to clutch, he felt alone and hungry for a partner of his own. That was a discovery he hadn't been aware of or ready to accept. For so long, he had rebelled against what was expected and ordinary. He had found comfort in being different.

As he buried his head against the pillow, the rebel was willing to admit that he had been wrong.

Six

One week later

"Jillian. Jillian? Something wrong?"

She heard the voice beside her as she stood there, but she was unable to speak. For her, time, and everything along with it, slowed as she looked across the distance with no doubt. Her body was sure of him, even when her eyes were not. Shock, pleasure, and fighting the urge to run to him with the fancy of a child left her spellbound.

Cole, she mouthed as she watched him work from his large navy-colored food truck that was a showpiece all its own.

As he handed someone their order, he raised his head as if he had heard her call his name—but that was impossible because it had been less than a whisper. His eyes widened at the sight of her. He was just as surprised as she was.

Did he also feel the pull to eat up the distance between them? The urge to be near her?

It nearly suffocated her.

"You okay, Jillian?"

"Yes," she lied to her former first husband, hating the hand Warren placed at the small of her back as he stood beside her.

Cole's expression changed. Hardened as he'd turned his head and focused on taking an order from the next person in a very long line of customers waiting to purchase his food.

"I'm glad we met up, Jillie," Warren said, using her childhood nickname.

He would know it well. They had been high school sweethearts who had married right after graduation and then divorced a year later when marriage, college and finances had not mixed.

She looked up at him with a genuine smile. "Me, too, Dr. Long."

When she'd been told that significant renovation would close the restaurant for two weeks, she had been more than happy to post on social media that she was headed home to the east coast. Warren had reached out to let her know that he had moved back from Texas. That he'd taken an esteemed position as an attending cardiothoracic surgeon in Manhattan.

A day enjoying good music and a bevy of good eats at a food truck rally in Prospect Park in Brooklyn had seemed the ideal place for a friendly reconnection. They'd spoken here and there over the years, often via social media, but both had long since released ideas of reconciliation and were just happy for friendship and nothing more.

"The only thing missing to make me feel like I'm

home truly is *pizza*," she stressed, ignoring the nervousness she felt at just what Cole thought of her being there with another man.

"It would be bagels for me," Warren said, easing his black-framed glasses up on his nose as he looked around. "There're still a good number of trucks on this side. I wish I wasn't on duty tonight."

"It's cool," she said, shifting her eyes to Cole's truck. He had the most massive crowd awaiting a chance to order from the well-known celebrity cook. "I know that chef, and I'm gonna jump on board to help."

"Really?" he asked. "Cool. You have a way home?"

"Warren, I'm a grown woman, not the high school girl you first met," she reminded him.

"And you've survived a long time without me around," he said, sounding bemused.

"Same for you. I am so proud of you, Warren."

"And you're an executive chef," he said, looking down at his feet and then up at her. "We both are living our dreams."

"I think getting out of our nightmare of a marriage played a *huge* role," she said.

"I agree." Warren chuckled.

Following an impulse, Jillian reached up to pat his chest as she felt the twinkle in her eyes. "Go save lives, and I'll go cook," she said, feeling comfortable around him.

Warren gave her another smile before turning to stride away.

Jillian licked her lips as she walked over to Cole's truck. The smell of food mingled in the air with the music played on the main stage. She didn't know if she was crazy or not, but she followed her instincts and the road that led back to Cole. Her heart guided her.

"Excuse me," she said, easing between two women in line to climb the steps and open the door to the polished food truck. "Need some help?"

Cole did a double-take—maybe even a triple—as he paused with a handful of sliced green onions above an open takeout container. He knit his brows as he finished the dish and handed it to his customer with a smile.

It had been so long since he'd beamed that disarming tool at her.

"One moment," he said to the next person in line.

Jillian's heart hammered as she closed the metal door and reached for one of the black aprons hanging from a hook.

He walked over to her. "Get out, Jillian," he said coldly. "I don't want you here."

Her ego caused her spine to stiffen and she had to give herself a quick five count. *Fight for him. Don't give up.* "But you need me," she told him, shifting to his left to try to pass.

Cole moved to block her.

She looked up and their eyes locked. She released a little puff of breath to relieve the electricity she felt at being so close to him. Inhaling his scent. Getting lost in his eyes. Wanting to feel his touch.

She craved Cole Cress. It was a profound hunger fueled by love. She had to bite her lip to keep from revealing her heart to him. "You want to waste time arguing with me while your patrons wait, *Chef*?" she asked.

He turned and moved away from her with strides that revealed his annoyance. "You sure you're *allowed* to help me?" he asked as he grabbed a towel and looked down at his hands as he wiped them.

"Allowed by whom?" she asked, stepping to the small

sink to wash her hands before quickly surveying the ingredients in his fridge and the items offered on the menu.

The food truck was far more than that. It was a compact chef's kitchen with all the bells and whistles. She felt excited to play with his beloved toy.

"My mother…and *your* man," Cole grumbled.

He's jealous.

"Your mother does not own me, and the gentleman you saw me with was my ex-husband, not my current man," she said, shifting to stand beside him and smile down at a young woman. "What can I get for you?"

At that point, they were off to the races and spent the next few hours splitting the grill to make the orders and trim the order line down. Long after darkness descended and the towering light poles of the park had to bring illumination, the two worked in sync, even helping each other with a particular order and using a shorthand to get the job done, fast, efficiently and, most important, deliciously.

Jillian found it exhilarating.

The close quarters and having to brush past Cole had stoked her desire. At times, she would notice the muscles of his arms as he reached to hand a customer their plate, or the way he used a cloth to dab at the sweat dampening his forehead, or the scent of his cologne mingling with the onion and spices in the air. The fit of his jeans on his buttocks. The small of his back when he reached for something from the shelf above his head.

The smile he offered each and every person.

A charmer. *Her* charmer.

Or at least, he would be again.

She bit the inside of her cheek as she envisioned licking away the sweat dampening his chest. The impulse to be near him and to reconnect with him had been too tempting to deny. The very sight of him flooded her body with that undeniable warmth of love.

Jillian decided that she wanted Cole back in her life, no matter the consequences.

"All right. Thank you. 'Night," he said to his last customer before sliding the window closed and pressing a button to automatically lower the awning.

"All the bells and whistles," she said as she finished wiping and sanitizing the stainless-steel countertops. "This is top of the line, Cole."

He nodded as he removed his apron. "I only like the best of the best," he said.

"Oh. Well…thank you," Jillian said with a flirty curtsy.

Cole eyed her for so long with a blank expression that she felt foolish.

She threw her hands up in frustration.

"I was referring to things that are mine," he said.

"I'm not a *thing*," she shot back.

"Nor were you mine," he returned coldly in retaliation.

"I don't *belong* to anyone," she stated, stressing the word.

Cole smirked and dropped his head as he shook it.

"You treat me like we never shared a year—"

"Are you serious?" He balked with wide-eyed astonishment. "And you treated me any better? Don't be a hypocrite, Jillian. You chose your career over me—and didn't give me the respect to talk to me about it first."

"A big scene wasn't part of the deal. Be fair," Jillian said. "We were never meant to be serious."

Cole took a step closer to her. "What was part of it?" he asked.

Jillian leaned back against the counter as she looked up into his eyes. "What?"

"It. Us. Whatever we were," he said, his eyes dipping down to her mouth.

She licked at it with the tip of her tongue. "It was just sex. Great sex," she whispered into the heat rising between them. "No strings. Remember?"

"Oh. I remember. I wish I could forget," Cole said, looking tortured as he gripped her waist and easily lifted her to sit atop the counter.

She spread her legs and reached to press her hands against his shoulders before gripping his T-shirt. "Cole," she gasped in that hot little moment before he dipped his head to kiss her mouth.

The first feel of his lips was electrifying. She shivered and clung to him with the jolt as they pressed their upper bodies together and deepened the kiss with a moan that burst with their hunger for one another. With each passing second, their movements rushed—almost wild and desperate as they undressed each other. Unbuttoning. Unzipping. Pulling up, over. Yanking down. Until they were nude. And panting between kisses.

He put hands on either side of her atop the counter as he looked at her with heated eyes. She rubbed his sides with her knees as she leaned in to lick at his lips. He caught her tongue and sucked it deeply into his mouth before releasing it to press kisses to her neck and the deep valley between her breasts.

"Cole," she moaned in sweet agony, flinging her head back.

Each lick of his tongue against a taut brown nipple made her shiver and cry out.

Each deep suckle led to her arching her back as if to offer him more to taste. To enjoy. To have.

She reached between them to grip his inches—gasping at the heat and the hardness.

He hissed in pleasure as she stroked him. With a grunt, he rolled his hips, thrusting his tool against her palm as he wildly licked at her breasts. "Jillian… Jillian… Jillian," he moaned.

"Now, Cole," she gasped, needing him to ease the throbbing ache of desire. "Now."

He honored her demand and used his narrow hips to guide his smooth tip into her swiftly with one deep thrust.

She cried out and arched her back at the feel of him. The hardness. The heat. The perfect snug fit. The strokes. She ached and pulsed in places she had ignored as she had longed for only his touch and denied seeking pleasure with anyone else. And in the heat, it all was so achingly familiar. She leaned into it. Accepting the unique connection they shared—setting aside doubts and any promises or deals made to claim her desire for this man. Along with her passion, her heart swelled with emotion for him as she felt the wave of her climax rise.

No longer could she deny the truth to herself or to him. "I love you, Cole," she whimpered as she gasped with each of his deep, long, and strong strokes. "I love you *so* much."

Cole stiffened and stopped midstroke. Sweat dripped from his body onto hers as he stared at her.

Still releasing deep breaths with his hardness deep inside her as she clutched and released him with her walls, she looked up. Her eyes searched his as she waited for the next words that would come out of his beautiful mouth.

"Don't do that, Jillian," Cole said, his voice stern.

Damn.

There was no more glorious sight to Cole than Jillian naked, her eyes glazed, mouth panting, and breasts pointed high, his hardness buried deep within her. But she'd ruined it with her declaration of love. The very last thing he wanted was to be toyed with or placated.

When he'd first spotted Jillian with another man, his undeniable jealousy had rushed at him. It had conquered any other emotion and distracted him from his work. Thoughts of another man enjoying her sexuality had plagued him.

"Do what?" she asked as she continued to use the inner walls of her intimacy to clutch and release his inches.

"Use the love card," he countered with a quickness. "You didn't love me. Love would've led to you choosing me and not a job."

"I do love you. I didn't realize it until I'd lost you—"

"Tossed me aside," he countered.

"Cole, I didn't know," she said, sitting upright to press kisses to his chin and mouth. "I thought we could just walk away from each other and it would mean nothing, but it does. I can't stop thinking of you and missing you and wanting you. I dream of you inside me. Deeply. So deep. Just like now."

Her words, kisses and touches were irrefutable. His body was caught in her trap and he didn't want to escape. Her tongue dipped inside his mouth and touched his. That caused him to shiver. She began to work her hips back and forth, sending her sliding on his inches. He got harder.

"Jillian," he moaned into her mouth as he gripped her hips.

She pressed her lush breasts against his chest and wrapped her arms around his neck. "Did you miss me, Cole?" she asked, looking into his eyes.

He refused to answer even as he enjoyed the feel of her core easing back and forth on him.

Jillian kissed a trail to his ear and sucked the lobe. "Do you forgive me, Cole?" she whispered.

He shivered but bit down on his bottom lip to keep quiet.

"Don't you want me back, Cole?" she asked as she eased her core to his throbbing tip and paused to kiss it with her lips before easing down onto him again.

He flung his head back and released a hoarse cry. She knew all too well how sensitive his tip was.

Jillian smiled as she drew her knees up to her shoulders, causing her walls to tighten along on his hardness.

He drew his lips into a circle and gave her a long stare he knew was intense. "Jillian…" he warned.

"Oh, so you *can* talk," she said lightly before circling her hips clockwise and then counterclockwise.

Just the sight of the snakelike movement of her hips was an enticing as the feel of her. He winced as he pressed his hands to his face. No one knew his body, and how to arouse him, like Jillian. But, in turn, *he* knew her just as well. And he felt like being a little more in control.

He had to, or Jillian would know the truth that he could no longer deny.

The root of his anger was the aching of his heart.

He lowered his hands to her hips to stop the hypnotic, rhythmic motion.

Jillian leaned back to look at him.

Their eyes searched each other's faces.

Cole lowered his lids slightly as the look in her eyes shifted from desire to something more profound. More vulnerable. More revealing. Raw. Real.

His heart skipped a beat and he felt his feelings for her tighten his chest. The battle whether to trust her or not raged within him. "What more do you want from me? From my family?" he asked, his voice as hard as the inches still buried inside her.

Her eyes filled with remorse and glistened with unshed tears. "Let me love you," she whispered on a breath before closing her eyes and shaking her head with her regret.

Damn.

Her pain caused the same in him. It pierced.

Jillian opened her eyes, her lashes damp with tears she'd held in, and looked at him. She gasped and covered her mouth with her hand. "You really care about me, too, Cole," she said.

He shut his eyes.

She pressed her hands to his face and kissed his mouth. Gently. Lovingly.

"Don't you have a deal to keep with my mother?" he said. He tilted his head back to avoid her tempting kisses and to attempt to hold steadfast to anger that was fading.

"I choose you," she said.

"Too late," he said.

"Cole," she said, revealing a streak of frustration with him.

He surprised himself by the urge to chuckle and was relieved when he didn't.

Again, she started to rotate her hips. He was unable to deny that he missed her in his bed, but he also yearned for the sound of her laughter and her free-spirited nature in his life. "I don't believe you are in love with me," he admitted as he shifted his hands to grip her buttocks.

Jillian lowered one arm across his back and settled the other on his shoulder as she kissed one side of his mouth and then the other.

"I will prove it to you, Cole Cress," she whispered against his lips.

He lightly gripped the back of her neck and kissed her deeply, wanting to eat her words. She moaned from the back of her throat as he sucked her tongue and delivered a thrust that eased the rest of his inches inside her until she was full with him.

They moved in sync in a wicked back-and-forth motion. Desire and passion fueled them. Moans and pants and hot, whispered words of praise and pleading filled the air as they gave in to the attraction that had pulsed between them from the first sight of one another.

The months of denying himself the treats of another woman now had him feeling quite wild. He had to fight not to give in to it and perhaps thrust too hard or deep. The urge to leave love marks upon her neck and breasts filled him, but again he resisted the temptation to suckle and bite her flesh. He felt excitement and pleasure. His body began to seek and crave his release, but he eyed her intently as he honed in on a change in her intimacy that hinted she, too, was near climax.

He took the lead, delivering deep, slow strokes that made her eyes seem to glaze as she bit her bottom lip.

He raised one of her legs over his arm and shifted a bit to the left to match his thrusts with his racing heartbeat. Fast and furious. Her eyes widened and her mouth gaped as she dug her fingernails into his buttocks. He grunted and hissed as he felt her walls grip and release him.

She was primed and ready.

And so was he.

"You want it?" Cole asked, his voice deep and intense.

"Please," she begged in a hot little whisper in his ear.

He shivered as he shifted her leg he held on to his shoulder and turned his head to kiss her calf as he let loose a series of piston-like strokes to stoke the storm bursting to explode.

Jillian turned his face and licked at his lips. "Yes," she gasped against his mouth before she winced and cried out as her body shook with her release.

He met her on the apex, licking at her mouth before releasing a roar to match that of a lion as he got lost in white-hot spasms and euphoria.

They both breathed into one another's open mouth and stared in each other's eyes. When he stopped his thrusts, she took the lead in their explosive ride, wanting to push him right over the edge into madness. His rough cry was her reward as Jillian used her legs around his waist to keep him from running from her skill. She didn't stop until all of his hardness was eased.

Cole felt relief.

When a tear raced along her cheek as she clung to him, he pressed a comforting kiss to it and then to her neck.

"I do love you, Cole," she whispered beseechingly.

He just couldn't allow himself to embrace that emotion.

Not yet.

Jillian glanced at Cole as they worked in silence to clean and sanitize the food truck. Her cheeks warmed as she wiped down the counter where they had enjoyed each other for the first time in months. She noticed he moved with the same slowness that she did. They were drained. Truly, sleep was the only remedy after exhaustive and mind-altering sex.

He glanced up from sweeping the floor and caught her stare on him.

She locked her eyes with his and felt a surge of energy from his look. They shared a smile—a naughty one.

"You missed me," she said, just slightly teasing.

He chuckled and tapped the push broom against the tiled floor. "I missed you," he admitted.

She dropped the sponge she was using and closed the gap between them to wrap her arm around his waist as she pressed her cheek to his muscular back. "I'll be back soon. I just have to give my notice to the restaurant—"

"No, you don't," he said.

She froze and stepped back as he turned.

"Keep the position," Cole said.

That made her nervous.

"All I ever wanted was a choice in the matter and not to be treated like your personal sex slave," he said.

"And I'm ready to give us a serious try," she said.

"I'm not," he said, continuing to sweep the floor. "Plus, you may change your mind."

Jillian knew she had destroyed whatever trust he'd had in her, and she was determined to prove to him that he could trust in her and, in time, one day love her.

I hope.

"How do you suppose we see each other?" she asked, feeling some of her own fears about love resurfacing.

"If it matters to us, then *we* will make a way," Cole said.

She nodded as she finished ensuring all surfaces were sanitary to prepare food. Still, doubts plagued her.

Should I *trust* him? *Am I wasting my time?*

She released a breath.

Why is love so dang on complicated?

Cole came up to stand behind her. "What's on your mind?" he asked. "I can see it on your face."

Nothing.

But that was a lie and wouldn't help her build the same trust for which she yearned.

She leaned back against his strong body, wondering

how she'd missed how secure she felt in his presence and how observant he had always been to her moods. "Love wasn't a part of my plan, Cole, but here I am, loving you," she said, speaking her truth as she turned to look up at him. "And it scares me."

In the depths of his grayish-blue eyes, she saw the fear of her own reflected.

Cole wrapped his arms around her and bent his head to press a kiss to her forehead. "I will always be honest with you, Jillian, and that's all I'm asking from you," he promised. "I give you my word that I won't lead you on."

She nodded, enjoying the light massage he was giving her back. She felt her desire rising as his hands slipped under her shirt and pressed to her skin with warmth, but she couldn't run from her doubts and the fact that she already had two marriages under her belt.

The only thing she knew for sure was how much she missed Cole in her life, and having him back was worth the risk.

Because not having him had been torture.

Seven

Two weeks later

Cole's footsteps echoed inside the two-thousand-foot condo in the Chelsea section of Manhattan's west side. It was empty of furniture—save for the king-size bed in the owner's suite. The post-war nineteen-story building's structural design was evident in the modern lines, towering eleven-foot ceilings, polished teak hardwood floors, and views of the Hudson River via the expansive windows.

But it was the neighborhood that had clutched it for him. Chelsea offered a mix of culture, nightlife and art that suited him well. He didn't even mind the traffic noise that reached the ninth floor because it spoke the neighborhood's vibe. Art galleries, restaurants, shopping and gourmet food markets were in abundance among the new and old residential structures.

There was always something to do and to see.

His stomach rumbled in hunger.

"And to eat," he said.

Bzzzzzz. Bzzzzzz. Bzzzzzz.

He pulled his phone from the back pocket of his denims. His smile was not to be denied at a FaceTime call from Jillian. He answered. "Hello, Chef," he said, holding the phone up to his face as he took in hers.

She was beautiful as ever, with her curly hair piled atop her head and her face fresh of any makeup. Her brown eyes twinkled as she gave him a smile that beamed. "How are you, Chef?" she asked, standing on her terrace, the waterfront in the background.

Missing you.

"I know I'm missing you like crazy," she said, seeming to steal his thought. "I hated to leave you yesterday."

"Me, too," he admitted, walking down the long, wide hall to the owner's suite. "It was hard sleeping without you."

"Even in that big beautiful bed?" she asked.

He chuckled. "It felt bigger without you in it," he admitted.

"Then I gotta get back to it real soon."

Good.

For the last two weeks, they had been nearly inseparable and how they'd spent that time together ran the gamut. From long rides across the city on his motorcycle to mind-blowing sexcapades. Long conversations about their careers and their families. Cooking and feeding each other. Sometimes saying nothing and just enjoying the comfort of being together lounging naked in bed as the rain poured outside.

"You made a good choice," he said, eyeing the king-size structure that sat in the middle of his bedroom, the covers strewed everywhere.

"Thank you," she said as the San Francisco winds blew the escaped tendrils back from her face.

His feelings for her had deepened.

Jillian was making it impossible not to do so. She was putting on a full-court press to prove she loved him and wanted him in her life. Never had *he* been wooed with having his favorite meals prepared, surprising him with thoughtful gifts, and continuous declarations of her love as they invested time in each other.

And the sex.

He shook his head at how it had only intensified once deeper feelings had been added to the mix. Nothing felt better than looking down into Jillian's eyes as he stroked deep within her and seeing them flooded with her emotions and, at times, tears of sweet release.

It was addictive.

And he felt himself crave her.

"I just wanted to see that face before I headed to the restaurant," she said, walking back inside her apartment. "I'm excited to see the changes."

"Call me when you're done and tell me about it. I'll be up," Cole said, taking steps to the kitchen that centered the condo. He picked up the stack of takeout menus.

"Something to look forward to," she said as she leaned the phone against something to pull a lightweight jacket over the fitted long-sleeved tee she wore with her black uniform pants.

His doorbell rang loudly.

"Someone has company," she said, jerking a leather satchel over her head to settle on her side.

"Gabe and Mo wanted to see the place," he told her, walking over to the door.

"Speaking of family…" Jillian picked up the phone and walked down the hall to reach her front door. "My grandmother believes you're beautiful and wants to know if I didn't bring you around because I was scared she would steal you from me."

Cole chuckled, remembering and liking the feisty silver-haired woman with pink-painted lips. Dinner with Jillian's family had been a surprise that he'd enjoyed. Her mother was warm. Her father, a solid man. And her grandmother simply adorable with a quick wit and a flirty eye wink. "Beautiful, huh?" he asked as he stood by the condo's front door.

"Funny, you chose to focus on *that*," she mused.

They laughed.

"Enjoy your visit, and please check with your interior decorator on your *furniture*," she quipped before blowing him a kiss and ending the call.

Cole made a mental note to do that in the morning as he slid his phone into his back pocket and opened the front door. "Do I smell food?" he asked, looking down at the bags they carried.

"Wow. Hello to you, too, Cole," Monica said, rising on her toes to kiss his cheek before walking inside.

Gabe chuckled as he offered his brother his fist for a tap with his own in greeting. "Don't let her fool you. She is starving, too," he said, offering his future bride an amused look when she shot him a playful glare before looking up at the towering tray ceiling.

"This condo is *beautiful*," she said, making a slow turn to take in the abundance of floor-to-ceiling windows that offered a view of the sun descending on the Manhattan skyline.

Cole led Gabe into the kitchen, where he set the bags he carried atop the sizable marble island. "It will be better once Jaime gets it decorated," he said, opening the custom cabinets to remove plates.

The kitchen was stocked with essentials because he and Jillian had enjoyed staying in and cooking for each other.

"Jaime Pine Design?" Monica asked, removing the lightweight emerald-green trench she wore with matching slacks and a light silk sweater. "Good choice."

"I always liked what she did with the townhouse," Cole said as she took Gabe's navy jacket and set both garments atop the empty counter.

"Does Mother know?" Gabe asked, opening the containers of steaming Thai food.

"I didn't tell her," Cole said as he piled a plate high with saucy beef noodles, green papaya salad and *pak boong* sautéed in traditional spicy Thai flavors. Several small omelets made with shrimp and green onions made a food tower he planned to demolish. "The last thing I need is her interfering in my life again."

Gabe and Monica shared a look.

"You ready to talk about just what she did to end things with you and Jillian?" Gabe asked, leaning against the counter and taking a bite from a grilled pork skewer.

"She got between Jillian and me," Cole said, covering his lips with the back of his hand as he spoke with his mouth full—something his mother abhorred.

Monica smiled at him as she opened a bottle of white wine. "Who knew you were a note writer? It's so romantic."

Cole was surprised she knew that.

"I found one in the kitchen and I read it—felt scandalous for doing so—and quickly put it back," she said as she searched and found the cabinet holding wine goblets.

"Where was it?" Cole asked as Gabe looked on at their exchange.

"In her knife case," Monica said, giving him a playful wink before she poured half a glass of wine for each of them.

He bit back a smile and hung his head, remembering that particular note well.

The taste of you still lingers on my tongue.

The night before, he had spent nearly an hour savoring Jillian intimately while bringing her to one explosive climax after another.

"You didn't tell me you found a note," Gabe said to her.

"And you didn't tell me your little brother and the chef were doing the do," Monica countered.

Gabe raised his glass to her.

She touched hers to his.

"Touché," they said in unison.

Cole eyed them, loving their vibe together. Monica had softened his brother, and never had he seen him smile so much. Jillian did the same for him. His rebellious brooding was not as constant.

And his mother had contributed to taking that from him.

"Mom offered Jillian the chef position to end things with me," Cole said, filling the silence and giving in to the sudden need to share his frustration with their mother.

"Damn." Gabe frowned. "Are you sure?"

"She didn't know I was in Jillian's apartment, and I heard it all myself," Cole said.

The frown became a scowl.

"Perhaps it's time I share something." Monica took a deep sip of wine before moving over to wrap an arm around Gabe's waist.

He looked wary.

"She did the same with me." Monica finished dryly, "But *I* didn't get a job offer."

"What!" Gabe roared.

Monica winced as she held him tighter and recounted Nicolette's coming to the charity ball she threw for the nonprofit foundation she'd developed to help young adults aging out of the foster care system. "She warned me that our relationship would never survive. But she was wrong."

"You never told me that," Gabe said, looking down at her upturned face.

Cole shook his head at the indignity of his mother's behavior.

"I didn't because it was your mother that sent the invite to your grand opening that brought us back together," she said, pressing a hand to his chest.

"Doesn't change the fact that to interfere in the lives of her sons like that is nothing but hubris and ego." Cole's voice chilled as his anger resurfaced.

Forgiving was far easier than forgetting.

"I agree," Gabe said, tossing the rest of his skewer onto his plate as if his appetite had vanished.

Or been taken from him by his annoyance.

"I wonder what other secrets we're clueless to," Gabe muttered.

Cole thought of the huge one he carried about his father. He felt guilt at his complicity.

"Monica..." Gabe said.

Cole looked over at her face. She shifted nervously, and was avoiding his brother's eyes. It was odd and telling.

Uh-oh.

"At this point, anything you are keeping from me is a betrayal," Gabe said, his voice hard.

She closed her eyes and released a heavy breath. "But I signed a nondisclosure agreement when I was hired," she said.

Uh-oh.

Cole could only imagine the things Monica knew about the family, having worked as their housekeeper for five years. The NDA had been necessary. Like it or love it, they were famous and the press—the paparazzi—hungered for a break in the armor that shielded the family's privacy.

"Gabe…" he said, realizing she was in a terrible position.

"Monica," Gabe repeated sternly, ignoring his brother and keeping his laser focus on his bride-to-be.

"You can't say anything," she insisted, finally leveling her eyes with his.

Cole was curious.

"I once found a file in your parents' bedroom of all the brothers being under surveillance by a private investigator," she admitted, her words rushed and almost tumbling upon each other.

"What!" the men roared in unison.

If they had been in a cartoon, the walls and floors would have shaken.

Monica squeezed her eyes shut then opened one to look back and forth between them.

Gabe angrily paced.

Cole's grip on his wineglass threatened the fragile stem.

"Maybe it's time to flush out their secrets and give them as good as they give," Cole said, curious if his father's dalliances had continued over the years.

Gabe paused and looked over at his brother. "I wonder how much they would like a PI digging into their lives," he said. "I can't even believe the nerve of them. Our parents. Are we that big of a sheep to them that *we* deserve no privacy?"

Cole felt insulted. Indignant. Betrayed.

Again.

That stung.

And he was sick of it.

"Well, an investigator helped me with locating my mother," Monica said, referring to her trials to reconnect with parents who had given her up into the foster care system.

"What was her name again?" Gabe asked. "Bobbie…?"

"Barnett," she supplied.

"Are we doing this?" Gabe asked.

Cole firmly nodded. "Hell yeah."

One week later

Jillian was relieved to enter her apartment. It was nearly midnight. She was bushed and thankful to have the next day off. The restaurant's renovation and more updated look had increased bookings and the entire night she and her team had been swamped with orders. During the work, the fatigue had been beaten off with energy, a desire to perfect and a need to please each patron. Afterward, without work to fuel her, exhaustion was queen.

She eased everything to the floor by the closed front door, including the clothes she wore. Naked, she freed her topknot and shook her curls out as she made her way down the hall to her bedroom. Not even the pastel colors against a white backdrop gave her their usual boost as she entered the en suite bathroom and treated herself to a quick shower and washed her hair to free it of the smell of food clinging to her.

Once done, she stood in the shower and inhaled deeply of the steam now scented with her favorite soap and shampoo. The only thing she had left to do for the night was to call Cole. Looking forward to seeing his face and hearing his deep voice spurned her to open the fogged door to step out and wrap a plush white towel around her damp hair and then her body.

She retrieved her phone from her bag by the door. Quickly made her way back to the bedroom to sit cross-legged on the foot of the bed. She had missed calls and texts.

She chuckled at the funny meme her grandmother had sent of the sensual silver-haired man from the Dos Equis commercial—the most interesting man in the world. Ionie thought he was one of the sexiest men in the world and made no qualms about it.

Her father just wanted her to know he missed his daughter.

Her mother wanted a recipe for a meal to cook for her father for their upcoming anniversary.

Warren requested a call back when she had time.

With plans to call her family and friend the next day. Jillian returned Cole's missed call instead. She struck several cute poses as she waited for him to answer. She was disappointed when he never did.

Maybe he's asleep, she thought as she rose to plug the power cord into her phone before setting it on the turquoise-tinted glass bedside table.

Cole had always insisted she call to let him know she'd made it home safely. It would be the first night since her return from the east coast that he hadn't answered. She turned off the clear globe lamp and dropped the towel around her body to the floor before climbing under the covers, enjoying he feel of the cool, crisp sheets against her skin as she looked out the window at the half moon. Snuggling one of her plump pillows to her side helped in how much she missed Cole's body beside her, but not by much.

Never had she expected to long for him in her life. Love had not been a part of her plan, but here she was. And she loved him.

His humor.

His smile.

His advice.

His loyalty.

His strong hugs.

His kisses.

His lovemaking.

She pressed her thighs and knees together as the bud nestled beneath the lips of her intimacy swelled with life. Some attention from his clever tongue was just what she needed to send her into a deep sleep. Cole's loving was the epitome of the Energizer bunny.

And of her fear of being hurt.

It lingered but was repeatedly defeated as her methods at wooing him seem to succeed. Cole seemed more like himself. Fun, charming, and with a ready smile.

The job at CRESS III was affording her choices—more than she'd had in a long time. She was steadily paying down her insufferable debt, helping her parents with her grandmother's in-home nursing care, and able to treat herself a little. The job didn't bring her the same freedom and joy of working for herself, but the stability it offered was clear.

And after financial ruin, that was important.

Bzzzzzz. Bzzzzzz. Bzzzzzz.

Her heart jolted at the sudden loud vibrations of her phone against the glass. She flopped over to snatch it up and smiled at *his* contact picture on the screen. She an-

swered. "Hey, Cole," she said, touching the globe to il-
luminate the bedroom some.

He gave her the grin that made all her pulses race.
"You in bed already?" he asked.

"Not sleeping," she assured him, feeling a tiny nig-
gle of shock at how accommodating she was willing to
be for him.

The Jillian of old had only cared about having her
sexual appetited sated.

The new territory in which they'd ventured was still a
little frightful because she was phobic of love.

But the feeling of being in love was beautiful. Nicer
than she had ever thought or imagined it to be.

Will he ever admit to loving me back? Does he?

"Wait? Where are you headed?" she said, noticing
when the phone dipped that he was fully dressed—leather
jacket and all.

"Open the door."

She sat upright as her heart hammered and her stomach tightened. "Huh?" she said softly, tentatively tossing the covers back from her body. "Don't joke. It's not
funny."

Cole chuckled and the twinkle in his gray-blue eyes
against his shortbread-brown complexion was magnetic.
"My bad. Sorry," he said.

She made a face and flopped back onto her pillows.
"Got my hopes up, Cole Cress," she chastised him.

He just shrugged one broad shoulder.

Jillian arched a brow. "Wait. Huh?" she said as she
straightened. "Are you here or not?"

"Am I?"

Jillian ended the call and rushed from her bed. Her
bare feet lightly beat against the hardwood flooring as
she rounded the corner, jetted down the hall, and snatched

the front door open just as naked as the day her mother had pushed her into the world. But the hall was empty, and her disappointment stung.

Shoving the door to swing it closed, she turned. "I am going to tell Cole Cress something about tricking me!" she muttered, now in an intolerable lousy mood.

"Tell me to my face."

She spun.

Cole leaned in the doorway, his arm keeping the door from actually closing.

She covered her shock well and leaned against the wall to eye him. "You came this far, come a little bit more," she said in a sultry voice as she beckoned him with a wiggle of her index finger.

He nodded and hung his head for a moment before looking up to take in her nudity. His eyes smoldered and seemed to darken in color. "I flew across the country just to spend your day off with you," he countered.

A playful battle of wills.

"I can't believe you're here," she said, looking down the length of the hall at him as she fought like hell not to run and collide into him.

"Meet me halfway," he offered.

Jillian pushed off the wall and slowly walked to the midway point between them. She loved how his eyes did not miss the sway of her hips or her breasts. She was already bold and confident, but his attention made her feel simply divine. And when he stepped inside to close the door, dropped his leather duffel bag and then all of his clothing to join her mess on the floor, she gave him the same ogling—enjoying every moment and movement of his strong muscled frame.

It was the sway of his member back and forth across his thighs that was her undoing, and she moved to him, taking the inches into her hand as he encased her in his embrace and tasted her lips with hunger as she stroked him to hardness.

Cole picked her up, and she clung to his neck, pressing kisses to his shoulder as she guided him to her bedroom.

Atop her on the middle of the bed, and in her deeply, he made fierce love to her. Her fears were quieted and she felt hopeful this man—this beautiful, loyal and charming man—would be hers.

Long after explosive climaxes that had evoked cries from them both, she lay against his chest with her bent legs atop his and enjoyed the up and down movement of his chest as he took deep breaths meant to sustain him after such an exhaustive workout.

"What will we do tomorrow?" Jillian asked as she stroked her thumb across one of his flat brown nipples.

Cole lightly rested a hand on her buttocks and gave it a tap as he pressed a kiss to the top of her head. "Whatever you want. I just have a Zoom meeting with my team around nine, and then I'm yours for the rest of the day," he said, his deep voice seeming to rumble in his chest against her ear.

And hopefully for longer than that.

That thought caused her to stiffen in surprise. Love for Cole—she had accepted that fact. But more? Marriage? Forever? That was new. And startling.

"How's the revamp coming?" she asked, seeking a hiding place from her thoughts.

"Great, actually," Cole said. "When I took the position, it was more about family duty and obligation, but I have to admit my mother saw something in me that I am just discovering. I am enjoying the work and have a good eye for it. I want to succeed. Not to best my brothers for the CEO position my father will vacate, but to help make the best for whichever of my brothers succeeds him."

Cole. Ever loyal. And expecting nothing less. Even from her.

I will never let you down again, my love.

She rose slightly to look down at him and stroked the side of his face. "So, you've decided you don't want it?" she asked.

"I never did, but I'm ready now to officially step down from being in the race," he said before turning his head to press a warm kiss to her palm. "I'm learning that focusing on antagonizing my father is foolish. Perhaps in my need to best him, I am worried I will become him."

She kissed the side of his mouth and fought the urge to declare her love for him even as it nearly burst her heart. She so badly wanted to ask for the impetus for his broken relationship with his father, but she refrained. Knowing how close she was to her parents, she couldn't imagine what had caused such a deep fracture between them.

"Whenever you want to talk about it, I am here for you," she whispered, needing him to know that she would always have his back.

Cole looked up and locked his eyes with her own. They searched hers for so long. So intensely. She could only hope that what he sought he found in her brown depths. "You are making this harder and harder for me," he admitted with the hint of a smile.

She tilted her head to the side, feeling hopeful. "Good," she whispered down to him.

One week later

The silence in Cole's now beautifully furnished living room was stunning as he, Gabriel and Monica sat on the low-slung, dark blue suede sofa and eyed the woman sitting across from them on the matching piece. Nothing echoed but the crackle of the modern slate fireplace to the side of them.

Bobbie Barnett, a medium-brown woman with long, wild, loose ebony curls that floated beyond her shoulders, long black lashes and pouty lips glossed with brown, was beautiful. Still, it wasn't the private investigator's looks that held everyone captive.

It was the truth she'd just revealed to them.

"Well, damn," Gabe finally said, reaching for Monica's hand and holding it tightly.

Cole rose and walked over to the dining room, needing space and clarity. He hadn't known what secrets, if any, would be uncovered, but never had he expected to be told his father had an illegitimate son in England from when he was just eighteen. Before he'd even met their mother.

Another Cress son.

A brother.

What do we do with this information?

"What's his name?" Gabe asked.

Cole turned and crossed his arms over his chest as he awaited the response.

"Lincoln Cress," Bobbie offered, her voice soft and raspy.

Cole frowned. "Did he know? Our father. Did he know?" he asked, striding across the room to rejoin them.

Bobbie sat back and crossed her legs. "At this point, I doubt it. His name is on the birth certificate, but it's not signed," she said, opening the file she held in her lap. "I have a little info on your brother. On Lincoln. Do you want it?" She eyed them all.

Gabe and Monica shared a brief look.

Cole released a deep breath as he glanced at his booted feet and then back over to her. "I do," he admitted.

"Me, too," Gabe agreed.

Bobbie nodded and tossed her wild mane behind her shoulder as she cleared her throat. She removed a photo and set it on Cole's wide metal-trimmed stone coffee table. "He lives in England where he is a chef at his own Michelin-star restaurant," she said, pausing to look up at them at the similarity. "Single. No children. Well off. Well educated. And upon meeting him, without revealing to my true intent in being there, he is…uh…quite a character."

Cole reclaimed his seat and took the photo Gabe had studied and then handed to him. "Meaning?" he asked before looking down.

Their eldest brother resembled Lenny Kravitz. In good shape. Strong features. Handsome.

He could see similarities in this stranger and their father.

"A little moody," she said with an expression that made it clear their encounter had not been fun for her. "*Rude* comes to mind, but perhaps I caught him at the wrong time. Who knows?"

"I think we need to know more about him before we even decide what to do next," Cole suggested.

"I would recommend a blood test at some point," Monica offered.

The brothers nodded in agreement.

Bobbie set the folder on the table. On top was her bill, including fees for her trip to England. "I think it entails a trip back to London to really get at it," she said.

Neither man flinched at the hefty price or the next bill to come.

"Fine," they said in unison.

She rose and offered her hand to all three. "Good. We can do it week to week and, whenever you tell me it's enough, I'm headed home," she promised. "Don't worry, I won't charge extra for his bad mood."

Monica walked the other woman to the door while Cole and Gabe shared a long look as neither could do anything more than release heavy breaths.

Eight

One month later

"Six months," Jillian said, standing in front of the mirror and eyeing her reflection in her black T-shirt and matching uniform pants.

She'd given the position half a year and she still hated it. Not the ability and desire to cook delectable meals— that was an inherent part of who she was and had always longed to be. The rules of the corporate structure left her feeling restricted and her culinary gift now felt a burden.

For Cress, INC. to be started by two world-renowned chefs who had a bevy of sons, also just as skilled and well known in their field, was particularly irksome for her. Phillip Senior and Nicolette should understand more than anyone with just a business background that chefs needed the freedom to create, to evolve.

The decision to add a varying seasoning was watched

over by the manager with the eye of an eagle—or more
like a buzzard awaiting its next prey to fail and fall to
its death.

Jillian made a playful face before turning from her reflection. Quickly she grabbed her phone and her satchel,
being sure her beloved engraved knife set was snuggled
inside it. At the door, she retrieved her short, lightweight,
black trench from the closet and then walked out the door.
She considered driving the short distance to the restaurant but walked instead, enjoying the smell of the harbor.
She released a breath and eased her hands into the deep
pockets of her trench coat. Inside one was an envelope.
She stroked it with her fingers. She'd debated what to
do with the letter ever since she'd written it, carefully
folded it and sealed it inside. That had been a week ago.

It was her resignation.

Never had she felt such ill at ease about going to work.
She knew the feeling to be dread. Creativity could not
thrive in such an environment. Not even when her restaurant had begun to fail had she lost determination to
get in and fight for her dream. Never had she thought of
giving up.

Never.

But failure had taught her well. Spending profits and
not saving them for possible bad times ahead had been
so very foolish. *Never again*, she promised herself.

And, if she were honest, even the strict nature of
Cress, INC. had taught her something. About efficiency,
marketing, low turnover, and the need for a team outside
of making great meals, for a restaurant to thrive.

Her dread resurfaced as she eyed the towering restaurant at the end of the pier. The spacious parking lot
was empty, save the section set aside in the rear for employees. She rolled her eyes at the sight of Clark's yel-

low vintage Mercedes-Benz parked in his spot next to her empty one.

Her hand stroked the envelope again.

She had been diligent in paying down her debt and even had some money saved. All would not be lost if she used the six months of experience and took it to another restaurant or tried again at opening her own.

The last thought slowed her steps just as she reached the rear door leading directly into the kitchen.

Am I better prepared this time?

She sighed.

That, she didn't know. But what she was sure of was the feeling that she was missing out on so much by sticking it out in San Francisco. Her man. Her family. Her creative freedom.

It was not just the structure and conformity she disdained. Not being in New York with Cole and her family felt like a waste when she was so unhappy without them.

But what about my dreams?

Her grandmother had longed to teach. She had done so until she'd reached retirement age.

Her mother had yearned to marry her "Bear" and have a child. She had. Devoted herself to it. She hadn't gone to work until Jillian had graduated high school. Now she worked as a clerk at the county courthouse, but marriage and motherhood had been her everything.

Her father's love of cars was bred from childhood and now he was an auto mechanic for a dealership. Another dream realized.

Cole threw his all into everything. Be it his love of motorcycles, his food truck, or now a desire to succeed at his position at Cress, INC.

If I run home to them while they have lived their dreams, am I giving up too easily on my own?

Jillian turned and leaned against the rear of the building, looking up at the afternoon sun.

Maybe it is time for a new dream...

"Good afternoon, Chef."

She looked over and smiled at one of the waiters walking up to the restaurant to begin his shift.

"Afternoon," she said just as her phone vibrated inside her pocket. She removed it and looked at the screen.

Cole.

She swiped to answer his call. *"Bonjour Monsieur Cress. Ça fait plaisir d'avoir de tes nouvelles?"* she said, trying to use the French he was teaching her to let him know it was good to hear from him.

He chuckled. "Not bad."

"Considering you only taught me that and how to demand you get naked for me," she added.

"Say it."

"Rends-toi nu pour moi," she said, enjoying seeing his handsome face smile with pride.

"I wish I was somewhere private and then I would," he assured her, his voice deep and delicious to her ears.

Jillian paused in making a naughty comment at all of the bustling activity behind him. "Where *are* you?" she asked.

"Checking in on the preparation for the launch party tomorrow night." He looked back over his shoulder.

"Oh," she said.

He faced his phone again. "What's wrong?" he asked, knowing her so well.

"Nothing," she said.

Not getting an invite to the event was the side effect of their secret affair. She wanted nothing more than to buy a beautifully sexy gown and attend.

"You're more than welcome, Jillian," he said, as if

reading her thoughts. "I didn't want to put you in a position to have to choose between having me or having your job…again."

She forced a smile and nodded. "But what if I chose you?" she asked.

He looked surprised.

"Would you have me at your side as your guest? Your date?" she asked, hating that she wasn't sure he would.

His face became serious. "Without question."

Warmth spread over her chest.

"Then I do have a choice to make," she said, refraining from sharing with him another sentence she was teaching herself via her phone's translator.

Je t'aime de tout mon cœur.

I love you with all my heart.

Cole rubbed his hands together before checking his watch as he stood near the grand ballroom entrance of the luxury Manhattan hotel. He felt pride as he surveyed the crowd enjoying the lush party décor, open bar, and abundance of heavy appetizers as they listened to upbeat music and conversated. Tuxedos and sparkling gowns were in abundance. Press and peers were awaiting the new interactive website's relaunch at midnight—a costly feat he was confident was worth every cent.

He wiped his hand over his shadow of a beard and then smoothed his hands down the front of his dark navy tuxedo and matching shirt. He was surprised by his nervousness. Although they practiced the countdown to the launch numerous times, a flop at this point would be disappointing and embarrassing,

"Don't worry, you look amazing, and you know it."

He turned to find Barbara, a member of the Cress, INC. office staff, walking up to him with two glasses of champagne in her hands. She used to make subliminal advances to his brother Gabe before his relationship with Monica had ruled the papers once the former maid had inherited millions after the death of the famous father she had never known.

Barbara now gave Cole the extra touch and long looks.

In the past, he would have taken the invite and found a private space to give her the release she sought. Things were different. He was different.

Because of Jillian.

"No, thank you, Barbara," he said with emphasis as he eyed the glass—and whatever else—she offered him.

She arched a brow and shrugged a bare shoulder in her strapless dress before drinking one flute of champagne and then the other before turning and walking away.

He was glad to see her leave him be.

"Mr. Cress."

He turned to find a waiter holding a tray. A small envelope sat upon it. He knew as he reached for it that it was from Jillian.

She's not coming.

"Thank you," he said to the young server.

He held the envelope, letting his disappointment set with him. He had wanted her there but hadn't wanted to pressure her. His position at the door was not just to greet his guests but to ensure he saw her as soon as she stepped into the party.

Cole recognized her handwriting on the envelope and stroked his name as he strolled away from the door. He had taken a few steps and paused. "Wait," he said.

How would a handwritten note from Jillian even get there if she was thousands of miles away?

He opened the envelope and removed the note. "'You

are the sexiest man in the room. No question,'" he read aloud.

He turned. Then he smiled.

Jillian stood in the hall outside the ballroom, looking stunning in a chocolate cami maxi dress cut on the bias with a deep vee and thin straps. A delicate brown lace jacket, worn open, trailed behind her, perfecting framing her sultry body in the clinging silk. Her normally curly hair was pulled back into a sleek ponytail; her eye makeup was dramatic and her lips were covered in a nude gloss.

Beautiful, he mouthed, clutching her note as he walked over to her.

As he stood before her with his heart thundering at a frenzied pace and his entire body electrified by her very presence, he would be even more a fool to deny his feelings for her. They consumed him. They pushed him to reach for her and pull her body to his kiss as he lowered his head and feasted of her lips. The moan he released was pure hunger.

He broke their kiss with reluctance and looked down at her. "All your gloss is gone," he said.

She shrugged as she reached up to wipe the remnants of it from his mouth. "To *hell* with that gloss," she said.

"I'm feeling like to hell with this party," he said, his inches swelling to life.

"And miss your big moment? Never." Jillian lifted on her heels to taste his mouth.

"I'm having another big moment right now." Cole looked down at his rising erection.

"Oh, big indeed," she said with a sassy wink.

They laughed.

"So, I made my choice, Cole. I chose you," she said, pressing her hand to the side of his face.

"Me wanting you here was never about proving anything. I just wanted you by my side. Enjoying your company. Feeling your support. Dancing with you in my arms as I celebrate. Seeing you cheer me on," he admitted with total honesty.

Her eyes softened.

It struck a chord in Cole that rang loudly.

"But my mother will not be pleased," he said.

"The choice is hers," Jillian said, stepping back to open the small gold clutch hanging from her wrist.

He looked on as she replaced her lip gloss and checked her hair in the mirror of a compact. "Ready?" he asked when she snapped it closed and dropped it back in her purse.

She nodded.

He extended his hand and she slid hers into his. "Did you ever think we would be walking into a gala hand in hand together?" he asked as they entered the ballroom.

She chuckled. "Definitely not, *but* definitely happy to have been wrong," she assured him.

He raised the entwined hands and kissed the back of hers. He felt her shiver.

She closed her lace overlay to cover her breasts. "Hard nipples," she explained. "Don't want to poke anyone's eyes out."

He laughed.

Her humor was entertaining.

As he saw his parents moving toward them, he knew they would need it. "Here we go," he warned, bending to press a kiss to her temple.

Jillian's height seemed to rise a bit beside him and he knew she had straightened her back. He hated someone feeling a need to prepare themselves to match his mother, but he also knew the two women in his life were about to bump heads because of the deal they'd brokered about him.

Nicolette patted her gray-streaked blond updo as she gave them a perfect smile that was as fake as a fifty-dollar Hermès Birkin bag. "Hello, Cole. Your father and I weren't aware you were bringing a guest," she said.

"I wasn't aware that I needed to have a guest approved," he countered in a pleasant tone.

"Cole," Phillip Senior warned in a gruffly stern voice.

He eyed his father coolly. The desire to reveal his long-lost son to him dripped from his tongue. However, he refrained from the move for the love of his entire family and wanting to shield his mother still—as they awaited a new report from the private investigator.

When Phillip returned his look with a glare, Cole stepped into the familiarity of his anger and disappointment at his father, failing at growing beyond it.

"Needless to say. You're fired," Nicolette said to Jillian, her smile still in place as she looked around and waved at those whose eyes she found on them.

Jillian stopped a waiter, picked up two glasses of champagne and handed one to his mother. She reached into her clutch and removed her cell phone.

Cole looked on in curiosity as she dialed a number.

"Hello, Clark? Yes, this is Jillian. I'm here with Mrs. Cress—"

Clark? The manager of Cress III?

"Yes, *that* Mrs. Cress," Jillian said with a nod and lick of her lips. "Please confirm for her that I handed in my resignation, giving two weeks' notice, before I left last night."

Cole bit back a smile, loving her even more.

She put the phone on speaker. "Go ahead, Clark."

"I don't have time for your jokes, Jillian," he said, not believing her. "Some of us have to work."

"Cool. I no longer have time for you, Clark. You insufferable a-hole," she said. "Mrs. Cress just fired me, so you need to find a replacement ASAP. That two-week window just closed."

She ended the call and touched her champagne glass to Nicolette's.

Ding.

"Thanks so much for ending that even sooner than I thought," Jillian said with a bright smile.

Cole eyed his mother's face and was afraid she was going to have a stroke as her left eye seemed to blink uncontrollably.

"First Gabe and now you with this crap," Phillip Senior snapped.

"Exactly," Nicolette agreed with coldness.

And that pushed him to the limit. Seeing his parents judge and find Jillian unsuitable with such callousness was disturbing. So swiftly, he was reminded of the same disdain his father had expressed to Gabe when he'd first revealed that he was dating Monica.

There are women you wed and those you bed. Know the difference. And that goes for all of you. The anger Cole had felt back then was twofold now because it was Jillian his father was insulting.

"Jillian is the type of woman I can cherish and respect and be loyal to," he said, his eyes daring his father to say more. "A woman worthy of nothing but good, just like any other woman...including my mother."

His father's lips thinned to a line.

Cole was thankful for Jillian's tight grip on his hand as he was taken back to that moment the light he'd felt for his father dimmed all those years ago...

* * *

Cole hitched his book bag up higher on his thin shoulders as he climbed from the back of the family's limousine in the uniform of his private school. "Thanks, Franco," he said to their driver, who gave him a two-finger salute as he was surrounded by the loud and echoing sounds of Midtown Manhattan. Cole had boldly sneaked from home and left his brothers behind to finish their after-school studies while he hoped to help out in the kitchen in any way during busy dinner service.

His older brother, Phillip, was the sous chef. Sean had just finished his studies in culinary arts at Le Cordon Bleu that summer in Paris and worked there, as well. Gabe, at seventeen, had just begun culinary school and assisted in the bustling kitchen whenever he was home. Cole, at fifteen, wanted in on the action. Since they were young, their famous parents had taught them how to cook and praised them often for their skills.

This was a bold move but anything worth savoring was worth the risk.

Cole jogged up the concrete steps to the wide double-glass doors. He entered, barely paying attention to the towering adorned ceilings and elaborate Art Deco décor as he made his way to the kitchen.

"Hey, Chef, it's one of your boys," the burly pastry chef, Victor, yelled out. "Which one are you?"

"Coleman," he offered as his mother walked out of her office to give him a curious blue-eyed stare.

"I completed my homework during school so that I could help out today," he offered, his words rushed as he walked over to her, already towering over her by a couple of inches.

Nicolette gave him a chastising look even as she

pressed a kiss to his already chiseled cheek. "Mon beau fils rebelle," she said. My handsome and rebellious son.

He gave her a smile that already had girls sending him longing looks.

"Ask your father," she said with one last soft pat to his cheek before using the back of her hand to brush her blond bangs from her face.

He knew his mother would be easy. Up until she'd had Lucas, his little brother, he had been her undoubted favorite.

Cole moved to the sink to wash his hands, knowing his father would check because his rule was to wash hands as soon as any kitchen was entered. He felt nervous as he made his way through the large, bustling kitchen to the rear hall leading upstairs to a small apartment above the restaurant that his parents used as their joint office and storage.

He had already practiced his speech. "Dad, I finished my homework. Can I help out in the kitchen? Mom said it was up to you," he said, coming to a stop before the closed door.

Taking a breath and feeling confident, he reached for the knob and turned it before pushing the door open. His grip on the knob tightened as he eyed his father with his pants down around his ankles, rutting away between the open legs of some woman atop the desk.

It was more of his father than he needed or wanted to see.

Fueled by anger and bitter disappointment in a man who could do no wrong in his eyes, Cole rushed across the room and used both his hands to shove against his father's side with a savage grunt that only hinted at his hurt. He backed away as they cried out and rushed apart. The expressions on the faces of his father and on whom

he now saw to be one of the restaurant's long-time wait-
resses were of shock.

As they struggled to correct their clothing, Cole turned
and raced down the hall, then the steps, wishing he had
never dared to come to work. Or gone up the stairs. Or
opened the door.

Or had seen what he'd seen...

Things between them had changed at that moment.

Cole knew a huge part of his childhood had been lost
by his discovery…and in keeping his father's betrayal
a secret. "Judge not," he warned Phillip Senior before
walking away with Jillian close at his side.

Hours later, Jillian rolled over in Cole's bed and found
it empty. She raised her head from the pillow and looked
around once her eyes adjusted to the darkness. He stood
by the terrace doors, looking out at the cold, fall night,
still naked. She allowed herself a lingering moment to
enjoy the strong lines of his broad shoulders, defined
back and buttocks before climbing from the bed. Sharing in his nudity, she crossed the room and wrapped her
arms around him from behind as she pressed a kiss to
his spine. He covered her arms with his own as if welcoming the comfort she gave him.

The launch and the party had been a glorious success,
but she knew their heated interaction with his parents lingered, taking some of the shine from his event for him.
Long after they'd returned to his condo and showered,
he'd lain in silence in their bed. Not even seeking the explosive sex he usually craved.

"Why did you quit?" he asked, surprising her.

She frowned, now considering that her decision was
a part of his worries, as well. "I didn't care for the struc-

tured format, and it was so hard to not be here in New York when I didn't even like it," she said, easing around his body to stand in front of him, pressing her back and buttocks to the cold glass. "Not that I couldn't use the money. It was the reason that I took the job in the first place."

"What?" Cole asked.

"I never told you, but I tried—and failed horribly—at opening my own restaurant," she said. "After my ego was blown up by social media and being a private chef to celebrities, I thought I was ready. I wasn't. And it ruined me financially. I was on a quest to rebuild and recover. And that job afforded me that, plus, I could help my parents with my grandmother's medical care."

He looked down at her and the light of the full moon highlighted his eyes. "You never told me that," he said.

She looked away. "It's embarrassing. Who wants to admit to crippling debt, a horrible credit score and starting over until I thought I had it all?"

Cole used a finger beneath her chin to tilt her face back to him. "So *why* did you quit?" he asked again.

To be here with you.

Fear kept her from speaking her truth. At that moment, her actions felt desperate, especially when she'd yet to succeed at getting him to proclaim loving her. But that was how she had truly felt. Lost without him. In a way she had never felt with any other man. Not even for her previous husbands.

Am I a fool? His fool?

"Jillian."

She avoided his electric gaze.

Cole lifted her body against the glass so that her eyes were level with his own. "Did you come back for me?" he asked, his voice so deep. So captivating. So stirring.

"Yes," she whispered, pressing her hand to the top of his strong shoulders.

The truth wouldn't be denied. Not any longer.

"You got me," he admitted, wrapping his arms around her naked frame and pulling her soft body against his formidable strength.

Her gasp was visceral. The first feel of his mouth on hers sent a thrill across her body as she wrapped her arms around his neck.

"You got me," he repeated against her lips as he carried them to the bed. "My Jillian. My beautiful Jillian. You got me, baby."

He pressed her body down onto the foot of the bed with his own. His hands cupped the sides of her face as he pushed her hair back and examined her as if cementing every detail to memory. His smile was slow and warmed his eyes as he continued to study her.

The look made her breathless. Anxious. Adored.

"My Jillian. You *got* me," he kept saying as he pressed light kisses to her forehead then her cheeks, her chin and, finally, her mouth. Slowly. As if to savor.

Never had she experienced anything more exquisite.

Cole deepened the kiss with their eyes locked as she released his sides from her gripping knees to spread her legs and gently thrust her hips upward. A tender urging. To enter her. Fill her. Please her.

He obliged with a slight shift of his hips to find her center with his tip.

"Cole!" she gasped just as he thrust inside her. Swift and deep. So deep.

The lips of her intimacy kissed his hardness and she clutched him with her walls.

His grunt of pleasure into her mouth was her reward. There, on the foot of his bed, not sure they wouldn't tumble to the floor, they made love with aching slowness. Like a fine wine or a meal. Savored. Cherished. Needed.

Physically, it was familiar. Emotionally, it was all new. Different. Deeper. A fresh level of connection between them that shook her to her core. This was passion. Truly something she had never experienced before and could only hope to experience once again.

Cole placed his beautiful mouth near her ear. "Jillian," he whispered. "My Jillian."

Over and over again, captivating her.

She clung to him with her arms and legs, wanting him thrusting inside her forever. "Cole," she cried.

And when they trembled as they reached their climax together and their cries filled the air, Jillian knew that she was risking it all for her sexy rebel.

And he was worth it.

Nine

One month later

Cole's heart thundered as he quickly parked his motor-cycle in the lot of the hospital. On the entire ride up on the elevator, he found it hard to stand still. He felt concerned and a need to be reassured that all was well. His stomach had been in knots since he'd gotten the call. As he received his visitor's pass and directions to the hospital room, he was ready for an update.

Another elevator ride took him to the third floor of the massive structure. As soon as the doors opened, he stepped off and moved to the nursing station. "Excuse me. Room 304, please," he said.

The nurse didn't look away from the computer as she held up her ink pen to cease further conversation.

"Girl, look up," someone said to the nurse whose name badge read "Olive."

And Olive did, leaning back a little in her seat as her

emerald eyes took Cole in before she gave him a warm smile. "I'm sorry. What was your question?"

"Room 304, please," he repeated, his brows dipping slightly at how nearly all the eyes of the staff were on him.

Cole had no time to be eye candy.

"It's down the hall to the right," Olive said, pointing in that direction with her pen as she rose and leaned against the desk.

"Thanks," he said, turning to head off to where she'd pointed.

"No, thank *you*," Olive called behind him.

All thoughts of her and the giggling hospital staff were lost to him as he turned the corner. His steps faltered and then paused as he eyed Jillian and her ex-husband standing by the window. Warren was still in his scrubs and white coat.

Annoyance replaced Cole's worry. He wasn't surprised to see the man there at all. He worked in the hospital and, upon Jillian's return to New York, their friendship had continued. The cavemen DNA in him felt territorial and wanted to club the doctor. The evolved man who tried to respect his woman's relationships before him tried his best to keep the Neanderthal at bay.

But not successfully.

Cole grit his teeth, easing his hands into the pockets of the dark blue jeans he was wearing with a matching fisherman-knit sweater and brown leather boots. It's just that Warren's presence was becoming a norm. He seemed to always be in the mix. At her parents' house. On the phone. FaceTiming. Messaging funny memes.

He tried to reason that, before their marriage, they had been childhood friends.

Again, not successfully.

Jillian crossed her arms over her chest and leaned her head against the window as she looked out. His eyes shifted to Warren's tall figure. He frowned as the man looked at her profile with what appeared to Cole to be love and longing. Jillian chuckled and looked back up at him. Warren's expression instantly changed, keeping his feelings for her cloaked.

For him, his suspicions that Warren wanted to be her next and not just her ex were confirmed.

Jillian glanced down the hall and saw Cole. Her face filled with a light that warmed him as she came to him and seemed thankful for him to be there. He ate up the steps to reach her, wrapping her in his embrace and pressing a kiss to her forehead. "How's Ionie?" he asked.

"Stable," Jillian said, her arms wrapped securely around his waist as she looked up at him. "The doctor believes it was a stroke."

Tears filled her eyes and that wrenched his gut. "Hey, hey, hey," he said softly. "What I have learned about your grandmother is that she is a fighter. Right?"

Jillian smiled and bit her bottom lip. "I feel for the doctors when she's able to swing and wants to go home," she quipped.

They looked at each other and shared that kind of smile of intimacy and closeness.

He liked it a lot.

"I'm glad you're here. I need you with me," she admitted, pressing her hands to his back atop the sweater.

He raised her body up to lightly kiss her lips before setting her back down on her feet.

"Hello, Cole."

He stiffened and looked over Jillian's head at the other man. "Warren," he said, offering no warmth even as he gave him a forced smile.

Warren pushed his spectacles up on his nose and gave Cole a stiff smile, as well.

"Thanks for coming to check on my grandmother, Warren. You'd better get back to your rounds before you're missed," Jillian said as she released Cole and turned to her friend.

"Yeah, I gotta go. I have surgery in a little bit," he said, checking the time on his pager.

"She's in good hands," Cole reassured him as he placed his arm around Jillian's shoulders.

Warren nodded. "I'll check on you later," he said to her before walking away.

Keeping her grandmother's well-being paramount, Cole set aside his concerns about Warren's feelings for Jillian as they walked together to enter Ionie's hospital room.

"Good evening, everyone," he said, giving Jillian's parents a nod of greeting before moving to the side of the bed where Ionie looked less energetic.

She opened her eyes at the sound of his voice and then squeezed them shut. "Cole, you turn around until Jillie puts my lipstick on me," she said, sounding tired and talking slowly.

He chuckled and bent to press a kiss to her soft cheek. "Beautiful as ever," he said to her.

That made Ionie smile.

Jillian sat beside her grandmother on the bed. As Ionie kept them entertained with her quick wit, which wasn't harmed by her slow words, Cole eyed Jillian. Things between them were so serious. So intense.

So needing of ultimate trust and understanding.

But that wasn't easy for him, especially knowing her ever-present ex harbored love for her.

Over the years, he'd seen many relationships shatter because of infidelity—emotional and physical.

For so long, he had fought hard not to give in to the weakness that love could be. The vulnerability. The risk. The danger.

Does Jillian love Warren, as well? Is there more there that I'm missing?

His eyes shifted to Jillian's profile and his doubts gripped him.

He wanted it to work. He truly wanted them to be one of the few to make it.

His fear of betrayal just wouldn't allow him to believe it could be.

Jillian gently gnawed at her thumb as she swiped through online listings for chef positions, sitting at the kitchen table at her parents' house. Cole had taken them all to dinner after they'd left her grandmother to get some rest. Although she knew he wanted her to go to his condo, she had begged off to be with her parents instead.

When she was with Cole, she got too lost in him and would forget her anxiousness over being unemployed. Still. The last thing she wanted was to reveal to him that she had moments when she regretted leaving her well-paying job—mainly anytime she paid a bill and had to dip into her savings.

And now her grandmother's medical bills would increase; she would need physical therapy to fully regain her walking stature.

"Damn," Jillian swore, covering her face with her hands as she fought not to feel so overwhelmed by it all.

She'd chosen love, but love didn't pay the bills.

She picked up her phone and opened the text she'd received from Gunther Red, the award-winning musician, asking if she was available to chef for a two-week cruise around the Greek Isles. The money was great, the locale and freedom ideal, but his love of cocaine and pleading to see if she tasted as good as she looked had kept her from accepting.

Her thumb floated above the phone as she eyed the text and seriously considered dancing with—or rather avoiding—the devil for two weeks. Any hope his wife would help keep him from being handsy went out the window when the woman had made her advances for a threesome.

Jillian dropped the phone and ran both hands through her curls before gripping the soft hair in her fists.

Bzzzzzz. Bzzzzzz. Bzzzzzz.

She looked at her phone at the incoming text. Cole. She swiped to open it.

My Heart: I have a headache.

"Awww," she said as she picked up her phone to text him back.

Do you have a pain pill?

Bzzzzzz. Bzzzzzz. Bzzzzzz.

My Heart: Wrong head...

She laughed. The exchange reminded her of their no-strings sexual adventures when they would've been tearing each other's clothes off within an hour.

"What's so funny?"

Jillian set her phone down and looked up at her mother passing by her to wash her hands at the sink. "Nothing," she said. "Why are you up?"

Nora opened the fridge. "Your daddy got thirsty," she said, reaching in to pull out a bottle of water. "And why are you up? It's after one."

"Looking for a job," she admitted.

Nora looked at her as she eased the water bottle into the pocket of her fluffy, bright yellow robe. "You'll find something," she assured her. "You want me to take a look at your résumé?"

Jillian nodded. "Yeah, maybe so, Mom. Thank you. I'll email it to you."

"Good," Nora said, wrinkling her nose at her daughter affectionately before walking away.

Jillian picked up her phone, looking at both invites on her phone. One from the man she loved. The other from a man who seriously needed therapy and or drug rehab.

"Jillian."

She looked over her shoulder, surprised to find her mother standing in the archway. "Yeah?"

"What's going on with you and Warren?" Nora asked, coming back to take a seat at the table.

"Me and Warren?" Jillian balked, a frown on her face. "Yes."

The women eyed each other.

"Nothing. Just friendship. I'm with Cole, remember?" she said, reaching over to playfully tug her mother's thumb.

Nora eyed her. Studied her.

Jillian's frown deepened.

"Just make sure *you* remember, dear," Nora finally said. "And if you want something else, that's okay, but always be clear with your intentions. It's less messy."

Jillian waved away her mother's concerns as she rose to retrieve her own bottle of water from the fridge. "Warren and I are just friends. Plus, Cole is a grown man who understands that. Trust me. I got this."

Nora grunted. It revealed her disbelief in just how much her daughter "had it."

"Night, Ma," she said, reclaiming her seat and picking up her tablet as her mother took her leave. She searched the internet for Gunther Red and within moments her decision was made. The most recent articles were about a woman claiming he'd held her captive during a drug binge.

"Oh *helllll* to the no." Jillian picked up her phone to politely decline the private chef gig.

Dropping her phone back to the table, Jillian rubbed her bottom lip with her thumb.

Bzzzzzz. Bzzzzzz. Bzzzzzz.

She picked it back up and opened the text from Cole. It was a picture of him in bed. Ready and waiting, if she was willing. She eyed him in all his rugged glory. It was quite a temptation.

Jillian grabbed her devices and turned the lights off in the kitchen before making her way up the stairs to the guest bedroom. It had been hers until she'd gone to college. She removed her warm and toasty fleece pajamas and took a steamy shower. Once dried and then lathered in scented lotion, she eased her body into a slinky satin slip of bright emerald. It fell to her feet as she pulled on gold heels. She freed her curls from a messy topknot to arrange with nimble fingers before glossing her lips. Once she covered her sexy attire with a fluffy ostrich coat in the same green, she grabbed her phone and keys. As she prepared herself for yet another round of passion, the feel of the satin against her nudity was foreplay itself.

She felt sexy. Powerful. And she wanted him. Around her. On her. In her.

Jillian opened the front door and the late fall winds whipped around her, breezing her curls back from her face and tightening her nipples into buds that pressed through the thin material. She paused at the sight of a Mercedes-Benz Sprinter slowing in front of the house.

Cole.

In yet another of his vehicles he rarely drove.

He lowered the window just as surprised to see her leaving her parents' home as she was to see him pulling up in front of it. She came down the three levels of stairs, ignoring the cold, as she felt the heat of desire rise in her. She motioned with her head for him to park in the driveway.

He did.

When she neared the luxury van with its dark-tinted windows, the side door slid open. Cole was already sitting in the middle of the rear seat, in all black, his knees wide and his lap ready.

She stepped aboard and let her coat slide down her body to puddle at her feet as he closed the door and shuttered them from the frosty air.

He swore as he watched her with his beautiful eyes hooded as she came up the wide aisle to stand before him. His hands gripped her hips and then eased around to cup her soft buttocks. "I was just about to text you to come downstairs," he said, looking at her as she eased up the skirt of her slip to reveal she was bare beneath it before straddling his hips.

"And I was headed to bring it you," she whispered against his open mouth before lightly stroking her tongue against his bottom lip.

Cole trembled as he eased a hand over the curve of her bottom to slide his middle finger inside her core. He cried out at the wet feel of her.

Jillian tore at the button and zipper of his pants, glad when he raised his hips for her to jerk them down to his thighs. She freed his hardness. It was hot in her hands as she stroked him from the base to the smooth tip.

Cole sucked one of her nipples into his mouth through the material.

She arched and let her curls tickle her back and shoulders as he wrapped an arm around her waist. He lifted her with ease just to settle her back down on his lap, his hardness inside her.

With a wildness intensified by their desire and their locale, they got lost in their explosive heat and clung to one another as their bodies moved in sync for a fast and furious ride that just had to rock the luxury vehicle on its very wheels.

Cole sat back in his desk chair and crossed his legs as he eyed his brother reading the lengthy report Bobbie Barnett had sent them. He straightened the hem on his lined slacks as he waited for Gabe to finish the full story of their father meeting the mother of their half-brother Lincoln when Phillip was just eighteen and headed off to college. It included a background history on Lincoln and his mother. No stone had been left unturned.

"Bobbie's thorough," Gabe said, closing the file and looking up at his brother across his desk in his office at Cress, INC.

"Well worth the costly price," Cole agreed, shifting his watch on his wrist and arranging the sleeve of his tailored shirt to ensure it showed.

At Gabe's continued silence, Cole looked up to find his brother eyeing him oddly. "What?" he asked.

"Nice threads," Gabe said, failing at an attempt to keep from chuckling.

Cole stood and pulled the ebony tailored blazer over his matching shirt. He latched the lone button as he came from behind his desk to turn this way and that to show off his new suit. "Jillian suggested I look a little more professional coming to work," he said, raising his chin as he tightened the knot of his tie.

"Ah, the power of a pussycat," Gabe said, stroking his beard. "And stop primping. You're acting like Sean."

Now that made Cole howl with laughter. It was undeniable that their older brother, who favored the actor Daniel Sunjata, was the star of the family and knew it. In fact, he enjoyed starring in several of the culinary shows Cress, INC. produced, was friends with high-profile celebrities, and had been named one of *People*'s Top Ten Sexiest Chefs twice in a row. The charmer was as handsome and famous as he was a genius in the kitchen. And Sean knew it.

"Besides, I've seen you in a suit before, egomaniac," Gabe drawled, setting the file atop his brother's desk.

"Yes, but never in the office," Cole pointed out before removing the blazer and reclaiming his seat.

"Short of a DNA test to confirm things, it seems Lincoln Cress is indeed our brother," Gabe said.

"Our eldest brother," Cole corrected him.

Gabe shook his head and winced. "Phillip Junior won't like that."

Good.

Of all the Cress brothers, Phillip Junior was the most competitive and backbiting. He held an outdated belief that as the eldest son of the Cress family, he should be the undisputed heir to the company's throne. Learning that Phillip Senior had instead opened the opportunity up to all his sons had created a divisiveness among the brothers that was unsettling.

Cole removed his wallet and money clip from his pocket and counted off enough crisp hundred-dollar bills to cover his half of Bobbie's bill.

Gabe took the cash. "I'll cut her a check today," he said.

Cole nodded and rested his elbow against the arm of his chair before propping his chin in his hand. "Everyone needs to know about this," he began, thinking of the secret already weighing him down. "We have to call a family meeting."

"Do we speak to our parents alone or tell everyone at once?" Gabe asked. "You know, as hard as he has been on us, he was there every day—raising us, teaching us, reprimanding us. There are many things about our father that I doubt. But I know he loved being a father. Sometimes his sternness was this overreaching need to be for us what his father was not for him."

Cole shifted his gaze out the window as he fought with whether to share's his father's infidelity—a part of his father's life that was not in that file from Bobbie Barnett. And thus he took little comfort in her report of his current faithfulness. "Let's think about it and make a decision soon," he said, reaching for the file to carry it across his office to the safe inside his closet.

"Another Cress brother," Gabe mused, shaking his hand before releasing a light laugh.

"Maybe," Cole declared, locking the safe and returning to his seat.

They locked eyes.

Of all the brothers, Cole was closest to Gabe, who was older than him by just two years. And he knew they were thinking the same thing.

"A thousand," Cole offered, reaching in his wallet for another ten bills.

Gabe nodded and stood to remove his platinum money clip to do the same. "He looks just like us, Cole. He's our brother," he said. "Face it."

"I'm not against it. I'm just not as sure as you. That's all."

Betting was their thing since childhood. Be it a guess on what was for dinner or whether one would win the charm of one pretty girl over the other. The brothers had brought the act into adulthood.

Cole gathered the bills and slid them into a Cress-monogrammed envelope, removing the paper strip to reveal the adhesive as he sealed it.

"I should have bet you that you and Jillian would fall in love," Gabe said, remaining standing as he slid his hands into the pockets of his gray three-piece suit.

Cole put the envelope in the top drawer of his desk. There was another already sitting there. He opened it. There was five thousand dollars inside. "Who says I'm in love?" he asked as he tried to remember the reason for the cash.

"Are you not?" Gabe countered.

He showed his brother the envelope. "Did we bet on something and forget?" he asked.

Gabe chuckled as he strolled to the door. "I didn't forget. I lost. Your launch went off without a hitch," he reminded him over his shoulder.

Well damn.

Cole moved the money from the envelope into his money clip. "Gabe," he called before looking up.

His brother paused in the doorway.

"Would it bother you if Monica was still best friends with her ex-husband?" he asked, alluding to his doubts for the first time aloud.

"Ouch," Gabe said before wincing. "Um, I'm a good

man, but I'm not a perfect man, so I don't know how I would feel, *but* I'm happy as hell that I don't have to worry about that. *Also*, I do believe that if it's bothering you, you might need to admit what you feel for Jillian."

Gabe locked eyes with his brother. "I care about her," he confessed.

"I know," Gabe said with a smile before tapping the door frame and walking away.

The sounds of Beyonce's "All Night Long" echoed against the walls of Cole's condo as Jillian paused to do body rolls before checking on the baked macaroni and cheese in the stylish navy-blue Viking oven. In a great mood, she wanted to reward herself and Cole with a down-home Southern meal. The kind her grandmother Ionie taught her to cook before her entry into culinary school to excel at French cuisine. Baked turkey wings smothered in brown gravy with onion and peppers, chicken pilau rice, cabbage cooked down with fried pork jowls, the mac and cheese with five kinds of cheese, candied yams, and cornbread.

A Southern feast.

She paused, wondering if Cole had ever had a traditional Southern meal. She certainly had never prepared any for the Cress family when she'd been their chef. And it was well known that all of the Cress chefs favored French cuisine.

"Well, he's getting fed some tonight," she said, using silicone mats to remove the glass dish from the oven to set on a large trivet on the counter.

"Some what?"

Jillian looked up in surprise to find Cole walking into the dining room from the hall leading from his in-unit parking space. He held his suit jacket and house keys in hand. "Soul food," she said. "That 'down below the Mason-Dixon line' comfort food."

He crossed the spacious kitchen to press a kiss to her temple as he looked at the bevy of serving dishes on the countertops. "Looks good," he said.

"You ever had a spread like this?" she asked, bumping her bottom back against him as she removed lids to show off her skills.

"No...and good thing because I would have looked more like Lucas growing up," he said before opening his mouth as she offered him a spoonful of her candied yams.

"Your brother Lucas was chubby?" she asked in surprise. "Sure doesn't look it now."

Cole playfully swatted her bottom. "How does he look now?" he asked.

Jillian cut her eyes up to him as she sucked the rest of the yams from the spoon, playfully wiggling her shaped brows at him.

He laughed and picked her up by the waist to sit her atop the island before standing between her open legs.

"Don't worry, I have the Cress brother I want," Jillian reassured him. "Lucas who?"

All of the Cress men—including their father—were good-looking, but it was only Cole who had drawn her appreciative eye. From the moment she'd looked past his mother during her interview for the chef position and seen him standing there watching her, she had been caught up in the man's web. Trapped by his looks. Enticed by his flirtation. And hooked by his sex.

Cole kissed her mouth and squeezed the top of her thighs. "Why the big meal?" he asked, still tasting the sweetness of the yam's brown sugar, cinnamon and butter glaze on her lips.

"Good news. My grandmother finally got into the

rehab facility we wanted…" Jillian began as she undid his tie and loosened the top buttons of his shirt.

"Excellent," Cole said, truly looking pleased with the next step in her grandmother's recovery.

"And I got a new personal chef position," she said.

"Congratulations, beautiful," he said with enthusiasm.

"For Warren," she added, leaning toward him to press kisses to his neck.

Cole leaned back. A scowl lined his handsome face.

Jillian was shocked. "What's wrong?" she asked.

He turned and strode over to the Bose sound dock on the glass table behind the sofa. Soon the sound of Beyonce stopped mid-falsetto-note abruptly. He began to pace back and forth in front of the fireplace.

Jillian slid down from the island to join him in the living room. "Cole, what's going on? What's this about?" she asked.

He stopped his movement and eyed her. "Which is it, Jillian?" he asked. "Do you not see that Warren loves you? Do you not care that he loves you? Do you want him to love you still? What?"

"Warren does not love me, Cole," she said, waving her hand dismissively.

And instantly remembered giving her mother the same gesture.

What's going on with you and Warren?

She also remembered the grunt her mother had given her.

That grunt had said so much without saying a thing.

"He loves you. He wants you. Now, where are you with this?" Cole eyed her across the divide.

Jillian was confused by his anger. "Wait. What?" she asked. "You want me to turn the job down? Stay unemployed? Stay strangled by new debt? Not work? What?"

Cole wiped his hand over his mouth. "I would never try to control you like that, but I would like for you to be aware enough to understand when you are putting yourself in a compromising position," he said.

"A *compromising* position," she scoffed.

Cole jerked the hem of his shirt from inside his pants as if feeling restrained by it.

"Don't be blinded by jealousy, Cole," she said, shaking her head in disbelief. "I didn't even know you had a problem with Warren."

"Blinded by jealousy?" he snapped.

"Yes," she insisted, turning to walk back into the kitchen.

Cole followed.

She ignored him as she removed plates, linen napkins and cutlery from the cabinets and drawers to set the dining room table.

"Do you want a relationship with your ex?" he asked.

"Which one?" she asked sarcastically as she breezed past him.

"Jillian," Cole said calmly.

She set the dishes down on the corner of the table and looked to him.

"Do you want a relationship with Warren?" he asked.

"Definitely not," she insisted. "I see him as nothing but a friend. Damn near a brother, if we hadn't made the mistake of crossing the line from friends to more."

"He doesn't feel the same," Cole insisted.

"You're wrong. You don't know him. You're assuming," she said, now focusing on setting the table. "As a matter of fact, you're wrong about me. Why *assume* I would be inappropriate with an employer?"

"You were with me."

That felt like a blow.

She looked at him again, fighting an urge to toss something at him. "Really, Cole?" she asked, her tone accusing. "I guess I spread it out for everyone right along with the meals. Right?"

Cole released a heavy, harsh breath before pressing his fingers to his closed eyes. "I didn't say that."

"You said a lot," she charged.

Cole shoved his hands into the pockets of his slacks as he leaned his tall frame against the wall. "And what would you do if you found out I wasn't wrong and Warren loves you and wants you back?" he asked, his voice low and deep.

She frowned. "He doesn't. Damn!"

"What if he did?" he countered. "Would you still take the job?"

"Yes," she asserted.

He nodded in understanding. "At first, I hated the idea of you working for him because I was worried that something would happen. That you would betray me in a way I can swear I would never do to you…" he began. "But now, more than hating you being around him, I pity him because it's cruel, Jillian, to be blind to his feelings for you and to continue to hang around him while actively ignoring the heart he wears on his sleeve. Hoping for more than friendship."

"So now you're looking out for Warren?" she asked in sarcasm and disbelief.

He shook his head. "I remembered the offer my mother made and how you had no clue that I had any feelings outside of sex for you," he said, a chill entering his tone.

She swung between frustration with his assumptions and annoyance at him, clinging to the past. "I thought we were beyond that," she said.

"So did I. I was wrong."

Stunned.

That was the only word for how she felt at that moment.

They stared at one another. Cole looked away first.

That stung.

"Maybe I should give you some space," she said, even as she desperately yearned for him to implore her not to go.

"Maybe we should give each other some space," he countered.

That hurt.

It also spurred her to want to be away from him. Quickly.

She moved around the apartment, gathering her things and fighting not to let one single tear fall.

"What about the food?" he asked, still leaning against the wall from where he'd crushed her heart.

Jillian released a bitter laugh. "Please don't push me to tell you what you can do with that food," she snapped before snatching open the front door and leaving, wishing she could slam it closed.

She leaned against the door and hyperventilated, seeking control and not finding it.

The crash of dishes echoed through the solid wood and she froze at the shock. Turning, she pressed a hand to the door as she lowered her head.

What the hell just happened?

Ten

Two weeks later

"You ready, Cole?"

He looked up from the copies of Ionie's medical bills for her care at the rehab facility. Bobbie Barnett had been able to retrieve the paperwork for him, along with the accurate information on where to send payment. "One sec," he said as he opened his checkbook and paid in full the substantial bill that remained after the contribution by her medical insurance. He sealed the envelope and left it in his tray for outgoing mail that his assistant would ensure was handled.

In his and Jillian's brief time in a formal relationship, Cole had forged a cute relationship with her grandmother, Ionie, and he no longer wanted that financial burden on her or her family. A minimal loss to him could change the very fiscal outlook of their lives, and that didn't sit well with him.

And Jillian would be none the wiser. He had already included a request for anonymity.

They hadn't spoken since that day in his condo, and the last thing he wanted was for her to believe his gesture was a move to reconcile. He missed her, but his doubts about her relationship with Warren lingered. Be it she was complicit in the man's love for her or uncaring of it, neither was to his liking. Both hit too close to home with his own issues.

It was why he'd resisted serious relationships in the past.

"Ready," he said, grabbing his cognac leather bomber to pull over the navy dress shirt and denims he wore with polished brown boots. As the brothers walked together to the elevator, Cole removed a navy fitted sweater cap to cover his head and ears from the biting cold of winter outdoors.

"Welcome back." Gabe eyed Cole's return to more casual attire.

"Thank you," he said as they rode the elevator down to the lobby. "Now, if the weather will magically warm up so I can get some hours in on my food truck, I will be a very happy man."

"No, you won't," Gabe said as they strode across the massive, busy, sky-lighted lobby and through the automated glass doors of the Midtown Manhattan building.

Cole said nothing in response. There was nothing to say. It was true. He was miserable without her. Again. And this time at his doing.

The brothers climbed into the rear of one of the company's vehicles as the driver held the door open for them. "Thank you," both said to Harvey.

They fell silent as Harvey reclaimed his seat and eventually pulled away from the parking spot in front of the building. The mood was tense. Neither was looking forward to this visit to the Cress family townhouse.

It was time for the truth to be revealed.

Cole looked out the tinted window at the city as they neared the prominent and historic Lenox Hill section of Manhattan's Upper East Side. His brother was silent as well, the investigative file resting on his lap. But Cole didn't bother to wager what occupied Gabe's thoughts. He was too focused on his own.

This will not go well.

The driver slowed the SUV to a stop in front of the five-story, ten-thousand-square-foot townhouse. Both men opened their rear doors and exited before Harvey could. "Give us an hour," Gabe said as Cole stood on the pristine sidewalk and looked up at the towering structure.

For such a huge part of his life, it had been home.

Now he was a visitor.

He opened the wrought-iron gate to jog up the steps, glancing back as his brother did the same. He rang the bell.

"Where's your key?" Gabe asked, reaching into the pocket of his camel wool coat.

"Respect is earned when respect is given," Cole explained. "Do you want our parents to feel they can just stroll into our home whenever they please?"

Gabe made a face. "You're right," he said, releasing the key back into his pocket.

"Ain't I always?" Cole asked.

Gabe volleyed back. "Not lately."

Another Jillian reference.

"I'm regretting talking to you about her," Cole said just as the elaborate front door opened.

Felice, the new housekeeper, smiled as she stepped back to pull the door wide for them to enter the marbled vestibule. "Hello, Mr. Cress and Mr. Cress," she said. "It's good to see you both."

They gave her warm smiles in greeting before walking the length of the entry hall to step into their parents' lavish, spacious living room in its shades of light gray and steel-blue against the pale walls.

"Your coats?" she asked, already extending her arm.

Each removed his outer gear and turned it over to her.

"Mr. Cress is awaiting your arrival in the library," Felice said before turning to hang their coats in the closet. "Everyone is in their suite, preparing for dinner."

As the men made their way across the hardwood floor to the open kitchen and den area, Cole's steps slowed as he remembered the excitement he'd felt at knowing Jillian worked there. He had enjoyed teasing and flirting with her as much as when he'd finally bedded her. He smiled at the closed pantry door, pleased no one knew just how much fun he and Jillian had shared in there.

She was gone. A short and plump man in a red chef's coat was in her place.

The brothers rode the elevator upstairs to the second floor, where the movie theater and library were located. His parents occupied the entire third floor as their private suite, complete with a sitting room, massive walk-in closets, their joint home office, a pantry, and a spa bath. On each of the fourth and fifth floors, a huge den centered three-bedroom suites and another well-stocked pantry.

There was no denying the beauty of the home flushed with luxury and every creature comfort to be desired.

Cole and Gabe shared a last look before the elevator slowed to a stop.

Their father stood near the rear glass wall that ran the entire exterior of the home. He glanced over his broad shoulder to eye them before he turned. "Come in, boys," he said, his deep voice booming without even trying.

As they neared him, Cole saw his father's eyes dip to the file Gabe held. He didn't miss the way Phillip Senior rolled his shoulders back as if to steel himself.

"Are you staying for dinner?" Phillip Senior asked. "Chef is preparing Peking duck. I haven't had it in years."

"Listen, Dad, this is not an easy conversation to have, but it has to happen…" Gabe began, sitting in one of the leather armchairs and waving an invite to their father to take one of the seats across from him.

"Getting right to it?" Phillips Senior said with a chuckle. "I assume the file is the reason the two of you requested this private meeting that we couldn't have at the offices."

Cole eyed him, searching for the love and respect he'd once held for him years ago. "Did you have people in the family followed by a damned private investigator?" he asked with a hard stare.

"Cole!" Gabe snapped.

He had just blown their carefully crafted plan out of the water.

Phillip Senior did take the seat before looking over at Cole, who was still standing. "I should have known with *your* involvement, niceties would be amiss," he said.

"The question still stands," Cole said, summoning the same strength he wished he'd had that day when he had just run from the restaurant and walked home.

"When will the hate fade, son?" Phillip Senior asked.

Cole's emotions tightened his throat. "I wish I hated you, then I wouldn't be so damn disappointed."

Gabe remained silent as if sensing a long-overdue moment between his brother and his father.

Some emotion he couldn't identify crossed Phillip

Senior's broad face. He cleared his throat and shifted in his seat. "I never hired a private investigator in my life," he said.

Cole turned from him, trusting nothing he said to be the truth.

"Well, we did," Gabe said.

Cole glanced back just as his brother leaned forward to sit the file on the table between them. "We felt you were deserving because you pried into our lives—"

"I did not!" Phillip Senior shouted.

"Regardless, we have discovered something that you need to know."

Cole turned to face them as Gabe removed his hand from the file and sat back.

"You have a son, Lincoln—"

"Lies!" Phillip Senior roared, jumping to his feet and swatting the file away with the back of his hand. "How dare you accuse me of such a lie! Is that what you think of me, Gabe? I know *he* hates the very air I breathe but do you believe that of *me*?"

Cole released a bitter chuckle. "Ask me, do I believe it after walking in on you screwing a waitress while our mother was downstairs in the restaurant," he said, his words dripping with contempt and his eyes stinging with the heat of his anger.

"What?" Gabe stormed in shock.

Phillip Senior pushed his chair onto its side before taking two large steps across the floor to lunge at Cole. He grabbed the front of his shirt in his fists. "You don't know what the hell you're talking about!" he yelled in his face, spittle flying.

Cole released another bitter laugh before his eyes went cold. "Liar," he said in a quiet voice that was damning.

Gabe squeezed between them and pushed to put distance between them. "Enough," he said.

"More than enough."

The three men swung their heads in the same direction to find Nicolette standing at the top of the stairs. Each man's chest heaved from emotion and exertion. They each turned and walked away from one another, seeking the control they had lost. Silence reigned, but the tension was omnipresent.

Cole moved to stand at the rear wall and look out at the snow beginning to fall and coat the backyard below. His eyes went to the garden Jillian had begun and how it had been taken over by weeds and overgrowth.

Neglect had a way of doing that.

He let his forehead rest on the cold glass. His heavy breaths fanned it. He had denied himself Jillian's attention and was beginning to feel and look as abandoned as the garden.

A flash of blue against the glass caught his eye and he watched in the reflection as his mother went to his father's side. "I knew about the affair," she admitted, pressing a hand to her husband's cheek to stroke it lovingly.

Cole's eyes widened. It was his turn to be stunned. He turned to eye them—united and in love. He had been a fool, thinking he'd sheltered and kept her free from hurt when all the while she had long since given her husband the forgiveness Cole would not. He didn't know how to feel, but pleased was nowhere on the list of possibilities.

Cole turned from them and fought the urge to valiantly punch his fist through the glass until the entire rear wall shattered. Instead, he lightly tapped it against his leg.

"What affair? When?" Gabe asked.

"Fifteen years ago," Nicolette supplied as she guided Phillip Senior to another chair to sit.

"And did you know Cole knew about it?" Gabe asked. "Just how many secrets does this damn family have?"

"No, I didn't know Cole knew," Nicolette insisted.

That was of little reprieve.

"I've got to get out of here," he said.

Gabe blocked his path. "No! Don't run from it. Make them stand in their mess and realize it created more mess," he said before stepping past his brother to eye their parents. "You two have this weird bubble where first and foremost there's only the two of you. Even now, you comfort a man who betrayed you and ignore a son who protected you."

Nicolette look confused at first and then her expression changed as if Gabe's point of view was now her own. "My Cole Man," she said, reverting to her childhood nickname for him.

He shook his head, denying his mother the opportunity to appease her sudden guilt. He had feelings of his own with which to grapple. "I'm done. This is it for me. I will never keep another secret for anyone, so you have tonight to tell the family about Lincoln or I will," he said before turning and striding away.

His booted feet ate up the stairs as he descended them. Reaching the first floor, he moved quickly to the closet and yanked his coat from the wooden hanger, causing it to tumble to the floor.

"You good, bro?"

Cole glanced at Gabe coming down the last few stairs to also reach for his coat. He'd also picked up the hanger Cole had sent to the floor in his haste.

"Yeah," he lied. "You?" Discovering their father had once cheated on their mother had to have affected his brother, too.

"No," Gabe admitted, opening the door and entering the vestibule. "Affairs. You keeping one hell of a secret from me. A half-brother we have never met. No, I am not good."

Cole was glad to see Harvey already parked on the street and awaiting them.

"I called him," Gabe said, answering the unspoken question.

Bzzzzzz. Bzzzzzz. Bzzzzzz.

"Great," Cole said as he pulled his cell phone from the inner pocket of his coat.

For a moment, he wished it were Jillian.

He shook his head at his mother's number. "Nope," he said, sending the call to voice mail before dropping the phone back into his coat pocket as he bent his body to enter the back seat of the SUV.

He shivered from the cold and was thankful when Harvey slammed the door closed and rushed around the vehicle to do the same for Gabe.

"We never did get him to admit he had us all investigated," Cole said just as Gabe's phone rang. "Unless it was Mom."

"Actually, my bet is on her after the stunts she pulled with Monica and Jillian," Gabe said, pulling his phone from his pocket. "I'm glad to be out of there. I'm going home. Eat some dinner. Love on my woman and go to bed, because reality sucks right now."

Cole shook his head with a snarky laugh when Gabe showed him their mother was calling him now.

"Bonjour," Gabe said in greeting as he checked the time on his gold watch.

Cole ignored his brother's conversation in French as he looked out the window. He was stunned by the knowledge that his mother had been aware of his father's infidelity. Discovering that she'd known, forgiven his father, and seemed to still forge a loving relationship, was forcing him to rethink a lot of things—and to wonder even more.

What private circumstances could have led to his mother forgiving him?

That, he didn't know. But he was now well aware that the role of the blind hapless victim within which he'd placed his mother had been wrong.

How long had she known?

Cole pinched the bridge of his nose, ready to get home to nurse a bottle of rare Scotch from his well-stocked bar.

"Vous ne pouvez pas vous attendre à ce que nous prétendions que c'est tout normal et juste manger le dîner avec tout le monde qui est désemparé de ce qui se passe?" Gabriel said.

Cole gave him a glance, agreeing with what he'd said. *You can't expect us to pretend it's all normal and just eat dinner with everyone who is clueless to what's going on?*

He was sure his brothers had known of their arrival and were wondering about their speedy departure. He regretted not speaking to them and taking a moment to hug his niece. He had just felt an urgency to get out of there.

"Je suis d'accord avec Cole. Dis-leur. Ou nous le ferons. Plus de secrets!" Gabe's hand urgently slashed the air. *I agree with Cole. Tell them. Or we will. No more secrets.*

Cole pulled his phone from his pocket and swiped until he was looking down at a photo of Jillian the night of the relaunch of Cress, INC.'s website. Her smile was infectious, and that dress was burned into his memory.

What is she doing?

Hopefully, not Warren.

His grip tightened on the phone.

"Je vais lui demander," Gabe said, looking briefly in his direction.

"Ask me what?" Cole said as he tucked his cell phone away.

He listened as Gabe explained that their parents

wanted to read the report and reach out to Lincoln for a DNA test to confirm paternity before telling their other brothers.

"No. No more secrets," Cole said with a firm shake of his head. "We can all wait for the results together. We know. They should know. They *will* know, if it's left to me."

Gabe finished the conversation with his mother and ended the call. "Family meeting tomorrow night at the townhouse at eight," he said.

Cole nodded as Harvey brought the SUV to a stop in front of his condo and he let himself out.

Long after he entered his condo and lit the fireplace before pouring himself a stiff drink, he had a reckoning that would not be denied. He was plagued by thoughts of Jillian, their relationship, and where it had all gone wrong—and just what role his knowledge of his father's infidelity may have subconsciously played in that.

Jillian crossed her arms at her chest as she walked around the studio apartment in the Meatpacking District of Manhattan. It didn't compare with the moderate-size loft apartment she'd given up for her move to California, but it was more budget-friendly—and that was key. Most important, it was freedom from her parents' home where late-night giggles and a squeaky bed frame made her life a living hell.

Knock-knock-knock.

She turned from her view of the building across the street to stride the short distance to the door. She gave the movers a thankful smile for working during such frigid weather to transport her furniture from her storage unit after a request of just an hour ago. "Lunch is on me," she said to the two men, waving her hand at a large pot of chili and cheesy cornbread on the stove.

"Now that sounds like a plan," the muscled owner said.

Jillian jammed the door open with a wood wedge and moved out of their way.

Getting the key to the apartment that morning from the property manager had been the good news she needed. She sat on the window seat and pulled her knees to her chest as she looked out at the gentrified neighborhood that had shifted from its factory roots. Now it's where she called home.

At the sight of a tall man on a motorcycle parking in front of the building, she straightened and pressed her hands to the window.

Cole.

She felt foolish when the man pulled off his helmet, revealing he was not Cole at all.

Of course.

He didn't know where she lived and didn't seem to care to find out.

It was over.

She'd chanced it and lost. And it hurt. If Cole had dropped to his knees, asked her to marry him, she would have. Without question.

"And then I would have *three* ex-husbands," she muttered, resting her chin atop one of her knees as she settled back on the window seat.

"You said something, Miss Rossi?" one of the movers asked.

She glanced at the young man with skin as dark as midnight. He really was attractive. "Ms.," she corrected with the hint of a smile. "I have two ex-husbands making me anything but a Miss."

"Their loss," he said with an appreciative eye.

He was young and fit with a beautiful smile. Just the type to have a wonderful afternoon of fun with—if Cole didn't already occupy her thoughts, keeping her from letting any other man occupy her bed.

No matter how much she missed a man—one particular man—in her bed.

She gave him a shake of her head to gently curtail any attempt at his garnering her attention. He gave her a regretful look and another flirtatious smile before leaving the apartment.

She was thankful when the movers were done in the apartment, having finished setting her belongings where she liked and enjoying the chili she'd prepared. The space was so small that she'd felt cramped with the two men in it. As soon as she closed the door behind them, she turned to lean against it in relief as she looked around.

This was her new life.

A small apartment. Single. Heartbroken.

And lonesome.

Again.

She kicked off her fuzzy slippers and tucked her bare feet beneath her bottom as she sat on her leather sofa. She scrolled through photos of her and Cole. Smiling at some things. Laughing at others. Getting heated at a few that were X-rated.

She was so tempted to call him. Question him. Push back against his misconceptions about her.

Jillian looked at a photo she'd sneaked of him as he'd stepped out of the shower.

Plead with him.

Her eyes dipped down to his package. Sex was the only thing they could do right.

But she wanted more.

"I need more," she said, dropping the phone and once

again—for what seemed the millionth time—wrestling the urge to call him.

Love was in the mix and there was no more going back to casual sex when her heart was on the line.

She stood and walked over to her kitchenette to pour herself a glass of red wine. "*He* was wrong. *He* ended things. *He* should call me," she said before taking a deep sip.

He broke my heart.

She turned and leaned her buttocks against the counter.

He accused me of wanting more with Warren.

She took another sip.

And said I was being cruel to Warren.

Another sip.

And cut me loose as if I would ever hurt him.

And another.

Her emotions swelled as she remembered the look on Cole's face when he'd agreed that she should leave. Betrayals were difficult—whether done by someone else or self-inflicted when ignoring a resolve not putting one's heart on the line again.

Jillian felt foolish for giving her power away. She tipped her head back to empty the glass before looking into its emptiness and feeling a kinship. Her tears replaced the wine. They fell with far too much ease.

And that, too, felt like a betrayal.

With a cry that was as jagged as the cuts to her heart, she gripped the glass before throwing it against the wall to shatter.

Eleven

All five Cress brothers were sitting in the den of the family townhouse. There was no staff. The kitchen, living room and dining room were empty. Silence ruled the room.

Phillip Junior paced in front of the elaborate fireplace, lit to help heat the room.

Sean chuckled at videos on his cell phone as he lounged near the closed patio doors.

Gabe refilled his brandy snifter from atop the wide glass-and-brass bar beneath the seventy-inch television on the wall.

Lucas lounged in one of the light gray suede chairs as he texted away on his phone.

Cole eyed them from where he leaned against the entryway between the den and dining room.

"Does anyone know what this meeting is about?" Phillip Junior asked.

Cole and Gabe shared a look.

Lucas frowned, looking up just as they did. "Care to share?" he asked, his voice as deep as his brothers' and father's.

That drew the curious stares of the other Cress brothers.

"Maybe they're ready to announce the new CEO," Phillip Junior said, sounding hopeful.

Sean leaned forward to set his elbows atop his knees as he looked from Cole to Gabe. "Did you get it?" he asked Gabe, speaking everyone's awareness that the middle child—the good one—was favored for the position.

"Remember, I made it clear I don't want it," Gabe said before glancing at his watch. "My restaurant and the position I have at the company is enough on my plate."

All eyes landed on Cole.

"Really?" he asked in disbelief. "Me? Don't be foolish."

"Right." Phillip Junior looked reassured by the reminder that Phillip Senior and Cole had a turbulent relationship.

Cole frowned. Deeply. "I would point out the disgust I feel for you enjoying that I don't have the greatest relationship with our father, but you have enough to tackle tonight, big brother," he said, glancing at his watch.

"What the hell does that mean?" Phillip Junior exclaimed.

"Cole," Gabe intervened.

Footsteps echoed throughout the house. The men all shifted their gaze as their mother and father crossed the kitchen and stepped into the stylish den. Nicolette gave them each a soft smile, looking pretty and regal in the fuchsia pantsuit she wore with her hair pulled back into a low ponytail. In his three-piece suit, Phillip Senior's face seemed more severe as he placed an arm around his wife's shoulders and pressed a kiss to the top of her head.

"We have some news to share..." their father began, his British accent echoing.

If it were at all possible for a room to become more silent, then that best described the environment. Cole looked down at the tip of polished handmade boots as he awaited the reaction of his brothers.

"It has been brought to our attention that when I was eighteen, I unknowingly fathered a child," Phillip Senior said, sticking to his no-nonsense persona. "A son."

And, like the Fourth of July, the questions and exclamations fired off like fireworks in rapid succession.

"What!" Lucas said, his eyes wide and confused.

"Are you serious?" Sean asked.

Phillip Junior threw his hands up in the air. "What does this mean for Cress, INC.?"

"Ça suffit!" Nicolette exclaimed.

Cole, like Gabe, remained silent. He looked on as his brothers sat, expressions full of shock, as their mother pressed a hand to their father's chest when he clutched her closer to him.

Phillip Senior pressed another kiss to his wife's brow before releasing her to move into the center of the room and boldly eyeing each of his sons. "Yesterday, a preliminary DNA was done and the results came in today," he said. "So far, it has confirmed he is, indeed, my son. Your family. And once the results of the court-approved DNA results return in the next few days, he will also be an heir."

This time his words brought silence. It was stiff. And awkward. And uneasy.

Even Cole took a beat to accept his father's declaration. He had never assumed his father would turn over a key to the kingdom with such ease for a man he'd never known.

"Just like that?" Phillip Junior asked, his jaw stiffening.

"Absolutely, son," Phillip Senior said with a stern expression as he looked at him. "Maybe more so than *any* of you."

Cole's eyes pierced his profile.

"What does that mean?" Gabe asked, breaking his silence.

Phillip Senior shifted his stance. "You have all benefitted from the legacy your mother and I created. It has served each of you well. He received nothing from me and did it all on his own," he said, with a rare reveal of emotion.

That surprised Cole. And rattled him a bit.

Displays of affection from their father were only doled out to their mother once the brothers had become young men. With Phillip Senior, there had been nothing but sternness and a steadfast desire to raise men.

"I never turned my back on any of my sons, and I won't do it now," Phillip Senior said before looking directly at Cole. "*None* of you."

"And is this stranger eligible to be the new CEO of Cress, INC.?" Phillip Junior asked, sounding accusatory.

Phillip Senior turned his head to look at him. "'Stranger'?" he said, his voice filling with coldness. "He is your brother. The same as all the rest."

"I disagree with that," Phillip Junior said.

Steps against the hardwood floor suddenly echoed.

Everyone in the den turned their head just as a man stepped into the room. He was tall, with a shortbread complexion like their own, and a similar face to a twenty-years-younger Phillip Senior.

Cole recognized him from Bobbie's report before their father beckoned the man further into the room with a wave of his hand and introduced him.

"Phillip Junior, Sean, Gabriel, Coleman and Lucas... This is Lincoln Cress. Your brother."

Jillian pushed up her rarely used spectacles as she gave the sprawling double-height kitchen one last perusal before sliding her cutlery set into her satchel. She was done with her chef duties for the day and ready to get to her tiny apartment for a hot foot soak and then a bubble bath. "ASAP," she said.

Bzzzzzz. Bzzzzzz. Bzzzzzz.

She paused to remove her cell phone from the pocket of her chef's coat. "Hey, Ma," she said, tucking the phone between her shoulder and ear as she finished buttoning her overcoat before leaving the empty house via the mudroom.

She rushed to her beloved Mazda Miata as the brutal northeast winter wind whipped around. She was thankful there was no snow to tackle on her lengthy commute to Manhattan.

"I'm at the rehab facility with your grandma," Nora said. "I went to make the monthly payment at the billing office. The account balance had been paid in full. Did you do it?"

Jillian was too busy wishing she had cranked the car and warmed it up before getting into it to really pay attention to her mother's words. "Did I do what, Ma?" she asked as she leaned over to make sure the heat was coming on.

"Did you pay your grandmother's bill in full at the rehab facility?" Nora asked.

Jillian sat straight. "Definitely not," she said, shifting her eyes to her reflection in the rearview mirror.

"Maybe it's an error," Nora said, sounding concerned.

"Did you ask them who paid it?" Jillian asked as she reversed Cherry across the paved courtyard and accelerated forward down the long, winding driveway leading to the main road.

"They said an unidentified benefactor who wished to remain anonymous."

Cole.

"It was Cole," Ionie said in the background, echoing Jillian's thought.

Could he?

With ease. The sum would be of little consequence to him.

Would he?

That was the question.

Did he?

She shook her head. Why would he do such a thing when they weren't even speaking?

"*If* it was Cole, then we will have to pay it back," Jillian insisted.

"Of course," Norah agreed. "But still, *if* it was him, it was a very generous offering. So very gallant."

"Gallant?" Jillian drawled.

"Yes, it seems like the appropriate time to use such a word," Norah said.

She chuckled with her mother.

"Call him. Ask him. And if it was him—*thank* him, Jillie," Ionie said, her speech still a little hesitant.

Jillian pulled to a stop at a red light. She felt nervous at the thought of reaching out to Cole. It was a mix of excitement at hearing his deep voice and fear that he wouldn't answer. "I'll call him," she said. "Let me get back to you, Ma."

She ended the call and dropped the phone onto the passenger seat. As she continued her ride home in silence, she thought of every possible scenario of just what might happen when she called him. None of it ended well.

But why would he pay the bill—if he paid the bill.

There was only one way to know.

And I have to know.

She had not yet struck up the courage to call him by the time she reached home and gave in to her desires for a foot soak. As she drew a hot bubble bath in her clawfoot tub, her eyes kept going to her phone sitting on the edge of the sink. She *wanted* to talk to Cole.

And more.

Maybe we should give each other some space.

The last words he'd spoken had been enough to keep her from reaching out. She assumed he would decide the space between them was no longer needed. She hoped he would fight for her the same way she had laid her heart out on the line and fought for him. Wooed him. Chased him. Proved she loved him.

It hurt that he hadn't reciprocated.

She eyed the phone again. Curiosity was killing her like the cat. She raised her hand from the water and dried it on the towel hanging over the side before reaching for her phone. Her heart beat so rapidly as she pulled up his contact and dialed his number. She eased her knees up to her chest as the phone started to ring. When it went to voice mail, all of her fears rose along with tears of regret and sadness.

She set the phone back on the sink and rested the side of her face atop her knees. "To hell with love," she muttered, lifting a handful of bubbles to her mouth to blow them up into the air.

Bzzzzzz. Bzzzzzz. Bzzzzzz.

Her head shot up and she looked over at the screen of her phone. A picture of Cole was on it. She felt excited, like a middle school girl receiving a call from her first crush. And just as nervous.

She reached for the phone and answered his call. "Hello?" she said, wincing when it came out like the strangled cry of a rooster with a hand around its neck.

"Jillian?" he said.

He sounded uncertain even though she was sure her name had displayed on his Caller ID.

Unless he erased your contact.

She raised her wet hand to squeeze the space between her eyebrows. "Yes, it's Jillian. How are you, Cole?" she asked, keeping her tone measured.

"I'm good. You?"

Jillian closed her eyes. They sound so formulaic. So awkward. Stilted. So much like strangers than former lovers.

"Am I bothering you? Are you busy? With work…or someone?" she asked, unable to deny the desire to know if he had completely moved on from her.

The line went silent.

With every passing moment, her pulse increased, and her stomach was a pit of growing nerves. "I understand if it's none of my business—"

"I'm not seeing anyone," he said.

Great.

"And you?" he added.

"Do you care if someone else filled the space you asked for?" she asked, instantly regretting letting her hurt lead her.

"Wow. Really, Jillian?" he asked.

She sighed. "Look. I didn't call to argue. My mother says that my grandmother's bill at her rehab facility has been paid in full," she said. "I was wondering if it was you that blessed us in such a way?"

"You never said if you were with someone." Cole avoided her question. "How's your bestie anyway?"

The water had cooled and the bubbles were beginning to fade, so she stood and stepped out of the tub. Water dripped off her curves. "Warren?" she asked as she grabbed a towel to unfold with a snap before she held it in front of her body.

"Who else?" he drawled.

Jillian arched a brow. "Still concerned about him?" she shot back in sarcasm.

He chuckled.

She did not.

"About the bill, do I have you to thank for it?" she asked, directing him back to the question he'd evaded.

Silence.

"Also, my family and I insist on repaying you, if that's the case," Jillian added.

"I'd prefer to discuss it in person," he finally said.

She nodded as she used the side of her hand to wipe away the steam coating the large round mirror over the pedestal sink. In the reflection, her eyes were uneasy. "Uh. Yeah. Sure," she said. "When?"

"The sooner, the better."

She nodded even though he couldn't see her. "I'll be there within the hour," she said.

"See you then," Cole said before ending the call.

Maybe he wants me to sign a promissory note.

Her nerves did not abate as she dried off and dressed in an off-the-shoulder black sweater, with leggings and shiny black, thigh-high boots with heels. She took time with her makeup and hair and then put in her contacts instead of donning her spectacles. A faux sable coat, leather gloves and dangling gold necklaces finished her polished look.

She did not want to look like she felt: single, alone, and hurting from a breakup.

On the drive to Cole's part of town, she tried to prepare herself for seeing him again. He was a man with great magnetism. His looks. Those eyes. That body. Cole Cress was stylish and charming. His vibe was the essence of cool-and-in-control. His eyes could pierce with contempt or charm without question.

When she stepped up to his front door in the hall of the Chelsea apartment building, she truly thought she was prepared to feign nonchalance.

You got this! You. Got. This.

The door opened and Cole stood there looking at her, far too handsome in a navy V-necked sweater and matching cords.

Oh me. Oh my!

She'd been so wrong. So very wrong.

"Come in," he said, stepping back and pulling the door open wider.

She gave him a smile she hoped wasn't awkward as she moved past him. The scent of his cool cologne seemed to surround her and she bit her bottom lip with a wince as she held back a moan of heightened awareness. She jumped when she felt his hands on her shoulders as he helped remove her coat.

Relax, Jillie. Get it together.

But it was hard with his fireplace lit, the lights dimmed, and a few fat candles glowing around the room. Add him smelling good and looking good…

The heat Jillian felt had nothing to do with the fire-place.

"Hungry? I cooked some dinner," Cole said, hanging her coat in the closet and then moving into the kitchen.

That surprised her, but she just nodded as she walked over to the kitchen. "What smells so good?" she asked, acutely aware of feeling awkward and out of place in Cole's apartment. Somewhere she had once pictured would be her home, as well.

"What's wrong?" Cole asked.

She looked over at him. "Nothing," she lied. "Why?"

"You looked sad just then," he said, pausing in putting on mitts to take something out the oven.

His eyes stayed locked on her and she shifted under his steady gaze.

"I'm good," she said.

Their eyes met and held.

Her heart pounded. She felt breathless. Staring into Cole's eyes, being captivated by him again, was beyond words, thus leaving her speechless.

"Today I met my half-brother Lincoln," Cole said, finally offering a reprieve by turning away from her to pull a heavy-duty sheet pan from the oven.

Her eyes dipped to take in his buttocks.

"Wait! What?" she asked with two hard blinks as his words registered.

"When my father was eighteen and about to go off to college, he fathered a son with a young woman. He left England not knowing she was pregnant," he explained. "And today, we all met him."

She watched him as he set the pan of roasted Cornish hens and root vegetables with baby potatoes on the counter. "That must have been a shock. Are *you* okay?" she asked, having seen the battle of wills and might between father and son when she'd worked for them.

Cole eyed her again for long unsettling moments before focusing on taking the hens off the pan to rest and trap in the juices. "Yeah," he said, nodding. "There's still so much to question and understand, but Lincoln agreed to come back to New York for a little while to give us all time to figure out what it all means for the family. The brothers."

"How's Phillip Junior?" she asked with an amused expression.

"Traumatized," Cole countered. "I'm sure he skipped dinner and will whine to Raquel all night about no longer being the heir apparent to the Cress throne."

"And Nicolette?"

Cole retrieved a bottle of wine from his wine rack. "Composed," he said.

They shared a knowing look. Nicolette was the queen of composure but beneath the façade she may very well be close to blowing like a geyser.

"I've had some revelations about myself that directly correlate to my relationship with my father," he said, the muscles of his arms straining against the thinness of his sweater as he opened the bottle.

Jillian bit back a gasp that almost escaped her lips and cleared her throat as she followed him into the dining room. "Has that made things better between you?" she asked.

Cole suddenly stopped and turned.

She nearly bumped into him.

He looked down at her. "No," he said. "But it made me realize that I let my issues with him affect us. And I regret that, Jillian."

Everything inside her fluttered. Her heart. Her belly.

Her pulse. And the bud nestled between the lips of her intimacy.

"I thought I was here to talk about the medical bills," she whispered, seeking control when her body was ready to relinquish it. "Did you pay them?"

"Yes," he admitted.

"Why, Cole?" she asked, even as she felt light-headed from the intensity of his stare upon her face, the closeness of his body, and the reminder of his regrets about them.

"Because I love you," he said with a simplicity that shook her to her very core.

Jillian closed her lids and pressed a hand to her eyes as she took a step back. It was a reprieve from that pulsing and all too familiar energy between them. "I *can't* let you do that," she insisted as she turned and pressed her back to the wall.

She was overwhelmed by it all.

"You can and you will," he insisted.

Her body shivered, and she knew before she opened her eyes that he now stood in front of her. "Cole—"

"I won't have you focusing more on making money than on enjoying your gift so that you can pay a bill for someone I have come to care for myself," he said, reaching to stroke her cheek with his thumb.

A gasp escaped.

"My father once betrayed my mother and I caught him…" Cole began as his eyes caressed her. "Since I was a teenager, that betrayal that I kept—the secret that I held—shaped everything I thought I knew about love and fidelity. That, plus an ex I discovered only wanted me because I was a Cress, destroyed my trust."

She saw the emotions raging in the gray-blue depths of his eyes. "Oh, Cole," she whispered, reaching to gently hold his wrist and connect with him as he shared with her.

"I never wanted to fall in love and trust anyone with my heart…and then two years ago, I saw you during that interview with my mother," he reminisced. "I fell for you before I even knew it. That's why, when you chose the job over me—"

Jillian rose on her heeled boots and pressed a kiss to his mouth to halt his words in the hope of easing the hurt she now knew she'd caused him. His arms wrapped around her, pressing her body to his as he eased his face against her neck. The first kiss at her pulse brought shivers. The second softened her knees.

She was thankful when he took her up into his strong and able arms. She wrapped hers around his neck. "I have my own confession," she whispered in his ear, feeling him shiver as her breath stroked his lobe. "It's about Warren."

Cole stiffened.

"I spoke to him after what you said and he admitted that he was hoping he and I would get back together," she said. "So, I didn't take the job and told him maybe it was best we saw less of each other because I didn't want his hope to rise."

Cole relaxed. "I thought you were going to say y'all—"

"For the past two years, I have not been with anyone but you, Cole," she admitted.

He lowered her to her feet and then picked her up again, this time with her legs wrapped around his waist so that they were looking at each other. Eye to eye. Mouth to mouth. "Same here," he promised her, his words breezing against her lips.

She believed him.

With a light lick of her lips, she kissed him.

Cole released a moan of hunger as he deepened it with his clever tongue, turning to press her back against the

wall. She grabbed his costly sweater into her fists without a care as she kissed him with every bit of passion
she had been denied over the weeks. She was starved
for it. For him.

Wait!

Jillian jerked her head back to break the kiss. He
looked dazed, his mouth covered with her sheer-pink
gloss as his eyes filled with confusion. "If you had this
wonderful epiphany about us, why did I have to call you,
Cole Cress?" she asked, using her thumb to clean his lips.

"I have a surprise for you," he said, carrying her down
the hall to his suite.

She released a soft moan at the sight of the lighted
candles offering the only illumination in the spacious
room other than the moon's shine. Atop the bed were
rose petals and the scent of them burst in the air. In the
center of the array was another of his notes.

Cole carried her across the room and set her on her
feet as he started to undress her. Her eyes stayed locked
on the note.

"You did all this since I called. How?" she asked before her sweater went flying over his head.

"Wealth has its benefits," Cole said as he undid her
bra.

"This is nice. And *that* is very nice," she said, trembling as he sucked one hard nipple and then the other into
his mouth. "But why did I have to call you?"

Cole ignored her as he bent to unzip her boots before
removing each along with her sheer socks. He pressed
heated kisses to her hips as he slid her leggings and lace
thong panties down over her plump bottom and thighs.
He turned his head to suck her plump vee with a grunt
before giving it a gentle bite.

She cried out and arched her back with a gasp at the

pleasure. Naked and shivering before him, Cole looked on as he stepped back from her, his erection pressing against the zipper of his pants as he pulled his sweater over his head, revealing his chiseled chest and abdomen. She closed the gap between them to stroke the flat hairs on his chest before dipping her head to stroke one flat brown nipple with her tongue. "Can I have my note?" she asked as she undid his belt and zipper to work his pants and black boxer briefs around his hard buttocks and even harder inches.

Cole chuckled. "Yes," he said.

Jillian gripped his tool and gently guided him behind her to the side of the bed as she reached for the note with her free hand. Behind it was a red-velvet, heart-shaped ring box. "Oh," she said in surprise.

Cole wrapped an arm around her waist. "All of this I did tonight. But that, I purchased a few days ago," he explained, finally offering the proof of his intentions toward her before her call.

Jillian leaned back against his strength, releasing his erection to clutch her note with both hands as she emotionally choked up.

"I was trying to figure out some grand way to propose and then you called," he further explained. "I went with fate."

Tears welled from the joy of being loved by someone she loved and having him want to share the rest of his life with her. *But* her fears crept up—she couldn't deny that. Opening the note, she smiled at his words, caressing them with her fingertips as she read them aloud. "'I hunger for your love the same as I hunger for your body. Your presence is my comfort zone. Your smile is my light. Making you happy will be my goal for the rest of our lives, my Jillian.'"

Jillian closed her eyes as tears fell. Their affair had begun with a note and it was so romantic of him to propose with one, as well. She wanted nothing more in the world than to believe him. Memories of two failed marriages were her detractors. And she hated that, for Cole and for herself.

Damn.

Cole pressed one knee into the bed to pick up the ring box before turning to sit on the bed in front of her as he opened it.

The ring was exquisite. She loved its unique design and the brilliant sparkle of the large diamond. "Cole," she whispered, seeing the flicker of candlelight in his eyes.

He removed the ring from the box. "Will you—?"

"Wait," she said, reaching to cover the ring and his hand with her own.

He looked up at her, apprehension in his eyes.

Jillian pressed a hand to the side of his face. "Cole, I've been married before—"

"Do you love me?" he asked.

"More than I have ever loved anyone," she said with sincerity.

"Then how can you compare me and what we can build together—trust, love, a family—when you have never had the same love for those other men?" he said. "Who you are now is not who you were then. And I am not them."

"A family?" she asked, pressing her hand to her belly and envisioning it swollen with their child.

Cole covered her hand with his own. "Yes," he stressed.

"Girl or boy?" she asked.

"Girl," they said in unison.

"There're more than enough male Cress family members," Cole said dryly.

Jillian's eyes went back to the ring.

I do love him.

She reread the note.

And he loves me.

She remembered reading something Maya Angelou had said. "'Have enough courage to trust love one more time…'" she quoted the poet.

Cole rose before her. "We both have to leave our past in the past and trust in each other," he said before dropping to his knee. "Let's do it together. Marry me?"

I can't let the hurt caused by other men keep this love from me now.

With a building excitement like nothing she had ever felt, Jillian bit her bottom lip as she raised her left hand, presented it to him, hoping he could see and feel the love she had for him. And as he took her hand in his and slid the weighty jewel onto her finger, she pushed aside her fears, determined to claim her happiness with the man she loved.

Cole stood and kissed her before quickly grabbing her waist and turning her body to lay it down on the bed, sandwiched by the rose petals and his body.

His weight felt familiar. Comfortable. Perfect.

"And what about dinner, my love?" she said, rubbing her leg up and down the length of his as he pressed kisses to her neck.

Cole gave her a wicked smile before moving his body down between her legs as he spread them. "I have everything I want to eat right here," he said before lowering his head to blow a cool stream of air against her intimacy.

Jillian clutched at his head as she arched her back and closed her eyes at the pleasure of his tongue. She rolled her hips and Gabe moaned deep in his throat as his fingers gripped her buttocks. "Yes," she gasped in ecstasy as goose bumps raced across her skin.

She gave in to the pleasure and her love with the hope that they would cherish, honor, and trust one another in a way neither had before with anyone. She was hopeful. Even as she was driven to mindless passion by her love—who seemed hell-bent on pleasing her—she allowed herself to free-fall into the bliss of love and carry Cole—her sexy rebel—right along with her.

Hopefully, for forever and a day.

her hips and Gabe moaned deep in his throat as his fingers gripped her buttocks. "Yes," she gasped in ecstasy
as goose bumps raced across her skin.

She gave in to the pleasure and her love with the hope
that they would cherish, honor, and trust one another in
a way neither had before with anyone. She was hopeful.
Even as she was driven to mindless passion by her lover
who scented hell-bent on pleasing her—she allowed herself to free-fall into the bliss of love and carry Cole—her
sexy rebel—right along with her.

Epilogue

Three months later

Cole looked over his mother's head as they danced to
eye Jillian dancing with her father. There was a smile
on her face as she looked up at the tall, broad man with
the love a daughter has for her father. His bride looked
beautiful in a couture, formfitting, soft tulle gown scattered with delicate beading. The deep V-neckline and
detachable overskirt of layers of tulle made her hour-
glass figure more pronounced. The sheer blush color of
the gown was sexy and delicate. She was stunning. Cole
smiled and chuckled when Harry surprised her with a
dip and Jillian's eyes widened.

I love my wife.

Earlier that afternoon, they had wed at the courthouse.
Just the two of them. They had chosen to put their marriage and each other first above all else. They'd wanted

the focus on their marriage and not just a lavish wedding ceremony.

The reception was open to all their family and friends, and their wedding planner had magically converted the grand ballroom in the luxury Manhattan hotel to a floral wonderland—just the way Jillian had envisioned it. And that was his goal for the rest of his life. He wanted to make her as happy as she deserved to be.

"Are you happy, son?"

Cole looked down into his mother's blue eyes. In their depths, a genuine concern for him—even if her actions to destroy things between Jillian and him had been her misguided attempt to make his life as easy as possible.

Perhaps to save him from the heartbreak he was sure she'd felt at the discovery of her husband's affair.

"There is no one who could make me any happier," Cole said, giving her the smile he'd used as a young boy to charm her for an extra dessert after dinner.

Nicolette nodded as she blinked away tears. "Okay," she said, her voice soft and resigned to yet another of her sons being with a woman not of her choosing.

"Why did you forgive him?" he asked, his eyes studying his mother's profile.

For the briefest moment, Nicolette's body stiffened and she avoided looking up at him.

"A man's ego is a fragile thing," she said. "And having your wife win a trifecta of James Beard awards, for which both of you were nominated, can weaken a shaky foundation."

Cole saw a flash of pain in her eyes even as she attempted to keep from facing him. He bent his head and pressed a kiss to her temple. "Then he was a childish fool," he said for her ears alone.

Nicolette touched her head to his chest briefly. "I agree," she said, summoning a smile for her son.

The song for the parents' dance ended and everyone applauded before both Cole and Jillian moved toward each other. He wrapped an arm around her waist and pulled her close as he looked into her upturned face. "Ready for our honeymoon?" he asked, her hands stroking his neck as they danced to "All of Me" by John Legend.

"Yes. I can't wait for a week-long vacation in Greece," she said, her eyes sparkling with love and happiness.

"That sounds like you won't miss the food truck," he mused, raising her hand to spin her before pulling her body back to his.

"No offense, but I won't," she said.

Cole chuckled.

Jillian had left behind her coveted position as the private chef of a high-powered movie executive to fulfill her dreams of her own cooking establishment by operating the food truck during the week while Cole was busy with his duties at Cress, INC. On the weekends, they enjoyed working it together, combining their love of food and each other.

"Listen, Jillian…" he said.

"Yes, *husband*," she said.

"I never want you to worry if your light shines brighter than mine that I will resent you or harbor ill feelings toward you. A win for you is a win for us," Cole promised, again shirking ever taking on the bad traits his father possessed.

"A win for you is a win for us. Same difference," she assured him, easing her hands onto his shoulders.

"Always," he vowed before gripping her waist and lifting her to kiss her deeply and with all the passion he could muster without offending their now applauding audience with proof of his arousal.

"And forever," she whispered against his mouth.

* * * * *

HOLLYWOOD
EX FACTOR

SHERI WHITEFEATHER

One

Frustrated by it all, Zeke Mitchell unbuckled his seat belt, preparing to exit the plane. He'd just spent four hours and fifty-one minutes in the air, obsessing about his ex.

He should be glad to be home. But instead, he was stressing over Margot Jensen. She was an actress and one of his LA clients. She was also his occasional lover. But most important, she was his former wife. They'd started sleeping together soon after their divorce, which was going on three years now. An uncommitted affair, he thought.

Sporadic, sex-only hookups.

But that might be coming to an end. Margot had texted him last night, saying that she was having second thoughts about their affair and wanted to discuss it with him.

He stood and removed his carry-on from above his

seat, then disembarked with the rest of the first-class passengers and proceeded to the baggage reclaim area to collect the remainder of his luggage. From there, he headed outside to ground transportation, where he'd already arranged for a town car to take him straight to Margot's. She'd asked him to come by as soon as he could, but he was fine with that. He wanted to get their damned discussion over with.

He blew out a sigh. What did he expect? To have a fling with his ex-wife forever? At some point, their affair was meant to crash and burn. Then again, maybe he could convince her to be together one last time…

Damn it. Why did Margot have to affect him this way? Why couldn't he shake her from his blood?

He cleared his mind and scanned the cars lined up at the curb, searching for his driver. The sidewalk was busy, people rushing past him. Some of them glanced his way, but Zeke tended to stand out in a crowd. At six-four, he was packed with muscle. Not all bodyguards were his size. A lot of the agents he employed were able to blend in, to go unnoticed. That would never be the case with Zeke. In addition to his stature, his mixed heritage made him identifiable, too. He was Samoan and Choctaw from his dad's side and white from his mom's.

He located his driver, and within no time, he was riding in the back of a Lincoln, en route to the Hollywood Hills, where Margot lived. They'd sold the Redondo Beach house they'd owned together. Nonetheless, Zeke still lived in that area, making an oceanfront condo his current home.

About forty-five minutes later, he arrived at Margot's residence, an elegant three-bedroom, four-bath Spanish Colonial Revival surrounded by a wrought iron gate.

Zeke instructed his driver to wait for him, then exited the car. He opened the coded gate and ascended the red clay steps leading to the front door. He had a key to her house, but he never used it. It was strictly for security purposes.

Zeke and his partner operated Z-One Security, a personal protection company with over three hundred employees guarding celebrities all over the world. Whenever they took on a new or complicated assignment, Zeke would spend some time with the client, becoming familiar with their lifestyle and training the rest of his team accordingly.

He rang the bell, and Margot answered, looking soft and luscious in a billowy blouse and wide-legged jeans. He noticed that her nails were decorated in mismatched polish. She'd always had an eclectic fashion sense, with different looks to suit whatever type of mood she was in. Today, he surmised, she was in a state of uncertainty. Would that work in his favor? Or was he reading too much into it? She'd never been short on contradictions.

"Hi, Zeke." She greeted him with an anxious smile.

"Hey, Margot." He wasn't going to give her the satisfaction of a smile, anxious or otherwise. He was already pissed at himself for wanting her.

She wore her wild red hair in a low-slung ponytail with loose tendrils framing her face. Her bright blue eyes lent her an innocent quality. Her dimples, however, struck a mischievous chord. They'd served her well when she was a child actor playing a precocious character in *The Kid Years*, the family sitcom she'd become known for. She was playing an adult version of that same character now, in a sequel of the old show aptly called *The Grown-up Years*.

The job that had triggered their divorce.

When they'd first started dating, she'd given up acting, only to resume her career after they got married. A move that felt horribly deceptive to Zeke. He'd never wanted a celebrity wife. He'd grown up with a famous mother, and he'd struggled through every minute of it. As a kid, his only salvation had been his mom's security team. They'd provided a sense of stability in an otherwise chaotic environment, shielding his family from the paparazzi and obsessive fans who hounded his mom. For Zeke, becoming a security specialist when he got older was a no-brainer.

Luckily, Margot didn't need much of a security detail. Aside from the usual internet trolls who harassed celebrities online, there'd never really been any issues. But he wasn't taking any chances. He engaged a crew to monitor her social media accounts and keep an eye on the camera footage outside her house.

He was being filmed right now. Not that it mattered. As far as his employees knew, his visits with her were strictly professional. He hadn't told a living soul that they were lovers. Margot, on the other hand, had blabbed about their affair to Zeke's sister. The two women had been friends since they were kids, and now his sister was privy to his personal shit.

"Are you going to come inside?" Margot asked.

He nodded and entered the house, catching a glimpse of his dark suit and gray striped tie as he passed a mirror in the foyer. He preferred to wear business attire when he traveled. He would change into a pair of board shorts when he got home.

She escorted him to the living room, a space rife with wood floors, beamed ceilings, a stone fireplace and French casement windows. There was a view of the backyard, including a mixed garden, a pool, a spa and an artfully designed patio.

He glanced at the sofa, but he didn't take a seat. Neither did she. Flustered by their ever-present attraction, he shifted his stance. The energy between them was thick and tangled.

Confusing, he thought.

"Can I get you anything?" she asked.

By now, he was itching to kiss her, to touch her, to carry her to the master suite and do wicked things. "What did you have in mind?"

"Coffee, water, beer. Whatever you want."

He raised his eyebrows. "Whatever I want?" He waited a beat. "Surely you know what that is." He kept his voice low, quiet. Seductive, he supposed. He was making his move, scattered as it was.

Her reaction was just as scattered. In fact, she looked downright dizzy, as if being with him one last time had crossed her mind, too. But then she composed herself and said, "I didn't arrange this meeting for us to…"

"I know, but it's been a while since we…" He'd been away on an assignment for what had seemed like forever, eager to see her, to hook up with her again. "Six months to be exact."

"Yes, but that was before the adoption was finalized and Liam came to live with me."

Zeke had been wondering if this was about her son. The eight-year-old who'd become her priority. He didn't know young Liam, but he'd seen plenty of pictures. He had a security file on the boy.

In all honesty, the idea of her becoming a mom twisted him up inside. Once upon a time, they'd talked about having kids of their own. Of course, that was when they'd been madly in love. But those feelings no longer applied.

Zeke cleared the scratchiness from his throat. Now

that her kid had become part of the discussion, he was at a loss for words. Margot was silent, as well. But that was typical of them. Aside from getting naked, they didn't know how to communicate anymore. Their sexual escapades didn't even include spending any nights together. They just did the deed, then went their separate ways, like hot-blooded strangers hungry for a fix.

Suddenly, he needed a cold drink, something to take the edge off. "If your offer is still good, I think I'd like a beer."

"No problem." She gazed at his mouth, wetting her own lips in the process. "I'm thirsty, too. I'm going to get myself some water." She headed toward the kitchen. "I'll be right back."

Zeke watched her dash out of the room. In spite of the obvious tension, she was trying to act casual. But that did little to ease his mind—or his relentless desire for her.

Margot entered the kitchen and caught her breath. Why did ending her affair with Zeke have to be so painful? Why did she have to want him so badly?

She filled a glass with water from the fridge and drank half of it, telling herself to relax. She could do this. She could let Zeke go for good. It wasn't healthy for her to keep sleeping with him. For now, she needed to focus on her son. Liam was at school today. He was a great student, a smart boy who'd learned to adapt to whatever situation he was in. But his life, thus far, hadn't been easy. He'd spent most of his youth bouncing in and out of foster homes, hoping for a forever family. And now he had Margot.

She'd never intended to become a single parent, but when she'd met Liam at a children's charity, she'd connected with him instantly and knew he was meant to be hers.

She used to think that Zeke was meant to be hers, too, but their divorce had proved otherwise. And their affair? That was insanity. Who slept with their ex instead of moving on? Someday, when she was ready, she would start dating again. But next time she would have a normal relationship, not the turmoil she'd endured with Zeke.

She put her glass in the sink and almost left the kitchen without his beer. *Good Lord.* She grabbed it and returned to the living room. She handed him the bottle, and they both sat. He took the sofa, and she scooted onto an overstuffed chair. He opened the beer and took a long, hard swallow.

He met her gaze, and her heart banged against her ribs. He was a breathtaking man, imposing in his size, with rugged features and eyes that were nearly as black as his hair.

"Where's your water?" he asked.

"I drank it in the kitchen."

"And you're not thirsty anymore?"

"No." At least not for water. Slaking her thirst for him wasn't so easy, but she was determined to exorcise those demons.

She was thirty-three now, and he was thirty-eight. At this point, she'd known him for over half of her life. In addition to her friendship with his sister, she'd also had a close association with his dad. Caine Mitchell used to be Margot's agent. Her own father had walked away when she was seven, abandoning her without a care. She understood that Zeke's childhood was difficult on account of how famous his mother was. But she used to love hanging out at his parents' house and seeing them together. The Hollywood agent and the Hollywood star. They'd been a good match, even if their union had first stemmed from tragedy.

Zeke wasn't Caine's biological son. His birth father was a stuntman who'd been killed in a work-related accident soon after Zeke was born, leaving his mother devastated. In the midst of her grief, she'd married Caine, and he'd adopted her infant son. Bailey had come along five years later, making her Zeke's half sister. Caine was gone now, too. He'd died twelve years ago, leaving an emotional legacy behind. He was the glue that had held everyone together, and they all missed him terribly. Even Margot still brought flowers to his grave.

She looked into Zeke's eyes, those deep, dark hypnotic eyes. To keep things from getting too quiet, she said, "I was just thinking about Caine and how he adopted you."

"And now you have an adopted son." A muscle ticked in his jaw. "But you always wanted kids."

Margot's chest went tight. He'd wanted them, too. Before their marriage had gone awry, they'd talked about having babies. "Becoming a mom has been amazing. But it's still so new and different, and I'm still learning, figuring things out as I go."

"That's normal, I suspect. But I wouldn't really know anything about it." After an uncomfortable pause, he asked, "Are you going to hire a nanny or an au pair? If you are, I need to screen your applicants. Me or one of my agents."

"I'm not going to hire anyone. My mom enjoys watching Liam. She's available whenever I need her. Or she has been so far."

"That's good," he replied, pinning her with his gaze. He swigged his beer without breaking eye contact.

Margot tried not to fidget under his scrutiny. The way he was looking at her made her want to take him straight to bed. But she couldn't, she reminded herself. Not unless she was willing to get all jumbled up again.

Before she did something stupid, she said, "When I texted you last night and said that I was having second thoughts about our affair, I was still struggling with my decision. There was a part of me that wanted to hang on." A part that still did, she thought. Even now, her traitorous body ached for his. "But I need to create a healthy environment for myself and Liam, and I don't see how that's possible if I'm still sleeping with you."

He set his drink on the coffee table. "Then, this is it? It's over?"

"Yes." It had to be, she told herself. No more heart-thundering sex. No more lusty rendezvous.

He leaned back, his massive body sinking into the sofa. "I'm going to miss being with you."

"I'll miss being with you, too." She wasn't going to lie or pretend otherwise. "This wasn't an easy decision."

"Then maybe you shouldn't end it so soon. We can keep doing it for a while and see how it goes. Being a mom doesn't mean you're not allowed to have a lover."

"I know. But I'm trying to do the right thing, and sneaking off with you isn't going to help my cause. There's no future in it. We're divorced," she reminded him.

"I'm well aware of our relationship status." He tugged at his tie, as if the perfectly tied knot was starting to choke him. "But I never would've filed the papers if you'd held up your end of the bargain. When we first got together, you told me that you were done with acting. But then you took that damned sequel. Your old producer called, and you went running."

She narrowed her eyes, irked that he was inciting the same old argument, spinning the narrative to suit him. "I had a right to change my mind. Being an actor makes me happy."

"Oh, really? Then why were you so miserable half the time?"

"I was only miserable when it wasn't going well." She'd made it big at nine years old, and by the time her stardom had ended, she was a teenager, struggling to find her footing. A phase that had lasted through her twenties, when she'd fallen head over heels in love with him. A mistake, if there ever was one. "Everyone else wanted me to succeed again. My mom, your family. Everyone except you." She glared at him. "You're the least supportive person I know."

He loosened his tie all the way. "I supported you plenty. Besides, you knew that I never wanted to be married to a celebrity. That it was a deal breaker for me."

She huffed out a breath. "You didn't even try to compromise."

"Damn it, Margot, I wanted a conventional life with you. Not all of the TV-star hoopla."

"It's not hoopla. It's my job," she shot back.

"A job you chose over me."

"I didn't choose it over you. I wanted my old career back. But you refused to listen to my side of it."

"You didn't care about my side of it, either."

"Yes, I did." She'd taken his issues into consideration. She'd stressed and worried about his feelings. But she'd been foolish in believing that he'd loved her enough to make it work. "You divorced me, not the other way around."

"What was the point of staying together if all we did was fight? I did you a favor by leaving."

She mocked him. "Lucky me, having such a considerate husband. But you know what? You need to go now."

"Gladly." He stood, coming to his towering height.

At five-nine, Margot was considered tall, too. But with his size and strength, he was Hulk material. She used to tease him and say that she was going to paint him green. Now she just wanted to knock him flat on his ass.

He polished off the rest of his beer. "I'll bet that after I'm gone, you're going to run right over to Bailey's and bitch to her about me."

"I can share my feelings with her if I want to." She wasn't going to let him control her friendship with his sister.

"This is bullshit."

"If you say so." She gestured to the front door, but he didn't leave. Instead, he went into the kitchen to rinse out the empty bottle and put it in the recycling container below the sink.

She dogged him. "Look at you. Mr. Tidy."

"So, I'm not a slob. Not like you."

Margot gritted her teeth. "I'm not a slob. A little disorganized, maybe. But that's not the same as being messy."

"Are you kidding? You never clean up after yourself." He glanced at her sparkling counters. "At least you have a great maid service. It's obvious they were here this morning."

"Whatever." It was true, her housekeeper had been there. "Just get out of my sight and don't ever come back."

He rounded on her. "Are you sure you don't want to kiss me first? Or rip off my clothes and claw the crap out of me?"

Her pulse zipped through her body, going straight to the instant heat between her legs. A half-cocked smile spread across his lips. Could he tell that she was turned on by what he'd said? His security training made him a bit of an expert in that regard. He was good at reading people's emotions. Of course, he used to say that she was sometimes hard to gauge. A fact that both challenged and perplexed him.

She lifted her chin. "I never should've had an affair with you."

He stared her down. "Yeah, well, it's too late. You already did."

He didn't immediately leave like he was supposed to. He stayed put, keeping her hanging on by a thread. There was no way she was going to kiss him, or unclothe him, even if she wanted to. Idiot that she was, she would probably fantasize about him tonight: sighing, moaning, touching herself.

"This isn't fair," she said.

"What isn't? That you still want me? Or that I still want you? I wish I knew how to fix it."

"Me, too. It would be nice if we could find a way to get past it without being so angry." She searched his gaze, desperate for a solution. Neither of them should be suffering this way. "There's got to be something we can do." She studied him, her mind whirring. "Maybe we can try to be friends."

"Friends?" he parroted.

"Yes, you know. A platonic relationship between people who are supposed to like each other."

"Do you like me, Margot?"

"Sometimes," she replied honestly.

"I like you sometimes, too," he said softly.

She always got a little woozy when he whispered. To combat the feeling, she squared her shoulders. "We can use that as our starting point."

He looked worried, dragging a hand through his hair and spiking the short, thick strands.

"Do you really think that'll work?" he asked.

"I don't know." She wasn't any better at being his friend than he was at being hers. "But it's got to be less stressful than fighting." Or wanting each other, she thought. She needed to stomp out her hunger for him. To crush it to bits.

"I guess we can try. But how are we supposed to go about it?"

"I can come by your place on my way to the studio tomorrow morning and bring breakfast." That seemed friendly enough. Plus, her mom was already scheduled to take Liam to school that day. Margot didn't have to alter her routine to see Zeke. "We can figure out where to go from there. But I'll be there really early, so don't sleep in."

"Do I ever?"

"No, I suppose not." He was an early riser, a habit that had been formed from surfing. He used any excuse to hit the waves. Sometimes he even paddled out on moonlit nights.

He squinted. "I better go now, before we start arguing again and blow this whole deal."

"Good call." She agreed that it was safer for him to leave while they were on a positive note.

She walked him to the door, and the moment turned awkward. He leaned forward to hug her, but then he pulled back, as if it might not be a very platonic thing to do. In their case, he was right to keep his distance. She didn't need to feel his big, broad body next to hers.

"I'll see you tomorrow," he said.

"You, too." She watched him descend the steps and retreat to the town car waiting for him.

Was initiating a friendship with him the smartest course of action? She wasn't altogether sure, but she'd already made the offer, and she was going to follow through.

No matter how difficult it proved to be.

Two

After Zeke left, Margot headed over to Bailey's house. He'd been right about her wanting to see his sister. But she wasn't going there to bitch. She needed a bit of girl talk.

Bailey was a screenwriter who worked predominantly from home, and as long as she wasn't on a pressing deadline, she made herself available to Margot.

They both lived in the Hollywood Hills, only in different neighborhoods. Margot resided in Whitley Heights, a historic district built during the rise of the motion picture industry, and Bailey was in Laurel Canyon, a mountainous area rooted in the 1960s and '70s counterculture.

Margot took the winding road that led to Bailey's house, a woodsy cabin perched on a hill, surrounded by herbs, flowers and dense foliage. Zeke's sister valued her privacy, something she shared with her brother.

Neither of them had basked in the spotlight of their mother's fame. Zeke had reacted to it by building a personal protection empire, and Bailey took refuge in the isolation of writing.

Margot liked being in the public eye. She enjoyed posing for pictures and chatting with fans and walking red carpets. She was nowhere near as famous as Eva Mitchell, though. Zeke and Bailey's mother had been a world-renowned sex symbol in her day. Even now, she was still revered for her beauty.

Margot parked on Bailey's narrow street and made her way to the back of the cabin. Bailey said that she would be working outside today.

Sure enough, there she was curled up in a hammock with her laptop. She didn't look anything like Zeke. She didn't have his tense personality, either. Bailey was a petite, blue-eyed blonde with an easy nature. She sported a casual style, too. Sometimes she dressed up, but mostly she gravitated to sweats and sneakers, or cutoff shorts and sandals.

"I'm here," Margot announced.

"I know." Bailey glanced over and grinned. "I saw you out of the corner of my eye." She closed her laptop and got to her feet.

Margot moved toward her for a hug. Bailey always smelled so soft and natural. In her spare time, she concocted soaps and lotions and organic potions.

They embraced, and Bailey said, "I made lemonade." She gestured to the fruit trees in her yard. "Fresh from the source."

"Thanks. I'll try to make this visit short."

"No problem. I have time." Bailey removed the lemonade from a boxy little fridge in the entertainment area. She poured two glasses and placed them on a wood table surrounded by chairs decorated with floral-printed cushions.

They sat across from each other. On this bright spring day, the sun shined gloriously over the hills. In the silence that followed, Bailey tucked a strand of her honey-colored hair behind her ear. The silky strands were so long, they skimmed her tailbone. Margot had to work a lot harder on her hair, thick and wavy as it was, putting product on it to keep it from frizzing. But the unruliness suited her, so she didn't mind.

She gave herself another reflective second to breathe before she said, "I broke off my affair with Zeke."

"Oh, wow. You did it. You actually did it." Bailey paused. "I loved having you as my sister-in-law, and I wished your marriage would've worked, but I'm relieved that you finally ended that crazy affair."

"I knew you would be. You kept telling me how emotionally damaging you thought it was for me to keep sleeping with him."

"I told Zeke the same thing. In my opinion, it wasn't good for either of you. Of course, as hardheaded as my brother is, he wouldn't listen to a thing I had to say." She leaned forward. "How did he take it?"

"Not well at first. We got into an argument over the past, but then we decided to try to be friends."

Bailey's eyes went wide. "You both decided that?"

"It was my suggestion, but he agreed to give it a go. I'm going to stop by his condo tomorrow to talk more about it."

"No offense, but you better not end up back in his bed."

"No offense taken. And for the record, he tried to get me to be with him today, but I turned him down."

"I'm glad to hear it. But just be careful, okay? Old habits and all of that."

Old habits, indeed. Their affair had started on an evening where they'd met up to discuss business. She'd wanted to use a different security service after the divorce, but he'd insisted that she stay with his company. At some point, they'd gotten into a raging fight that had culminated in a wild bout of sex. "I swear, I'm not going to do anything stupid."

Bailey laughed a little. "Well, I think you being his friend sounds kind of stupid."

Margot laughed, too. But only for a moment. Turning serious, she said, "There came a point when he made the choice to stop loving me, and when I stopped loving him, too. But we never got closure after the divorce. Instead, we just kept sleeping together."

"So, if you learn to become friends, you'll both get the closure you need?"

"It's worth a try." Margot sipped her lemonade. "Remember that crush I had on him when we were kids?"

Bailey crinkled her nose. "How could I forget? He was all you ever talked about. I wanted to jump off a bridge whenever you cooed his name."

"I know. I'm sorry for putting you through that. But the first time I saw him, so tall and dark and broody, I nearly melted on the spot. He wasn't nearly as impressed with me."

"He thought you were a pest back then."

"I was, I suppose. A gangly fourteen-year-old, fresh from a canceled sitcom, mooning over my best friend's brother. He was a freshman in college, and there I was, giggling and acting silly, trying to get his attention."

"You finally got old enough for him to take an interest in you."

"Sometimes I think it would have been easier if we'd never gotten together at all. Having a crush on him was bad enough, but the way I loved him later on…"

His sister sighed. "Yes, but look at you now. A strong and successful single mom. I'm proud of how far you've come."

"Thank you. I appreciate you saying that." And once she tackled this friendship thing with Zeke, she intended to become even stronger, conquering her hunger for him for good.

The following morning, Margot was on her way, ready to face Zeke. She stopped at a trendy food truck near his place that specialized in healthy meals and gourmet coffee. The female server recognized her and asked for a selfie. She happily obliged, flashing her best smile.

She returned to her car and continued her journey. The home she and Zeke used to own together wasn't far from here, but she avoided going down that street. She didn't need the reminder that they were once married.

Zeke's modern-style condo faced the ocean. After she arrived, she approached his private deck, a low-maintenance area with a fire ring, a grouping of lounge chairs and a mosaic-topped table. He could've afforded to buy her out and keep their other house, but he'd decided to start over somewhere new. Hence, this cool, sleek bachelor pad.

She set everything down and rang the bell. She waited, but he didn't answer. Had he slept in after all? She tried a second time. Then a third. Seriously, how tired could he be?

She fired off a text. I'm outside your door. Where are you?

Again, she waited. But he didn't reply.

At this point, she was getting downright miffed. Zeke used to say that her fiery disposition matched her hair. But today she had good reason for being mad. She'd come all this way, only to be shunned by him.

She turned to gather the bags and leave, when she spotted him on the beach with his surfboard propped in the sand. She hadn't even thought to look for him out there, even if it was the most logical place for him to be.

As she watched him peel off his wetsuit, her heart began to pound. He was wearing shorts underneath, but just the act of him undressing was enough to send her into a tailspin.

He turned and noticed her. They stared at each other from across the distance. He headed in her direction, and she unpacked the food, setting up their meal on the table.

When he got closer, she noticed how tight his shorts were. Well, of course they were snug. They were Lycra. He never wore board shorts under his wetsuit; they bunched too much.

"I'm sorry if I kept you waiting," he said.

She was doing her damnedest not to drool. All that brawny muscle. All that masculine beauty. Was it any wonder that she'd kept sleeping with him after the divorce? "I texted you. But I didn't realize that you were on the beach."

"I didn't bring my phone with me. Do you want to come in while I get dressed?"

"No, thanks. I'll stay here." She didn't want to be anywhere near him when he took off those skintight shorts. She was already struggling to block that image from her wayward mind.

He gripped his board. "I'm not going to shower. I can do that later."

She actually would've preferred that he showered. To her, the scent of the sea on his skin was just another aphrodisiac. "You don't have to rush on my account."

"But I kept you waiting. I'm just going to put on some clothes. I'll be right back."

He entered the condo, leaving her alone with her thoughts. She sipped her coffee and gazed out at the ocean, trying to stay calm. Her mind was still misbehaving. She couldn't stop thinking about his body-hugging shorts. The surfer-boy smell of his skin. The affair she was already missing.

He returned, dressed in faded jeans, a dark blue pullover and slip-on sneakers. Margot was wearing a standard gray hoodie. It was a chilly spring morning, but it was supposed to warm up later.

"How long do we have?" he asked.

She blinked. "What?"

"Before you have to leave for the studio."

She checked her phone for the time. "About thirty minutes." Which seemed like an eternity now.

He sat across from her. "Thank you for this. I'm starving. I don't have any groceries in the house. I plan to go shopping later, though."

She watched him attack his food. They were having the same thing to eat: egg-and-cheese burritos, sautéed sweet potatoes and fresh fruit. Their drinks were different. Hers was a café mocha, and his was a dead eye: a regular coffee with three shots of espresso. She knew his tastes. The man definitely liked it strong.

He finished chewing a mouthful of burrito and gulped his coffee. "Can I ask you something that I've been wondering about for a while?" He placed his cup back on the table. "Have you been with anyone else, besides me, since the divorce?"

Margot nearly flinched. That was what he was curious about? Other partners? "We agreed back then that our affair wasn't going to be exclusive."

"Yeah, but now that it's over, I was hoping it would be okay to talk more about it."

Stalling, she took a small bite of her potatoes. She hadn't been with anyone else, but she didn't want him to perceive it as loyalty. Or some sort of misguided feelings for him that still lingered.

Rather than respond to his question, she turned it around on him. "What about you? How many women were you with while you were sleeping with me?"

He answered outright. "None. It seemed too complicated to be having an affair with you and be seeing other people, too."

"It was the same for me. You were the only one. But now neither of us has to worry about that complication anymore."

They just needed to learn to quit lusting after each other.

He took another bite of his burrito. Then he asked, "Does Liam know that you're divorced?"

More personal questions, she thought. More discomfort. "Yes, but I only mentioned it to him in passing. I didn't go into the specifics, other than I used to be married to Bailey's brother and that you own the company that provides our security." Which seemed specific enough, she realized. "I wouldn't have said anything to him at all, but he's really close to your sister, so I thought it might come up at some point anyway. He adores Bailey. She's one of his favorite people."

Zeke drank more of his coffee, gazing at her from across the rim of his cup. "How did they get so close?"

"Aside from her being my best friend?" Most people would have assumed the obvious, Margot thought. But not her analytical ex. He was always looking for deeper meanings. And in this case, he was right. "Bailey has been helping Liam write a children's book that they're going to self-publish. It's about a dog that adopts orphaned kittens. The concept was his idea. He's really excited about it. He wants to give the proceeds from the book to the foster charity that helped him and me become a family."

"That must make you proud." Zeke seemed impressed by her son's sensitivity. But there was something else, too. Something she couldn't quite name. Until he said, "I'd like to meet Liam. I'd like to get to know him."

"For security reasons or on a personal level?"

"Both, if that's okay with you."

"Can I think about it?" She wanted to be careful not to rush into anything. "You and I are just starting to get to know each other again, and I don't want to confuse Liam by introducing him to you too soon."

"Just let me know what you decide. I'll be around for a while. In fact, I'm taking the next month or so off. My last assignment was pretty grueling, and I need to relax before I jump back into another one."

As a small breeze kicked up, she tucked her napkin under her food container to keep it from blowing away. "I'll be free soon, too. Once we wrap up this season, we won't start filming again until the show is officially renewed by the network."

"Then it sounds like we have plenty of time to see

each other." He grabbed his napkin before it took flight. "And do whatever friends do."

She glanced at her phone, suddenly eager to leave. Zeke was studying her a bit too closely, reminding her of the past, of the pain, of the children they should've had together. "I should probably get going." She closed her food container. "I'll take the rest of this with me."

"Has it been thirty minutes already?"

She rose from her seat. "No, but it's close enough." And she needed to get her emotions back on track. She didn't want to show up at work all rattled.

He walked her to the edge of the deck, and they stood a few torturous feet apart. His proximity made her want to kiss him, to taste his luscious mouth, to press herself against him.

"You can go take your shower now," she said, as the wind whipped between them. "Not that you need my permission," she quickly added. "I was just..."

"I know..." He hesitated. "I'll wait to hear from you about when we should get together again. Or when I can meet Liam or whatever happens next."

Margot pushed a strand of hair away from her face. Would she be stronger the next time she saw him? She hoped so. If not, she was just going to have to keep trying, for however long it took.

Margot spent the evening with her mom and Liam. After Liam went to bed, she and her mom went back to the kitchen so Margot could clean up.

She made a point to load the dishwasher rather than leave the dinner dishes in the sink the way she sometimes did.

But mostly she was stealing glances at her powerhouse mom.

Sixty-five-year-old June Jensen was a sturdy brunette who loved the entertainment industry with a vengeance. She'd hired Caine to be Margot's agent while she'd managed Margot's career, but she was happily retired now and living in an active fifty-five-plus community with other Hollywood diehards. At the moment, she stood at the counter with a pair of rhinestone readers perched on the end of her nose and the latest copy of *People* magazine at her fingertips. She still liked to read the old-school way, flipping through the glossy pages until she got to the cover story. Margot had never been on the cover of *People*, but she'd been featured inside, something that had thrilled her mom to no end.

Typically, nothing fazed June. Or that was the impression she gave. Margot knew otherwise. Her mother had been devastated when Margot's daddy up and left, crying herself to sleep on long, lonely nights.

Margot had cried, too. She'd spent years thinking it was her fault, that if she'd been a better daughter, he would have stuck around. Even before he left, he'd seemed indifferent, leaving her longing for his affection. Once she'd landed *The Kid Years*, she'd been certain that he would come back to be part of her life. Only he never did. He'd made his child support payments on time, but that was where their connection ended. These days, he was remarried and living in Costa Rica with his much younger wife. He had absolutely nothing to do with Margot. He didn't even follow her on social media.

Her mom, on the other hand, was her biggest fan. She'd gotten Margot into the business when she was just a baby. To some people June had seemed like a typical stage mom, pushing and prodding and trying to make her kid a star. But for Margot, the attention had felt good, especially with her dad's lack of interest.

It was strange how her celebrity affected her family. Her mother loved it, her father didn't care, Liam thought it was cool and Zeke had divorced her over it.

Of course, now she had the pressing issue of being his friend and deciding how and when to introduce him to Liam.

"Can I talk to you about something?" she asked her mom. At this point, she wanted her mother's advice, even if she was only going to give her bits and pieces of the story.

"Sure. What is it?" Her mom removed her glasses and set the magazine aside, settling in for their discussion.

"I had breakfast with Zeke this morning. But it wasn't a security meeting. He and I are working toward being friends."

Her mom cocked her head, her hair falling at a blunt angle against her chin. "I know you've maintained a business rapport since the divorce. But you want to be friends now?"

Margot nodded. "We thought that we could hang out and do a few things together." Except for being lovers, she thought. But she couldn't mention that part.

"Well, there's certainly nothing wrong with socializing with him. Lots of exes in this town do that. It's more common than people think. But I'm curious why you sound so trepidatious. He's not pressuring you, is he?"

"Not at all. It was my idea. But I do have some concerns about Liam. Zeke wants me to introduce them, and I'm afraid that it might confuse Liam to see me hanging around with Zeke."

"Confuse him how? You're a single adoptive mom, making an effort to be friends with your ex-husband. I think that's a healthy approach to divorce and a positive lesson to teach your child. Granted, Zeke hurt you when he walked away. But you were smart enough to get over him."

Smart? Margot would've laughed if she didn't feel so utterly dumb right now. "You're right. I'm probably making a bigger deal out of it than it is. Maybe I'll text Zeke tonight and try to set something up for him and Liam to meet over the weekend." At least then she could quit fretting over it.

Her mother leaned against the counter. "I admire you for being a modern woman and approaching this the way you are. And as much as I disapprove of the way Zeke ended your marriage, I appreciate that he still cares about keeping you safe. You shouldn't have a problem hanging out."

"I'm glad you see it that way." She summoned a hurried smile. "I hope us being friends works in our favor." Far more than she could possibly explain. "But maybe I should get back to the dishes now." She didn't want to talk this to death or slip up and give herself away, revealing that she still had sexual feelings for Zeke.

No matter how hard she tried not to.

Three

On Wednesday afternoon, while Zeke was at his mom's house, he called and checked in with his partner at the office. Although Zeke had started Z-One Security with his share of the money that he and Bailey had inherited from their dad, he hadn't done it alone. He'd recruited Vick Rossi, one of his mom's old bodyguards, to join him.

"How's Eva doing?" Vick asked.

"I don't know," Zeke replied. "She hasn't come downstairs yet." He was in the parlor, waiting for his illustrious mother to join him.

"What about Bailey?" Vick asked.

"She's not here yet, either." The three of them had arranged to visit today, but he was the only one on time. Was this how Margot had felt when she'd showed up at his door and he wasn't there?

"Your mom is probably still putting on her face and

deciding what to wear, and your sister will probably rush in with a messy braid and smudged mascara."

"That sounds about right." Those two women had absolutely nothing in common. Eva was a glamour queen who'd been dubbed the sex kitten of her era, and Bailey was anything but. "You know my family well."

"I cared for them like my own."

"You most certainly did." Vick had protected the Mitchells with his life. He was in his seventies now and had contacts in every sector of law enforcement. He made a damned fine partner for Zeke.

"I'll bet you're really missing your dad on days like this," Vick said.

"That's for sure." Zeke loved his mother and sister, but sometimes their energy drove him crazy. "I'm going to hang up now and pour myself a drink."

"Enjoy it while you can."

"Will do." He ended the call and approached the bar. He chose a single-malt scotch and added a dash of spring water. His dad had taught him that water helped bring out the aroma of the scotch.

As he sipped his drink, he sank into a chair and glanced around the lavish room. His mom favored French furniture, ornamental pieces designed for a king and his court. Or a queen and her court in her case. She definitely lived like a royal. There'd been a throng of housekeepers and cooks and assistants who'd worked here over the years. Some of the most loyal still remained.

Overall, the estate rested on five acres, with an eighteen-bedroom, twenty-four-bathroom main house, a guesthouse, a guardhouse and a ten-car garage. When Zeke was a kid, his favorite part of the mansion had been the game room. He'd spent plenty of time in the pool and spa, too, soaking up the Southern California sun.

He'd hated going out in public with his parents. He'd relied on Vick and the rest of his mom's security team to make those occasions more bearable. Red carpet events used to be his greatest nightmare. His mom would drag him and Bailey to them whenever she'd starred in a PG-rated movie that she thought was age-appropriate for them to see. She'd made a handful of madcap comedies, where she played the dumb blonde. At least those silly things were tolerable. What bothered Bailey the most were the nude magazine spreads. Zeke had learned to let those roll off his back. But since he was a guy, people didn't compare him to Eva or pick him apart, not like they did to Bailey. He'd always felt bad for his sister because of that.

Footsteps echoed on the polished wood floors, signaling that someone was headed toward the parlor. He knew it was his mom, even before he saw her. He recognized the click of her high heels.

He stood to greet her, and she moved forward, reaching out to embrace him. Even as tender as their hug was, he was still careful not to press too hard and wrinkle her outfit. A habit from his youth.

They separated, and he took a moment to analyze her appearance. At sixty-two, she was as shapely as she'd ever been, courtesy of a private trainer and her dedication to yoga. Her platinum hair was still bleached to perfection, and she was still capable of giving smoldering looks to a camera, even if she wasn't required to do that anymore.

Although she'd aged well, she hadn't aged naturally. She got regular Botox treatments. She'd had plenty of little nips and tucks, too. Today she was wearing a silky pink dress that matched her lipstick.

"You look amazing, Mom," he said, feeding her delicate ego. She'd always needed a lot of attention. But she also had a kind and giving heart. She volunteered at women's shelters and donated millions to the cause.

"My handsome and brilliant son." She touched his cheek. "You look so much like your other daddy."

She was referring to his birth father, the stuntman who'd died when Zeke was a baby. But at least he knew his "other" daddy's family. He'd been visiting his paternal grandfather in Samoa since he was a kid. He loved it there.

"Can I fix you a drink?" he asked, taking charge of the bar.

"I'll just have some cranberry juice."

He poured it over ice then handed her the glass. "To the lady of the manor," he said, toasting her with his scotch.

"I'll drink to that." She sipped her juice. "Where is that sister of yours? I thought she'd be here by now."

"You know Bailey. She marches to the beat of her own drum."

"I worry about what a recluse she is."

"She has Margot to keep her company. Those two will always be as thick as thieves." Far thicker than he would've liked.

"So it seems." Eva stood beside the white marble fireplace with intricate scrolls and a curved base, almost as if she was posing next to it, her shoulder resting against the lightly veined mantel. "Have you seen her?"

He finished his scotch. "What? Who?"

"Margot. Have you seen her since you got back?"

"Yes, but we always touch base whenever I come

home. For business and whatnot," he added. The "whatnot" used to be sex. Hot, secret sex. Or almost secret. It still irked him that his sister knew about the affair. She'd even had the gall to tell him how much she disapproved of it. "Margot is supposed to introduce me to her son this weekend." She'd already texted him with the day and time, moving faster than he'd anticipated.

"I haven't met him yet. Bailey says that he's a doll. They're working on a children's book together."

"Yeah. Margot told me about that." Zeke was anxious about meeting Liam, but he sure as hell wasn't going to let it show.

"It's nice that you and Margot are on decent terms. Considering how volatile the end of your marriage was, I never thought you'd speak to each other again."

"We got past that." By tearing each other's clothes off, he thought. "We're trying to be better friends now." *Better* made it sound as if they already were friends, but his mom didn't seem to notice. She wasn't as observant as Bailey.

Speaking of his meddlesome sibling, she finally came dashing around the corner and into the parlor. She wore her ultralong hair in a flyaway braid, just as Vince had predicted. Her mascara wasn't smeared, but that was only because she wasn't wearing any makeup.

"Bonjour, Maman." She greeted their mother in French, using the language in affectionate jest, poking fun at the furniture. When Bailey was little, she'd gotten into trouble for scribbling on a console table in this very room.

A second later, she smiled at Zeke and said, "Hey, big brother."

He raised his eyebrows. "What? No foreign language for me?"

She hugged him instead, taking the opportunity to whisper in his ear. "It's the only running joke I have with Mom."

That was true. Most of her interactions with their mom were strained. "Are you happy now that Margot ended things with me?" he whispered back, chiding her for getting involved in his affair. She was the last person who should've been doling out relationship advice. She'd never been married. Hell, she'd never even had a serious boyfriend.

Bailey pulled away from him before their mother could notice that something was amiss. It was all Zeke could do not to glower at his sister. She grabbed his glass and sniffed it.

"Maybe I should have one of these," she said. "Will you fix it for me?"

Yeah, whatever, he thought. He walked over to the bar.

"Make it a double," she called after him. "No, wait, on second thought, I'll have a ginger ale, a splash of grenadine and two cherries."

He rolled his eyes. She'd just requested a Shirley Temple, her beverage of choice when they were kids. He mixed her mocktail and made his next scotch a double.

After the three of them settled in to chat, Eva said, "Just so you know, I'm scheduled for surgery on the twenty-fourth."

Bailey reacted with a start. "Oh, my goodness, why? What's wrong?"

"Nothing is wrong," their mother quickly replied. "I'm having my implants replaced."

Zeke figured it was something like that. Bailey should've assumed as much, too.

"Really?" his sister asked. "Another boob job?"

"Don't get all testy about it. They're supposed to be replaced every ten years. This time, I'm having them lifted, too."

Bailey sighed. "If you're going to all that trouble, then why don't you just have them removed?"

"Because I'm used to having implants. Besides, at my age, why should I have to compromise? My own aren't nearly as big."

Zeke all but winced. This wasn't a conversation he wanted to be part of. He walked over to a window, letting the women hash it out.

He opened the drapes and gazed out at a picturesque view of the garden maze. The elaborate design had been inspired by the labyrinth of Versailles. It had also been the site of his and Margot's wedding. She'd looked like a princess that day, draped in a beaded gown. She'd even worn a tiara with a veil attached. He'd felt like the luckiest guy in the world, lifting that veil, kissing her, claiming his bride.

And now they weren't even lovers anymore.

Would their friendship prove futile, too? He didn't have a clue what to think. But it wasn't helping, getting wrapped up in that damned maze. He closed the drapes, shutting it out.

He tuned back into the squabble his mother and sister were having. By now, Eva had conned Bailey into staying with her for a couple of days after the surgery, even if she already had a house full of people to look after her. But that was how their disagreements typically went, with Bailey losing the battle. Zeke moved away from the window and rejoined them.

A short time later, their visit ended. Their mother retreated to her suite to relax, and Zeke and Bailey exited the mansion together.

They lingered in the circular driveway. She was at least a foot shorter than him, so it was easy to peer down at her.

"Why do you even bother arguing with Mom?" he asked.

"Someone has to. Besides, it's easier than arguing with you." When he blew out a flustered breath, she said, "Come on now, don't be mad at me over you and Margot. It was her decision to end your affair, not mine."

"Yeah, but you kept encouraging her to do it."

"That's only because I didn't want to see either of you get hurt." She squinted as the sun got in her eyes. "Truthfully, I would've preferred seeing you stay married. But you're the one who destroyed that."

"She destroyed it first." But he wasn't going to stand here and battle with his baby sister over the emotional schematics of why he'd gotten divorced. "I need to go. I have things to do." That was a lie. The rest of his day was free. He just wanted to escape with his emotions intact.

"Okay, but don't be mad at me," she said again.

"I'm not, I guess." Deep down, he knew that she only had his best interest at heart. But that didn't help ease his frustration over Margot. The woman he'd married in a maze, he thought. The ex-wife who still consumed him.

Margot sat next to Liam at the dining room table, watching him create a submarine with one of his Lego sets. He was making an entire world under the sea. He loved the ocean and everything in it. Like Zeke, she thought.

Was that the only interest they had in common?

Probably, she thought. Whatever the case, she hadn't even told Liam that Zeke was visiting today. But she couldn't withhold that information much longer. Zeke would be there within the hour.

"We're having company soon," Margot said.

"We are?" Her son glanced up from his project, his blondish-brown hair falling onto his forehead. He wore it in a simple style, but he had a couple of cowlicks that could make it tough to manage. His eyes were big and brown, so big, he often reminded her of a saucer-eyed anime character.

"Who's coming over?" he asked.

"Bailey's brother," she quickly answered.

His enormous eyes lit up. "Is Bailey coming, too?"

"No, just Zeke."

His shoulders slumped. "Why isn't she coming?"

"She's working today. Besides, I thought it would be nice if you got to meet Zeke on his own. He used to be my husband, but he's also my friend." Or so she hoped.

Liam set his submarine aside. "What if it gets boring with just me and you and him?"

Being bored was the least of her worries. "Then we'll think of something fun to do."

"What kind of stuff is he into?"

"He lives at the beach, so he loves the ocean. He's an accomplished surfer. It's one of his favorite things to do." She gestured at Liam's creation. "He'll probably think that's cool."

He grabbed one of his Lego fish and made it cruise through the air. "Maybe we can go swimming when he's here."

"Sure, why not?" Anything to make this easier. "I'll text him and tell him to bring his trunks. We can eat by the pool."

"What are we having?"

"Zeke is bringing tacos." He'd insisted on providing lunch. "But I'm going to make some banana pudding for dessert." Her son was a bit of a banana freak. His favorite sandwich was peanut butter and banana. Sometimes she even fried them for him.

He smiled. "I can help you make the pudding, Mom."

Her heart went warm. She loved hearing him call her Mom. He'd started saying it as soon as the adoption was finalized. Although Liam didn't remember his birth mother, he knew that she was gone. That much he'd been told.

Margot knew the details, of course. Daisy had been a troubled, drug-addicted teen from an abusive home. At eighteen, she'd gotten pregnant with Liam. She quit doing drugs and tried to be a good mom, but two years later, she started using again and lost her little boy to foster care. When he was four, she died from an accidental overdose. Liam's father had never been in the picture. He was a hookup from a party and someone Daisy never saw again. But that didn't mean that Liam wasn't curious about his birth parents. Just last week, he'd asked Margot if she had any pictures of them. She couldn't help him with his dad. No one knew his identity. But she gave Liam a photograph of Daisy that she'd gotten a while back from his old caseworker, and he seemed thrilled to have it. He kept it tucked away in his room like a treasure.

Z-One Security had the same picture in their files. Margot had provided Zeke's company with information about Liam. They knew everything there was to know about her son. And about her, too, except for the part where she'd been sleeping with Zeke after the divorce.

She texted him and got an immediate reply. He was

totally up for a swim. He included water emojis for effect.

Liam's attention span in the kitchen was short. He helped her slice the bananas, then ran upstairs to change. He was starting to seem excited about Zeke coming over. Or maybe he was just excited about going in the pool.

Margot finished making the pudding and went to her room to slip on her swimsuit. She chose a simple blue bikini with white polka dots. But for now, she covered up with a sundress. She reapplied her lip gloss and fluffed her hair, for whatever that was worth.

She returned to the kitchen and gathered plates, flatware and napkins. After setting the patio table by the pool, she went back inside and waited.

Zeke arrived about ten minutes later with a big bag of food. He was dressed in a pineapple-print shirt, board shorts and flip-flops.

Margot took the bag, while Liam inched forward and stared at the stranger in front of him. For now, they remained in the living room.

"It's nice to meet you," Zeke said, breaking the awkward silence.

"You don't look like you'd be Bailey's brother," Liam replied, still gaping up at him.

Zeke shifted his stance. "I'm her half brother."

"Which half?" the eight-year-old asked.

Zeke glanced at Margot, and they exchanged a smile that made her heart go pitter-pat. She pressed the bag closer to her chest.

"Bailey and I have the same mother," Zeke said to Liam. "But neither of us looks like her. I look like my dad, and Bailey looks like her father."

"I think you look like Aquaman."

"Really?" Zeke bent down to talk to Liam, putting himself at a less intimidating level. "Your mom always told me that if I was green, I would look like the Hulk."

"No." Her son shook his head, quite serious in his assessment. "You're more like Aquaman. Except you don't have long hair and a beard like the guy in the movie. Yours is more like stubble or whatever it's called."

"I don't have his magical trident, either," Zeke said. "But I wish I did."

Liam only nodded. Aquaman was his favorite superhero, and now he seemed starstruck, almost as if Zeke was the real deal. But it was easy to be awed by Zeke. Margot had been that way for years.

"Should we go outside and have our lunch now?" she asked.

"Sure." Zeke moved toward the French doors that led to the backyard and the patio. Liam followed him like a puppy.

When they got to the patio table, Margot unpacked the bag. In addition to the tacos, there were rice and beans, and guacamole and chips.

"What do you guys want to drink?" she asked. "The fridge out here is jammed with sodas and bottled water and juice."

"I'll take a water," Zeke replied.

"Me, too," Liam said, even if he rarely drank water. He normally wanted something sweet. Her kid definitely had a case of idol worship.

They sat down to eat, and Zeke opened a slew of hot sauce containers—the fiery stuff—and doused his tacos. Margot glanced over at Liam, hoping he didn't mimic Zeke again. Luckily, he didn't. Liam would've gagged on something that hot.

The meal was relatively quiet, but things got noisy

in the pool afterward. Liam and Zeke had loads of fun, swimming, splashing and goofing around. Liam was right. Zeke was more Aquaman than Hulk. Liam could've been an Atlantean, too. They both should've been born with fins.

Margot was pleased to see them getting along so well, but deep down, it hurt, too. Zeke would've made a great father, if he'd given their marriage a chance. Only now, she was a single mom watching her son fawn all over her ex.

She decided not to join them in the pool. Instead she sat on the edge of the shallow end, still wearing her sundress and dipping her feet in the water.

"Come in, Mom!" Liam yelled out to her. He and Zeke were playing water basketball, with Zeke lifting Liam up to help him make the shots.

"I'm good where I am."

"Come on!" Liam prodded her again.

She shook her head. "You guys are doing just fine on your own."

"Zeke can make you come in," Liam said. "He's big enough to pull you in the water."

She gazed past Liam and made eye contact with Zeke, cautioning him not to do it.

"I won't pull you in," he said, heeding her silent warning. "But it would be nice if you'd join us."

"*Please*." Liam begged.

"All right." He deserved a mom who was willing to be part of the fun. Besides, she was supposed to be establishing a friendship with Zeke, not sitting around being tormented by him. "I have to put sunscreen on first."

She walked over to the table, where the lotion was. Then, without a moment's notice, Zeke emerged from the pool with water dripping from his body and puddling at his feet.

"What are you doing?" she asked, under her breath.

"I'm going to help you with the sunscreen."

"I can do it myself."

"You can't get your back by yourself. And that's the part of you that sometimes burns the worst."

So much for not being tormented. Just being near him was giving her goose bumps. She handed him the lotion and peeled off her sundress, holding her breath, anticipating his touch.

Thank goodness Liam wasn't watching. He paddled around the basketball hoop, cheering for himself and pretending to be an NBA star.

As Margot turned to face the pool, Zeke moved to stand behind her. She heard him opening the bottle and squeezing the lotion into his hands, warming it up.

He started at her shoulders and worked his way down, applying the sunscreen in circular motions.

"Just making sure I don't miss a spot," he said.

She couldn't find the words to respond. Every nerve ending in her body came alive, tingling wherever he touched. He went all the way down to her tailbone, and she nearly moaned.

Liam finally looked over at them. "Hurry up, you guys!"

"Almost done," Zeke called back, fumbling just a bit.

Margot felt his fingers slip on her skin, as if he'd just gotten caught doing something horribly forbidden. Which, in a sense, he had. They both knew better.

He came around to hand her the bottle, and they gazed uncomfortably at each other. "I'll let you finish up," he said.

Yes, she would do the rest of her body. But the damage of him touching her had already been done, the intimacy giving rise to carnal urges she couldn't afford to indulge.

He cleared his throat. "I better get back to Liam."

She nodded, wondering how she was going to survive Zeke's company for the rest of the afternoon. One thing was for sure: she was never going to let him put his hands on her like that again.

He dived into the pool, making a huge splash and getting the ball away from Liam. Her son laughed, and they resumed their game.

Margot slathered on the rest of the sunscreen, putting it everywhere she could reach, protecting herself from the sun. If only there was a lotion that could protect her from Zeke and the scorching heat he incited.

Four

Zeke spent the next hour stealing glances at Margot while she swam and splashed and got beautifully wet. Being around her was painful. But he thrived on it, too. His fingers still tingled from where he'd touched her.

By now they were having races, paddling from one end of the pool to the other on inflatable floats. He'd won two rounds until Margot and Liam cheated and ganged up on him, pushing him straight off his alligator-shaped float.

It was weird, but somewhere in his warped mind, it almost felt as if he and Margot were married again and Liam was their kid. Yet thinking along those lines was ludicrous. Goofing around in the pool with her son didn't make them anything even remotely close to being a family. Zeke was just caught up in the moment, getting dragged into Margot's seductive clutches.

Would he ever get over his desire for her? The fact

that neither of them had been with anyone else after the divorce seemed proof that they were both still a bit too tied up with each other.

"Can we have our dessert now?" Liam asked his mom.

"Oh, yes, absolutely." She paddled to the side of the pool on her sparkly mermaid float. Zeke couldn't stop himself from watching her.

She glanced over at him. "Do you want some pudding?"

What he wanted was to eat her alive. He could only imagine how good she would taste.

"Yeah, sure," he said, fighting a frown. "Pudding."

She grabbed a towel and dried off. "I'll bring it to the table."

While she went into the house, he climbed out of the pool and got a canned iced tea from the beverage fridge, needing to cool his libido. He flipped the top and chugged it down, finishing it in two seconds flat.

Liam appeared at his elbow, and he handed him a can, too. Margot's son was a cute little guy, chasing Zeke around like a mini-me. Margot used to chase him around when she was a teenager, but that had been a whole other thing.

She returned, carrying a tray with the pudding. They served themselves, eating out of clear-plastic bowls.

"How long were you guys married?" Liam asked suddenly.

Zeke hadn't expected this line of questioning. Clearly, neither had Margot; she paused midbite. But maybe they should've been better prepared.

A moment later, she replied, "We were married for three years, but we knew each other a long time before that."

Liam had a perplexed expression. "Then how come you got divorced?"

"Sometimes people are better off being friends."

She glanced at Zeke, and he nodded, hoping her statement was true. For now, the friendship angle was still new.

Liam accepted her answer, only to turn to Zeke and ask, "What's it like to own a security company?"

He was surprised but thankful for the change of subject. "I like keeping my clients safe, so it feels good to me. Sometimes I work directly as their bodyguard, but that part isn't always as exciting as it sounds. I spend a lot of time just driving them around, accompanying them on their day-to-day activities."

Young Liam thought about it for a second, then asked, "Have you ever been my mom's bodyguard?"

"No, I haven't." But there were plenty of agents in his company who were available to her. Nonetheless, she used to say that she thought his bodyguard persona was hot. Too bad he didn't feel the same way about her being a celebrity, even if she did look beautiful in the shimmery gowns she sometimes wore.

Margot shifted in her chair, and Zeke glanced over at her, feeling a sudden rush of heat. Or was it discomfort? He barely knew the difference anymore.

Either way, he broke the tension by changing the subject yet again. He said to Liam, "You're a really good swimmer. Who taught you to swim like that?"

"One of my old foster moms. She was a swim instructor. She gave lessons at her house. But the pool had a big fence around it so none of the little kids would fall in." The boy rocked in his seat. "Mom said that you like to surf. I've never tried it. But I want to someday."

"I started bodyboarding when I was around your

age. That's easier than surfing at first." Zeke's dad used to take him to the beach. His mom rarely went along, unless they were on a private holiday in a secluded location, where they could avoid the public and the paparazzi. "I can teach you to bodyboard if you're interested. We can do it at my house." Because the invitation slipped out before he could run it by Margot, he added, "Your mom can be there, too, of course."

"That would be so much fun!" Liam turned to his mother and implored her. "Can we go to his house and do that? Can we, please?"

She calmly replied, "Yes, but we'll have to arrange a time when it's convenient for all of us. We can't rush into it."

"Okay!" In spite of her levelheaded tone, her son was still excited. "Can I go back in the pool now? I want to pretend that I'm bodyboarding."

"Go ahead." She smiled, teasing him. "You can use the mermaid float."

"Very funny." He got up and grabbed the dolphin he'd been riding earlier. Then he changed his mind and went for Zeke's alligator.

While Liam was off doing his thing, Margot tucked her hair behind her ears, and Zeke noticed how enticing it looked, curling around her face. It was still damp from the pool.

"I'm sorry if I put you on the spot about the bodyboarding lessons," he said. "I should've waited and talked to you about it before I said anything."

"It's okay. It'll be nice for him to learn a new sport." She fussed with her hair again. "He wasn't too thrilled about you coming over at first. He was worried about being bored. But you're probably the most exciting person he's ever met."

"It's been an exciting day. Lots of activity." More than Zeke had even bargained for.

Margot's phone signaled that she'd received a text, and she glanced at the notification. "Will you give me a second?" After she read the message, she said, "It was my assistant reminding me about a charity ball next Saturday that I agreed to attend. She's going to email me the tickets. It's a dinner and auction with an Old Hollywood theme, but I completely forgot about it." She heaved a sigh. "Between finalizing Liam's adoption and you coming back to town, I got sidetracked, I guess."

"You still have time to prepare for it." With her resources, she could pull it off. "You've always loved that sort of thing." And he'd always detested it, serving as yet another reminder of why they didn't belong together.

"I know, but now I have to rush to find someone to go with me. I can't ask Bailey because she's attending a writers' retreat that weekend. Maybe I'll call Jordan and see if he's available."

"Jordan?"

She nodded. "Jordan Nichols. You remember him, don't you?"

"The guy from your old acting workshops?" He didn't like the sound of that. He'd always suspected that Jordan had a thing for her back in the day. Not that he should concern himself with it now. Yet it still bugged him. "When's the last time you saw him?"

"He made a guest appearance on my show last season, and we've had coffee a few times since then. He just got cast in a new spy thriller."

Zeke didn't care if Jordan was going to be the next James Bond. Suddenly he was jealous of him again. "And now you're going to invite him on a fancy date?"

She shook her head. "It wouldn't be a date. He and I are just friends."

Feeling much too impulsive, he said, "If that's the case, then I can go with you as a friend."

"You? Mingling with my crowd?" She gaped at him. "You hate industry parties. You never attended anything with me when we were together, so why would you do it now?"

It was better than Jordan going with her. He didn't trust that dude not to turn it into a date. "What's the point of us being friends if we don't step out of our comfort zone?"

"Are you sure you're ready to step that far out of it?"

"I know how to behave in that scene. Some of the guests might even be Z-One clients."

"That's true." She appeared to be mulling it over. "But you've always made a point of staying in the background, and now you're offering to be front and center with me."

"I used to attend red carpets with my mom. Big major events. This can't be any worse than that."

"Okay. Fine. You can come with me," she reluctantly agreed. "But it'd better not turn into a disaster."

"Quit worrying. I already told you that I can handle it." Or he hoped that he could. If not, he was going to be trapped in one of the longest nights of his life.

Margot glanced around her bedroom, with its eclectic decor of chrome and glass and painted woods. How many times had she hooked up with Zeke here?

Too many, she thought.

Sometimes they never even made it to the bed. They would just go at it wherever they stood, bumping into the furniture and knocking things over. No finesse. Only urgency and lust.

She frowned at the vintage-inspired gowns her stylist had sent over, bunched together on a portable rolling rack. The ball was only four days away, and she was struggling with what to wear. At least Bailey was helping her decide. It was still weird, though, knowing that she was bringing Zeke.

Bailey reached for a sparkly green number loaded with sequins. "This color would look good on you."

"It's too flashy." Margot wasn't drawn to it, at least not for this occasion. "Do you think I'm making a mistake?"

"By not wearing something flashy?"

"No. By letting your brother escort me."

"That's tough to say. It could strengthen your friendship or it could backfire and seem like a date. Fine dining, drinking, dancing..."

Margot studied a purple dress with a plunging neckline. She definitely wasn't wearing that. "I never said that I was going to dance with him." She remembered how beautifully they'd glided across the floor together at their wedding reception, but that wasn't something she should be rehashing. Memories of their wedding always left her pained. She'd loved him so much back then, she'd thought they were going to be together forever.

Margot scowled at the dresses again. "Normally I enjoy doing this. But I just can't seem to concentrate today."

"I know how you feel. I have a lot on my plate, too. The day after I return from my retreat is Mom's surgery."

"It's nice that you agreed to help look after her."

"What was I thinking, letting her talk me into that?" Bailey shook her head, making her antenna-style ponytail swish. "I must be crazy."

"You are, but that's why I love you."

"I love you, too. But you need to get your rear in gear and choose a dress. At this rate, you'll be going in the nude."

"That's all I need, to be naked in front of your brother after ending my affair with him."

"That would be a bit of an issue. Maybe you should wear a really ugly gown to throw him off your scent. The yellow monstrosity with the feathers ought to do the trick."

Margot laughed. "I'll look like a bird."

"No kidding. I mean, seriously, did your stylist include that as a joke?" Bailey flapped her arms and made clucking sounds. "Instead of ballroom dances, you can do the funky chicken."

"I won't be dancing at all, remember?" Margot chose three gowns that held possibility, hanging them side by side. "Hopefully one of these will do." She proceeded to strip down and try on the first dress, a flirty silhouette with a snug bodice and full skirt.

"Do you need help with the zipper?" Bailey asked.

"No. I got it." It closed on the side, under her arm. But the dang thing was still too tight. She could barely breathe, and one thing she needed to do when she was around Zeke was breathe.

The second gown had too much fabric. It overwhelmed her, bunching in places it shouldn't.

And the third one...

"Now we're getting somewhere." Bailey approached her. "That looks amazing on you."

Margot stood in front of the cheval mirror, angling

it to get a better view. The gold satin dress hugged her waist and flowed at the hemline, with one long, lean slit that showcased her legs. It was definitely flattering. "Hair up or down?" She held it up, then dropped it back down.

"I don't know. You'll have to work that out with your hair person. Who are you going to use on such short notice?"

"I already booked Martell Johnson. He's new, but he's good. He's going to do my makeup, too."

"Is he coming to the house?"

"Yes. I wanted to skip the salon."

"I'm always up for skipping the salon. God, I hate those gossipy places." Bailey stood behind her and met her eye in the mirror. "What about your jewelry and shoes and all that?"

"Maybe I can wear emerald earrings. I have a pair that dangle a bit. I also have gold pumps and a gold evening bag I can try, as long as the shades match."

"You'll figure it out." Bailey moved away from the mirror. "You always put yourself together so well. I wonder what type of outfit would be good for our high school reunion."

Margot shrugged. "Who cares? We're not going anyway."

"I know we agreed to skip it, but I've actually been thinking about going."

"Seriously?" Margot couldn't imagine a worse idea. It had been fifteen years since they'd graduated, since that particular hell had ended. They'd both been bullied something fierce in high school. The other kids picked on Bailey because she was the awkward daughter of a sex symbol, and they'd made fun of Margot because they thought the sassy character she'd played on TV was stupid. Prior to the cancellation of her show, she'd been tutored on set, and that didn't help her social skills, either. But Bailey had experienced even more trouble. She used to stutter when she got nervous. Sometimes she still did. "What made you change your mind?"

"I guess I want to prove to myself and everyone else that I've changed. That I'm stronger now than I was back then. But I have some time to think about it. The reunion is still four months away."

"It sounds daunting to me. But I understand where you're coming from, having something to prove." Margot had done her fair share of touting her strengths, of showing the world that she'd changed. But attending their reunion? "You're braver than I am."

"I guess we'll see. I haven't decided for sure." Bailey sat on the edge of the bed. "I wonder if Wade Butler will be there."

"Now, there's a blast from the past." Wade had been a fellow student, an oddly quiet computer nerd who'd gotten bullied, too. He rarely interacted with anyone, but he still came to Bailey's defense whenever he saw someone picking on her. "He was your hero."

Zeke's sister sighed. "I really liked him, despite how withdrawn he was. I think he liked me, too, but he never asked me out or did anything about it."

"It's probably just as well, with how things turned out for him back then." At the end of their senior year, Wade had gone to prison for hacking into the FBI and solving some of their cyber division crimes. But not before he'd bragged about it online under the white-hat alias he'd created.

"He's a big-time tech billionaire now."

"He is?" Margot hadn't been aware of his progression.

Bailey nodded. "I saw a feature on him in *Entrepre-*

neur. He lives in San Francisco. It's probably dumb to think that he might go to the reunion."

"It's not dumb." To Margot, it made sense. "He might want to prove himself to the jerks who bullied him, too."

"I think he's already proven it. Even the FBI forgave him and started using him as a consultant. He's a philanthropist now, too. He does all sorts of good in the world. The article I read about him was impressive."

"Maybe so, but he's still an ex-con, and that might weigh on him. They arrested him at school, right after first period, hauling him away in handcuffs. That's not something he's likely to forget."

"Remember the long black coat he used to wear and those big scruffy combat boots? I always thought he seemed more like a goth guy than a computer nerd. He looks pretty stylish now, in the pictures I saw of him, anyway."

"I guess you'll find out how much he's changed if you attend the reunion and if he's there, too."

Bailey shrugged. "Maybe I'm fooling myself into thinking I should go. As much as I like to think that I've changed, I'm probably still a dork."

Margot smiled. "If you're still a dork, then so am I."

"A dork who's going to a ball with my brother."

"At least I'll be wearing a fabulous dress." Margot made light of her situation. But deep down, she was getting butterflies about seeing Zeke again. And in spite of her earlier claim, she actually wanted to dance with him.

Far closer than she should.

Zeke stood on Margot's porch landing, dressed in a black tux with a white limo waiting on the street. He'd yet to ring the bell. Instead, he asked himself what he was doing, taking her to a charity ball.

He'd been worried about her bringing another guy, he reminded himself. That was the only reason he'd jumped into this glitzy ordeal.

He finally rang the doorbell, not wanting to get caught too long on camera, just standing here. Margot's mom, June, answered it.

She flashed an appreciative smile. "Well, check you out. My daughter's security man. Or should I call you her BFF now?"

He laughed a little. "I think my sister would have something to say about that."

He'd always appreciated June and her pragmatic nature. She'd never told him off about the divorce, even if she didn't agree with his reasoning.

She invited him inside, and as soon as he entered the house, Liam came skidding around the corner, dressed in a pair of baggy pajamas and eating a cookie.

"Hey, Zeke! Guess what? Grandma baked these." He held up his half-eaten treat. "Do you want one? They're oatmeal raisin."

"No, thanks. I'll be having dinner at the party I'm going to with your mom." He glanced around. "Where is she?" He didn't see Margot anywhere.

"She's in her room," the boy answered. "The guy who does her hair and makeup just left, so she's probably getting dressed now. Right, Grandma?" He turned toward June.

"That's right." She looked at Zeke and said, "You might as well have a seat and wait." She gestured to the living room.

"Sure thing." He adjusted his waistcoat and settled into a spot on the sofa.

Liam plopped down on the floor in front of him, and June took a wingback chair by a window. The kid ate more of his cookie, dropping crumbs onto the ornamental area rug. He was naturally messy, like Margot. Zeke suspected her bedroom was in full-blown disarray about now. She tended to toss things all over the place when she got ready to go out.

About five minutes later, she came sweeping down the staircase, like a goddess in gold. Zeke stood to watch her entrance. Liam and June hopped up, too.

Her gown shimmered in the light, hugging her long, lean body. Her hair tumbled across one shoulder in thick, shiny waves, reminiscent of Veronica Lake or Jessica Rabbit or whomever the style had been patterned after. Either way, it was hot. But elegant, too. Emeralds winked glamorously at her ears.

"You're the prettiest mom ever," Liam said, fussing excitedly over the woman who'd adopted him.

To Zeke, she was the prettiest damned ex-lover ever. He struggled to keep his eyes off her.

"You do look gorgeous," he said. "Really stunning."

"Thank you, both of you." She curtsied to her son, then met Zeke's gaze for a highly charged moment. "You look incredible, too."

He shrugged. By now, he was starting to feel like an anxious teenager on a fussy prom date with a girl who only wanted to be his friend.

June moved forward and said to her daughter, "You're an absolute vision. I love what Martell did with your hair and makeup."

"It fits the theme." Margot batted her fake lashes. "Theatrical eyes and full lips."

Lust-tinged lips, Zeke thought. Red-hot and passionate. But this wasn't the night for kissing them. "Are you ready to head out?" he asked. He wanted to get this show on the road. Or better yet, skip it altogether.

She nodded and hugged Liam goodbye, pulling him tight against her. She didn't seem concerned about him getting cookie crumbs on her dress. Luckily, he managed not to. Her gown remained as sleek and sexy as when she'd first glided down the stairs.

As soon as Zeke and Margot were outside, he took a cleansing breath. Yet it barely made a dent in his anxiety.

He walked her to the limo, and their driver opened the door so she could climb into the car. Zeke followed her into the back seat, and once they were on their way, he closed the privacy panel and opened the moonroof. The ball was being held at a nearby hotel, so they didn't have far to go. But now that it was just the two of them, they both fell silent.

He searched for something to say, but all he could come up with was, "Do you want a drink?" The limo had a stocked bar.

She shook her head. "I'll have a cocktail when we get there."

"Yeah, me, too." Again, more silence. He glanced out the window. "Well, this is awkward. Us being so quiet."

"I can pick a fight if you think it'll help."

"Smart aleck." He relaxed a bit, losing interest in the window and turning back toward her. "What do you want to fight about?"

"Oh, I don't know. How about the way you were staring at me back at the house? It's a good thing my mom didn't catch you drooling over me."

He scoffed. "I wasn't drooling." He paused and shifted, the leather seat creaking below his butt. "Well, maybe I was a little. Your lipstick is sexy." He could still feel the heat of how kissable it made her look. "You smell good, too." He leaned closer, getting a sultry waft of her perfume; he detected a mixture of night-blooming jasmine mingled with cedar or cypress or something deliciously woodsy. He couldn't remember the brand, but she'd worn it in the past. He recognized the scent. "Will you dance with me tonight? We haven't danced together in a really long time."

She fidgeted with the slim gold chain on her glittery bag. "I already told myself that I wasn't going to. That it wasn't a good idea, even if I wanted to. But ask me again after I've had a cocktail or two."

"You need liquid courage to dance with an old friend?"

She met his gaze, staring straight at him. He stared back at her, too. If their affair hadn't ended, he would be sliding his hand along the slit in her dress, reaching up to cop a sweet feel of her panties. Then again, if this had been happening during their affair, she probably wouldn't even be wearing them.

"You're not an old friend," she said.

"A new one, then." He moved away from her, pulling back to modify his position. He'd already been leaning too close. "I'll do what you said and ask you to dance later." He would allow her to build up the courage she needed. He could probably use an alcohol-infused boost, too.

Or maybe he'd come to his senses and not dance with her at all.

Five

The ballroom shimmered in black and white with touches of red, the Old Hollywood theme evident in its decor. The nameplates on the tables were shaped like clapper boards, and brightly painted stars embellished the floors. Popcorn stands added bits of whimsy, surrounded by movie reel confetti. Champagne towers were everywhere. The guests milled around during the cocktail hour, checking out the memorabilia up for silent auction.

In this day and age most of the bigger auctions involved entering the bids on handheld digital devices, but this was being done the old-time way where bids were written on sheets of paper.

As Margot sipped her champagne, she tried not to worry about the rest of the evening that was still to come. Dinner would be served by a waitstaff in vintage uniforms, and during dessert—something decadent, no doubt—the dance floor would open up with a live band playing music from the golden age of Hollywood.

She glanced over at Zeke. He was handling himself quite well, drinking scotch and water and chatting with Lenny Newberg, a prominent director who was at least twice his age.

When that conversation ended, Zeke returned to Margot's side, and they stood in front of a glass display containing a prop from a 1930s horror film.

"What's up with Lenny?" she asked.

"He's an old acquaintance of my mom's. He knew I was her son and asked me to give her his regards. He belonged to the same golf club as my dad, too. I gave him my contact information and reminded him that I was in security and that he could call Z-One if he ever needed me."

"It's good that you're networking."

"The potential for new clients is endless."

"Have you come across any of your current clients?"

"Yes, and they seemed surprised to see me in this capacity as a guest. But it stands to reason that they would be. Normally I'd be wearing an earpiece and standing in the back of the room, instead of attending the party with a drink in my hand."

"I'm glad you came with me."

"Are you?" he asked, a bit roughly.

"Yes, I am." She thought he was the most compelling man at the ball. But he was making her nervous, too, with how big and strong and serious he was.

He turned to study a colorful brooch once owned by Ann Sheridan. "Are you going to bid on anything?"

"I was actually thinking about bidding on that brooch. My mom always said that I reminded her of Ann Sheridan." She gestured to a cardboard cutout of the actress next to the display. "You can't tell by that photograph, but she was a redhead, too."

He made a curious expression. "I'm not familiar with her work. What types of roles did she play?"

"She could be sweet or sultry. A girl next door or a femme fatale."

Zeke released an audible breath, the chandelier above them casting a film noir glow. "You're definitely like that, too. Sometimes I think those qualities in you were my downfall."

Margot got a racy chill. He was gazing at her with memories of passions from the past in his eyes.

"I'll bid on the brooch for you," he said.

She shook her head. "You don't have to. I can do it myself."

"No, let me. Then if I win the bid, I can give you the brooch as a gift. And if I don't, then it'll just be one more uncertain thing about this night."

She blinked. "Uncertain?"

"I still don't know if you're going to dance with me, or if I should even pursue it, regardless of how many drinks either of us have."

Her pulse pounded at her throat. "My champagne glass is still half-full. Or half-empty, depending on one's perspective." She didn't know which way she was leaning.

He wrote down a bid for the brooch. There didn't appear to be anything she could do to stop him, other than bid against him. But that would only create an unnecessary competition.

"I'll keep checking back before it closes and increase my bid if I have to," he said. "I'm going to try my damnedest to get it." He paused. "It's for a good cause."

Did he mean the charity? Or was *she* the cause he

was referring to? Margot glanced away, struck by his impact on her. Trying to distract herself, she said, "Maybe I'll bid on some items for my mom."

Going up and down the aisles, she scoped out five different things. If she won them all, her mom would have a sizable bounty. After she placed the last bid, she and Zeke returned to the party.

They wandered around together, stopping to talk to other guests. Mostly, it was Margot who embarked on those conversations. Zeke had gone quiet. Would he ask her to dance later? Or would he let it go? She couldn't tell by his behavior.

As the cocktail hour came to a close, they proceeded to their table, but all she could think about was the uncertainty of that dance and how it would feel to have his body pressed against hers.

The meal was exceptional. Zeke chose the steak and seafood platter, and Margot went for the vegan option even though she wasn't vegan. He never knew what to expect from her. She kept him guessing.

Some of her castmates from *The Grown-up Years* were there, sitting at their table. By now, they'd gotten the gist that he and Margot had become friendly exes. But they didn't know that he still had the hots for her. As always, Zeke's desire for Margot ran rampant. He had to stop himself from staring at her while she ate.

She chatted with the female news anchor sitting on the other side of her. Mostly they talked about their children, showing off pictures from their phones. The topic was foreign to Zeke. He couldn't exactly chime in. He'd always been the big silent type, anyway. It sounded like a cliché, but it suited him, especially in his line of work.

Would Margot have been better off marrying another

actor? And what about Zeke? What type of woman should he be with? When he'd fallen for Margot, she'd seemed perfect for him. But there was nothing perfect about the way it turned out. Even this ball didn't make sense. He shouldn't be here with her. He should've just let Jordan What's-His-Face take her.

By the time Zeke finished his dinner, he was frowning. He excused himself to check on the brooch.

He wandered over to the auction area and saw that he needed to increase his bid. If he wasn't so pigheaded, he would let someone else win it. Yet he was determined to acquire it for Margot. The last piece of jewelry he'd given her was the diamond-studded wedding band he'd placed on her finger, which she no longer had cause to wear. So why should this bauble matter?

Because it represented her in a way that made him ache, he thought. Her innocence. Her wildness. Everything that made him crave her.

He cursed under his breath and raised his bid, almost as if he was raising the stakes on his feelings for her.

He returned to the table and resumed his seat next to Margot. She was indulging in the dessert that had just been served: a lavishly frosted black forest cake with cherry filling.

"This is delicious," she said.

"I can tell." He thought she looked downright orgasmic, going after another bite.

"Are you going to eat yours?" she asked.

"Maybe just a little." He sank his fork into his cake, and she watched him taste it.

Damn, it was good. Thick and gooey and bursting with flavor. He ate a bit more. He'd always had a sweet tooth that he struggled to contain. But he worked off the calories in the gym. Staying fit was part of his lifestyle.

A waiter came by, offering coffee, tea or port. Zeke and Margot both chose the wine. Soon after, the band took the stage and opened with, "I'll Never Smile Again," a song Frank Sinatra had crooned in his youth with the Tommy Dorsey Orchestra. Zeke's dad had been a Sinatra fan, so he'd heard it before.

As the tune continued, Zeke sipped his port, letting it warm him from the inside out. The next song was equally slow and melodic. He didn't recognize it, but he appreciated the soft sound.

People got up to dance, swaying to the old-fashioned beat. Was Margot waiting to see if he would make his move? Or would she prefer that he didn't? There was only one way to find out.

"Have you had enough liquid courage to dance with me?" he asked.

She hastily replied, "I never finished my champagne from before, and I've only had a few sips of this." She fingered the stem of her glass. "I'm not impaired."

"Neither am I." He was on his second unfinished drink of the night, too. "Do you plan on getting tipsy later?"

"Probably not. What about you?"

"I'd rather keep my wits about me." He stared longingly at her mouth. "But I think we should dance together, regardless. Then we won't have to keep obsessing about it."

"Maybe you're right." Her voice turned breathy. "But you can't kiss me when we go out there. A friend wouldn't kiss a friend."

"I never said anything about kissing you."

"No, but you look like you want to."

He quit staring at her mouth. "I'm not going to try anything. I'll be the kind of friend you need." Someone she could trust, someone who would keep his yearnings in check. "I won't take advantage of you."

"I won't do that to you, either. No flirting. No encouragement." She removed her napkin from her lap, folding it neatly beside her dessert plate. Was she giving herself time to calm her nerves, preparing to let him hold her?

He knew the feeling. But he stood and offered her a hand, escorting her onto the dance floor.

Margot swayed in Zeke's arms, lost in an attraction that she wished would go away. He'd promised that he wouldn't kiss her, and she believed him. But was she as trustworthy as he was? Would she stop herself from enticing him?

A part of her wanted to seduce him, to charm him back into bed. But she needed to respect her own boundaries.

She'd never danced to old songs like this before, and now that she was in the midst of it, she imagined that she and Zeke were being swept away to another era. Would life have been simpler for them then? Somehow, she doubted it. The same problems that existed between them now probably would've surfaced in those days, too. When it came to romance, the world was a complicated place.

She lifted her chin. Their faces were close enough to kiss, to do exactly what they'd agreed not to do.

Could he tell what she was thinking? Did he know how badly she wanted to taste him? Would it cause a scene if they kissed here? This wasn't a heavily publicized event, but it wasn't completely private, either. Photographs were permitted.

Margot leaned closer into him, making the dance

more intimate. The only barrier between them was her shiny little evening bag, draped across her body and resting at her hip. Zeke had taught her to never leave her belongings unattended.

He met her gaze, and her imagination took flight. Was he still bewitched by her lipstick? She hadn't re-applied it, but the formula had staying power. She suspected that her lips were still a wild shade of red, much like the cherry filling in the dessert they'd eaten.

Everything they did together tonight seemed sexual, every second of every moment. Heaven help her, but she missed their affair. The erotic feeling of having him inside her.

She pulled back. "I think I need some air."

"Do you want to go outside for a bit?"

"Please." She was desperate to cut and run. But it was her own fault for wanting what she shouldn't have.

He led her to the courtyard attached to the ballroom, and they stood off by themselves. Although the temperature was mild, Margot felt a chill. Zeke removed his jacket and gave it to her, clearly aware of her shiver.

"Thank you." His jacket was big on her, but it made her feel safe. Which was weird, considering how threatened she was by her attraction to him.

"Are you okay now?" he asked.

"Yes." She cuffed the sleeves of his jacket, rolling them up several times, so she didn't look like a scarecrow. "It's pretty out there." On the other side of the courtyard was a garden surrounded by twinkling lights. "Lots of flowers."

He nodded. "From what I recall, carnations were always your favorite. Do you see any of those?"

"I can't tell from here." From her vantage point, all she could see were some tall leafy blooms. Larkspur, maybe. "But you're right about carnations being my favorite. They're not fancy or exotic. But they're hardy, and that's what I like about them."

"The garden at my mom's always reminds me of our wedding. That damned maze." He frowned into the night. "Sorry, I shouldn't have brought that up."

"It's all right. We can't pretend we don't have a past or that reminders don't come up. Being honest with each other is probably the only way to get comfortable with being friends."

"Then honestly, us dancing together was a mistake. It just made me miss our affair."

"I know. Me, too." She couldn't deny that she'd had the same reaction. "But maybe in time, things like that won't matter anymore."

"I hope so." He quit frowning. "It's nice talking to you like this."

She was calmer now, too. "You know what makes it easier? That neither of us ever says that we miss being married. We only ever say that we miss the affair."

He tugged a hand through his hair. "The affair was less painful. But I did get a family-type feeling when I was in the pool with you and Liam. It almost seemed like you and I were still together and Liam was ours. But it wasn't as big a deal as it sounds. That feeling only lasted for a second."

She could do little more than stare at him. "But why would you even get a feeling like that?"

"I don't know. I think I was just caught up in the moment. But I'm not under any delusions about us being a family. We're divorced, Margot, and nothing is going to change that."

That was true. Their marriage was over, and she wasn't going to worry about him getting caught up in one little moment. "Thank you for telling me about your feelings in the pool. With the way we're opening up to each other, we might actually be on our way to becoming genuine friends."

A slight smile appeared on his face. "I really want our conversations to get easier."

"Me, too." She smiled back, grateful that they'd come this far without imploding. "What happened with the brooch?"

"I increased my bid, but I should probably check on it again. The bidding is supposed to close at ten." He glanced at the Rolex on his wrist, the classic timepiece perfectly complementing his formal wear. "That only gives me about five more minutes. I can check on your stuff, too."

"Okay. But you don't have to increase my bids. I'll take my chances with what I offered."

He dashed off, and she stayed in the courtyard, gazing across the fence at the garden. It wasn't anywhere near as elaborate as the location where she and Zeke had gotten married. His mother had spent a fortune replicating the labyrinth of Versailles, and Margot had been thrilled when Eva had suggested using it for the ceremony. It had seemed so magical at the time, a storybook wedding for a dreamy bride. The honeymoon had been equally spectacular. They'd gone to Samoa, traveling throughout the islands, the tropical air caressing their naked bodies at night. But that wasn't something she should be thinking about. Even as dazzling as everything had been in the beginning, their life together hadn't been a fairy tale.

Zeke returned shortly. He approached her and said, "I won the brooch. You only nabbed one of your items. The autographed still from *Citizen Kane*."

"That'll make my mom happy. She loved that movie."

"They said that we can pick up our stuff before we leave tonight."

"When do you think we should go?"

"That's up to you. This is your scene, not mine."

She nodded. The ballroom was filled with her crowd. The people he knew were either Z-One clients or associates of his mother's. Not anyone he would typically socialize with. "Maybe we can stay for a bit longer." She wasn't ready to leave just yet. "I'm enjoying the night air."

"You don't mind standing, do you?" He glanced around. "All of the benches out here are taken."

"I'm fine. I like looking at the flowers." She noticed that other guests were strolling the garden path, carrying their after-dinner drinks with them. "It's soothing."

"This is going to sound like a stupid question, but did your wedding bouquet have carnations in it? I can't remember what it looked like."

She remembered, all too well. "It was pink carnations, white roses and baby's breath. Your boutonniere was a rose."

"I was so excited that day."

"Me, too. But things didn't turn out the way we planned." Far from it, she thought. "I still have our wedding album, though. I stored it in the garage."

"I'm surprised you didn't throw it away."

"I never toss things out. That's probably part of why you think I'm so messy. Me and my clutter."

"I shouldn't have criticized you for that." He reached out to skim her hand with his. "Did you keep anything else from that day?"

"I have everything." Her dress and veil, her bouquet, her engagement ring, her wedding band. She could've sold those, she supposed. The princess-cut diamond on the engagement ring was huge. "I'm a glutton for punishment."

"We both are or we wouldn't have started sleeping together. The ink on the divorce papers was barely dry, and there we were, fighting and fu—"

He didn't finish his statement, but she knew what word he was going to use. "We weren't thinking clearly then." Yet they'd hooked up whenever they could, keeping it going for three excruciating years.

He didn't respond. She turned silent, too. The breeze had picked up, making her even more attached to his jacket.

"Do you want to go for a walk in the garden?" he asked. "The pathways appear to be well lit."

"Sure. A walk would be nice."

They left the courtyard and entered the garden through an open gate, her stilettos echoing on the concrete. They didn't talk. They just followed the trail they were on, plants swirling around them.

Finally, they stopped near a weeping willow bursting with fairy lights and took a moment to admire it. With the way its branches draped, it looked downright haunting.

"When am I going to see you again after this?" Zeke asked, drawing her attention away from the eerie tree.

"You want to plan our next get-together?"

"Isn't that what friends do?"

"How about next Saturday? You could give Liam his first bodyboarding lesson." She knew how happy that would make her son. And if he was happy, so was she.

"That works for me." Zeke moved closer to her, making room for another couple headed toward them from the other direction.

Margot had to move closer to him, too, in order to let the other man and woman pass by. They all exchanged pleasantries. But now the walkway seemed too narrow.

One little misstep, and she could easily get locked in Zeke's arms. Her pulse jumped, an urgent desire washing over her. If only she could kiss him, just once, to curb the craving. Except that once would never be enough.

"Maybe we should head back now," she said.

He agreed, and they followed the other couple to the courtyard, keeping a polite distance behind them.

Once they were inside the ballroom, they headed over to the auctioneers to collect their goods, which had been placed in charity-themed gift bags for easy carrying. After that, Margot sought out the other cast members of her show to let them know she was leaving, even though she'd barely spent any time with them.

The limo ride was quiet. Zeke leaned back in his seat, and Margot took possession of the bags. They arrived at her house without incident, except for the turmoil in her mind. She was still thinking about the kiss that wasn't going to happen.

He walked her to the door, and she removed his jacket and returned it to him.

"Thanks for going with me," she said. "And thank you for the brooch."

"Sure. Anytime. I'll see you next week. I'll get Liam a board and a wetsuit, plus the other gear he needs. Just text me his height, weight and measurements."

"I will. Oh, and I'll pack a picnic lunch for the beach, if you don't mind peanut butter and banana sandwiches. That's what Liam will probably want."

"I'm not picky." He took a step back. "Night, Margot." He said her name softly.

"Bye." She unlocked the door and slipped inside, her heart beating way too fast. If this had been a date, they would've kissed for sure. But this wasn't a date. Or anything that warranted a kiss.

"Bye." She unlocked the door and slipped inside, her heart beating way too fast. If this had been a date, they would've kissed for sure. But this wasn't a date. Or anything that warranted a kiss.

Six

Margot spent the next six days plagued with thoughts of Zeke, still struggling to get a handle on her attraction to him and fearing that it might never subside.

But on this sunny afternoon, she was keeping busy hanging out at Bailey's house. Zeke's sister stood on a tall, metal ladder in her woodsy yard, attaching a swing to one of her massive trees, and Margot remained below, looking up at her.

"I always wanted one of these when I was little," Bailey said, as she hoisted the rope over a sturdy branch. "But we already had a playground at our house with a swing set, so Mom refused to consider it. Do you think Liam will like it? I was hoping he could use it, too."

"I think he'll love it." Margot's son thrived on outdoor activities. "He already thinks your house is like something out of a *Swiss Family Robinson* movie."

"Has he ever read the book?"

"Not that I know of."

"I'll have to get him a copy." Bailey finished attaching the ropes and descended the ladder. "It looks pretty good, huh?" She moved the ladder out of the way.

"It's lovely. Very old-world charm." Margot was impressed. She never would've accomplished something like that on her own. She wasn't the handywoman type.

Bailey sat on the wooden seat to test it. "This is going to be fun." She pumped her feet and got the swing going, soaring higher and higher. "I wish I had a vine I could grab on to. Then I could be like Tarzan, swinging through the jungle."

Margot teased her. "Wasn't he your secret crush when we were growing up?"

"No, smarty. But there have been some hotties who've played him. I wouldn't mind having me some of that."

"I'll bet." Margot switched to a more serious subject. "How is Eva, by the way? How did the surgery go?" Bailey had spent the earlier part of the week on caregiver duty.

"Everything is fine. I think she appreciated having me there. Boy, she's a diva, though. She ran me ragged. I swear, I waited on her hand and foot. Her household staff is looking after her now, but they always do."

"How long is the healing process?"

"Six weeks, give or take. I hope this is her last procedure."

"I doubt it will be." Margot couldn't imagine Eva putting up with the ravages of time. "She's going to fight getting older for as long as she can."

"Not me." Bailey quit swinging. "I'm going to embrace every wrinkle or saggy boob I earn. But I guess it's different for my mom. She was the *It* Girl of her generation. Other women aspired to look like her. Her beauty is her identity."

"We all have something that we think gives us our identity. Mine is my acting. There was a time when I identified as being Zeke's wife, too."

"Yeah, until he put an end to that." His sister sighed. "So, what's happening with you two? How was the ball?"

"It went well. Or as well as could be expected. I messed up and danced with him, but I won't ever do that again. Even he thought it was mistake and was sorry that he'd suggested it. It was just too tempting for both of us. Too sexy, I guess. And that's the last thing we need."

"At least you both know your limitations."

"I'm seeing him again tomorrow. Liam and I are going to his house so he can teach Liam to bodyboard."

Bailey cocked her head. "Why do you look worried about it? Are you afraid that Liam isn't ready to ride waves yet?"

"No, he's a great swimmer, and I think he'll make a great bodyboarder and surfer someday, too. It's Zeke who's got me rattled. Do you think I'm ever going to get over him? I mean, *really*, *really* get over him?"

"As in not wanting to sleep with him anymore? God, I hope so or you're going to drive me nuts about him, like you did when we were teenagers."

"Speaking of which, have you made a decision about our high school reunion yet? Because if you go, maybe I should go with you. It doesn't seem fair to let you tackle that on your own. Plus, it might be good for me to get over that part of my life, too." She needed to grow and change, especially now that she was back to obsessing about Zeke.

"That would be great. I'd love for you to go with me. But like I said before, it's not for a while, so there's no hurry for either of us to decide. There is something else I want to share with you that I'm really excited about. I'm going to launch a nonprofit that helps kids who are being bullied. I'm thinking it could be a hands-on organization, with events for the kids and their families."

"That's a wonderful idea. Just let me know if you need anything from me. I'd be glad to do what I can. But I wonder if you should contact Wade Butler about it. Maybe reach out to him on social media? The last time we talked, you told me that he was a philanthropist and a billionaire, so wouldn't it behoove you to have him in your corner? Considering how badly he used to get bullied, I think he would take an interest in it."

"Maybe so, but I haven't even created a business plan. I'm not ready to make any formal presentations. I'll just wait and see how things go, and if Wade shows up at the reunion, I can talk to him about it then."

"But you just said that you were still undecided if you were going. How can you talk to him if you're not even there? Besides, aren't you curious to get to know him and find out what he's like now?"

Bailey made a tight face. "I'm not launching this charity so I can reconnect with Wade. That's not what this is about."

"I'm sorry. You're right. I was jumping the gun." She didn't need to push Bailey into conversing with her old crush. Margot had enough man troubles of her own. With the way things were going, she would probably spend another restless night, steeped in ex-husband anxiety.

Bailey got up off the swing. "Do you want to have a go at this?"

"Sure." Margot could use the diversion. Anything, she thought, to help her quit stressing about Zeke.

Margot sat on the beach in a canopy chair, watching the bodyboarding lesson. Liam looked cute in his wetsuit and fins. He'd morphed into an Atlantean, after all. Or a hybrid or whatever half-humans would be called in Atlantis. She wasn't an expert on lost worlds.

But she was an expert on lost hearts. She sighed, thinking about herself and Zeke. They'd both taken a for-better-or-worse vow, but he hadn't held up his end of the bargain. He'd bailed when things had gotten too complicated for him. Yet here she was, letting him be part of her son's life.

Liam was already getting attached to Zeke. That much was obvious. But as time went on, would he start to think of Zeke as a father figure? And would Zeke take on that role without even realizing it? She hoped none of that happened. It wouldn't be good for any of them.

She gazed at her son, out there in the ocean. He had a big happy smile on his face, even when he struggled to catch a wave. Overall, he was doing pretty well. He'd gotten the paddling techniques down and had already learned to duck dive, even if he needed more practice to perfect it. Either way, he was a natural. He had a great instructor, too. Zeke was being patient and kind, educating Liam about the ocean and teaching him to respect it.

When the lesson ended, Liam rushed over to her, running ahead of Zeke. "Did you see me?" he asked. "Were you watching?"

"Yes, I most definitely was, and you were amazing."

She was proud of her boy. "But I figured you'd get the hang of it right away."

"Me and Zeke are going to store our wetsuits at his house, then we'll come back here to eat. I'm going to build a sandcastle, too, using the bucket and those little plastic shovels I brought. Oh, Mom, bodyboarding is so much fun. I wish we lived at the beach."

She wasn't about to respond to his last comment. Nor was she going to tell him that back in the day, she and Zeke had owned oceanfront property together.

Zeke walked up to her, carrying the bodyboard he'd been using. "Are you getting enough shade?" he asked.

"Yes, I'm fine." Along with the canopy chair, she was wearing a big floppy hat. "I'll have lunch waiting for you boys when you get back." She'd packed more than peanut butter and banana sandwiches. She'd also brought an assortment of fruit and a variety of snacks.

"I'm totally down for lunch." He stood in front of her, creating a whole other block of shade. "But, Margot?"

She adjusted her hat. "Yes?"

"I'm not a boy."

She blinked. "What?"

"You called both me and Liam boys."

She roamed her gaze over him, hoping that he didn't peel off his wetsuit in front of her. "It was a figure of speech." And now she could scarcely breathe.

He shrugged, smiled, tunneled a hand through his hair, slicking it away from his forehead. "I was just kidding around. You can call me whatever you want."

Except her husband, she thought. Or her lover. Or anything other than a friend. She glanced over at Liam. He'd already removed his wetsuit.

"Come on, Zeke," he said impatiently.

"Hold on, buddy. Give me a sec."

Zeke moved away from Margot to strip down, but she could still feel the effect he had on her. The emotion, the lust, the hurt of being divorced. With any luck, she would get herself back on track while he and Liam were gone.

She didn't turn around and watch them leave. Instead, she removed a bottle of water from the cooler and took a thirst-quenching swallow. After that, she spread out a blanket and unloaded the food, getting ready for "the boys" to return.

When they showed up, they were hungry as bears. Liam sat down and placed one sandwich, two bags of chips and three cookies in front of him. Zeke took two sandwiches, a shiny red apple and a mountain of crackers and cheese. Margot sampled a bit of everything, including the yogurt no one else touched.

"These are good," Zeke said about the sandwiches. "Filling."

"They're the best." Liam took another massive bite of his as he plowed through his lunch. Margot suspected that he was hurrying so he could rush off and build his sandcastle.

Within no time, he left the blanket to work on his project. He moved closer to the shore, where he had better access to the water. He didn't want any help. By now, he was content to be by himself.

Zeke and Margot remained where they were, and she studied him, mesmerized by how powerfully the sun glinted off his skin. He wasn't her first lover. She'd lost her virginity to someone she'd dated before she and Zeke had gotten together. If she'd known that she was going to marry Zeke someday, she might've waited and let him be her first. Then again, maybe it was better that he wasn't. She already had enough sexual connections to him.

"We're going to have to do this again soon, so I can give Liam more lessons," he said.

"There's plenty of time for him to learn."

"Yeah, but it's going to be harder to arrange our schedules once you and I go back to work."

"We'll figure it out." She tried to keep her voice light, steady. "But do me a favor, okay? Don't ever let that feeling come back."

He sent her a confused look. "What feeling?"

"What you told me about at the ball. That when you were in the pool with me and Liam, it made you feel as if we were a family."

"I said that it *almost* made us seem that way." He frowned at the half-eaten apple on his lap. "And I thought we already settled that issue at the ball."

"We did. But you and Liam are getting so close."

"That doesn't mean I'm going to start having a bunch of family-type feelings. It was just a mixed-up emotion on that first day. I'm not losing sight of what my relationship with you or your son is."

She fidgeted with the yogurt spoon in her hand. "I just wanted to clear the air and mention it."

He snared her gaze. "Then is it clear now?"

"Yes." But there were other issues still floating around in her mind, like the sexual tension between them that wouldn't go away. But she wasn't going to bring that up.

They sat quietly, finishing their food. Neither of them started a new conversation as the uncomfortable silence stretched out between them.

Finally, she glanced in Liam's direction. "I'm going to check on how the castle is coming along."

She got up and walked away, leaving Zeke on the blanket. She ventured toward Liam and stopped when she reached him.

"That looks great," she said. So far, he'd created a single-story structure with a square roof and domed accents.

He glanced up from his handiwork. "Thanks. It's not done yet, but I'm putting some shells around the moat to make it prettier."

"Yes, I see." She knelt down beside him. "Maybe you'll be an architect someday. You're certainly good at building things."

"Grandma says that, too." He wiped his hands on his trunks. "But I might want to be a writer."

"Like Bailey," she remarked.

"Uh-huh." He pushed his hair out of his eyes. "Do you think Zeke can come over tomorrow so I can show him a draft of the book me and Bailey are writing?"

After the discussion she'd just had with Zeke, she had no idea what his reaction to the invitation would be. But she wasn't going to deny Liam the chance to see him again. "He might have other plans. But you can ask him."

"Cool. Can I ask him now?"

She nodded, and Liam ran toward Zeke, leaving Margot and his castle behind.

Soon, both boy and man came over to where she was. Liam spoke first. "He says he can come if it's *for sure* all right with you."

"It is," Margot reassured Zeke, talking directly to him. She removed her hat, letting her hair fly around her face. For now, she just needed to stop worrying so much. Eventually Zeke would go back to work and start traveling again. He wouldn't be around much to see Liam later on, anyway. "It's totally fine."

"Then I'll be there for certain." Her ex stayed a cautious distance away from her. A moment later, he said to Liam, "That's a mighty fine sandcastle. After you're done, you can offer it to the sea as a gift for welcoming us today."

"Do you think there's mermaids and stuff like that out there?" Liam asked him.

"I'd like to think so." Zeke bent down to draw a mermaid in the wet sand at his feet. He gave the creature wavy hair, similar to Margot's, which was whipping wildly in the wind.

When he stood, he met her gaze, sending a sensual chill down her spine, the way he always did.

Zeke sat next to Liam on the sofa in Margot's living room, paging through Liam's manuscript. Margot was in the den, and Zeke assumed that she was purposely leaving them alone. Was she trying to prove that she'd made peace with him getting close to her son? Or was she merely trying to respect Liam's privacy and let him show off his writing by himself?

"At first I wasn't sure what kind of dog to make Nina," the boy said about the canine character he'd created. "But I chose an Irish setter because they're smart and affectionate, and they get along with kids and other animals. I wanted Nina to be like that. I did research on all kinds of breeds before I picked one. Bailey said that was important. She researches the stuff she writes."

"My sister has always been a stickler for detail. But when she was younger, she used to spend too much time alone. It was good when she and Margot became friends. They needed each other."

"I have a new friend at school. He might be my best friend someday. I make friends pretty easy, but I'm used to having to do that."

Zeke couldn't imagine being in foster care, going from home to home, adapting to different environments. Zeke's childhood hadn't been ideal, but it beat the heck out of Liam's. Up until the adoption, Margot's son had been at the mercy of strangers. "It's nice that you know how to make friends."

The kid smiled. "You're my friend now."

"Yes, I am." He thought Liam was an awesome little dude. Wise for his age, but tender at heart, too. Zeke glanced at the manuscript. "Are you going to do the illustrations for this?"

"Heck, no. Bailey is going to hire someone. But I get to tell them how I want them to draw Nina. Another reason I made her an Irish setter is because that breed has red hair."

"Like Margot's?" Zeke figured that was an easy call.

"And my birth mom's. Her name was Daisy."

Zeke was aware of who Daisy was. He had information about her in Liam's security file, along with a photograph that Margot had provided. But unlike Margot, Daisy wasn't a natural redhead. Her short choppy locks had been dyed. "Did Margot tell you about Daisy's hair?"

"No. She gave me a picture of her. I keep it in my room, but I can go get it." The kid gazed expectantly at him. "Do you want to see it?"

"Yes, I absolutely would." It was probably the same one that he had on file, but he didn't want to deprive Liam of the act of showing it to him.

While the exuberant eight-year-old headed for the staircase, running and skidding across the floor, Zeke remained on the sofa. Margot should've told him that she'd given Liam his birth mother's picture. From a security standpoint, things like that mattered. But Zeke would discuss it with Margot later.

Liam returned shortly, carrying an eight-by-ten of a pale, thin young woman with bright copper hair and soft brown eyes. It was definitely the same image.

The boy plopped back onto the sofa, scooting in tight. "This is her."

Zeke took the picture and said, "You have her smile. Her eyes, too. It's a nice combination."

"Thanks." Liam moved even closer. "Can I tell you a secret?"

"I suppose it depends on what it is."

"It's about my mom."

"Which one?"

"Margot."

Well, hell. "Yes, you can tell me. But if I think it's something that you should share with her, I'm going to encourage you to tell her."

"All right." Liam squirmed a little. "Before she became my mom, I met her at a foster kids' charity thing. Lots of other celebrities were there, too."

"I know how you first met and how the adoption came to be."

"Oh, okay. But here's the secret part. I already liked Margot from her TV show before I met her. I even streamed her old show, the one where she was a kid in it. She was my favorite person on TV, and I used to imagine having a mom like her. But I never told her that I was one of her fans."

Zeke knit his brows. "Why not?"

"Because I don't want her to think that I only wanted her to be my mom because she's famous. She knows that I watch her show now, but she doesn't know that I've always been watching it."

"You should tell her. I think she would be flattered that you imagined having a mom like her, too. It might even be fate that brought you together."

"What is fate? I hear people say that all the time, but I don't know what it means."

"It's when something is meant to happen."

"Will you be there when I tell her?"

"If it'll be easier for you. It's important that she knows how you feel." Zeke's own feelings about Margot's celebrity didn't match Liam's, though. Their marriage had dissolved over the sequel of her show. Yet for Liam, seeing her on TV had factored into his dream of a perfect mom.

"I don't remember Daisy. But do you think that somehow I remembered the color of her hair? So that when I saw Margot on TV, I imagined her as my mom?"

"That's entirely possible. But the bond you have with Margot goes beyond that now."

"I love her a lot."

"And she loves you."

Liam leaned forward. "Should I talk to her now?"

"If you're ready, sure." Zeke placed Daisy's picture on the coffee table and they went to find Margot.

She was still in the den, sitting in a puffy gray armchair with her legs tucked under her, surrounded by floor-to-ceiling bookcases.

She glanced up from the iPad she'd been scrolling. "Are you done showing Zeke your book?" she asked Liam.

"Sort of…" the boy stammered, letting his nervousness show.

She frowned. "What's going on?" She turned to look at Zeke. Did she think that he was responsible for her son's sudden anxiety?

"There's something Liam needs to tell you," Zeke said. "A secret he's been keeping."

Now she seemed even more concerned. She got up and went over to Liam. "What is it, honey?"

He replied, "It's about your show." He went on to explain, giving her the details, repeating what he'd told Zeke.

Tears filled Margot's eyes. "I think that's really sweet." She pulled Liam to her, hugging him. "I'm so glad I became the mom you always wanted." She gazed at Zeke and mouthed, *Thank you*, letting him know she appreciated him encouraging Liam to come clean.

Mother and child continued to embrace, and Zeke stood back, out of their way. Finally, when they separated, he said, "I should go home now." This tender scene was starting to become too much for him, making him feel like the outsider he was. But at least he wasn't getting that family feeling again. He sure as shit didn't need that, especially with the fuss Margot had made about it at the beach.

"Will you come back soon?" Liam asked. "Maybe some night this week? You can help me with my science project. I'm supposed to make a map of the solar system. I have to do a written report, too, and read it in front of the class."

"Sure, I'd be glad to help. I like astronomy."

"Cool." Liam gave Zeke a hasty hug goodbye.

After the boy left the room, Zeke asked Margot,

"Will you walk me out? There's something I need to discuss with you."

She nodded, and they stepped onto the porch landing. "Is something wrong?" she asked. "You look like I did something I wasn't supposed to do."

In a sense, she had. "Liam showed me Daisy's picture. But you should have told me that you gave it to him."

"Why does that matter? You already have a copy of it."

"It's a security issue, Margot. If he posts her picture online and announces that she's his birth mom, it could attract unwanted attention from someone from her past. Daisy lived a troubled life with some unsavory characters around her, and now her son has been adopted by a celebrity."

"Oh, my goodness. I should have considered that. But I don't allow Liam to go online without my supervision. I set parental controls on all of our devices."

"Maybe so, but that doesn't mean his friends' devices are secure. He could easily use someone else's. You're in the public eye. Being extra cautious comes with the territory. I'm not saying that he doesn't have a right to Daisy's picture. I'm just saying you should have told me ahead of time, so the team assigned to your security can monitor the situation."

"Thanks for letting me know. I won't do anything like that again without talking to you first."

"I just want to keep your son safe. And you, too."

"It's scary to think of the people out there who might take a nefarious interest in Liam. Not just someone from Daisy's past, but strangers, too."

"I'm not going to let anything happen to him. I'd die before I'd ever let anyone hurt either of you."

She caught her breath. "You don't need to die for us, Zeke."

He could've been dying already. Not in a literal sense. But suddenly, he was dying to touch her. To kiss her. To do more than keep her and Liam safe. She never failed to leave him in a state of bewilderment. She was gazing at him with confusion in her eyes, too. Between the two of them, their emotions were a mess. Sex had been so much easier than being hungry-for-each-other friends.

"What night should I come by?" he asked, trying to get himself back on track.

She only stared at him. "What?"

"To help Liam with his project."

"Oh, yes, of course. How about Tuesday? That'll give me time to prepare and get whatever art supplies he needs for the map. I still need to look over the guidelines his teacher sent home."

"Tuesday is fine." He would make himself available then.

But he had no idea what he was going to do about Margot, short of ending their friendship and never seeing her again. Only there was no way he could do that. He would miss her too much.

Seven

Margot busied herself in the kitchen, making zucchini bread from one of her mom's old recipes. But mostly, she was trying to keep her eyes off Zeke. He was at her house, sitting at the dining room table, helping Liam with his science project.

While Liam created a big colorful map of the solar system on poster board, Zeke did online research, printing information for the written report. Liam had checked out a library book from school that was pertinent to his subject, but he had to go through that himself. Margot wasn't going to allow him to slip by, letting someone else do all the work. Basically, his assignment was to write about why Pluto had been reclassified as a dwarf planet and what the criteria were for being a full-size planet. He was also supposed to include how Pluto got its name, and that's what Zeke was working on now.

"Was it because of the Disney dog?" Liam asked.

"Nope," Zeke replied with a bit of a chuckle. "It came from the Roman god of the underworld. In fact, it was an eleven-year old girl who suggested the name Pluto. She was the granddaughter of the man who discovered it."

"Really? Oh, wow. That's cool. Thanks for looking that up. It's fun having a research assistant."

Zeke chuckled again. "Is that what I am?"

"Yep." Liam grinned and went back to his drawing.

Clearly, her son adored Zeke. He wanted Margot's ex around as much as possible. And unfortunately, so did she. She was consumed with him, day and night, night and day. He was practically all she thought about.

"That bread smells good," Liam called out to her.

"It should be ready soon," she called back, hoping that was the case. She'd forgotten to set the timer, and now she couldn't remember when she'd put it in the oven. Being around Zeke was turning her brain to mush. Her body, too.

When she'd showered this morning, she'd fantasized about how they used to shower together. His mouth on her wet skin. His soapy hands. She'd relived every exhilarating memory, wishing that he was there with her. But she needed to break that cycle and stop having those types of thoughts.

Would it help if she got involved with someone else? If she took the plunge and started dating again?

She wasn't ready for a major relationship, but she could take it slow. She considered her options and how to go about it. Although there were exclusive dating sites designed for celebrities and other high-profile people, she didn't want to meet someone online. That was too nerve-racking.

What about someone she already knew? Should she

call Jordan and invite him out? They were just friends for now, but he used to be interested in her. For all she knew, he still could be. It was worth a try.

She needed a diversion, and she trusted Jordan. He was a good guy. Besides, she'd already contemplated bringing him to the charity ball until Zeke had intervened.

She glanced across the kitchen and into the dining room to study Zeke. He looked up and caught her watching him.

Her entire body went warm, almost as if she was having hot flashes. She turned away and realized that she'd forgotten about the zucchini bread again. Heavens, could she be any more distracted? Annoyed with herself, she grabbed a couple of pot holders and opened the oven. She tested the bread with a toothpick. Thankfully, it wasn't overdone. If she'd neglected it any longer, it might've come out hard as a stone.

She removed the pan and set it on the stove top. She waited until it cooled a bit to slice it, slathered some with butter and brought two plates to the table.

"Thanks, Mom." Liam pushed his poster board out of the way and dived into the bread.

Zeke thanked her, as well. But she got the feeling that he would just as soon take a buttery bite out of her.

Neither of them had a handle on their lust. But at least she was going to try to do something about it, as soon as she possibly could.

Two days later, Margot and Bailey strolled along the trail near Bailey's house that overlooked the canyon. Although it was a common path for hikers and runners, it was quiet this morning. They walked at a leisurely pace, sipping coffee from travel mugs filled to the brim.

"I'm glad you're doing whatever you need to do to make your life easier," Bailey said.

"Thanks." Margot watched the sun rise over the hills. "Jordan seemed excited when I invited him to dinner, and it feels good to have gotten that part out of the way. Can you believe it? It'll be my first date since the divorce."

"Are you nervous?"

"No. But Jordan doesn't make me nervous the way Zeke does." He didn't make her body tingle or her heart pound, either. But she was still struggling with her hunger for Zeke. "I'm even nervous about telling Zeke that I'm going on a date."

Bailey clutched her coffee in both hands. "Why do you have to give him a heads-up? It's none of his business what you do."

"I know, but with as much time as we've been spending together, it seems only fair. I wouldn't feel comfortable seeing Jordan or anyone else without saying something to Zeke. I thought about calling him, but that's kind of chicken. I think I should do it in person."

"Really? Because I think telling him at all will just cause a big, nasty fight. Let's be realistic here. How would you feel if the tables were turned and it was Zeke who was planning on dating someone else?"

"Honestly, I'd be hurt and jealous. But we're only supposed to be friends, so it doesn't matter how it would make me feel." Margot glanced over at the prickly brush flanking the sides of the trail. "We can't keep having those erotic feelings for each other. It's causing too much stress."

Bailey heaved a sigh that drifted into the canyon. "If it was me, I'd go the chicken route and tell him over the phone."

"He's probably going to get mad no matter how I do it. But at least my conscience will be clear if I make the effort to see him in person. Besides, I think I'll be able to calm him down, and we'll be able to talk rationally. Now that we've become friends, we're learning to communicate."

"That's good. Because the last big blowup you two had triggered your affair."

"Don't I know it." Margot sipped her coffee, taking refuge in the caffeine. "But no matter how he reacts, it's going to be different this time. I'm never going to sleep with him again. That part of our relationship is over. I'm going to go see him tonight. But I'm just going to show up and take my chances that he'll be home. I think the element of surprise will be best. If I text him first, he might figure out that something's up. He's clever that way."

And on this uneasy occasion, Margot was determined to have the upper hand and be the person in charge.

At 7:00 p.m., Zeke's doorbell rang. He wasn't expecting company. In fact, he'd been getting ready to settle in and stream a movie. He was supposed to be on a break from work, but he'd spent most of the day on Zoom calls with his international team, reviewing their assignments.

He checked his security system and saw Margot on the screen. He answered the door, wondering why she was here.

She looked soft and breezy, wearing a casual spring dress and strappy sandals. But she seemed anxious, too, playing with the ends of her hair.

"Come in," he said, with concern.

She crossed the threshold into his condo, with its rugged furnishings and indigenous accents. Zeke's place reflected who he was, right down to the gourd pottery, bamboo window coverings and distressed wood floors.

"I'm sorry for barging in like this," she said. "But there's something I need to talk to you about."

He gestured for her to take a seat, and she headed for a chair and scooted to the edge of it.

Zeke stood near the bar. He should have offered her a glass of wine or a soda or whatever, but he was too impatient to hear what she had to say first. "What's going on?"

"I'm going out with Jordan on Saturday."

Damn it, he thought. He hadn't trusted that guy all along. "What the hell for?"

"I invited him to dinner. I decided it was time for me to start dating again, and I thought I'd start by going out with a friend and see where it leads."

He glared at her. "Where it leads?"

"Romantically. And please, stop looking at me as if I just said I was going to cheat on you. We aren't a couple anymore, and I didn't come here to fight with you."

"Don't lecture me on what we are or aren't. And don't play the pacifist, either. You're as good at fighting as I am."

"But that isn't my intention."

"Then what is?" His gut clenched, twisting and turning into a colossal knot. "To flaunt another man in my face?"

"No. Absolutely not." She remained seated, clasping her hands on her lap. "With how deeply our friendship has been developing, I just thought I owed you the courtesy of telling you what's going on."

He didn't want to be her friend anymore, not if it

meant getting hurt by her. "Why are you so interested in dating all of a sudden?"

She lifted her gaze to his. "Because I'm trying to shed my struggle over you. The lust you always make me feel."

"And that's supposed to make everything all right?" He didn't follow her reasoning. "You're battling feelings for me, so you go chasing after someone else? What does Jordan think about that?"

"I didn't tell him. The problem I'm having over you is personal. It isn't the sort of thing I can share with someone."

He scoffed. "I'll bet you told my sister."

"That's different." She zeroed in on the bar. "Do you think I could have a drink? My mouth is a little dry."

"Help yourself." He wanted her to get up, to come closer. He still stood near the bar. "Take whatever you want."

She glanced a bit shakily at him, as if his last statement was a double entendre. But she made her way to the bar and rattled around, searching for whatever he had available. She settled on pineapple juice.

When she tried to return to her seat, he blocked her path, trapping her behind the bar.

"What are you doing?" she asked.

Being territorial, he thought. But he couldn't seem to help it. Even if Margot didn't belong to him, he still couldn't bear for her to be with someone else. "I'm not going to let you go out with that guy."

"You don't have the authority to stop me. Now step back and let me pass. I already told you that I didn't come here to battle with you."

Too bad, because he was trying to egg her on, to make her feel what he was feeling. The rage. The hunger. The lust she was trying to avoid. He didn't want to be the only one suffering. "What if I want to fight? What if I want to show you who's the boss?"

She came toward him. "I mean it, Zeke. Get out of my way so I can drink this and go home."

He refused to budge, glad that he was finally making her mad. "You can finish it where you are."

"Fine." She guzzled the juice and slammed the empty glass down. "Now you can move."

Fat chance of that. "Sorry, but I'm just dandy where I am." He flashed a cocky smile, pissing her off even more. She looked like she wanted to take a swing at him. But it would take a bulldozer for her to knock him down, and she knew it.

She hissed like a cat. "Screw you, you big jerk."

"Is that the best you got?" He mocked her, baiting her to call him every name in the book.

She narrowed her eyes. "I don't need this crap from you."

And he didn't need her coming to his house, telling him that she was interested in another man. As far as he was concerned, that made them even. By now, he should have let her pass. But instead, he shrugged and said, "It's not going to work, anyway."

"What isn't?"

He looked her straight in the eye. "You using Jordan to get over me."

"I'm not using anybody." She defended herself, a bit too vehemently. "That isn't what I'm doing."

"I'm just calling it like I see it. Nothing is going to cure you of me, except me."

She tossed her wild red hair over her shoulder. "If that's your way of trying to get me to sleep with you, you can go straight to hell."

"Fine. You win." He retreated, allowing her the freedom to get away from him. Only she didn't dash out the door. She remained where she was, as if a supernatural force was keeping her there. They stared uncomfortably at each other, a tense silence engulfing them. "Go," he said, reminding her that she could leave.

Her breath shuddered. "Do you really want me to?"

"No." He ached for her to stay, for her to touch him, for him to touch her. "But it's your choice. I'm not your jailer."

"Yes, you are." Her voice hitched. "You've always controlled some part of me."

"Not purposely." He waited for her to make the first move, to come closer and let the moment explode. They were on the verge of another affair. He could feel it in the air, like storm clouds gathering in the sky.

She inched toward him. "Am I going to regret this when it's over? Am I going to hate myself for it? Or is this going to feel so good that I won't care?"

"I can't answer those questions for you." But he sure as hell hoped it was the latter. All he wanted was for her to pounce, for the rain to break free. He could barely breathe just thinking about it. He even counted the seconds in his mind, watching her, waiting.

One one-thousand, two one-thousand...

She rushed forward, slamming her body against his. He sought her mouth, and they kissed as if they might die if they didn't. She tasted like everything he'd been missing: his old lover, the woman he craved. He wrapped his arms around her, and she dug her nails into his T-shirt, trying to connect with his skin. They kissed some more, hot and desperately carnal.

When they came up for air, he said, "Take off your dress."

She did his bidding, letting the garment slide to the floor. "Now what should I do?"

"Nothing. I'll do the rest."

He lifted her up, setting her on top of the bar. She looked sexy as hell in her pink bra and blue panties, her sandals dangling from her feet. He carefully slipped off each shoe, pretending that he was going to take his time. But before she knew what hit her, he grabbed her panties and yanked them down. She gasped, and he suspected that her heart was beating like a runaway bride. She met his gaze, and he flung her underwear away, not caring where they landed. Her bra came off next.

He tugged her to the edge of the bar top and got down on his knees. He was tall enough to make this work, and he intended to have a nice, naughty feast.

He parted her with his fingers, and she moaned in excitement. She wanted this as badly as he did.

He knew her sexual preferences because they matched his own. She was the most compatible lover he'd ever had. The most responsive. Everything about her was positively sinful.

He buried his face between her legs, and she rocked against his mouth and made breathy sounds. He glanced up and saw that she was thumbing her own nipples, making them as hard as bullets. Was it any wonder that he couldn't get her out of his system? He could do this for the rest of his life and still want more. She was slick and wet, and he relished the taste of her.

She watched him through vivid eyes. So blue, he thought. So powerful. The lanterns above the bar were giving her an unearthly sheen. She reached out to touch him, putting her hand against his face. He pleasured her with every fiber of his sex-starved soul, and she arched her body, bending like a bow that was about to snap.

Or a woman who was about to come.

He grazed her thighs with his beard stubble and she shivered all the way to her toes. The sounds she made were wild now. She opened her legs as wide as she could, shuddering through her orgasm.

He stayed on his knees, absorbing her climax in the most intimate of ways. When it ended, he got to his feet, and she kissed him luxuriously on the mouth, melting all over him.

It was too late, Margot realized. She couldn't go back and undo it. She'd already let Zeke take her to delectable heights. They both were standing now, facing each other, her mind spinning, her heart pounding.

"Why can't I stay away from you?" she asked, still reeling from what he'd done to her.

"For the same reason I'm hooked on you. We're good together this way."

She knew exactly what he meant. Sex was their common ground, the thing that never seemed to fail them. She couldn't even begin to think about regret. She didn't want to hate herself for being with him, either.

She skimmed his cheek with her fingertips, fascinated by the rugged angles of his face. "It's your turn to get naked."

He agreed, and she helped divest him of his shirt, exposing his chest and abs, those to-die-for muscles. He peeled off his shorts. He was already half-hard. She rubbed him, making him fully erect.

He tipped his head back, and when she dropped to her knees, he nearly shuddered on the spot.

"Fair is fair," she said. She wanted to give him the same kind of raw pleasure that he'd bestowed upon her.

"You'll have to stop when I tell you to."

She looked up at him, this big, tough guy who stood before her. "I haven't even started yet, and you're already giving me orders." But she wasn't going to listen. Margot was determined to be her own woman, even if she was getting dangerously involved with him again.

She flicked her tongue against him, and he shifted his stance, watching her, getting ready for more. She took him in her mouth, and his stomach muscles jumped and flexed.

He tasted beautifully familiar, and she savored every solid inch. She took him deeper and deeper, as far as her throat would allow. He slid his hands into her hair, tangling it around his fingers, pulling and tugging.

"Damn you." He groaned, his excitement mounting.

Damn him, too, she thought. No doubt about it, he was her drug of choice, the needle in her arm, the habit she couldn't break.

They created a rhythm, with him moving inside her mouth. He kept watching her, and she increased the pace, her head bobbing back and forth. She could only imagine how deliciously dirty she looked to him, still naked and sticky from her own orgasm.

He was close. She knew the signs. She'd done this to him many times before.

"You better stop," he panted.

She kept at it, digging her nails into his butt, getting more aggressive with him. He cursed, his voice sounding parched. Sandpapery, she thought. He tried to make her stop again, but she refused. She enjoyed torturing him this way.

He gave up the fight and jerked forward, spilling into her. She let the feeling overtake her. Being the source of his pleasure nearly made her come again, too. She waited a few minutes, letting the moment swirl around both of them.

He helped her up off her knees, and she smiled.

"You look like the cat that ate the big bad canary," he said, his voice still crackly.

"Or the kitten that lapped up all the cream." She smiled again, teasing him, feeling full of herself. "I should get dressed and go now."

"What? No. We're not done yet. I still want you in my bed."

"You'll need time to be ready again."

"It won't take long." He reached for her. "We can cuddle or something in the meantime."

She was tempted, so damned tempted. Except that cuddling with him was about the worst thing she could do. They hadn't spooned since they were married.

Pulling back, she made an excuse. "My mom is watching Liam, and she's probably already expecting me back by now." She searched for her underwear. She found her bra on the floor, but she had no idea where her panties were. A second later, she located them on a nearby chair.

He climbed into his shorts, snapping the elastic against his waist. "You better cancel that date with Jordan or I'm seriously going to climb the walls."

"Do you actually think I would go out with him now?" She'd blown her entire plan of seeing someone else, of severing her sexual tie with Zeke. "I'm back to having an affair with you."

He bunched his T-shirt into a ball. "Then let's have dinner together on Saturday like you were going to do with him."

She hooked her bra and shimmied into her dress. "That isn't necessary."

"Then will you at least come over on Saturday?"

"Yes, I can do that." But she still needed to be careful, keeping herself from cuddling, from caring more than she should, from getting too attached to him.

Ever again.

"then will you at least come over on Saturday?"
"Yes, I can do that." But she still needed to be careful,
keeping herself from cuddling, from caring more than
she should, from getting too attached to him.
Ever again.

Eight

On Saturday morning, while Liam was out shopping
with her mom, Margot worked in her vegetable garden.
This year, she'd planted tomatoes, bell peppers and a
variety of herbs. She wasn't a master grower. It was
more of a hobby.

About an hour later, she dusted herself off and relaxed on the patio, sipping iced tea garnished with mint.
She'd learned the hard way that mint could spread and
take over a garden, so she contained it in pots now.

As she poked around on her cell, scanning the latest
news articles, her phone rang. Bailey's name appeared
on the screen. Margot hesitated, apprehensive about answering the call. She hadn't told Bailey about her latest
rendezvous with Zeke. As far as Bailey knew, Margot
was having dinner with Jordan tonight.

Problem was, if she let the call go to voice mail, Bailey would text. And if Margot ignored the texts, her BFF

would worry. They never went more than a few days without checking in with each other.

Dang it.

She answered her phone with the customary "Hello?" as if she hadn't actually been stressing about it.

"Hey, you," Bailey said. "I just wanted to touch base and wish you luck on your date."

Should she lie and pretend the date was still on? No, she couldn't do that. She needed to be honest. "Thanks, but I canceled it. When I went to see Zeke to tell him about Jordan, it didn't exactly go as planned, and I—"

"Oh, my gawd." Bailey cut her off. "You slept with him."

Margot winced. "More or less." She forged ahead and added, "I'm seeing him again tonight."

"Are you serious?" Bailey sounded as if she wanted to shake her silly. "You're going back for more?"

"I know it sounds crazy, but I'm afraid that if I end it too soon, I'll never stop obsessing about him." She plucked the mint from her glass, sucking directly on the leaves. Just thinking about him stirred her blood.

"You shouldn't have told him about Jordan in person." Bailey's voice came over the speaker, loud and clear. "If you'd done it over the phone, none of this would've happened."

"I know, but I'm not going to beat myself up over it. Being with Zeke is exciting. But it's not going to last forever. Eventually it'll be over for good."

"So, your hunger for him is just going to fizzle out? Poof, like magic, and it'll be gone? What if you start falling in love with him again?"

"That isn't going to happen. Believe me, I'm staying out of the danger zone." She'd already warned herself about getting attached, and she intended to tread carefully and heed her own advice. "I realize that things have changed a bit, and Zeke and I are friends now. But that doesn't mean I'm going to let myself be vulnerable to him. Our affair is just going to be about sex." Mind-numbing, body-blasting sex, she thought. "Just like it was before."

No, that wasn't completely true, she thought. Their affair wasn't just like before. Their friendship was creating a new bond. And to top it off, Zeke was becoming friends with Liam, too. He was good with her son. Nonetheless, she wasn't going to fall for Zeke again. She couldn't afford that type of pain. Nor would she put Liam through it. He didn't need to see her falling for her ex. Margot was determined to protect herself and her son.

Margot arrived at Zeke's place, but before she approached his door, she took a moment to gaze out at the ocean. She appreciated its moonlit mystery, the water rolling and foaming onto the shore, the aroma of salt and sea. She even imagined mermaids splashing in the waves.

"Do you want to go for a swim?" a disembodied male voice asked.

Startled by the intrusion, she spun around and spotted her lover sitting in a darkened corner of his courtyard.

She quickly said, "You scared me."

"Sorry." He stood and came toward her. "I was out here waiting for you, and when I saw you staring at the beach, I kept quiet and watched you. It made me feel like a voyeur."

She caught her breath. "Is voyeurism a new fetish of yours?"

"No. But it could be, if the subject I kept watching was you." He moved closer. "You didn't answer my question about swimming. I was thinking we could skinny-dip."

Her skin tingled beneath her clothes. "It's not a private beach. One of your neighbors could see us. Or record us."

He stood close enough to kiss her, without actually doing it. "Then it'll be your first nude scene."

He was teasing her, she thought, and using their conversation as foreplay. He had no intention of creating a public scandal with her.

He escorted her inside, and as soon as he closed the door, he kissed her for real. She moaned, clinging to him like a reed in the wind. In the chaos of the kiss, her purse slipped off her shoulder and onto the floor. He nearly stepped on it, but she didn't care. She ached to have him inside her, to have the roughest, rowdiest night of her life.

He scooped her up and carried her to his room, dropping her straight onto his oversize bed. He'd left it unmade, for this purpose, no doubt, and she landed on the mattress with a thud, the sheets bunching around her.

He crawled on top of her, pulling at her blouse, tugging at her boho skirt. Her shoes were trendy flats. He got rid of those in two seconds.

She wasn't able to divest him of his clothes, because she was pinned beneath him while he went after hers. Her itty-bitty panties aroused the beast in him. He nearly tore them in his attempt to yank them off. Once she was naked, he went down on her, lifting her legs onto his shoulders.

He used his tongue, and she writhed against him.

This time oral sex was the appetizer, not the main course.

She reached back to grip the posts on the headboard, struggling to think beyond what he was doing to her. He worked his magic, and she tightened her grip on the posts, her vision blurring, her body feeling like it was splintering into fragments.

He made her come so fast, she barely knew what hit her.

He released her legs from his shoulders, and she sprawled out like a sacrifice before him. She couldn't seem to keep her thighs together.

He peeled off his T-shirt and ditched his jeans. He wasn't wearing underwear, and his erection sprang free. She reached for him, and he kissed her, his mouth covering hers.

At some point, he pulled away to grab a condom from the nightstand and put it to good use. Then, as he braced himself above her, he said, "I want to make this last."

Was he referring to this specific encounter or the longevity of their actual affair? She didn't ask him to clarify. Eventually, it would all come to an end.

He entered her, and she lifted her hips to meet his generous thrusts. They kissed; they moaned; they rolled over the bed and knocked his pillows onto the floor. The room was softly lit, a glass-domed lamp providing a nighttime glow.

They kept changing positions, bending and shaping their bodies to fit. At some point, she landed on top, straddling his lap. She felt like a dancer, and he looked like an athlete. The strength of his arms, the definition in his legs, the ripple of muscle along his abs. Was it a six-pack? An eight-pack? She didn't know, but she rode him with lust and fury.

He reared up to kiss her, and soon he was on top again, thrusting with heat and passion. She moved with him, matching his rhythm.

Margot came first, bucking and convulsing and clawing his back. He followed her, immersed in his own fiery pleasure and making primal sounds.

A few quiet minutes later, he got up to dispose of the condom, and she steadied her breathing.

When he returned, he stood beside the bed and stared at her. She leaned against the headboard and stared back at him.

"Are you hungry?" he asked, breaking the silence. "I can fix us a snack."

"Sure, why not?" She wouldn't mind having a little something. "Should I wait here or do you want to eat at the table?"

"You can wait here." He rummaged through his dresser, removed a pair of boxers and climbed into them.

After he left the room, she put her bra and panties back on, then returned the pillows to the bed and fluffed them. Zeke's bedroom was as striking as the rest of his condo, decorated in bold colors and aquatic artwork, showcasing big, bright paintings of the sea.

A short while later, he reappeared with a tray of food. She took one look at their snacks and sputtered into laughter. He'd made Dagwood sandwiches, the ingredients piled hilariously high between three slices of bread. In lieu of toothpicks, he'd used bamboo skewers to hold them together.

He grinned. "What can I say? I worked up an appetite."

"No kidding. But how am I supposed to eat that? First of all, that's way too much food for me. And secondly, I don't take ginormous bites out of stuff the way you do."

"I know. But you normally pick everything apart, so I figured you'd dissect it, anyway, and just eat the parts you like."

She shrugged, deciding that he was right. She'd always been a fussy eater. "What kind of drinks are those?" She couldn't see the labels on the canned beverages he'd brought.

"Flavored water." He tossed her one.

She caught it, hoping it didn't explode when she opened it.

He handed her a plastic plate with a sandwich. She didn't bother asking what was in it. She would find out once she started taking it apart.

He sat across from her and opened his water.

"Can I have that one?" she asked.

"Why? They're the same flavor."

"It's carbonated, and mine got shaken up."

He switched cans with her. She sipped from the safe one, and he flipped the top on the questionable one. Only it was fine. No fizzy overload. He smiled and toasted her with it.

Smart aleck, she thought. She removed the skewer from her sandwich, got rid of the extra slice of bread and pulled some of the meat and cheese out. It was a messy business, and when she got avocado and mayo on her fingers, she licked it off. She glanced up and felt her cheeks go hot. Zeke was watching her.

Just as she reached for a napkin, he said, "I want our affair to be exclusive this time."

She hastily replied, "Neither of us was with anyone else last time."

"I know. But we left it open so that we could've been. And I don't want to take the chance of you dating someone else while you're with me. Not just Jordan. You already said that you weren't going to see him. But other guys, too."

"I'm not interested in anyone else." She had no desire for another man. "I need to get my fill of you first."

"I need to do that with you, too." He gave her a possessive look. "I guess that makes it official, then. Our affair is exclusive."

"Yes," she replied, and they both went quiet.

He lifted his sandwich and took a hearty bite, and she continued picking at hers. By the time he was almost done, she'd barely made a dent in hers. But she didn't want any more, anyway.

"Do you know what time it is?" she asked. She didn't see a clock in his room. "I told my mom that I'd be home by eleven."

He leaned over to retrieve his phone from the nightstand drawer. He glanced at the screen. "It's nine thirty-eight. Does your mom know that you're hanging out with me tonight?"

Margot shook her head. "I didn't want her to get suspicious of us spending too much time together, so I said that I was going out with some friends from my cycling class."

"Does Bailey know what we're up to again?"

She nodded. "I couldn't bring myself to lie to her. She isn't pleased about it, but I knew she wouldn't be."

"I don't care what she thinks. I just want to do wicked things with you." He roamed his gaze over her. "Do you want to have another go at it?"

Her pulse all but jumped. "There's no time. I need to make myself presentable before I leave, not go home looking like some unknown man ravished me."

"We can make it quick. Besides, I like ravishing you."

"I like it, too." Way too much, she thought. "But maybe I should get ready to go now, before you tempt me into taking chances I shouldn't take." Determined to keep her wits about her, she asked, "Will you get my purse for me? I left it in the entryway, and it has my makeup in it. I packed a wide-tooth comb for untangling my hair, too."

"Sounds like you came prepared. But are you sure I can't make you change your mind?"

"Please, Zeke, just get my purse and bring it into the bathroom. I really need to get ready to go."

"All right. But you can't blame me for trying." He headed for the door. "I'll be back in a flash."

She went into the master bath, and while he was gone, she took inventory of his toiletries: his liquid soap, his cologne, the electric razor he used.

He returned with her purse and set it on the counter. But he didn't leave. He stood behind her, so they were both reflected in the mirror.

"What are you doing?" she asked.

"Admiring you." He moved closer. "You're beautiful, Margot. So damned beautiful."

Her hair was tousled, her mascara was smeared and her lipstick was gone. She looked like what she was: his reckless lover. And now she wanted him again.

"Is your offer still good to make it quick?" she asked, her voice going breathy, her common sense flying out the window.

"Hell, yes." He opened the medicine cabinet, showing her that he had a box of condoms in there.

"Then do it." She was still in her panties and bra, easily accessible to him. She focused on the mirror, eager to watch.

In the next wild instant, he pulled her panties past her hips. He shoved his boxers down, too, and snagged a condom, cursing when the wrapper took too long to open. Finally, he sheathed himself, and Margot pitched forward, getting ready for him. He thrust into her, and she gripped the sink and gazed ravenously at their reflections.

He moved in and out, nibbling on her neck, behaving like a stallion covering a mare. She turned on the water and splashed herself, getting him wet, too. But he didn't lose his stride. He maintained the pounding rhythm.

He took her so hard and fast the room began to spin. She could barely see straight, let alone watch their activity in the mirror anymore.

She came in a flurry, shaking while he spilled into her.

After he was done, he wrapped his arms around her, anchoring her so she didn't slump to the floor. She still needed to right her appearance and go home.

As if nothing had happened at all.

Zeke wasn't sure what was happening. The only thing he was certain of was an overwhelming need to see Margot again. But what did he expect? They were friends as well as lovers and that was a powerful combination. Besides, he liked her kid, too. So here he was on Monday evening, hanging out with her and Liam. He'd come to Hollywood tonight to meet with a prospective client, so he'd stopped by her place afterward, using the old "I was in the neighborhood" excuse to show up at her door.

She sat next to him on the sofa, and they formed Liam's captive audience. The boy was reading his Pluto report to them, the way he was going to have to do in front of his class. His project was due tomorrow.

After he finished rattling it off, his mom said, "That was really good. But try it again, and slow down a bit. You were going a little too fast."

"Okay." He took a big, exaggerated breath and went through it one more time.

He enunciated the words he'd missed before, making everything sharper. He looked cute, too, his sandy-brown hair filled with static electricity from where he'd been rubbing the back of his head against the wall. He grinned when he was finished, and Zeke shot him a thumbs-up.

"That was perfect," Margot said. "I'm so proud of the work you've done on this. You wrote a really informative report, and the map you did is wonderful, too. But I think you better go take your bath and get ready for bed now."

Liam made a disgruntled face. "Can't I stay up a little longer?"

Margot shook her head. "No, sorry. It's a school night. Besides, you need to be refreshed for tomorrow."

"I guess." Liam gathered his papers. "Can Zeke tuck me in after my bath? I can come down and let him know when I'm ready."

"I think that would be okay." Margot turned to Zeke. "If it's all right with you."

"It's totally fine." He didn't mind tucking her son into bed. He imagined tucking her in, too, or just flat out spending the night with her. But he knew that wasn't possible. They might be having an affair, but it wasn't a relationship. They weren't heading back into something deeper. They both knew better than to get too wrapped up in each other. But for now, the sex felt damned good. He couldn't help but crave more time with her.

"I'll be back." Liam dashed upstairs, leaving the adults alone.

They stayed silent, until Margot moved closer to Zeke and asked, "Did you really have a meeting in the neighborhood?"

"Yes, I did. But it was also a good excuse to see you. Truthfully, I could've let Vick take the meeting." His partner had been available to do it. "But you know what would be fun? If you and I could arrange for a few days together. It would be great to go away some-where, instead of me finding excuses to come here or you sneaking over to my place. But only if you're okay with leaving Liam with your mom. I wouldn't want you to do anything that would upset him."

"Liam loves being with my mom, and she adores being with him. She already watches him for me when I work or whenever I go out, so I don't see why it would upset him. He'll probably think it'll be fun with the way she indulges him." She hesitated. "But if you and I slip away, where would we go?"

"There's a remote house in the mountains that I've booked for some of my clients. It has a grotto and a lagoon-style pool, surrounded by forest. We could go skinny-dipping there, without having to worry about anyone seeing us."

She smiled. "You do have a one-track mind."

He smiled, too. "I just want to get naked with you, however I can." He searched her gaze. "So, will you talk to your mom about watching Liam?"

"Yes, but I'll need to come up with a story about where I'm going. I can't exactly say that I'm spending a few days with you. That's just a little too close for comfort." She sighed. "I guess I could say that I'm doing some spa days at a private resort."

"Whatever works. But let me check first to see what dates are available. I might have to pull some strings to make it happen sooner rather than later."

"All right. Just let me know. But we shouldn't keep talking about this. I don't want Liam to come back and overhear us."

They switched to another topic, and by the time her son showed up in his pjs, they were acting as casual as could be.

Zeke had never tucked a child into bed before, but he was going to give it his best effort.

He headed upstairs with Liam, doing his damnedest not to glance back at Margot or shoot her a hungry look. He couldn't wait for their clandestine getaway. He was going to try to arrange it as quickly as possible.

He cleared his mind and entered Liam's room, a big, bright space full of movie and sports posters, crates of toys, shelves of comic books, a snazzy entertainment center and a metal bunk bed.

Liam said, "I sleep on the bottom because it's bigger. The top is for when I have a friend stay over. There's also a trundle under here." He gestured to the area below the bottom bunk. "It's for guests, too."

"Have you had any friends stay over?"

"Not yet, but Mom said I can have pool parties and sleepovers in the summer." Liam crawled into the bottom bunk and pulled up the covers. "Did you have your own room when you were a kid?"

Zeke sat on the edge of the bed. "Yes, I did. Bailey

and I grew up in a mansion in Beverly Hills, so there were lots of rooms. Our mother is an actress, and our dad was her agent."

"Really? Is your mom famous?"

Zeke nodded. "Very much so. Her name is Eva Mitchell. But you might not know who she is because her movies are from a long time ago." In the really early days, when she'd first started getting famous, she'd used her maiden name. But Zeke doubted that would make a difference to Liam.

The boy went quiet for minute, giving Zeke a baffled look. "I thought you and Bailey had different dads."

"We do. I told you that before."

"Yeah, but now you're making it sound like you have the same one. You just called the guy who was your mom's agent *our* dad."

"I'm sorry. I should have made that clear. My father died when I was a baby, and my mom married her agent, a man named Caine Mitchell. He adopted me and gave me his last name. Then they had Bailey about five years later."

"Oh, wow." Liam's eyes grew wide. "You're adopted, like me."

"I most surely am. I loved my adoptive dad. He was everything to me. I was really sad when he died."

"Does it make you sad that your first dad died, too?"

Zeke nodded. "I have lots of pictures of him. He was a movie stuntman, and he was even bigger and taller than I am. I got my features from him. He was Choctaw and Samoan." When he realized that Liam didn't have a clue what that meant, he explained, "The Choctaw are a Native American tribe, and Samoans are indigenous Polynesian people from the islands of Samoa. My dad was born there. It's a beautiful place. I've been visiting my grandfather there since I was a kid."

"That's nice," Liam said thoughtfully. "But are you ever going to get married again or have kids?"

"I don't know." The question threw him for a loop. How was he supposed to consider that while he was messing around with Margot?

"Do you think my mom will?"

"I have no idea." He didn't want to think about her acquiring a new husband. He'd already gotten jealous of that damned date she was supposed to have.

Liam sank his head deeper into his pillow. "I'd like to have an adoptive dad someday if my mom ever gets married again. Brothers and sisters, too. I used to help with the younger kids in foster care."

"I bet you were really good at it." But this wasn't a conversation Zeke wanted to have. It was starting to make him tense. Or sad. Or some damned thing. "You should get some sleep now. Your mom isn't going to want you staying up half the night, talking to me. She was already worried about you being rested to give your report tomorrow."

"Yeah, she gets like that." Liam smiled up at him. "Thanks for tucking me in."

"You're welcome." He ruffled the boy's hair and got up to turn off the light and close the door.

Once Zeke was in the hallway, he shook away his feelings. He shouldn't be tense or sad or anything else. Margot's future and whatever it entailed was none of his concern. Nor was he going to dwell on it. But still, how would he handle it if their affair came to an abrupt end? Would he and Margot struggle to remain friends? Would her son get caught in the middle? Or would the boy be none the wiser?

Zeke didn't have a clue what to expect. But before he got too overwhelmed, he needed to get his emotions in check and take one cautious day at a time.

Nine

The house in the mountains was incredible. Not just the stunning glass-and-timber architecture, but the woodland that surrounded it: trees as far as the eye could see, wildflowers blooming on hilltops, a narrow creek flowing over branches and rocks. Nature, Margot thought, at its finest.

She inhaled the fragrant air while Zeke removed their bags from his SUV. Both of them had packed light since it would be a short stay.

"Are you ready for the grand tour?" he asked.

"Yes." She fell into step with him, and he unlocked the front door and ushered her inside. "How many times have you been here?" she asked.

"Just once, when I first checked it out to see if it was suitable for my clients. I didn't stay here, but I learned all about it from the caretakers."

"It's amazing." The cream-and-gold living room

showcased a magnificent view of the lagoon-style pool that Zeke had mentioned before. She walked over to the sliding glass doors to admire it. "It's so tropical." The yard overflowed with greenery.

"The pool is the focal point of the house." He joined her at the door. "It's accessible from the bedrooms, too."

"That's good to know. Thanks for suggesting this place. I haven't been out of the city in ages."

"It's my pleasure." He took her hand. "Come on, I'll show you the kitchen. I asked the caretakers to stock it with ready-made meals, so we didn't have to worry about cooking for ourselves."

She smiled. "I guess it's safe to assume that ordering out isn't exactly feasible."

He laughed a little. "This is definitely off the grid. You certainly wouldn't want to get stranded out here with someone who got on your nerves."

She squeezed his hand. "Then it's a good thing that you don't annoy me anymore."

"Same here." He leaned in to kiss her on the mouth, quickly, playfully.

Her pulse fluttered. She relished being kissed by him, even when it was just a brisk tease.

They entered the kitchen by way of a sunny breakfast nook.

She opened the fridge to poke around at the meals that had been premade for them. "There's some gourmet food in here."

"I wanted this to be a glamorous trip. But outdoorsy, too. The best of both worlds."

"Then you succeeded." She closed the fridge. "Where do the caretakers go when guests stay here?"

"They have a cabin on the other side of the mountain. They're a husband and wife team."

As opposed to the divorced couple that she and Zeke were?

"Will you show me the bedrooms now?" she asked, struggling to clear her mind.

"The master is on this level. The other two are downstairs, in a fancy basement setting with additional living quarters."

"Then I'll just see the master for now." She could check out the rest later.

He retrieved their luggage from the entryway and took her to a room with a cherrywood decor. The bed sat on a sturdy platform, and across from it was a luxurious seating area and media center. There was a kitchenette stocked with nighttime snacks, too.

The adjoining bathroom had an old-fashioned tub and a modern shower, big enough for an orgy. Or two hungry exes, she thought, who couldn't seem to get enough of each other.

Zeke placed their bags on matching valet stands and asked, "Should we change into our swimsuits and check out the yard?"

"I brought three different bikinis. I wasn't sure if I would need them, though. You kept talking about wanting to skinny-dip."

"I figured we would work our way up to that. By the way, there's a cave in the grotto where guests are encouraged to draw or paint or write on the walls. They keep art supplies down there for that purpose. The man who built this place is an artist and a bit of an eccentric, so that's where the graffiti idea came from. He used to live here, but he got too old and moved back to civilization. From what I've been told, he's fussy about who stays here. He prefers actors and artists and the like."

"Then I guess I fit right in." She waited a beat before she said, "Just so you know, I went back on birth control."

His eyes grew wide. "You did? When?"

"This week. I thought it would make things easier."

"You mean we don't have to use the condoms I brought? This is going to sound excessive, but I panicked about being in the middle of nowhere and shoved a full box of them into my bag."

She couldn't help but laugh. "One of the big boxes?"

He laughed, too. "A thirty count, I think." He turned serious. "But thanks for making the commitment that you did."

"Like I said, I thought it would make things easier." Nonetheless, she was uncomfortable that he'd referred to her choice as a commitment. She doubted that he meant it the way it sounded, but it still made her feel as if she was devoting herself to him somehow. Before she lingered over her anxiety, she said, "I'm going to put my swimsuit on now. But I'm going to change in the bathroom." She needed a moment of privacy to collect her scattered thoughts. She rummaged through her bag, nabbed the first bikini she saw and ducked into the bathroom. She hated that she still got nervous around him. After all these years, after being married and divorced, she should be calmer than this.

She removed her clothes and slipped on her bikini, a floral-print number that pushed up her breasts and barely covered her rear. Not that her skimpy attire mattered. By the end of the day, she would probably be naked, anyway.

She returned to the bedroom. Zeke had donned a pair of seafoam green board shorts. He looked like his usual self, tall and tanned and breathtakingly handsome.

"Damn," he said. "Check you out."

"What? This old thing?" She took a brave spin, modeling her suit. She'd bought it specifically for this trip.

He gazed unblinkingly at her. "You're a temptress."

"I try," she joked. "But should we go now?" She was eager to break his stare. He was still making her nervous.

He agreed, and they went outside. The yard was even more magical up close. The rock formations around the pool had shiny pink stones embedded in them.

"What are those?" she asked.

"They're rose quartz. The owner I told you about believes in crystal energy. According to the caretakers, rose quartz is said to promote love." He frowned. "But people don't fall in love because of a stone."

To her, anything seemed possible at this oddly beautiful house. But in reality, she knew he was right. Those glittery pink stones weren't capable of casting spells. Or at least not on her or Zeke. Neither of them would be falling in love this weekend.

He pointed to a copse of sago palms and said, "There's a sauna through there and a row of outdoor showers." He motioned to a set of moss-covered stairs. "Along that ridge is a fire pit, and a little farther up is an impressive display of chainsaw carvings."

"There's so much to see." Almost more than she could take in. "This yard is certainly going to keep us busy."

"It's even crazier than the maze at my mom's house."

"A lot crazier." But she didn't want to think about the place where they'd gotten married. They'd already talked about it too many times before. She changed the subject. "What do you want to do first?"

"Let's swim and do some graffiti art in the grotto."

"I'm not a very good artist," she forewarned him.

He shrugged. "Neither am I."

"You're better than you think you are." She recalled a wild-haired mermaid he'd drawn in the sand at the beach that had looked pretty darned good.

"I'm all right. But it's just for fun, anyway. There's body paint we can experiment with, too."

"Really? And you're just mentioning that now?"

He flashed a sexy smile. "Are you game?"

She nodded, her heart picking up speed. "Where is the grotto, exactly?" The pool had all sorts of nooks and crannies. She couldn't begin to figure it out.

"It's supposed to be below the center waterfall."

"You lead the way, and I'll follow." She stood off to the side and watched him dive into the deep end.

He surfaced, treading water and waiting for her. She took a big breath and dived in, too. Once she came up for air, he turned toward their destination. Margot swam after him, feeling as if she was going to a place of no return, a land of the lost. When in actuality, it was just a man-made grotto—a cave, designed for play.

Once they passed under the waterfall, it was easy to find. The cave was bigger than she expected, with separate coves and connecting pathways. Some of the areas were dimly lit, others were bright and easy to navigate. She walked next to Zeke, exploring their surroundings.

The artwork was everywhere, on walls, floors and ceilings. The people who'd come before them had expressed themselves in all sorts of wondrous ways. She noticed pictures in the styles of surrealism, impressionism and realism. Quite a bit of it mimicked prehistoric art, telling pictorial tales.

"This place is amazing," Zeke said.

Margot nodded. She liked the prehistoric imagery the best. As for the body art, there was a section of the cave set aside for that. It even had a shower, a mini waterfall of sorts, to remove the pigments from your skin before you returned to the pool.

"What sort of graffiti should we do?" she asked.

"How about if we just write our names? Then we don't have to worry about trying to compete with any of this."

"Okay, but only our first names. I don't want to reveal exactly who I am."

"Why?" He snared her gaze. "Are you afraid that someone might figure out that you had sex with me down here?"

Margot sucked in her breath. "We haven't done anything."

"Not yet. But it's only a matter of time." He used a black paint pen, writing ZEKE in big, bold letters.

She chose a lighter, more feminine script. As an afterthought, she drew happy faces on either side of her name, giving it a cute little flair.

Zeke raised his eyebrows. "Is that how good girls do graffiti?"

She shrugged. "I never claimed to be good."

"Sometimes you are, and sometimes you're not." He took her hand and led her to the body painting area. "And right now, you're going to be bad. We both are."

Mercy, she thought. Her pulse was already pounding in unspeakable places. She was excited to be bad.

The body painting kits came with a variety of brushes, water containers for cleaning the brushes and soft white cloths. Zeke decided to use his fingers. He wanted Margot naked, so he told her to remove her bikini. She undid the ties and let the top fall off. She peeled her bottoms down, slowly, giving him a show. She knew how much he enjoyed the smoothness of her skin. She'd always gotten full Brazilian waxes because it turned him on.

He dipped into the paint. He chose red for his first color. He followed the shape of her curves, applying the pigment in sleek lines. From there, he put flowers around her nipples, using purple and blue. He was careful not to smear the colors together. He rinsed his hands after each application and wiped them on a cloth. On her stomach, he painted green, leafy vines.

When he got on his knees and placed a pretty pink heart on her pubic area, it made her think about the rose quartz. Were those stones casting their spell, after all?

No, she thought. The heart he'd drawn translated to sex, not love. Lots and lots of sex.

He circled around back. She had no idea what he was doing, until he planted his hands on her bottom. He was making palm prints on her butt cheeks. Was that his way of being territorial, of marking her as his lover?

His final touch was a lightning bolt that traveled down her spine. She could feel the zigzag motion.

"What color is that?" she asked, trying to picture it.

"Silver, with specks of glitter." He came around to face her, looking into her eyes.

They kissed, but only for a second. She wasn't ready to get sidetracked. She wanted to paint him, too.

His big, broad chest made a strapping canvas. She used a brush and drew symbols that represented his love of the beach. She made wavy lines for water, a chevron for a seashell and a linear shape with stylized wings meant to look like a seagull flying in the distance. She wanted to add a dolphin, but she wasn't sure if she would get it right, so she did the basic outline of a fish.

She tugged his board shorts down, and he stepped out of them. She debated what to do next and decided on a sunburst around his navel, using orange, yellow and flecks of gold.

He looked like an ancient god come to life. If she'd been a better artist, she would've given him tribal tattoos. Zeke wasn't inked. Someday he would be. Tattoos were prevalent in both of his indigenous cultures, and as far as she knew, he was waiting for the right time in his life to honor those traditions.

"Are you done with me?" he asked.

"Not yet." She wrote a message in the V-shaped portion of his abdomen, right above his pubic region. An obscenity meant to arouse him.

He glanced down and read it, and she smiled at his reaction. It worked. He got instantly hard. He reached for her, and they kissed, rubbing their color-streaked bodies together.

He backed her toward the shower until they were standing beneath it. They kissed again, only longer this time, thriving on each other.

She rinsed away the artwork she'd created on him, making it disappear. Within no time, there were no symbols on his chest, no sunburst on his navel, no obscenities near his penis.

Zeke washed her, too. The colors streaked and ran, and she watched the pink heart dissolve into nothingness.

He nudged her closer to the wall, out of the spray of water. He bent his knees, grasped her hips and thrust into her. He moved at a thundering pace, making it seem as if there was no tomorrow. But maybe there wasn't. Maybe there was only today: this hour, this minute, this second.

He backed her into a corner to get more leverage. The cave wall was porous and bumpy, and Margot was pressed roughly against it. But she didn't care. She liked the jagged feeling. She wanted more.

And so did he. He lifted her off the ground, and she held tight, with her legs wrapped around his waist and her arms looped around his neck.

He didn't stop. He kept moving, stroking, pushing harder and deeper. He beckoned her to come. But what choice did she have? His manipulations sent shivers through her core.

Her orgasm erupted, and he watched her, his expression filled with intensity. When he shuddered and spilled into her, she felt his essence rush through her.

Like liquid fire, she thought.

Everything seemed so fast, so hot, so volcanic. She could barely catch her breath. He breathed heavily, too.

He lowered her legs to the ground, and she felt herself wobble. He steadied her, ever so gently, slowing the moment down. The fire was gone, but the sweetest of sparks remained.

An afterglow, she thought. A gentle sensation.

She put her head on his shoulder, and he stroked her water-drenched hair. This was a common feeling between lovers, she told herself, and nothing to worry about. The world wasn't going to explode if she cuddled in his arms.

Allowing herself the luxury of being tender with him, she closed her eyes and accepted it for what it was.

A romantic side of their affair.

Ten

In the evening, Zeke suggested a bottle of pinot grigio and a fruit and cheese platter, and now he and Margot were in the living room, eating and drinking.

As she spread a dollop of brie over a multigrain cracker, he thought about how much he was enjoying this trip and how soon it was going to end. Returning home to an empty condo was going to suck. He didn't like the idea of being alone anymore.

Would it get easier once he went back to work and started traveling again? He'd been spending most of his free time with Margot and maybe that wasn't such a good thing.

He scowled at his wine. Then why did it feel so good to be with her? Not just the sexual stuff, but the moments in between, too?

"What's wrong?" she asked.

He glanced up. "Nothing."

She gazed at him from across the sofa. "But you're frowning."

Damn, he thought. He knew better than to be so transparent. "I got some crumbs in my wine." Dumb as it sounded, he couldn't think of another excuse.

"I didn't realize you were so picky about your pinot."

"I'm not, normally. But this is a great vintage." That part was true. It hailed from a family-owned winery famed for its whites. The process they used produced light, crisp flavors. "Do you want more?"

She extended her glass. "Thanks."

He refilled hers and topped his off, too. He set the bottle back on the coffee table and noticed an angry red mark on the back of Margot's shoulder, near the edge of the ribbed tank top she wore.

"How did you get hurt?" he asked.

She didn't crane her neck to see what he was talking about. Clearly, she knew the mark was there. "I think it happened when we were…"

Having sex in the cave? When he'd been pressing her against the wall? "I'm sorry. I didn't mean to…"

"It's not your fault."

"I should've been more careful. It's probably going to bruise."

She waved away his concern. "I'm fine. Besides, I've done worse to you with my nails."

"That's different." Or it felt different to him. "I'm supposed to be protecting you. It's my job to keep you safe."

"Our affair isn't part of your job, Zeke."

"I know, but I'm responsible for you while you're with me, and I should be taking better care of you."

"It's all right. Really, it is." She finished her crackers and brie and went after a strawberry. "Don't worry about it."

Don't worry? As if he could stop himself. He was still stressed about going home alone and being separated from her.

What the hell was wrong with him? The only other time he'd experienced these types of feelings was when he'd first fallen in love with her. He'd been desperate back then to spend every waking moment with her. In those days, he couldn't live without her. And what about these days? he asked himself. Was history repeating itself? Was he falling back in love?

Even if he was, it would never work. She was still a public figure, and he was still a guy who didn't want a celebrity wife. Just thinking about being in the center of that world made him panic. He'd spent his entire childhood in a fishbowl, and the last thing he needed was to spend his adulthood trapped in one. But that's what he'd be facing if he and Margot became a true-blue couple again. He had no business loving her. Or thinking that he *might* love her.

Struggling to breathe, he gazed out at the nighttime view of the pool. The lights were on outside, showcasing the yard.

"I'm going to go for another swim," he said. "But I hope you don't mind if I go alone." He needed to get a grip on his emotions, and he couldn't do that if she was with him.

"No, I don't mind. I'm nowhere near the swimmer you are. I'd rather stay inside, anyway. I'm pretty beat from earlier."

He came to his feet, ignoring the rest of his wine. He sure as hell wasn't going to drink it now. He needed to stay grounded. "I'll probably be out there awhile." For as long as it took, he thought, to get his head on straight.

"Then I'll see you in the bedroom later." She stood and smoothed her top. "But how about a kiss before you go?"

"Maybe just a quick one." He moved forward, closing the gap between them and intending to keep it simple. But as their lips met, she rocked against him, pulling him under her spell. She tasted light and crisp, full of flavor, like the pinot. He could've gotten drunk on every inch of her. He gripped her waist, holding her as if he might never let go.

Before he went too far, he ended the kiss, trying to knock some sense into himself. He didn't want to love her again. He didn't want to revisit all of that old pain.

He stepped back. "You don't have to wait up for me."

"I am a little tired, but I guess we'll see." She bit down on her bottom lip, sucking it between her teeth.

Now he wanted to kiss her again. But their chemistry wasn't the problem. It was his heart that was getting in the way. Still, he wished she didn't look so soft and sweet. He didn't need the distraction.

She gestured to their leftovers. "I should probably clean this up now, if we're both done."

"I definitely am." He hesitated. "Unless you need some help."

She smiled. "No, thanks. I've got it." She reached for the food platter and headed for the kitchen, leaving the wine for her next trip.

While she was gone, he went outside, stripped down to his boxers and dove straight into the pool, anxious to escape.

He surfaced, surrounded by waterfalls and rock formations. He ignored the rose quartz, refusing to give credence to the power it was supposed to possess. Whatever was happening to him wasn't because of those stones.

Zeke swam for what seemed like hours, taking long bold strokes, determined to feel better. Only his plan wasn't working. No matter how hard he tried, he couldn't seem to shake his anxiety. It didn't matter if he was a strong swimmer, or if he could cut through the water like a knife. He was still drowning, immersed in the fear of love.

Zeke awakened next to Margot, with the morning sun streaming into the room. She hadn't waited up for him last night. She'd been asleep when he'd gone to bed.

Was she awake now? Her back was to him, and all he could see was her tousled hair and the shape of her body, covered with a sheet.

He swept her hair off to one side and checked the mark on her shoulder. It was purple now. A definite bruise.

To go along with his tortured heart?

As frightening as his feelings were, Zeke wasn't able to deny them. He knew that he loved her. But what did he expect? If he'd loved her before, then he was certainly capable of loving her again.

"What are you doing?" she asked groggily, proving that she was awake.

"I'm just making sure you're okay." He kissed the spot where she was injured, touching his lips lightly to her skin, wishing she hadn't bewitched him.

She made a soft sound. "What time is it?"

"I have no idea." And he didn't want to move away

from her to check. "You can go back to sleep if you're still tired."

"I think I'd rather stay awake." She rolled over to face him, smiling sweetly. "I'm sorry I crashed out last night."

"It's all right. I wasn't expecting you to stay up. You had a long day yesterday. You don't handle the outdoors as well as I do."

"The curse of being a redhead. But at least I didn't get a sunburn." She adjusted the sheet, keeping it over her. "How long have you been up?"

"Just long enough to wake up beside you." He gazed into her eyes, nearly seeing a reflection of himself in them. She was the only woman he'd ever loved, who'd ever affected him this way. He reached out to skim her cheek. "You're always so pretty in the mornings."

"And you're always so intense, no matter what time of the day it is."

"I can't help it. It's just who I am. Besides, isn't that why you developed that old crush on me?"

She nodded. "Silly little me. I got caught up in the dark and broody."

"You're still caught up in it, still sleeping with me, still sharing a bed." He lowered the sheet until her naked body was exposed. His, too. They were both bare.

She reacted by pulling him closer, and they kissed long and deep. She rubbed against him, and all too soon he was braced above her. He couldn't make his feelings for her go away. Not this time. They were like a boomerang, always coming back. He damned her in his mind. But mostly he damned himself.

She parted her thighs, offering herself to him, and he slid inside. She was warm and wet and inviting, and he accepted what she gave him, struggling with whatever semblance of sanity he had left. Her hands were everywhere, all over his body, seeking whatever parts of him she could reach.

He increased the pace, moving fast and hard. She joined him, meeting his dominant rhythm. He lowered his head to lick one of her pointy, pink nipples. He licked the other one, too, then blew air across it, making her shiver.

She grabbed ahold of the sheet, twisting the fabric between her fingers. She looked wild and messy, free and passionate. But she'd always been an uninhibited lover.

She wrapped her legs around him, squeezing him with a viselike grip. Moans and groans filled the room, sounds of passion, hunger and heat. Her climax ignited his, and they came together, erupting feverishly.

He held her afterward, and she rested her head in the crook of his shoulder. Her hair tickled his chin, a silky sort of scratchiness, a sensation he remembered from when they were first married, back when snuggling with her made sense. He should let go of her. But he stayed where he was, keeping her in his embrace and wondering what came next.

Was he supposed to tell her that he loved her? Or dig a grave and bury his feelings in the dirt? Neither scenario appealed to him.

He glanced down at her. She'd barely moved since the sex had ended. She looked groggy again, her eyelids fluttering.

But it didn't matter if she drifted off. There was no hurry for them to get up, nowhere they had to be, nothing pressing they had to do. His only worry was the gut-clenching ache of being in love.

Her eyelids closed all the way. She was definitely

falling back asleep. Cursing his weakness for her, he stayed awake, holding her unbearably close.

Later that day, Zeke's emotions remained on high alert. Nonetheless, he was trying to act casual, especially since Margot seemed so refreshed. At this point, they'd already lingered over lunch, and now they were going to go for a walk in the woods. But just as they were on the porch preparing to leave, her phone rang.

She checked the screen. "Will you give me a minute? I need to take this."

He nodded, and she headed down the steps without him. Clearly, it was a private matter. He stayed on the porch, but he could still see her, standing off by herself, engaged in conversation. Based on her expression, she'd just received some distressing news. Was it work related? Or was it personal? He couldn't begin to guess. Nor was he going to try.

Once her conversation ended, she returned to him and sat in one of the wooden chairs out front, as if she was still trying to digest the call.

He sat next to her. "What's going on?"

"It was about my show." Her voice quavered. "The network and the producers got into a dispute, and the network cancelled us. I never saw this coming. I thought for sure that our contract would be renewed and we'd be doing another season. And maybe more seasons after that. Our ratings were good. Everything seemed fine. But now I'm out of a job."

"I'm so sorry." He didn't know how to comfort her. Margot's association with *The Grown-up Years* had been a point of contention for him, the reason he'd divorced her, and now the series was gone. "Are you going to be okay, moneywise? I can loan you something if you need it."

She shook her head. "Thanks, but I have enough to get by for a while. I've been careful to make investments and put something away for a rainy day. But it just feels like I'm floating now, like my career might slip back into limbo."

He considered the timing. Was it a coincidence? Was it fate? Or something in between? "Maybe this is a sign."

She frowned. "Of what?"

"Of making a change in your life." And maybe going back in time and giving their relationship a second chance, he thought. Was that possible? Could it happen? Or was he grasping at straws? He couldn't be sure.

She stared him down. "Are you suggesting that I give up acting?"

"You did it once before."

"And it made me miserable."

"But it's different this time. You have Liam now. Maybe it would behoove you to consider a different line of work. Lots of former actors have created successful lives outside of the entertainment industry."

"I can't believe you're trying to talk me into throwing in the towel."

"Yeah, but you just said that your career might slip back into limbo, so what difference does it make?"

She blew out a breath. "I need encouragement, not my ex-husband spouting his old rhetoric."

"I'm not trying to start a fight." Arguing with her would only make everything more painful, and he was frazzled enough already. "I just…"

Her frowned deepened. "You just *what*?"

Should he say it? Should he admit that he loved her? That all of his old feelings had come back?

"Maybe we should take that walk," he said. Then he could decide if he should tell her. "It might do us both some good."

"Okay, but first I need to fix my hair. It keeps getting in my eyes." She removed a green scrunchie from her pocket and pulled her unruly mane into a high ponytail.

Zeke caught himself smiling. "Is that from the '90s?" She used to wear those when she was a kid. "Something you shoved away in a box somewhere?"

"No, smarty. They're back in style again. Some people are even donning them on the red carpet."

"Really? Damn. I need to pay closer attention to the trends. You always looked cute in them, though." Her hair spilled out over the scrunchie. He leaned over in his chair to plant a quick kiss on her cheek.

She flinched. "What was that for?"

"It's just me letting you know that I like being around you." That was a lot easier than saying that he loved her.

"I like being around you, too, when you're not doling out advice about my career. But it's not your fault that my show ended. I wish they hadn't canceled it."

And he wished that he wasn't tied up in knots over her. He stood and reached for her hand, and she took it, hugging him when she got to her feet.

Without getting into another conversation, they exited the porch and entered the woods. The property was surrounded by ponderosa pines, rugged trees with a sweet smell. The trails were wide enough for them to walk side by side, the ground covered with twigs and fallen leaves.

They took an elevated path and headed higher into the hills. As squirrels scurried through the trees and a red-tailed hawk soared above them, Zeke glanced over at Margot. She plucked a long-stemmed bloom from a tall flowering plant and worked it into her ponytail, adding a spot of yellow.

When they reached a ridge that spread into a flat plane, they stopped to appreciate the view.

"This is beautiful," she said. "I'd love to bring Liam up here. But I'd have to rent a cabin or something. The house where you and I are staying doesn't seem geared for someone his age."

"I agree. It's more of an adult sanctuary, for artists and lovers and whatnot. But if you want me to ask the caretakers if they know of a kid-friendly cabin in this area, I'd be glad to check on that."

"Thanks. That would be nice. I don't know if Liam has ever even been to the mountains. There's still so much I'm learning about my son. He likes to chat at night, before bed, so that's when I seem to get to know him best."

"He was talkative on the night I tucked him in. He asked a lot of questions, too."

Curiosity lit up her eyes. "What kinds of questions?"

Zeke winced a little. "He asked me if I was ever going to get married again or have kids. He asked me the same thing about you."

She blinked. "He did?"

"He's hoping that you'll get married again someday. He expressed an interest in having an adoptive father and some brothers and sisters."

"Oh, my goodness. I had no idea that he was having those kinds of thoughts." She furrowed her brow. "As attached as Liam is to you, I was worried that he might start thinking of you as a father figure." She leaned forward. "He didn't mention you becoming his dad, did he?"

"No. He just talked about you marrying someone else. And that was a bit hard for me to take. I know we're divorced, but I never really counted on you having a new husband."

She sighed. "I'm not ready for anything like that anyway. I'm in the midst of the affair with you, and I just lost my job. Things are complicated for me right now."

"For me, too. I was okay when we first got here, but then last night, I started getting jumbled. That's why I went for a swim and why I needed to be alone."

She fussed with the flower in her hair. "What are you talking about? You're not making yourself clear."

He studied her, summoning the strength to tell her the rest of it. "I didn't mean to get this close to you. It was only supposed to be sex. And friendship." He couldn't discount that part. "But for me, it's turning into more." He paused, felt his pulse spike. "I love you, Margot. I fell back in love with you. But truthfully, I don't have a clue what I'm supposed to do about it."

Eleven

Margot couldn't speak. She needed a moment to keep her knees from buckling, to stop her hands from quaking.

Zeke loved her?

A fear rose inside her, a panic that she was in danger of loving him, too. Just hearing him say it, just knowing that he felt that way created a tunnel to the past and all the years that she'd loved him.

She met his gaze. He was looking at her, watching her.

She finally summoned the courage to speak. "I understand that you're conflicted," she said, struggling to steady her voice. "But what prompted you to tell me how you feel? It seems odd that you're mentioning it on the same day I lost my job."

He shook his head. "I didn't know your show was going to be canceled."

"But you never wanted me to be part of it. You never wanted an actress for a wife."

"Yes, and why would I? I spent my youth living in the chaos of my mother's fame—the never-ending paparazzi, the invasion of my family's privacy, strangers stalking us, tracking down our phone numbers, going through our trash."

"I'm aware of all that." He'd drilled it into her since the beginning. She'd seen firsthand how Eva's celebrity had affected Bailey, too. "I'm not naive about how difficult it was for you. But I had a right to pursue my dreams and goals."

"I wasn't trying to take your happiness away from you. But I couldn't spend my days worrying that your star was going to rise or that you'd become as famous as my mother someday."

"You shouldn't love me. It's not good for you. It's not good for me, either."

"I know, but I can't help how I feel. If things were different, I'd ask you to marry me again, to start over, to have the opportunities we missed. But nothing has changed, and it still hurts as badly as it did before."

His admission made her ache, and so did the tortured way he was looking at her. She wanted to touch him, to connect with his pain somehow. But she kept her hands at her sides.

"I'm afraid of loving you," she said. "Of letting myself stumble back down that path. But even if I loved you, I wouldn't give up my career or stop being who I am. That would destroy me."

"That's what makes it so hard. We already went through this in the past, and it made us hate each other."

"We don't have to hate each other now." She inched closer to him. "We can stay friends."

"What about our affair?" He moved closer, too. "Do you want to keep sleeping with me?"

She shivered, goose bumps covering her arms. Continuing to be intimate with him now would only create more pain and suffering. Yet she foolishly replied, "Maybe we can keep it going."

He shifted his stance, leaves crunching beneath his feet. "For how long?"

"I don't know." Margot fought the heat building inside her. She was playing with fire, and sooner or later, she was bound to get torched. "But I can't bear to give you up just yet."

"I'm not ready to let go, either. But damn it, I should be." He glanced up at the sky. Was he searching for divine intervention, for something or someone to set him straight?

The only thing she saw were clouds shielding the sun. "We're both mixed-up."

"Yeah, we are. But I really want to kiss you right now."

"Just kiss me?" She wanted to have full-blown sex, even if it was a dangerous thing to do. She was conflicted, from her heart to her soul, but she couldn't seem to control her perilous urges. "I think we should do more."

Zeke reacted cautiously. "Are you sure this is the time and place?"

She glanced around. "Here in the mountains, among the flowers? This seems like a perfect time and place."

He leaned toward her. "Then who am I to disagree?"

Grateful for his acquiescence, she tugged him to the ground, and they kissed, over and over, wrapped in pain and fear and lust. A restless combination. A whirlwind of emotions. Already, her head spun with it.

She moved quickly, stripping off her boots and jeans and panties. She was wearing a tunic top that fit like a minidress, which she left on.

He shoved his jeans and boxers down, and she straddled his lap. There was no one around to see. They were alone on a hilltop in the middle of nowhere.

He was hard and ready. She was ready, too. So damned eager to be with him. She impaled herself, her breath hitching on a moan.

"If only..." he whispered.

She knew exactly what he meant. If only they could build a life together, if only their differences wouldn't get in the way. But she didn't want to talk about that. She just wanted to focus on the sex. Yet as she moved up and down, rocking her body and creating a sinuous rhythm, she realized that she loved him, just as he loved her.

But it didn't matter if she shared his feelings. It didn't change who they were. She wasn't going to marry him again. She wasn't even going to keep sleeping with him. This had to be their last day as lovers, the end of their affair. It was different now that love was part of the mix. In the long run, it would only cause them pain. They were two people who didn't belong together.

She rode him with the passion that clamored inside her, that made her scratch her fingers into the dirt, getting little pebbles under her nails. Tomorrow she would tell him that it was over, that she couldn't do this anymore.

They were going home tomorrow, anyway. This trip was almost done. But for now, she just needed to lose herself in the hunger and make both of them come, as hard and fast and desperately as she could.

* * *

The following morning, Margot woke up late and discovered she was alone. Zeke wasn't next to her in bed, but she didn't ponder his whereabouts. Instead, she packed her bag, preparing to go home. Of course, she had to steel her emotions, too, and figure out exactly what she was going to say to him.

Should she admit that she loved him? Or just state her case about ending their affair? She decided that it was only fair to tell him everything. It was strange, loving him again. But maybe she'd never really stopped. Maybe she'd been repressing it all these years, claiming not to care when she actually did. But did it matter? Love wasn't the answer to their problems. There was no future for them, other than being friends. They'd both gone too far, and now she had to step back and hope for the best.

After she bathed and got dressed, she wandered through the house, looking for him, anxious to get her feelings off her chest. She didn't find him, but she discovered that he'd made a pot of coffee. She poured herself a cup, then diluted it with hot water. Zeke always made it too strong for her. She added her usual sugar and milk, still wondering where he was.

She could text him, assuming that he had his phone on him. But instead, she went outside to look for him by the pool.

Sure enough, he was there. He sat in a patio chair, in a faraway corner of the yard, gazing out at the water. He looked sullen but sexy, dressed in a plain white T-shirt, holey jeans and black sneakers.

Margot approached him, and he glanced up. She was going to miss being with him. Even now, she wanted to lure him back to bed and give their affair one more day.

"Join me?" he asked, interrupting her thoughts.

When she didn't respond, he gestured to the empty chair next to him. Fraught with nerves, she took the seat and put her coffee on a side table. One more day wasn't going to make a difference.

"I'm sorry I disappeared," he said. "I couldn't stay cooped up inside."

She merely nodded. "How long have you been out here?"

"Since daybreak. I watched the sun come up."

"Have you eaten?" It was a mundane question, but she couldn't think of what else to say.

"I had some toast and jam. What about you?"

"Just the coffee so far. I'm not really hungry." But enough of the small talk, she thought. She needed to broach the truth. "Zeke?"

His gaze connected with hers. "Yes?"

"What happened to you happened to me, too. The love thing," she clarified, forcing herself to stay strong.

"Damn." He released a rough, tremulous breath. "Really?"

She nodded. "But I think it's been going on for a while. It seems feasible that I never really stopped loving you, only I didn't realize it or own up to it until now."

He leaned forward in his chair. "Maybe that's what's been going on with me, too."

"Maybe. But love isn't going to save us. Our affair has to end for good this time. What's the point of us sleeping together when it will only hurt worse later?"

He frowned, his eyes dark and hooded beneath his brows. "I don't want to keep hurting, any more than you do. But I still wish we could be together for real. Can't you reconsider your job situation?"

"And give up acting just because my show ended? That didn't work the first time, and it's not going to work now."

"But where are you going to go from here? Most of your career has been centered around playing the same character."

"I know. And it's scary to think that I'll never play her again. But maybe losing my job was a blessing in disguise. It might work in my favor to try something new." She considered her options. "I always wanted to transition into film, and this could be my chance to get cast in a breakout role."

"And break free of me while you're doing it? God, I feel like I'm getting divorced all over again."

"Me, too." She ached just remembering it. "But we're being civil to each other. Last time, we fought like feral cats and rabid dogs."

He sent her a sad smile. "We weren't friends then like we are now. So that's saying something, at least." He glanced toward the hills. "When we get back to the city, I'm going to book a flight out of LA."

She started. "And go where?"

"To Samoa. I think I need to spend some quiet time with my grandfather. He's always been good for what ails me."

She had incredible memories of Samoa from their honeymoon. The dreamlike beaches, the rainforests, the romance of being a new bride. Images she struggled to grasp now. "Will you give your grandfather my regards?"

"Of course." Zeke stood, coming to his towering height. "I should go throw my things together."

"I already packed, so I'll just stay here and finish

my coffee." She'd barely touched it. "I'm sorry for the way things turned out."

"So am I. But maybe we shouldn't have risked having another affair to begin with." He started to walk away, but then he turned back to look at her. "I'm probably always going to love you. But man, it's awful, loving someone I can't have."

She battled the urge to cry. "It's the same for me." Loving someone who couldn't handle her career choice, who couldn't be the lifelong partner she needed. Zeke would always be the husband she'd loved and lost.

When Margot got home from the mountains, she found out that Liam was sick.

Was this her fault for going away? For lying to her mom about where she was? For trusting that Liam would be okay without her?

In the midst of her guilt, she asked her mom, "Why didn't you call and tell me that he wasn't feeling well? I would have come back right away."

"He just started feeling ill today. But I think it's just a cold. He doesn't have a fever or a sore throat or anything alarming. His nose is stuffed up, so I gave him a decongestant and told him to rest."

Margot was still worried. This was her first experience with Liam getting sick. "Is he asleep?"

"I doubt it. When I checked on him, he was sitting up in bed, searching for something to stream."

"I need to check on him, too." Margot dashed up to his room. His door was ajar, so she peeked in and saw him leaning against a bunch of pillows and watching TV.

She knocked to let him know she was entering his

space. As soon as he caught sight of her, a big grin spread across his face.

"Hi, Mom!" He put the screen on pause.

"Hi, baby." She sat on the edge of his bed and smoothed his quilt. "Grandma says you have a cold."

"Yeah. But I just started watching these funny old cartoons. There's this wolf that keeps chasing this really fast bird that beeps like a car. But the wolf never catches him."

She smiled in amusement. "That's not a wolf. It's a coyote, and the bird is a roadrunner. Those are really old cartoons. They were around even before I was born."

"Really? Wow. Did you have fun at your spa thing? Grandma said you went to get pampered and stuff."

She didn't know what to say about her phony spa weekend. She certainly couldn't admit that she'd lied about where she'd been or how badly she was hurting over Zeke. "I'm just happy to be home with you now."

"I'm glad you're back, too. I'm getting kind of hungry, though."

"I'll fix you something. How does soup and crackers sound?"

"Good. But can I have one of those parfait cups with the whipped cream and strawberry goop, too?"

"You got it. Soup and goop coming right up."

She returned to the kitchen and prepared his food, running on nervous energy. Her mom hung around instead of going home. Was she waiting for Margot to calm down a bit?

After everything was ready, Margot brought Liam his tray. She'd given him two parfait cups and lots of crackers.

"It's chicken noodle," she said about the soup.

"Thanks." He smiled. "I love you."

"I love you, too." Such an easy kind of love, she thought. So different from the tortured love that she and Zeke were feeling. "I'll leave you alone now. But text me if you need anything else." She'd given him a kid's watch that allowed him to communicate with her. It even had a GPS so she could track him. He didn't always wear it, though. Sometimes he forgot. She walked over to the door. "Bye, sweetie."

"Bye." He spooned into his soup and returned his attention to the cartoon. Coyote was lighting a stick of dynamite that was about to explode in his face. Not exactly the best subject matter for a child, but Liam was old enough to know that it wasn't real.

She went into the living room, expecting her mom to leave now. Only she still wasn't ready to go. In fact, she plopped down on the sofa as if she meant to have a chat. She'd even reapplied her lipstick while Margot was gone. Her no-nonsense mother wasn't a glamorous lady, but she still took pride in her appearance.

"What's up?" Margot asked her.

"I was just thinking that for someone who just spent two and a half days at a resort, you don't seem very rested."

Because the spa hadn't been real, Margot thought, struggling with another bout of guilt. "Why would I seem rested? I came home to my son being sick."

"That's understandable. But you seemed out of sorts before I told you that Liam wasn't feeling well. I noticed it the moment you walked in the door."

Why was she still pretending? Margot asked herself. By now, there was no point in protecting her secret. "I'm sorry, but I've been lying to you. I was away on a trip with Zeke. We've been…"

"Dating?" her mom politely asked.

"No." She made the truth clear. "Just sleeping together. I realize how blunt that sounds, but I can't think of another way to say it." She was beyond the lies now. "We had an affair before, too, for years after we split up."

"Oh, my. How did I miss all of that?"

"I was good at hiding it. We still love each other, but it's not going to work." She explained why their relationship was doomed.

Her mom's shoulders tensed. "Those are the same reasons you got divorced."

"And this time I don't even have a job. On top of everything else, *The Grown-up Years* was canceled. The producers had a beef with the network."

"Oh, honey. I'm so sorry. I remember how devastated you were when *The Kid Years* was canceled and now this show, too. You've been through so much already. It isn't fair."

"It's an awful feeling, believe me. But I'm going to tell my agent that I'm interested in other projects. Not sitcoms, though. I'd like to do films. I need a change in my life." Something to make her feel new and fresh.

"I'm glad you're picking yourself up by your bootstraps. But it's such a shame that you're hurting over Zeke. Why does he have to be so damned stubborn? Why can't he see the mistake he's making? He should be fighting for you, instead of letting it end all over again."

"He's never going to be able to handle my career. His issues with fame run too deep." When Margot's eyes flooded with tears, she turned away, not wanting her mom to see her cry.

Zeke wasn't going to alter his perspective. There was already too much anguish inside him, years of turmoil that couldn't be fixed.

Twelve

Zeke stood alone on a strip of white sand, gazing out at the water. He'd been in Samoa for nearly a week, and normally this place gave him peace. Only this time, it wasn't working.

His grandfather—or Tama as Zeke called him—managed a resort on the south coast of Upolu. Guests could lounge on the beach, swim, snorkel and charter fishing boats. There was a restaurant, bar and onsite gift shop. Yet none of those activities was able to ease Zeke's mind. Surfing didn't help, either, and he was just a ten-minute boat ride to some of the best breaks in the area.

He couldn't stop obsessing about Margot. She was in his head, day and night, and the more he thought about her, the lonelier he felt.

Tama walked up beside him, and he turned to look at his grandfather. They were around the same height. Tama's hair was long and gray, and his skin was deeply weathered and heavily tattooed, the artwork on his body a show of pride. These days, he lived in a bungalow the resort provided, but when he was a boy, he'd grown up in a nearby village and lived in a traditional *fale*, a house with pebble floors, a thatched roof and no walls.

Tama had met Zeke's grandma here in Samoa. She'd come to the island with a group of friends, and she and Tama had fallen madly in love. Within no time, they got married and had a son named Joseph. In Samoan he was called Sefa. But he didn't stay on the island. Sefa was a restless guy, a charming daredevil who moved to the States, became a well-respected stuntman and married a famous Hollywood actress.

And then I came along, Zeke thought. The product of that fateful union. Soon after that, his dad died. His grandma had passed away during that era, too. Zeke had no recollection of either of them.

"How are you doing?" Tama asked.

Zeke shrugged. "The same as when I first got here."

The older man frowned. Typically, he was a bright and playful man. But he could be serious, too. "What do you want out of life? What's the most important thing to you?"

"Truthfully? I don't even know anymore."

"Then what was the most important thing to you when you first married Margot?"

"Just being with her and creating a life together. I imagined us having kids and doing whatever else families do." Zeke sank his feet into the sand. "But that was before everything went awry."

"Do you remember me teaching you about *Fa'a Samoa* when you were young and how important it is?"

"Of course. It's the Samoan way." Traditions that went back thousands of years. A complex cultural code designed to teach people how to conduct their lives and attain happiness.

"And what's at the heart of our ways?"

"Family. *Aiga*," Zeke added, using the Samoan word.

"Family is the heart of the Choctaw people, too. Your grandmother came from a tight-knit society, and she instilled her beliefs in your father. But he practiced the Samoan way, too. He had to learn to walk in both worlds. Sometimes he faltered, though, and struggled with his identity. That's one of the reasons he left and went to America. He was trying to find himself, but he found your movie star mother instead."

Zeke went silent for a second, trying to imagine it all. "What kind of relationship did my parents have? I know they met on the set of one of her films and had a whirlwind romance. But I don't know much about their day-to-day life. My mom never talks about that part. I think it makes her too sad."

"She loved your father very much, and he loved her, too. Their relationship was good, strong and happy. They spent as much time together as they could. But after they got married, he began to worry about how famous she was becoming. Everyone wanted a piece of her, but he just wanted her to himself."

This was news to Zeke. "I had no idea that my dad struggled with my mom's career. How did he overcome it?"

"He wasn't willing to lose her over it, so he didn't even share his fears with her. He just became the husband she needed, without her ever knowing that those things had crossed his mind."

"I'm glad he was able to do that. For both their sakes. But I can't get a handle on my fears the way he did."

Tama shook his head. "You're the last person who

should be afraid of having a famous wife. You protect celebrities. You support them and their families. You give them the best part of yourself. So why can't you give that to the woman you love, too?"

"Because I need my private life to be calm and quiet, not centered around her public persona. I realize that this is probably going to sound like psychobabble to you, but I already knew from the beginning that I never wanted a celebrity wife. That it would be too difficult for me."

"Yet you wed an actress."

"She wasn't acting when we got married. She'd already left the industry then." Zeke watched a boat bobbing in the water. "After Margot rebooted her career, I was so hurt and angry over what she did, I could barely see straight."

"Maybe you should talk to your father about this. He was a young man, like you, when he resolved his issues."

Zeke expelled the air in his lungs. His grandfather didn't believe in a separation between life and death. He conversed regularly with his deceased loved ones, treating them as if they were still alive. But Zeke had never quite gotten the hang of that. "I'm sorry, but I can't go to him with my problems, not the way I can with you."

"You most certainly can. Your father didn't die here, but he is buried here, and now this is where his spirit remains."

"Yes, but if I talk to him, is he going to respond? Is he going to tell me what to do? Or how to cope?"

"He might," Tama said. "But you'll never know if you don't try." The old man patted him on the shoulder, then turned to leave. "I have to go back to work.

But there's nothing more I can say, anyway. Whatever happens now is up to you."

Zeke watched his grandfather go, feeling more alone and conflicted than ever. He dragged a hand through his hair, wondering if he should try to talk to his dad.

But how would he go about it?

He couldn't do it here. A group of tourists had just arrived. He could see them heading in his direction, traipsing along with their snorkeling gear.

Happy vacationers, he thought.

Other people were playing and having fun, and he was scouting the best location to converse with a man he'd never even met.

Should he find a secluded spot near the lagoon? Should he sit beneath a coconut tree? Or simply go back to his room?

Zeke chose the latter. He made his way to his bungalow and stood outside the door, staring at it, not having the slightest idea where to start.

Maybe he should give himself a bit more time. He couldn't force a conversation, not if he wasn't ready.

He decided to head over to the gift shop instead. He always brought trinkets home from the island, mostly for his mother and sister. But maybe this time he could buy something for Margot and Liam, too. He was still friends with Margot. A painful friendship, but one just the same.

The lady at the gift shop greeted Zeke with a smile. Her name was Lucy, and she'd been running the store for as long as Zeke could remember. She was a strong-boned woman with a broad face and sparkling eyes. She'd grown up in the same village as Tama and had a slew of grandkids.

She left Zeke alone to browse. He chose a kava bowl

for Bailey, a coconut leaf fan for his mom, and a T-shirt with a tribal design for Liam. Finding something for Margot wasn't quite so easy. Nothing felt right. He lingered, looking at everything. Finally, he zeroed in on a little basket filled with painted stones. He sifted through them.

They had Samoan words and phrases on them, with English translations on the other side. He spotted *welcome*, *good day*, *please*, *yes*, *no* and *thank you*. Another grouping pertained to family: *father/grandfather*, *mother/grandmother*, *brother/sister*, *aunt/uncle* and *cousin*. *Husband* and *wife* caught his eye, too, striking an emotional chord inside him.

Still, should he get them? They reminded him of the conversation hearts Margot had always favored for Valentine's Day. She never wanted chocolates. She preferred those silly hearts.

Zeke sorted through the stones again. There was even one that had *love* written on it.

Rather than overthink it, he brought them up to the counter, along with his other purchases. Lucy took his money, his *tala*, and placed everything in a bag and wished him well.

On his way back to his bungalow, Zeke decided to talk to his father, out loud, right then and there as he strolled along the sand.

"Hey, Dad, I'm sorry I never confided in you before. It's all so new to me, trying to figure out what to say." He continued walking and talking. "I used to be married, but maybe you already know that. Maybe Tama told you about my wedding years ago." He glanced at the bag in his hand. "Anyway, I just got my ex-wife a gift." He waited a beat before he added,. "I'm still in love with her, and I want to be with her, but I'm struggling with what she does for a living. She's an actress, like Mom. Tama said that you had a hard time with Mom's fame, but that you worked it out."

Zeke went on to explain his childhood and how chaotic it had been for him. He was still talking by the time he entered his bungalow.

He sat on the bed, removed the stones from the bag, tipped the basket they were in and dumped them out. "This is what I bought for Margot."

He didn't get a reaction from his father. He didn't hear any voices or notice any spiritual stirrings. But when he looked in the mirror across the room, he saw a troubled version of himself. A man who'd hurt the woman he loved.

Was that what his father wanted him to see? The message he was receiving? A message that had been there all along, Zeke thought.

He broke eye contact with himself and stared at the *husband* stone, ashamed of the kind of husband he'd been. Margot had deserved better, so much more from him.

He said to his dad, "You were a good husband to my mother. You did right by her, proving that you loved her, and she doesn't even know the sacrifice you made." Regret stabbed Zeke straight in the chest. "I wasn't like you. I failed my wife. She's my heart, my everything, and I walked away from her."

He picked up the *love* stone. "I want to be there for her now. I want to be the kind of man I should've been from the beginning. To prove that I love her, not just by saying it, but by my actions." He closed his hand around the stone. "But will she accept me? Will she trust that I can change?"

Zeke knew that he could change. He felt it in his

blood, in his soul. He'd spent too many years worrying about how Margot's celebrity would affect him, instead of focusing on the love and commitment he'd pledged to her on their wedding day.

It was different now. He was prepared to do whatever it took to win her back, to stand by her side, no matter how famous she became.

Yet the possibility of her rejecting him scared him senseless. But after the way he'd wronged her, he feared the worst.

"Do you think she'll take me back?" he asked his dad, without expecting a response. Even Zeke couldn't foretell the future. In this case, only Margot had the answers.

On the day Zeke returned to LA, he decided to swing by his mother's house. He figured that his sudden urge to see his mom had something to do with his attempted communion with his dad. Nonetheless, he was going to make it a quick visit, a few minutes at best. He couldn't handle much more than that. He was overwhelmed with thoughts of Margot and when he should reach out to her. Tonight? Tomorrow? He was anxious, but nervous, too.

He parked in the circular driveway and entered the mansion. He was greeted by a housekeeper, who told him that his mom was preparing for a small afternoon tea party. Apparently, his timing wasn't so great, but he ventured to the garden anyway.

He found her fussing over the table. She looked elegant, as always. Today she wore a ruffled top and a linen skirt, her hair swept into an updo.

"Zeke!" She smiled. "I thought you were still in Samoa."

"I came back early. I'm sorry I didn't call ahead. I

just wanted to stop by and tell you that I had a good visit with Tama." And with his father, but he figured that was a conversation for another time. He couldn't just spring that on his mom and then dart back out the door. "I also wanted to give you this." He handed her the coconut leaf fan.

"Thank you. It's beautiful." She placed it on the table next to a basket of flowers, making it part of the centerpiece. "But I think I should warn you that your sister is on her way over, and she's bringing June and Margot with her. That's who this tea party is for."

His pulse nearly jumped out of his skin. "Then I better go." It wasn't his intention to intrude. He hesitated for a second. "I guess it's safe to assume that you know about my bungled affair with Margot."

She nodded. "June called me. She was worried about her daughter. That's part of why I planned this tea, to try to help ease Margot's pain and have a women's chat."

"That's nice of you." He was glad his mom had Margot's best interest at heart. "I messed everything up, but I want to get back together with her. I want to support her hopes and dreams. I want to marry her again and be the husband I should've been the first time around. But this isn't the right time for me to talk to her."

"Oh, my dear son. Anytime is the right time to tell a woman how you feel."

"Then you wouldn't mind if I stayed?" By now, he couldn't bear to leave.

"Of course not." She put her hand on his cheek. "I have faith in you."

But would Margot have the same faith? "I hope she doesn't think we ambushed her."

"I'll explain that you just happened to come by. It's the truth, after all."

Within no time, Bailey, June and Margot arrived. But he only had eyes for Margot. She looked soft and sweet in a pale yellow dress fluttering around her ankles. As soon as she saw him, she stopped in her tracks, surprised by his presence.

His mom jumped right in, as promised. "Zeke just got back from his grandfather's and came over to bring me a gift. He didn't know I was having this tea."

"Then you're not staying?" Margot asked.

"I am, actually. But not for the tea. Now that I'm here, I was hoping we could talk. Maybe go for a walk in the maze." The location of their wedding, he thought. That seemed like a fitting place for him to lay his nervous heart on the line.

She agreed to accompany him, and they left the rose garden and headed into the maze. In addition to the hedges, it boasted thirty-nine fountains and hundreds of metal sculptures.

Margot glanced over at him, but he hardly knew where to start. She was being quiet, waiting for him to say whatever was on his mind. By the time they reached the first fountain, he was even more nervous. But he couldn't stall. He needed to speak.

He started off by saying, "I made so many stupid mistakes in the past and did so many hurtful things. I'm so sorry for all of that. Truly, I am. But I'm ready to give you what you need. I want to support your career and stand by your side."

She flinched, the water from the fountain shooting up behind her. "Since when?"

"Since I did some soul-searching in Samoa. My fear of having a celebrity wife ruined our marriage. It debilitated me when it should've given me strength and made me a better husband. I didn't rise to the challenge.

I didn't believe in our love the way I should have." He explained further, going deeper, telling her the whole story, including the part that involved his dad. He even mentioned the gift he'd bought her and how the words on the stones factored into it.

She softly replied, "It's wonderful that you made a special connection with your father and that the gift you got me was part of it. But how can I be sure that if we get back together, you won't freak out again?"

"Because I'm stronger now." He led her to a bench, where they both sat. "I swear, I am."

"I don't know, Zeke. I mean, think about it, really think about it. What if I go into film and my career takes off beyond my wildest expectations? What if your worst fear comes true and I become as famous as your mom?"

"Then I'll increase your security. I'll become your personal bodyguard, not just your husband. I'll do whatever it takes to give us a semblance of normalcy without compromising our relationship."

She twisted her hands on her lap. "In theory, that's an amazing concept. But if it doesn't work, we'll be facing another breakup. I'm afraid of making a commitment to you and things ending up in shambles." I can't let that happen to Liam, either."

"The last thing I want is to make a mess out of either of your lives. I love you, and I love your son. I'd be honored to adopt him and become his father. But you have to believe in me, Margot. You have to trust me. I need your help to erase the past and start over."

"This is all I ever really wanted from you, but now it just seems so surreal. Like a dream that could shatter."

"I understand." He couldn't force her fears away. He'd just learned to tackle his own. "We can take it slow if that makes you feel better. We could start dating again and going to public places together. Then you could get a feel for what a new relationship between us would be like." If it was up to him, he would marry her tomorrow. Only it wasn't up to him.

"I appreciate everything you're saying and everything you're offering, but whether we go fast or slow, the end result could still be the same."

He put his hand on her knee, needing to touch her if only in some small way. "I'm willing to chance it."

Her breath rattled in her throat. "But I don't know if I am. I need more time to think about it."

"Then I'll give you as much time as you need." There was nothing more he could say to convince her to be with him. Nothing more he could do, except hope that she loved him enough to decide that he was worth the risk.

Margot returned to the rose garden alone. Zeke left without seeing Bailey and their moms again.

Back at the gathering, tea and scones had already been served. All three women anxiously gazed at Margot when she arrived.

"Where's Zeke?" Bailey asked, leaping up from her chair.

"He went home." Margot planted her feet on the flagstone patio, trying to stand strong but afraid she might fall over. "He's giving me time to think. To sort through my emotions."

"You didn't take my boy back?" Eva asked, speaking in a gentle tone about her son.

"No, I'm sorry. I didn't. I love him desperately, but my head is spinning." Her pulse was racing, too. Everything was moving at a dizzying pace. "Zeke says he's changed, but I'm afraid that the problems we faced in the past could arise again." She'd spent too many years going back and forth, loving him, losing him, having two affairs with him. "It's all so confusing."

"Maybe you should sit and try to relax," Bailey said. "Do you want some tea? I can pour it for you."

"Thank you." She took an empty chair and scooted closer to the table, accepting the cup her best friend handed her. In the silence that followed, she could feel everyone watching her. They were all seated now. After a few sips of the Earl Grey, she said, "Zeke wants to marry me again and adopt Liam. But how can I marry him, feeling the way I do?" She looked across the table at her mom. "I remember how shattered you were when Daddy left, how you cried when you didn't know I was listening."

Her mother sighed. "It's devastating to have the person you love walk away from you. But your father never came back. He left for good."

"Zeke keeps coming back to me in some form or another. But all I can think about is the pain of another breakup. I mean, how can I be sure that he's actually changed?"

"You can't," her mom replied. "Sometimes you just have to believe what someone tells you. You have to trust them."

Eva nodded in agreement. It was obvious that both moms wanted Margot to give Zeke a chance. But she didn't know if that was possible.

Margot turned to his sister. "What do you think?"

"Me?" Bailey glanced up from the fragile teacup in her hand. "I just want you to be happy, no matter what you decide. I want Zeke to be happy, too. In a perfect world, you'd be together. But perfect worlds don't just happen. There's a lot of work involved, and in your case, it would mean letting go of the past." She reached for a scone and tore a piece of it off, dropping crumbs onto her plate. "I've never been in love or had a relationship like yours. But I've spent a portion of my life watching you and my brother trip and stumble."

"Only Zeke isn't stumbling anymore," Margot said. "He claims to have found his footing." The man she loved was offering her his heart in a way that he'd never offered it before, trying to give her everything she'd ever wanted. Yet she remained on shaky ground, still horribly afraid of getting hurt.

Thirteen

A week later, Margot woke up one morning in a state of distress, still fighting the future. But this much she knew: her fear of getting hurt was tied to abandonment issues, starting with her dad leaving and escalating with her divorce and losing Zeke. She'd wanted so badly for their marriage to work, for him to support her career the way she'd supported his, to live up to their wedding vows, to make compromises.

Margot pushed away her covers and climbed out of bed. She slept in pajamas when she was alone, not naked like when she was with Zeke.

She walked over to her dresser, where the Samoan stones were tucked away in a drawer. Zeke had left them with Bailey to give to her, along with a T-shirt for Liam. Bailey had dropped everything off yesterday, but Margot hadn't given Liam his gift yet. Mostly, she was still trying to deal with the way her gift made her feel.

Those pretty little stones reminded her of the rose quartz at the mountain house, and in that regard, they made her nervous. But everything pertaining to Zeke was causing her anxiety.

Desperate to clear her troubled mind, she went into the bathroom. She washed her face, brushed her teeth and banded her unruly hair into a ponytail. Still clad in her pjs, she wandered into the kitchen to pour herself a cup of coffee. She'd set the timer last night to have a pot ready this morning. It was Saturday, and she was going to spend the day with her son, but she hadn't decided what they were going to do yet.

She leaned against the counter and sipped her coffee. She'd already told Liam that her show had gotten canceled, and he'd taken the news surprisingly well. But she'd assured him they'd be okay until she found other work. Her finances weren't a problem. Luckily, she didn't have to take the first thing that came along.

At this point, Margot yearned to play different parts, not get typecast as the same wisecracking character she'd been playing since she was a child. It was a risk and might not happen easily, but she was willing to take her chances.

She frowned at her cup. She was willing to take a chance in her career, but not in her relationship with the man she loved?

"Hey, Mom."

She glanced up and saw Liam. He looked cutely disheveled, his pajamas rumpled, his cowlick-stricken hair matted and messy.

"Hi there." She smiled at him. "You're up early."

"I couldn't sleep."

"Me, neither." She'd barely slept all week. "How about some breakfast?"

"Okay, but can I make it?"

"Sure." She appreciated his sudden interest in cooking. "What do you want to fix?" No doubt she would have to help him.

"Just fruit and cereal."

That he could do on his own. "Hot or cold cereal?"

"I like the cold stuff better."

"Me, too. I'll have a bowl of whatever you're having."

He chose his favorite brand of puffed rice and went to work on the fruit, a mixture of strawberries, blueberries and bananas. He rinsed and peeled and diced. Margot was enjoying watching him.

He looked up and asked, "How come Zeke hasn't been around lately?"

She scrambled for an answer. "He was in Samoa, and he just returned last week. He got us some gifts from there. I'll give you yours after breakfast."

"Cool. Was he visiting his grandpa?"

"Yes." And now he wanted to create a family with Margot. Her heart ached from the thought of it. An ache that could be soothed, she reminded herself. All she had to do was reach out and accept Zeke's offer.

But was she ready to do that?

Liam dumped the fruit in a bowl and said, "Zeke told me that Bailey's dad adopted him after his first dad died. It's weird that his mom is so famous. Him and Bailey seem so normal, not like they used to live in a mansion or anything."

"Actually, their childhoods weren't very normal. Photographers followed their family around all the time."

"Do you think that'll ever happen to us?"

"I don't know. But if it does, Zeke will beef up our

security." He'd offered to do a lot more than that. But she couldn't tell Liam the whole story.

He plucked a blueberry from the bowl and ate it. "Has your agent gotten you an audition yet?"

"No, but those things take time. I'm not expecting it to happen overnight."

"Maybe you could be in a superhero movie. That would be amazing. I could tell everyone that my mom fights crime. Unless you play a villain. But that would be okay, too." He cocked his head. "Are you going to miss being Fiona?"

She smiled at his use of her sitcom character name. "There will always be a fondness in my heart for her. But I want to prove that I can be someone other than Fiona." Just as Zeke wanted to prove that he could be a different version of himself. Only he wasn't acting or playing a character.

He was proposing the real deal.

Margot's heart clenched. She needed to believe him, to trust him, to shed her fears and take him back into her fold. If she was willing to take risks in her career, then shouldn't she be able to take a chance on the man she loved?

The man she'd always loved, she thought. It didn't get any deeper than that. She needed Zeke Mitchell, as much as he needed her. Living the rest of her life without him seemed impossible. Screw her abandonment issues. She wanted Zeke.

"Are you okay, Mom?"

She gazed expectantly at her child. He had a potential father waiting for him. Just as she had the husband of her dreams, waiting for her.

"I'm fine," she replied, a sense of warmth spiraling through her. No fear. Only love and trust and strength.

"How would you like for us to hang out with Zeke today?"

He grinned. "That would be great."

"I'll text him to see if he's available." Knowing Zeke, he was checking his phone at regular intervals, hoping to hear from her. "We should all go somewhere and do something fun."

Excited, Liam wiggled where he stood. "How about the museum with the dinosaur bones?"

"You mean the Natural History Museum?"

"Yeah, that's the place. I was sick the day my class went there on a field trip. That was last year, before you adopted me. But I always wanted to see it."

"Then that's what we'll do." Her son could learn and explore, and she could be near Zeke and tell him how she felt.

Zeke stood at the entrance of the museum, waiting for Margot and Liam to arrive. Margot had texted him earlier and invited him to spend the afternoon with them. She'd also said that she had something important to tell him.

It had to be good news. She wouldn't have included him on an outing with Liam if it was something bad. But without knowing the details, Zeke was still anxious.

Was she accepting his offer to start dating, to go slowly, to see how things unfolded? Or was she ready for more?

For all he knew, this was a test of some sort, a meeting in a public place to see how he handled it.

No, he thought. She wouldn't test him in front of her son. Zeke just needed to relax and trust her judgment.

As soon as he saw her and Liam headed his way, his heart picked up speed. Liam waved and ran toward him. Margot walked at a regular pace, but the tender expression on her face said it all. Yeah, Zeke thought. This was good news, for sure.

Happy news. Loving news.

And at that moment, he knew exactly what she was trying to convey by inviting him to join her and Liam today.

She wanted them to be a family.

Suddenly everything seemed right in the world. Or in Zeke's world, anyway. The woman he loved wanted him in every way that mattered.

"Hi, Zeke!" Breathless, Liam stopped in front of him. He was wearing the T-shirt Zeke had gotten him in Samoa.

"Hey, buddy. It's good to see you. I'm glad the shirt fits."

"Thanks. I really like it. Did you know that they have dinosaurs here? And a huge collection of ocean biology stuff, too?"

Zeke smiled, imagining Liam as his son. His and Margot's. "It's nice that you're excited about being here."

"They have tons of stuff for kids to do. I wonder if we came here at night, if it would be like those *Night at the Museum* movies, where everything comes to life. Wouldn't that be weird?" Before Zeke could respond, Liam turned around to urge Margot on. "Hurry up, Mom! I want to go inside."

Zeke wanted her to hurry, too, just so he could be near her. She made her way over to him, and their gazes met and held. She reached for his hand, and he thought he might die. It was just a light touch, but it meant the world to him.

"Thank you for inviting me to join you," he said softly.

"Always," she replied.

Yes, he thought. *Always*. Her meaning was clear. Liam had no idea what was going on, though. He was still chomping at the bit for his museum adventure.

"Come on, you guys," he said.

"He's right," Zeke said to Margot. "We need to go in."

She nodded, and their first unofficial day as a couple began. But about thirty minutes later, while Liam played in one of the kid areas, Margot made it official.

"Have you already figured out what I wanted to talk to you about?" she asked Zeke.

"Yes," he replied. "But I need to hear you say it."

"Then listen when I say that I love you, and I want to spend the rest of my life with you. That you're worth the risk. That I trust you. That I believe in you." She moved closer to him. "I think you're going to make a wonderful husband and father."

He let out the breath he'd been holding. "I'll be a better husband than I was before, I promise you that. And I'm honored that you're going to let me be Liam's dad."

"I want to have more kids someday, too. But I'm going to focus on my career first."

"I'm good with that. I'll support you, Margot. I'll be the partner you need. I also think it would be better if I didn't travel as much as I used to. I can have someone else work with the out-of-town clients. There's plenty of jobs in LA for me, plenty of local clients to keep me in this area."

She smiled. "With your family."

"Yeah, with my family." God, he loved the sound of

that. He glanced over at her son playing with the other children. "When are you going to tell Liam?"

"I think I should do it today. We can go back to my house later, and we can talk to him together."

"That sounds perfect to me."

"You can spend the night tonight, too, if you want. I'd love for you to sleep over. To start getting Liam used to having you around as much as possible."

"I'll be there. Tonight, and every night, until we figure out our living arrangements."

"I think we should buy a place together. We can find a location that's convenient for both of us. I know that Liam would love to be at the beach. But wherever we live, I want to keep him in the same school. It's a private school, so it won't be a problem."

"We'll make it work. But just so you're aware, there's a lady in the corner, snapping pictures of us." Zeke gave a slight tilt of his head. "She obviously recognizes you. But she's pretending to take pics of the exhibit behind us."

"I don't mind, do you?"

"Not at all. This is what I signed up for when I asked you to marry me again." Zeke was prepared for having a celebrity wife, for accepting everything that came with it.

"She probably thinks you're my bodyguard. But with the way I'm looking at you, she might be wondering if there's something else going on between us. If she's a die-hard fan, she might even know that you're Eva Mitchell's son and that you're my ex."

"I'm not your ex anymore." He was her soon-to-be husband again. "I'd kiss you right now, but if Liam turns around and sees us, that wouldn't be fair to him. We need to talk to him first."

"I can't wait to tell him."

"Me, too." He wanted nothing more than to start their new life together, committing himself to her in every way.

Margot reclined next to Zeke in bed, too excited to sleep. Their talk with Liam had gone wonderfully. He was thrilled that Zeke was going to be part of their family. He'd actually jumped around the living room, shooting Zeke high fives.

"Liam's reaction sure made me feel good," Zeke said.

"Me, too. His energy is infectious." She turned onto her side to face her fiancé, the man she was going to marry all over again. "What kind of wedding do you think we should have this time?"

He leaned on his elbow, looking at her in the same awed way that she was looking at him. "If it was just you and me, I'd say to keep it simple, but I think that we should do something bigger and more festive for Liam. It would be nice for him to have everyone together."

"I agree." Wholeheartedly, she thought. Liam was a foster kid who'd never been part of a big, happy gathering that he could call his own. "Maybe we could do a beach ceremony. I can call an event planner and see what sort of oceanfront venues are available. I think a dusk wedding would be pretty. The sun setting over the water, flowers, seashells, a driftwood arch for us to stand under to say our vows." Her mind was filled with ideas. "But most importantly, I think Liam should walk me down the aisle." At their last wedding, they'd forgone that tradition. Back then Margot didn't want anyone giving her away or taking her father's role in the ceremony. But now she had a young son who belonged at her side. "I'd love to have that experience with him.

As happy as I was at our first wedding, a part of me was still hurt and empty over my dad. But I'm learning to separate myself from that now."

"We've both grown and changed. It just took us a while to get there." He softly added, "Your dad might be gone, but I'm never going to leave you again."

"It's strange, but in some ways, we never really split up. How many divorced couples keep sleeping together?"

"We told ourselves it was just sex. But it was more than that. We needed to stay close, so we used our affairs as a way to stay connected."

"We're definitely connected now."

"We most definitely are." He leaned forward to kiss her, slow and sweet.

They were already naked, so there were no clothes to shed, no barriers to get in the way. He ran his hands along her body, making her feel loved. But it wasn't just a feeling. It was a vow. She knew that he meant to keep his promise about never leaving her again. In her heart of hearts, she trusted him. Whatever obstacles they faced, she and Zeke would tackle them together.

He kissed her again, and she moaned her pleasure, eager for more. Not just sex, but the life they were going to live. When he entered her, she held him as close as she possibly could.

She breathed him in, luxuriating in how familiar he felt. He whispered in her ear, and she sighed. He'd just told her that he loved her in the Samoan language. He knew how to express it in Choctaw, too. Zeke wasn't fluent in either dialect, but he knew enough to get by. More than enough, she thought, when it came to whispering words of love.

She wrapped her legs around him, content in the

weight of his body pressing down on hers. They'd left a night-light burning, and it flickered with a dusky glow, creating shadows on his handsome face. Yet as shadowy as he looked, there was nothing hidden, nothing to fear. He'd opened himself up to her, just as she'd done with him. They'd made an emotional pact to treat each other right.

He gazed down at her as if she was the most perfect woman on earth. And in some ways, she was. Perfect for him. Perfect for herself. She clasped hands with him, arching her body, moving in time to his rhythm, lost in the beauty of becoming one.

weight of his body pressing down on hers. They'd left a night-light burning, and it flickered with a dusky glow, creating shadows on his handsome face. Yet as shadowy as he looked, there was nothing hidden, nothing to fear. He'd opened himself up to her, just as she'd done with him. They'd made an emotional pact to treat each other right.

Epilogue

Life was good, Zeke thought. By now, he and Margot were searching for a house together. He was also back to work and staying with her while she went out on auditions. On their days off they hung out at his condo, where he continued Liam's bodyboarding lessons.

Today they were at his mom's, though, partying with family and friends to celebrate their engagement. Eva had insisted on hosting the gathering and making it a glamorous outdoor event, with catered food and floral arrangements floating in the pool.

It was an interesting mix of people. Most of Margot's friends were actors, and most of Zeke's were surfers or security specialists. Eva's crowd were Hollywood bigwigs.

His mom was in seventh heaven. She loved flaunting her celebrity. But someday Margot might surpass her. His fiancée was determined to revamp her career, and he was determined to help her. The complications from their past seemed so easy to overcome now.

He gazed across the patio and sent her a loving smile. She'd helped Liam get dressed up for this party, and the kid looked damned fine in his summer suit. He'd brought some school friends along, and they were oohing and aahing over the mansion. Zeke suspected that his mom was going to spoil Liam, treating him like her royal grandson. But that was okay with Zeke. Liam deserved to become a prince.

Zeke finished chatting with a colleague and approached Margot. She looked gorgeous in a long blue gown. She was also wearing her old engagement ring, the big shiny diamond he'd given her years ago. He'd offered to buy her a new one, but she wanted to wear the original one, saying that it had sentimental value. He agreed about how significant it was. He would always remember the first time he'd proposed and how excited he'd been, asking her to be his bride. He was excited to marry her all over again, too.

Once the cocktail hour ended and dinner was served, everyone sat down to eat. Zeke and Margot joined Eva, June and Bailey at the main table. Liam and his friends had their own special table.

Zeke reached for Margot's hand, and she leaned closer to him. Their wedding plans were in full swing. By now, they were opting for a fall wedding. Early fall, when the weather was still nice.

"This is a lovely party," she said to him. "And did you know that we're having banana fritters for dessert? Your mom got the recipe from your grandfather. But I was involved, too. I called your grandfather and told him how much Liam liked bananas, and he suggested *panikeke*."

"I love those, and I think Liam will, too. They always

tasted like doughnuts to me. But you can put different toppings on them."

"That's what your grandpa said. I think it was sweet of your mom to design the dessert around Liam, but also with a Samoan flair."

He glanced over at the table where Liam and his buddies were behaving like perfect little gentleman. "I'd love to take Liam to Samoa. I'd like to take him to the Choctaw reservation, as well." Zeke's grandmother had been from the Mississippi Band of Choctaw.

"I'm sure he would enjoy that. You're going to give him a good life. We both are."

He looked over at Liam again, feeling like a dad already. He would be adopting the boy soon after the wedding.

As the dinner progressed, Zeke cut into his prime rib and shifted his attention to his mom and Margot's. They were busy chatting with each other.

And then there was Bailey, he thought, sitting quietly across from him. She glanced up from her plate, and they exchanged a siblings' smile. She was helping Margot plan the wedding. She'd done that the first time, too. But weddings weren't always Bailey's strong suit.

Zeke said to her, "Remember when I told Mom and Dad that you wanted a bridal doll for your birthday? And then they gave you that wedding set you hated? The bride, the groom, the flower girl, the whole works?" He chuckled at the lunacy of it. "You were so mad at me for that."

She rolled her eyes. "It was the year I told you that I never wanted to get married."

"What the heck did you know? You were only seven."

"I was eight, and I'm still not sure if I ever want to prance down some aisle. Not like some people I know, doing it twice."

Zeke shrugged. "Yeah, well. I'd take notes if I were you. You'd be lucky to get a guy as awesome as me."

"Awesome? You?" Bailey gaped at Margot. "Can you shut him up, please? Like seriously, wipe that puffed-up expression off his face."

Margot laughed. "I could kiss him. But that might not be the way to keep him quiet."

"Yes, it is," Zeke replied. As much as he'd been enjoying his silly banter with Bailey, he was far more interested in Margot's kiss. "It's the only thing that's going to shut me up."

"Are you sure?" she asked, teasing him.

"Absolutely."

"Oh, brother." Bailey groaned, and went back to her food.

Zeke didn't care about his meal anymore. All that mattered was Margot. He leaned into her, and when her lips touched his, everything went still. Even his heart. It was just a simple kiss. But it was filled with love and commitment, with every wondrous thing he and Margot meant to each other.

And he couldn't ask for anything better than that.

* * * * *

We really hope you enjoyed reading this book.
If you're looking for more romance, be sure to
head to the shops when new books are
available on

Thursday 13th
May

To see which titles are coming soon, please visit

millsandboon.co.uk/nextmonth

A ROMANCE FOR EVERY READER

MODERN

Prepare to be swept off your feet by sophisticated, sexy and seductive heroes, in some of the world's most glamourous and romantic locations, where power and passion collide.

HISTORICAL

Escape with historical heroes from time gone by. Whether your passion is for wicked Regency Rakes, muscled Vikings or rugged Highlanders, await the romance of the past.

MEDICAL

Set your pulse racing with dedicated, delectable doctors in the high-pressure world of medicine, where emotions run high and passion, comfort a love are the best medicine.

True Love

Celebrate true love with tender stories of heartfelt romance, from the rush of falling in love to the joy a new baby can bring, and a focus on th emotional heart of a relationship.

Desire

Indulge in secrets and scandal, intense drama and plenty of sizzling hot action with powerful and passionate heroes who have it all: wealth, status good looks…everything but the right woman.

HEROES

Experience all the excitement of a gripping thriller, with an intense romance at its heart. Resourceful, true-to-life women and strong, fearless n face danger and desire - a killer combination!

JOIN US ON SOCIAL MEDIA!

Stay up to date with our latest releases, author news and gossip, special offers and discounts, and all the behind-the-scenes action from Mills & Boon...

 millsandboon

 millsandboonuk

millsandboon

Experience all the excitement of a gripping thriller, with an intense romance at its heart. Resourceful, true-to-life women and strong, fearless men face danger and desire - a killer combination!

MILLS & BOON
True Love
Romance from the Heart

Celebrate true love with tender stories of heartfelt romance, from the rush of falling in love to the joy a new baby can bring, and a focus on the emotional heart of a relationship.

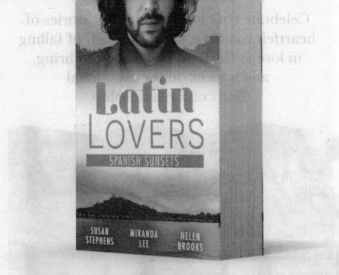